ROAD KILL:
TEXAS HORROR BY TEXAS WRITERS VOL 4

16 Horrifying Tales

**Compiled & Edited by
Bret McCormick**

A HellBound Books Publishing LLC Book
Houston TX

A HellBound Books LLC
Publication

Cover and art design by
Kevin Enhart for
HellBound Books Publishing LLC

www.hellboundbookspublishing.com

Printed in the United States of America

CONTENTS

Foreword

For four years now, E. R. Bills and I have been beating the bushes and peering into abandoned wells, seeking out the most terrifying tales the Lone Star State has to offer. We've left no stone unturned, no attic unexplored and no grave undesecrated. Our diligence has paid off. *Road Kill Volume 4* is the grimmest yet. You hold in your hands a grand collection of goose-flesh-inducing prose. Don't take my word for it. These sixteen stories speak – or perhaps scream – for themselves.

A peace-loving liberal, caught up in World War III, is transformed into a relentless killer in *Nia* by E.R. Bills. Local cops are befuddled by the mummified corpse of a man who was alive and well only three days earlier in James H. Longmore's *Harvey*. William Jensen intimately examines the insanity of one man's hellish legacy in *You Can Outrun the Devil If You Try*. Grampa's caught every kind of fish that swims in Lake Tawakoni and tonight something may be fishing for him in Patrick C. Harrison III's tale, *From These Muddy Waters.* *Buzzard Luck* is the only kind of luck he's ever had, but this optimistic single dad will find it hard to see the bright side on Halloween night in a chilling tale by W.H. Gilbert. True love conquers all – that's what these star-crossed lovers thought— until they encountered Jeremy Hepler's *Dark Rift*. To what extremes of endurance will one young man go in order to remove a stain from his town's history? Find out in *Hometown Hero* by Dan

Fields. In ***His Death Offers No Respite*** by Thomas Kearnes, Avery finds out love hurts, but wonders if revenge will ease the pain. Andrew Kozma's ***The Chauffeur*** explores the soulless mentality behind a corporate vulture's behavior and the inadvertent boost he receives from high-tech automation. In Sylvia Ney's ***Lights Out***, a woman's love leads her from ecstasy to despair and beyond. Mark A. Nobles reveals that ***The Year Walk*** is a time-honored mystical tradition, but can Elwanda shift between dimensions without bringing destruction to her family and community? Elliott Baxter paints a vivid picture of the sordid side of life and allows us to stumble into a gateway to hell in ***Two Nuns Walk into A Bar***. Satellite technology has allowed us to map the world in great detail – even so, Russell C. Connor's ***Smile for the Camera*** makes it abundantly clear that there are places and entities that do not allow prying eyes. Ralph Robert Moore reaches down the throat of reality and turns it inside out in ***The Fear All Women Have***. When life heaps one challenge after another onto the shoulders of a kind, but determined young woman, it's bound to create friction and when it does, as Carmen Gray shows us, ***The Smoke's Gotta Go Somewhere***. They say picking up hitch hikers is a dangerous thing to do and Corey Lamb's ***The Girl in the Car*** is the most dangerous of all, because she's dead.

Happy reading and good luck sleeping.

Bret McCormick, October 2019

ROAD KILL:
TEXAS HORROR
BY TEXAS
WRITERS
VOL 4

The Girl in the Car.
Corey Lamb

"Throw the shit in the car! Come *on*!"

I heard the barred door of the corner store come to a rickety slam as I hauled the two cases of beer into the Jessie Palmer's '72 Camino, tripping over myself as I lunged into the backseat. The tires spun before I even closed the door behind me, just as the elderly attendant hobbled out after us, waving his cracked baseball bat around in the air like he was swatting at a wasp's nest just out of reach of his liver-spotted arms. You'd think after the second time he'd been ripped off for a few packs, the guy would consider buying a rifle. Or at least learn enough not to take a twenty-minute dump when he's the only one behind the counter. Lucky for me, and by the grace of God, he hadn't.

"You grabbed the fucking *Lucky's*?" Dwayne Rogers yelled from the seat next to mine as he slapped me in the back of the head with his bony fingers. I knew Dwayne from Little League baseball. That is to say, when Dwayne was thirteen years old, he played on my team of ten-year-olds to avoid progressing into the live-pitch games. My dad was the coach, and I guess he knew Dwayne's dad from work. Therefore, I spent two and a half baseball seasons watching Dwayne's stepmom halfheartedly cheer for the fact that Dwayne had somehow managed to barely stand out among a crowd of inattentive children who weren't yet old enough to grow armpit hair. Now, Dwayne found himself in the shady company of Jessie Palmer and her much older boyfriend Tommy Simpson. Though, to be fair, so had I.

"Tell me he didn't get *Lucky's*," Tommy mumbled through the lit cigarette in his mouth. The guy had to be in his thirties, but I never had the nerve to ask. It was the caterpillar moustache. Or maybe the cracks around his eyes. I often wondered how he and Jessie ever met.

"It's what we drank last weekend!" I spat, still catching my breath from the run. "I remember the label!"

"Yea," Tommy sneered, "when we had to pay for it."

Dwayne grabbed the back of my neck and pulled my head closer to his.

"When you steal booze," he whispered, loud enough for the whole car to hear, "you steal motherfucking *booze*. Not this pisswater bullshit."

He threw my head back at the opposite end of the seat, almost slamming my face into the window.

I looked to the passenger-side mirror. Jessie was checking her makeup. She hadn't noticed.

"We might as well drive your ass right on back to the store," Tommy said, flicking his cigarette out the window. "Pop that cherry a little harder."

Dwayne snorted at this.

"Yea, it's only a bat," Dwayne laughed, cracking one of the beers anyway, "You can dodge a couple of swings, eh Stevie-boy?"

Sure, I'll just pretend I'm a baseball, and he's you at thirteen.

"You really only gotta dodge the one, before the old man's hip goes out," Tommy snickered.

"Right," I said, laughing along for some reason. But I knew they weren't laughing *with* me.

Jessie Palmer leaned back in her seat, reaching an arm out to Dwayne for a beer, opening and closing her hand in a *gimme* motion. Dwayne swatted it away and grabbed one of the *Lucky's* for her. She smirked at me—upside down—and I glanced away immediately, covering with an awkward smile, as I searched for a way to deflect attention from myself.

"Hey, a deer!" I said, gesturing out the window as my heart continued to race. There was a group of three of them—doe, from what I could tell—hanging out on the side of the road. Eating grass. Or flowers. Or whatever it was that deer did.

Tommy bit down on his cigarette and sped up, veering the car towards the trio, until the right side of the vehicle edged off of the pavement and started picking up dirt. The deer raised their heads in unison, paralyzed in the Camino's high beams.

"Twenty points for the little one," Dwayne barked, finishing with a large slurp of *Lucky's*.

Tommy pressed on the car horn several times in rapid-fire until he jerked the wheel and pulled us back into our lane again, laughing through his teeth as the terrified deer scattered into the woods.

"Don't be a dick," Jessie said, though with an unmistakable smile. Jessie was the reason I was there that night. She was the reason I did a lot of things.

"*What?* I thought our new friend back there wanted to see one *up close*," Tommy said, though I might as well have not been in the vehicle.

"*Hey, a deer!*" Dwayne said in a horrible mock-voice, sticking out his uneven front teeth and crossing his eyes. "*Let's all look at the deer!*"

Dwayne back-handed my shoulder. Hard.

"You've lived in East Texas how long, dip-ass?" he added, jeering.

I shouldn't have said a goddamn word.

"That's all right," Tommy said, taking a long drag of his cigarette, "he don't strike me as the huntin' type."

I caught Tommy's eye in the rearview mirror. I shook my head.

"You see," he carried on, holding a hand out to frame his statement. "They're mindless creatures, put here for our benefit. They eat, they sleep, they *fuck*…and they multiply. Too much for their own good. So, we keep 'em in check."

Dwayne slurped his beer again, laughing, but ultimately contributing nothing.

"They're nothin' to *stare* at," Tommy finished.

"Yea, and what does that make us?" Jessie asked, nudging Tommy's arm several times with her fist.

"*Killers*," Tommy growled, winking as he took another drag.

Jessie folded her arms and looked back out the window.

"Well, *I* wouldn't want to kill one," she mumbled.

Tommy watched her, staring for a moment before glancing back to me in the rearview mirror.

"Aw, see what you did, Stevie? You got her all worked up."

Jessie pulled herself away from the window.

"Leave him alone," Jessie said, slapping Tommy's arm playfully. "He's just a kid."

The funny thing was, I was older than Jessie by a full three months.

"And I'm *fine*," Jessie said to Tommy, before turning back to face me. "Thanks for the beers, Steven," she said, giving me a wink that momentarily justified the whole trip. "Really."

I smiled in return, doing my best to pretend I didn't like the wink as much as I did. She turned away just as I was starting to forget where I was.

"Might wanna be careful, Jess," Dwayne hissed. "I think you just gave him a stiffy."

The smile instantly drained from my face as Tommy laughed, choking a bit on his cigarette smoke. I shot a quick glance to my pants, and then to Jessie. I felt the blood rushing back to my face. Thankfully, it was dark out, so no one could tell.

"Dwayne, you're such an asshole," Jessie said, turning to punch him in the leg. He reached out to grab her arm, but was swiped away before he got the chance. "Don't pay any attention to him," she said, craning her neck to face me. "He's a repressed homosexual."

Tommy snorted through the end of his third cigarette and started coughing again – heavily. Dwayne slowly sat backwards into his seat, glaring at Jessie as she stuck her tongue out. I couldn't help but laugh along, however slightly.

"And just what the fuck are *you* snickerin' at, dipshit?"

Dwayne turned to face me, apparently choosing me as the easiest target of the bunch. I got the distinct impression that he wouldn't have dared say the same thing to Tommy.

"I–I, uh," I began, hoping I'd find the rest of the sentence along the way.

"I'll bet I've gotten more action in one *night* than you've gotten your entire life."

"Steven isn't into *dudes*, Dwayne," Jessie laughed, causing another death glare from Dwayne. She then started to quiet down before finally adding, "*Right?*" and turning to face me.

"NO. No, I'm not," I said, a little too quickly. "Girls. Definitely girls."

"You ever *boned* a girl, Stevie?" Tommy asked, rolling his window up. Jessie playfully slapped his shoulder again. Then, she turned around to gauge my reaction.

"Well…I…I don't–"

"Hell, I'm bettin' he's never even kissed a girl," Dwayne growled. "Not. A. One."

My face felt as though it would explode. I reached for one of the boxes of *Lucky's*, but Dwayne pulled it away, scoffing.

"You haven't, have you?" Jessie asked, smiling slightly.

"Holy, shit!" Dwayne spat, choking out a laugh in between words. "I was just fuckin' with ya! That's fuckin' pathetic!"

Dwayne's laughter shook the car, as I turned my head away from the group and to the window. This was the exact opposite of how I hoped tonight would go.

How did *I expect tonight to go? Jessie and I would ditch Tommy and Dwayne? Listen to some music, maybe? Go for a walk?*

"Jessie, kiss the kid," Tommy growled through yet another cigarette. I could *hear* the grin on his face.

Wait. What did he say?

I jerked my head back to face Tommy. I was sure I had misheard him. Jessie giggled, then leaned her head back over the gap in the center of the front seat. Her blonde hair cascaded down, practically touching the floorboard.

"How 'bout it, Stevie?" she said, puckering her lips and making a sloppy kissing sound. "Make an honest woman out of me?" she laughed.

Tommy smirked and blew smoke at the dashboard.

"Aw, he ain't gonna do it," Dwayne taunted, his eyes bouncing back and forth between Jessie's lips and me.

All I could think to do was smile at Jessie. As much as my insides were burning, I didn't have it in me to kiss her right then and there. She knew it. I knew it.

Jessie winked at me, then pulled herself back into her seat.

"You sure you're not some kinda queer, Steve?" Dwayne asked, composing himself however slightly. I'd say he was making fun of me, if the question hadn't felt genuine.

I choked. I had an opportunity to kiss Jessie Palmer. And I'd choked.

"He don't want to be kissin' another man's girl," Tommy said, reaching over to pat Jessie's leg. It was something in between a question and a statement. And then there was a pause, followed by, "I can respect that."

Earning Tommy's respect wasn't something I thought I wanted, until then. *Yea, that was it. Another man's girl. That's why I couldn't do it. Not because I'm a pathetic chump. Not at all.*

Dwayne leaned forward in his seat. "You know, Jessie, I ain't ever kissed a girl, neither."

"You can kiss my fuckin' ass," Tommy said, eyeing Dwayne through the rearview mirror.

Jessie, ignoring Dwayne, propped one of her bright red sneakers on the dash and poked at Tommy's shoulder.

"Gimme a smoke," she said in a faux-New-York accent. I smiled, though there was no way for her to know.

Tommy shifted around in his seat, grunting as he shoved a hand into the pocket of his jeans and pulled out an empty pack of Marlboros.

"Dwayne," Tommy barked, tossing the empty pack into the back seat.

"Fresh out," Dwayne said, though I had to wonder if he was telling the truth.

"Course you are," said Tommy, before flashing me a quick glance as the car rolled to a stop at one of the town's intersections. "And, I'm gonna go out on a limb here and guess our little tag along buddy back there doesn't have any smokes on him, either."

After a moment of wondering if Tommy was finished with his statement, I spoke up.

"Uh...no. Sorry."

I hadn't thought of cigarettes. I'd never so much as held one that wasn't made of sugar, but had I known I'd be asked for a pack, I'd have brought three.

Tommy grabbed the wheel and took an aggressive right turn.

"Well then," he said straightening the wheel, "looks like we're making another pit stop."

My stomach sank into my seat. I was still recovering from the *Lucky's* heist.

"Ooooh, I love this song!" Jessie yelled, throwing herself toward the radio to crank up the volume loud enough to drown out my awkward squirming. I happened to catch Dwayne's eye with the corner of my own. He was staring at me. Waiting for me to object. To ask to be taken home.

But I knew that I wouldn't. I couldn't. Not now.

You said you want to reach the skyyyyy...

Jessie threw her head back and raised an invisible microphone to her lips, belting the lyrics into the roof of the Camino.

So get up.

She turned back to point at me, bobbing her shoulders up and down, one at a time. I felt a bit of the color run back into my face.

The feeling's right, and the music's tight on the disco nights...

"Hey Jess, why don't you leave the singin' to the pros?" Dwayne snarked, pretending to snatch at the invisible microphone. But Jessie pulled it back, wagging a disapproving finger at Dwayne to the rhythm of the song.

The feeling's right, and the music's tight on the disco nights...

Tommy laughed through his teeth. Jessie looked back to me, grabbed my hand, and sang the lyrics to me in an exaggerated production.

The feeling's riiiight, the music's tiiiight on the disco niiiights...

I could think of nothing but to smile back, nervously. Damn it.

Jessie climbed in her seat a bit more and leaned in closer to me, singing a bit louder now. She squeezed my hands tighter.

The feeling's riiiight, the music's tiiiight on the disco niiiights...

I felt my gaze fall to her lips, but I jerked them back to her eyes almost instantly. I don't think I'd ever been so close to Jessie Palmer, the girl I had been crushing on since naps were a regular occurrence on the classroom itinerary. The girl I'd just stole two cases of beer for, and was probably about to steal cigarettes for.

Jessie gave me another wink and continued to sing. Tommy glanced back to the two of us, laughing again. Probably making fun of me. But I was in a trance.

The lyrics stopped for a moment as the beat carried us on to the next verse. Jessie was leaning in closer to me and pulling away, back and forth, to the rhythm. She was getting so close; I could smell her shampoo. Or maybe it was her hair spray. Coconut. No, almond. Both.

She lifted my chin with the tips of her fingers, mouthing the words of the song. I was jello in her hand.

My heart pounded into my throat. Maybe it was from the beer heist. Then again, maybe not. I wondered if she could feel it.

She winked again. And before I could stop myself...before the gravity of the situation really registered in my brain...I kissed her. I kissed Jessie *fucking* Palmer.

She fell silent. Everyone did. But...she hadn't pulled back. Not immediately. For the briefest moment, quick enough for anyone to attribute it to shock, but long enough for me to know better...Jessie Palmer *kissed me back*.

Dwayne stared in disbelief. Tommy's eyes were fixated on me, giving me a look that was neither anger nor approval. It was certainly a shift from his attitude five minutes prior, when he had outright told Jessie to kiss me. I wondered what was different now.

"What the fu–" Tommy began, but was immediately cut off by Dwayne's screaming.

"TOMMY, ROAD!"

But it was too late. Tommy jerked his head back to the front of the vehicle and pulled the wheel hard, but not before whatever it was that Dwayne saw rolled up and over the hood of the car, cracking the windshield straight across. Tommy slammed on the brakes, and we slid to a rigid stop in the center of a floating cloud of gravel.

Nobody said a word for the first few moments. We just sat there, breathing in shaky spurts. Tommy cut the silence by beating on the steering wheel. I thought he was going to break it off.

"Shit! SHIT! FUCK!" he spat, his hands vibrating against the wheel.

"What was that?" Jessie asked, trembling, and looking only at Tommy and not back to the object. But we all knew what it was. A thick dread swelled in my gut. I knew what we hit.

"Who," said Dwayne definitively, inhaling more than he was exhaling. "*Who* was that?"

Tommy spun around to face Dwayne, throwing a hand to his throat. "Don't you fucking say that! Don't you *fucking* say that!"

"Tommy, stop," Jessie said, placing a hand on his shoulder, which prompted Tommy to turn on her, shoving her against the passenger door as Dwayne gasped for breath.

"*You* shut the fuck up," Tommy yelled at Jessie, the corners of his mouth twitching. "If you had stayed in your fucking seat, I wouldn't have–I mean *we* wouldn't have–"

I opened the car door instinctively, which clicked the dome light on, illuminating everyone's horrified faces for the first time.

"And where the hell do you think *you're* going, lover boy?" Tommy asked, wide-eyed.

I didn't know. I was too scared to think. Too scared to breathe.

"I'm...gonna go check...on..." I gestured back behind the Camino, to what was lying the street. I couldn't even say it.

"The fuck you are!" Tommy fired back, raising himself more in his seat.

"It wasn't your fault," Jessie said. "It's dark. You didn't see it. We didn't do anything wrong. But if we leave–"

"I'm going," I said, stepping out of the car and staring at the ground. I'd made it only a few paces before Tommy kicked open his own door and came charging out after me.

"You get your fuckin' ass back here!" he roared, but it didn't matter. Nothing mattered to me but the sight of what was lying in the road, fifty feet from the car. A person. A woman.

Tommy ran up and grabbed my arm, but his grip slowly loosened as his eyes fell on the same sight.

She was a young girl, maybe fifteen or sixteen, in what would have been a white gown not unlike a wedding dress, now soaked in blood. A fringed bonnet managed to stay tied around her head. And as I watched, holding my breath, she inched her head toward us.

"Oh fuck," Dwayne whispered as he approached Tommy and me. "She's alive."

Tommy took a few deep breaths and paced back towards the car, his hands on his head. And then, without turning back to us, he spoke. His voice was cold. Commanding.

"Put her in the car."

"I'm not touching her–" Dwayne said.

I looked back to the poor girl. She wasn't moving. Just staring. Right at me.

I did this to her.

"We need to get help," I said, transfixed at the sight of the blood pooling around her. "We shouldn't move her. What if we…make it worse?"

It was like hearing someone else talk through me. I couldn't have spoken. The words meant nothing to me.

Tommy turned back to Dwayne and me and charged the two of us, huffing through his nose.

"*You*," he said, shoving Dwayne towards the girl. "And *you*," he said, shoving me even harder, "go grab her and put her in the *goddamn car*."

His jaw trembled as he gritted his teeth. I couldn't decide if it was out of fear or rage.

Dwayne stumbled over to the girl as Tommy stared a hole through my soul. I knew if I didn't help Dwayne, it wasn't going to end well for me. So, I obeyed.

"We're taking her to the hospital, right?" Jessie asked. She was bracing herself against the car, as if her legs were giving out.

Tommy said nothing, marching to the driver's side of the Camino.

"The *hospital…right*?" Jessie repeated, the concern in her voice was unmistakable.

"Yea," Tommy muttered, sitting back down.

I lifted the girl's feet as Dwayne carefully heaved her torso upward. At this, the girl's head rolled to the side, revealing a sizable red spot seeping through the bonnet, just above her ear. The stain travelled all the way down her cheek and oozed out onto her neck from the cloth. Dwayne refused to look at it or me as we carried the girl to the Camino. He just stared down at the gravel, watching his feet as we shuffled closer.

She was heavier than she looked. Like carrying sheets of roofing tile.

Jessie popped open the back door of the car, which pulled Dwayne's attention from the road.

"Whoa, whoa, whoa, hold on," Dwayne protested, stopping just short of the Camino. "If she's going back there…where are *we* going to sit?"

I wanted so badly to drop the girl's feet, but I knew that as long as Dwayne was holding her, I couldn't. As guilty as I felt for thinking it, considering what I was carrying, I didn't want to look weak in front of Jessie. Or, even worse at that moment, Tommy.

"Put her in the trunk," Tommy said, just loud enough for us to hear.

"Tommy–" Jessie began, but didn't finish.

Dwayne took a step back in compliance, pulling at the girl to get me moving. And then I felt–just enough to sink my stomach–the poor girl's leg twitch.

"Stop."

I looked back into the girl's eyes. They were fixed on me. She was at our mercy. *My* mercy.

It didn't matter if it pissed Tommy off.

"Backseat," I ordered Dwayne. "Come on."

Tommy stepped out of the car again, but I kept my eyes on Dwayne. I heard the gravel crunch beneath Tom's steel-toed boots as he approached us. My arms were going numb under the weight of the girl, and I felt them starting to shake. But I needed Dwayne on my side. I couldn't put the girl in the trunk. I wouldn't.

Tommy shoved a key into the lock of the trunk and yanked the lid open. He then turned around to face me, grabbing one of the girl's legs and forcing his line of sight into my own.

"It's *my* fuckin' car. And *she's* going in the fuckin' trunk."

It wasn't Tommy's car, though. It was Jessie's. But I wasn't about to bring *that* up. As much as my forearms hurt, I tightened my grip on the girl's legs.

"What if we get pulled over?" I said, my fingers slipping from the sweat. "We robbed a liquor store.

Your window's *smashed*. And you want to throw a dying girl in the trunk?"

Tommy's eyes darted from my own to my hands, to the girl's dress, and then back to me. He raised a hand to wipe the sweat from his lip. He opened his mouth, but Dwayne spoke first.

"Maybe Steve's right," he said, and Tommy turned to face him. "If someone finds this girl…bleeding out…in the trunk–"

Tommy looked back to the girl again, and then quickly down at the road. After a moment of agonizing silence, he let go of the girl's leg and slammed the trunk shut.

"I guess she's sitting in your lap, then."

As Tommy walked back to the driver's seat, Jessie stepped to me and took the girl's other leg. And not a moment too soon.

"Come on," Jessie said, and the three of us slid the girl into the back seat. I inched my way in after her, lifting her legs into my lap. Dwayne followed suit on the other side, resting the girl's head and shoulders on his thighs. With the way she was propped up, there was no mistaking the fact that she was still staring at me. I looked away as soon as I noticed, but not before the corner of her lips curled into a wince. Or, as it looked in my peripheral view…

…a crooked smile.

Tommy started the car up again, and the radio kicked on.

–sic's tiiiight on the disco–

Jessie didn't let the lyric play out before she cranked the volume down to a bleak silence. It was funny…I hadn't realized we were listening to a cassette tape. No wonder Jessie knew all the words.

"Shoulda just kicked the window out," Tommy muttered just under his breath as he picked up speed. "Can't see shit."

I looked back at the girl. To her dress. To the blood pooling in the seat beneath her. And then back to her face. Her eyes had closed.

"Was she just out there…*alone*?" Jessie asked, turning to face the three of us.

"Must've been," Dwayne said. "Didn't see no one else out there."

"But…*why* was she alone? Who just walks around in the road by themselves in the middle of the night…"

Jessie gave the girl's outfit another scan. She reached out like she wanted to touch it, but decided against it.

"…dressed like that?" Jessie finished, lowering her hand.

It's true, it was weird. The girl was wearing a white lace gown, now greyed from the pavement, with wrinkled frayed sleeves extending just beyond her forearms. She was also barefoot–the bottoms of her feet caked in dry mud–like she'd been walking through the woods for hours. Or through a ditch.

"Maybe she's …one of those Southern Amish…or something," Dwayne guessed, adjusting his legs beneath the girl's upper half.

"There *are* no *Southern Amish*," Jessie said. "That doesn't make any sense."

"Will you two shut the *fuck* up?" Tommy interjected. "What difference does it make?"

The girl's leg twitched again. Harder, this time. Through the outline from the hanging gown, I could trace the shape of her legs. And one of them was bent the hell up, like a doll's leg, a doll a child had cast aside. I looked at her arms. Her wrists. It was obvious they were broken.

"How far is the hospital from here?" I asked, checking one of the snapped wrists for a pulse.

"Jesus Christ," Dwayne said, apparently seeing her wrist for the first time.

"Few more miles," Tommy mumbled.

I felt a soft pulse and sat her wrist back into the seat. I looked to Dwayne, who nodded his head toward the girl's feet. I looked back down to see one of her big toes throbbing up and down, bending and pointing. Then, the toenail started scratching at my door. I wished more than anything for it to stop.

"Pull her leg back," said Dwayne after a few moments of the scratching.

"I can't," I said, laying a hand on the girl's foot. "It's broken."

The scratching got faster. By the look of it, the girl's toenails hadn't been clipped for months.

"Well, do *something*," Jessie said, staring out the window. "I can't take much more of that."

I patted the girl's foot with my hand–as if to say "it's going to be okay", but the bending and scratching with her toe only worsened. And then, though I wish I hadn't, I looked up at her face. There, looking back at me, unmistakably, was a bloody smile. Teeth and all.

At that, I pushed the girl's foot away from the passenger door, which pulled the hem of her gown up her leg just enough for me to catch the edge of something written on her skin, barely visible by the occasional streetlight. A word, wrapped around her ankle. A tattoo.

I glanced back to Dwayne. He was looking out the window, clearly pretending a dying girl wasn't sprawled across his lap.

After I was certain that nobody was looking, I lifted the hem of the girl's gown with my pinky finger and brushed it back up her leg a bit more, revealing not *a* word, but words–sentences–paragraphs of unintelligible text. In Italian–no, Greek. No…Something else.

Words after words of nonsense.

"You fuckin' perv!" Dwayne yelled beside me, and I jerked the gown back over the girl's leg.

"No, it's not…I–"

"What's goin' on back there?" Tommy asked, eyeing me through the rearview mirror.

"This little horn dog's coppin' a feel!" Dwayne barked, leaning over to shove me into the car door.

Jessie turned in her seat to face me, horror etched in her expression.

"Steven, are you serious?" she asked, sniffling a bit.

The blood rushed back to my face. I stammered.

"N-No! She's got…" I took a deep breath, "…tattoos. Everywhere."

"Yea well, you'd know, huh?" Dwayne sneered. I could tell he was getting off on calling me out. Or distracting from the reality of what we were doing.

"No, I mean…she's got…*weird* ones. All over her legs. Look!"

I pulled back the gown again, only a little further this time, noticing how high the tattoos were coming from. My eyes flickered between Jessie and the girl. To my relief, Jessie was looking at the girl's legs.

"What the fuck…" Dwayne said, staring. And then he pulled up one of the sleeves of the girl's gown.

"What?" Tommy asked, turning his head to us and back, periodically.

"It's all over her arms, too," Dwayne said, tracing a finger over the tattoos covering the girl's bicep. "Bunch of weird words. Moors…toe…gah? Gay? Veetah…cuh…veena?"

"Well, don't *read* it!" Jessie yelled, reaching over to pull the girl's sleeve back down.

"Why not?" Dwayne yelled back, imitating Jessie's tone. "We hit her with our car. I don't think she gives a fuck."

"Just…stop! You're freaking me out!"

"Have any of you…seen her…" I gulped, "looking at us?"

"Huh?" Dwayne looked down, but the girl had long closed her eyes. "The hell do you mean?"

I looked at Jessie. She seemed just as clueless as Dwayne.

"She, uh…the girl…keeps looking at me. She keeps…smiling."

After a lengthy pause, Dwayne forced out a laugh.

"You're fuckin' nuts."

I wasn't sure, but I thought I felt the car speed up a bit.

"She…looked at you?" Jessie asked, eyeing the girl and waving a hand out in front of her face.

"You mean when we found her," Dwayne said, "in the road, right?"

I shook my head.

"Here. In the car. In your lap."

Dwayne and Jessie eyed each other, gauging each other's reactions. Neither had any idea what I was talking about.

I cleared my throat. Or what was left in it, at least.

"You...never saw that?"

I felt my tongue swelling. I needed a drink.

"She's got ink on her chest, too," Dwayne said, cutting the silence we were all stewing in for what felt like an eternity. "All the way up to the neckline. Under the dress."

The girl's leg twitched again. All three of us noticed it that time.

"I don't like this," Jessie said. "Something's not right."

She turned back to face the front of the vehicle.

"Wait, Tommy..." Jessie said, looking back and forth from her window to the windshield. "You...passed the hospital."

"Passed it a little ways back," Tommy said, staring ahead. I could tell he was chewing on the inside of his cheek. And I realized he'd been quiet for a little while.

"What the hell, man?" Dwayne yelled, shifting around from beneath the girl.

"Who are those people?" Jessie asked, looking out the window.

I glanced out my own and watched as we passed three tall men in black gowns, similar to what the girl was wearing. They were staring at us from the side of the road. Pointing at the car as we sped by.

"I don't know," Tommy said, tapping on the steering wheel with his pointer finger, "but those aren't the first of 'em. While the three of you were blabbin' and touchin' her ink, I started seeing 'em.

One or two at a time, at first. Pointin' at us from the roadside."

Tommy took a deep breath, his eyes bouncing from the road to his mirrors. "There's a lot of 'em," he mumbled, wiping his forehead.

I looked out the back window as the three men faded into the night, watching us speed away.

"I think they're with *her*," Tommy finished.

"Jesus Christ," Dwayne said, looking out his own window. "Who the fuck did we hit?"

"About ten of 'em were waitin' in front of the hospital," Tommy continued, his voice now a monotone hum. "Right outside the entrance. They were waitin' on us to get there. I didn't know what to do. But pullin' in seemed like a bad idea."

"You think they want to hurt us?" I asked, to nobody in particular.

"Maybe they want to hurt *her*," said Dwayne. "They're all in black. She's in white. She was all alone."

"Do you think she was running from them?" asked Jessie, looking at me for an answer, for some reason.

But before I could guess, Tommy tapped the brakes. Hard. It was almost enough to roll the girl off of Dwayne and me–if we hadn't both grabbed her.

"Fuckin' bullshit," Tommy spat, and the rest of us looked out to the road. Several men–*and women*–in black gowns were now standing *in* the road, all pointing at us as Tommy swerved around them, blaring his horn.

"We gotta get the fuck outta here," Dwayne said, his voice a pitch higher than usual.

"The hell do you think I'm tryin' to do?" Tommy growled, straightening the Camino out to drive clear down the center of the road, straddling the yellow dividing lines.

But the black gowns were still appearing. We passed three more of them in the next few moments. Six more in the next minute. They were standing closer and closer to the center of the road, to the point where we'd collide with some of them if any one of us opened a door.

"What do they want?!" Jessie cried as Tommy zigzagged through another handful of pointers.

"If you ask me one more time, I'm throwing you out of the fuckin' car," Tommy said through his teeth. "One more word from any of you, and –"

Tommy slammed on the brakes again. A line of black gowns stood in front of us, stretching across the road. Seven of them in total, all holding hands with one another. All staring at us with wide eyes.

In the beam of the Camino's still headlights, I realized that the black gowns were split vertically down the middle, exposing the naked torsos of the men and women beneath them. Exposing the legs. The bare feet. The genitals. Everything.

Tommy threw the Camino in reverse, but to our horror, a second line of black gowns had formed behind us. None of us said a word as Tommy slowly put the car in park, turned the key off, and took a deep breath.

"Get her *the fuck* out of this car," he said to Dwayne and I, with the quiet intensity that might as well have been punctuated with a knife. Jessie did nothing but shake as she stared out front towards the dozen eyes staring back. They did not blink. They did not move.

"Fuck you, I'm not opening the door," Dwayne said, pressing the mechanical lock down and securing it in place.

"They're obviously following us because of *her*!" Jessie yelled, still watching the black gowns in front of us. "Get her out!"

I wanted to say something. Anything. But I couldn't. How did this happen? Why did I ever get in the car with them?

Because of Jessie. Because I wanted to seem *cool*.

Tommy threw his door open for the third time that night and leapt to Dwayne's side, nearly ripping the handle off of his door before pounding on the window until it practically gave out.

"I'm going to kick the shit out of you, Dwayne!" Tommy yelled, before rounding the back of the Camino and heading towards my door.

I looked out at the line of cloaked bodies staring back at us. I heard Tommy kicking up gravel and swearing as he reached my side of the car. I didn't lock my door. Maybe I was too scared. Maybe I wanted the girl out of the car, too.

Tommy yanked my door open and grabbed me by the shirt, pulling me out of the vehicle and tossing me to the ground. From the pavement, I looked back into the Camino at Dwayne, who was hanging his head off to the side. And then at the girl, who still wouldn't take her eyes off of me.

Tommy grabbed the girl by her legs and pulled her from Dwayne's lap. Her leg twitched again, but Tommy didn't seem to notice or care. He dragged her out of the car and dropped her to the pavement, beside me. But as he turned to head back to the driver's seat, the girl grabbed his pant leg with her broken fingers.

Tommy looked down at her and shook his leg, but she didn't let go. He looked back to the line of black gowns, who now marched towards us, and he sent a heavy kick right to the girl's face. And yet, her hand still clutched the hem of his jeans. Tommy glanced at me, quickly pulling his view back to the girl...and he stomped her again. This time, her grasp loosened.

Without hesitation, Tommy leaped into the driver's seat again, slammed the door behind him and started the Camino. I had no choice but to jump back into the car, wiping the gravel off of my hands and onto my jeans.

I looked again at the swarm of gowns. To my horror, the lines of eyes were closing in around us. We had maybe twenty yards until they reached us.

Tommy revved the engine, yelling at the interlocked people to clear a space. But they didn't. Instead, they started *singing*...all in the same operatic pitch. And all through open, smiling mouths.

A softer voice then joined in the chorus. To my right, through the window, I saw the dying girl sprawled out across the road. She was once again staring at me, smiling. And singing along.

Tommy shifted gears and revved harder.

...*just say you will...just do what you feel...I'm for real!*

I'd just noticed the music had started again with the car.

"Go, Tommy!" Jessie screamed. "Do it!"

"Punch it!" yelled Dwayne, and Tommy threw the Camino into drive. We were off.

"Wait!" I yelled, but it was too late. In seconds, we had run clear through four of the black gowns, spraying bodies like bowling pins in our wake.

...the music's full of joy and laughter. And it's such a thrill...

"Whoooo!" Tommy cried out as we sped off into the night. The other two were laughing and cheering, too. Mostly out of nerves, I assumed. I didn't know what to feel.

I turned to look at the wreckage behind us, but the black gowns were impossible to spot against the dark backdrop of the night. I couldn't even see the girl we had hit.

"I say," Dwayne began, cracking another beer, "we drive to the next gas station. No...Two gas stations down...and—"

"We're going to the next *town*," Tommy interrupted, hitting the gas a little harder. "And I'm not stopping 'till we get there. I don't care what we—"

"DEER!" Jessie screamed as a single doe skipped across the road, stopping right in front of the Camino to stare us down. Tommy hit the brakes, but not before clipping the creature and swerving off of the road...and into the ditch.

The impact was quick.

...music's tight-music's tight-music's tight-music's tight-music's tight—

I came to as the tape began to skip. Or maybe it had been skipping for some time. I didn't even know they *could do* that.

The car lay motionless, yet it was spinning all the same, and there was an odd pain behind my eyes, like someone was lightly pressing on them from the inside. I went to rub them, and felt a jolt in one of my shoulders. I could barely turn my head.

–music's tight-music's tight-music's tight-music's tight-music's tight–

No one else was moving.

"Is everyone–" I began, but stopped at the sight of Dwayne. His head had been thrown through the window. He was draped over the door, immobile. It was tough to say how much of the blood in his seat was his–or how much belonged to the girl in the white gown.

Tommy was crumpled into the driver-side floorboard. Dead.

–muuuusic's tiiiight-muuuuuusic's tiiiiiight-muuuuuuuuuuuusic's tiiiiiiiiiiiight–

The song was slowing down. And if it wasn't my imagination, the words were getting louder.

I *knew* cassette players couldn't do *that*.

"S-Steven?" Jessie whimpered. I couldn't see her from behind her seat. I lifted myself up, to the best I could, but still...

"Yea," I groaned. "You okay?"

"I hit my head," she said...and left it at that.

I reached for my door and pulled the handle. Because of the angle of the Camino, the door opened on its own. I took a deep breath and pulled myself out, collapsing into the dirt in the process.

–mUUUUUUUUUUUUUsic's tIIIIIIIIIIIIght-mUUUUUUUUUUUUUsic's tIIIIIIIIIIIIIght–

"Hang on," I called up at Jessie, realizing my shoulder had been dislocated in the crash. I couldn't see anything beyond a dim glow coming from the buried headlights of the Camino.

"I'm coming," I said through gritted teeth, attempting to stand as I clutched at my limp arm.

And then, the singing began again. That horrible, dreadful singing. Like an opera with no words. Haunting. Ceaseless. Coming from every direction.

mUUUUUUUUUUUUUUUUUUUUUUUUUsicstI IIIIIIIIIIIIIIIIIIIIIIIIIIIIIIIIIIIght–

As my eyes struggled to adjust to the darkness, shapes began to form. Cloaked figures. Naked bodies. White eyes.

Dozens of fingers…*pointing at me.*

mUUUUUUUUUUUUUUUUUUUUUUUUUsicstI IIIIIIIIIIIIIIIIIIIIIIIIIIIIIIIIIIIght–

Jessie's sobs barely cut through the monotonous wailing. Still, I could hear them. God help me, through it all, I could hear them. Even through the sounds of Dwayne's and Tommy's doors opening…and their bodies being pulled out. I could hear them.

To the backdrop of her screams, through the hellish ambience of the choir as it moved in on me…

…I wished I had never kissed Jessie Palmer.

Corey Lamb is a writer hailing from the murky depths of Baytown, Texas. Holding a degree in physics and punching a clock to pay the bills, Lamb breaks through the monotony by writing horror in his spare time. Though he has self-published several short titles under a pen name, *'The Girl in the Car'* marks the first piece of fiction published under Lamb's actual name. He is currently working on his first full-length novel.

Nia
E. R. Bills

Nia, Terry, Shen, Rudy, Mrs. Burgess.
Those were the names.
Those were *their* names.

I kicked up ash and watched it settle. The feather-like flakes folded and drifted, testing gravity. I walked through them holding my breath.

The fallout was still everywhere, forming a loose grit in the eviscerated buildings and rubble-filled streets. Patrolling Austin was like sifting through the remains of a shattered burial urn.

We only returned to the urban areas to scare up supplies or flush out renegade Klanners. For the most part, resistance had been reduced to scattered acts of terrorism; but the Klanners were still a problem. You could tell who most of them were by the Swastikas crudely branded on their foreheads.

They used coat hangers fired by red-hot coals to make the marks.

World War III had been exclusively pushbutton. No one knew exactly who pressed what first or why, but after the election in late 2020, nations with nuclear capabilities suddenly launched everything they had at us. We retaliated and won (maybe survived is a better word) because we had more than the rest of the world put together. I'm not sure there's anything left of Europe.

The final, conventional phase of the war was civil—civil war, I mean. All the boots-on-ground, blood-and-guts fighting was between Americans.

After the radioactive clouds lifted and the looting began, what remained of the Trump Nation fled to the relative security of Neo-Nazi and White Nationalist survival camps and shelters. Neo-Nazi and Klanner types had been prepping for doomsday for decades, and when the bombs fell, they went underground. When they re-emerged, they came back on top.

For years they had stockpiled provisions and arms in subterranean bunkers, and after the radioactive dust settled, they were sitting on what amounted to the largest store of uncontaminated food and water in the country and no small arsenal of munitions.

In no time at all, the Klanners filled the power gap. Preaching fire and brimstone, they treated surviving persons of color, immigrants, liberals, academics and the LGBT community to exactly that. "Taking the country back" was no longer a slogan. The central government and the American military had suffered devastating losses in targeted missile strikes, and their struggle to regroup gave the Klanners an opening. By the time the government and the Armed Forces were fully operational again, the Klanners were entrenched.

Nia, Terry, Shen, Rudy, Mrs. Burgess.

I suffered a severe head injury several klicks back. The doctors said it could cause a condition known as post-traumatic amnesia. My case wasn't as serious as all that sounds, but I was careful to follow the doctors' orders, and they said making and keeping lists and checklists was helpful. Written lists were best, but patrols weren't conducive to list-making, so I recited my chief list, my key, in my head. It was the last people I recalled being important to me. It helped me remember.

I was in graduate school when the war started, and I wasn't terribly surprised. Things had gotten completely out of hand under President Trump. Half the country no longer believed in America, much less the ideals it was purported to be founded on. Ideology had vanished, leaving only frustration and anger. When the press and congressional leaders attempted to curb Trump's abuses, it was just a matter of time before disgruntled MAGA zealots expanded infrequent, semiautomatic killing sprees to atrocities on a larger scale. They torched Muslim communities and businesses. They executed suspected immigrants, anyone they imagined had not been born on American soil. Thousands perished. Atrocity begat atrocity. Catastrophe begat cataclysm.

When the sirens sounded and the shelter designations came over the P.A., I was sitting in the Porter Henderson Library at Angelo State

University. I shook my head, wondering if we weren't finally getting what we deserved.

A handful of library employees—most of them students—ignored the shelter designations like me, and made their way to the library basement. We barricaded ourselves in and survived on what was in the student lounge kitchen and the candy and coke machines.

Rudy was a freshman political science major from College Station. He came to Angelo State with the intention of transferring to Texas A&M after he had a solid year of studies at a smaller school under his belt. I'd been in an Anthropology class with Nia my sophomore year. She was a skinny black girl with dark eyes. I was surprised she recognized me.

Shen was a Physics major from South Korea. Petite and cheerful, she'd only been in Texas for a few months. Terry was a Mexican American student from San Antonio. Sandoval was his last name, I think. He was stocky and fierce-looking, but as soft-spoken as a monk.

Mrs. Burgess, a research librarian and a widow—at least thirty years our senior—immediately assumed a matriarchal stance, and that was okay. It seemed to help her cope. The rest of us were disparate millennials, more traumatized by the disconnection we felt from the internet than our actual relationships with parents or siblings or each other. But this changed very quickly.

Nia, Terry, Shen, Rudy, Mrs. Burgess.
The Klanner hold that HQ Intelligence had sent me to find was reportedly maintained by 2-4 hostiles who were possibly in possession of a hostage.

Austin was a Dali landscape, especially the downtown. It looked like it'd been put in a microwave and cooked on "High." Anything that didn't melt or boil, burned or exploded. The handful of topside survivors—leftovers—looked like grisly wax figurines, hairless and dripping. Bleeding. There were very few of those still around.

The shelter survivors looked like emaciated ghosts. There were certainly no longer any concerns about keeping the town weird. It was bizarre enough for everyone, now. And it would likely remain that way for a long time. Maybe forever.

Patrolling was difficult, especially on foot. The long hills, the alleys. There were lots of tricky lines of sight.

Not much movement there, though. And that was good.

I was rescued by U.S. Marine regulars when the Klanners stormed the basement of the Porter Henderson Library, where we had holed up in a huge storage area that housed the Unprocessed and Special Collections. That's why the Klanners came. With everything offline and most utilities still inoperable, combustible materials became extremely valuable and even life-sustaining in the winter. Resources placed or stored aboveground had a greater radioactive imprint and residue; stuff in the subterranean shelters and storage was considered safer, cleaner. And we were surrounded by hundreds of thousands of books. All radiation-free.

It was a new take on *Fahrenheit 451*. Libraries became really popular again.

Nia, Terry, Shen, Rudy, Mrs. Burgess.

"I noticed you," Nia said.

"I didn't know," I replied. "I wasn't even sure you'd recognize me."

"I knew who you were before I noticed you.'

"How?"

"Something you did."

"What?"

"It's not important."

I kissed her.

We had our own little hiding place in the stacks. Near the boxes, piles and shelves of the Unprocessed Collection—we tried to stay away from the Special Collections. Everyone did.

We had all found our own spots. Shen was with Terry near the microfiche stations. Rudy was with Mrs. Burgess in one of the Study Rooms near the doors. He still had a girlfriend somewhere. Maybe. Hopefully. Mrs. Burgess was good company for him.

Nia finally kissed me back.

I smiled. "You kept me hanging."

"Oh, you white boys are insufferable. Nothing wrong with a little adversity."

"White boys? You mean I'm not your first?"

"I didn't say that. I'll neither confirm nor deny it. It's irrelevant."

I pulled her close. She put her arms around me. "What about the black guys?" I asked.

"I haven't seen any around. You'll have to do."

I kissed her again. "Just glad to be of service, ma'am."

"You know," she said, "one of my friends, a white girl. She said she'd been with you your freshman year. One-night thing, but no hard feelings."

"Yeah? And?"

"She said you were nice. And hung."

"Oh?"

"Yes."

"Am I?"

"You're not bad for a white guy."

I laughed.

"Fair enough," I responded, crooking my eyebrows. "But there's no need for the reverse discrimination."

Nia smirked. "Ha. Right. This is more like reverse affirmative action, *Mr. Chalky*. Is that white fragility in your pocket or are you just happy to see me?"

We sank then, undressing. Eager and maybe even a little reckless. Never could tell who might walk up. Mrs. Burgess would chastise us if she caught us. But only in a good-natured way.

It wasn't every day the world came to an end.

Nia, Terry, Shen, Rudy, Mrs. Burgess.

On patrol, something scurried ahead on the left side of the street. South Congress. I scanned the area. Small and not moving fast, whatever it was. I resented the break in my reverie.

I stepped over a discarded scooter. It was in decent shape and clean. Someone else was in the neighborhood.

I lowered myself to a crouch and listened.

I could hear leaves or light paper refuse being moved across a stretch of pavement or sidewalk by the light breeze. But no voices.

Then, a stray memory.

I'd come to Austin once as an undergrad. Sixth Street was a madhouse and we'd partied all night. It was an unsettling juxtaposition to what I was seeing now. More eerie than weird.

Two-thirds of the United States' population had died in the initial blasts and immediate fall out. Half of the last third suffered from terminal radiation exposure and would expire in the next several months. The entire country was filled with ghost towns.

Nia, Terry, Shen, Rudy, Mrs. Burgess.

When the Klanners came, we did our best. Or as much as we could do without actual weapons.

Mrs. Burgess braved the main entrance and she was a real handful. She fearlessly accosted the Klanners, accusing and scolding, all of it loudly, to warn us. She played the cards she had. Her indignance was palpable, but she held her contempt in check.

"Who do you think you are, young man? What is your name?"

Mrs. Burgess kept her hands on her hips and glared. "This is a public library. A *protected* facility. We are guarding these resources for future Americans. *For future Texans!* Didn't you grow up around here?"

It worked initially, befuddling the first two Klanners who came in. But the third unceremoniously silenced Mrs. Burgess with a gunshot to the center of her forehead.

Mrs. Burgess had tucked Rudy away in a mop closet. But when the Klanners shot her, he burst out of his hiding place with a broom, the handle of which he had whittled down to a sharp point. He rammed the makeshift spear through a Klanner's chest, just below the sternum. He must have worked on the broom handle in his spare time. It was a good idea. I wished I'd thought of it. The next Klanner that entered gunned Rudy down.

Nia and I hid, pursuing a half-baked plan to separate a Klanner from his gun if we could isolate one. Two walked into our trap instead of one and I hesitated, looking to Nia for direction. When I was spotted, she didn't hesitate. Before he even had a chance to raise his gun, Nia slammed him over the head with the spine-side of a giant, crisp new copy of *The World Book Atlas*. I clutched a massive compendium of the *Holy Bible*. It was that or a large, meticulously annotated hardback edition of *Moby Dick*.

Nia's *Atlas* knocked my would-be assailant out cold.

When the second Klanner came forward, Nia was bent over, in the process of striking the unconscious attacker in the head again. I clumsily telegraphed my swing, and the second assailant ducked away. I dropped the compendium and grabbed him just as he fired. I felt a pinch in my side and slipped behind him, wrapping my arms around his neck. I locked my right arm with my left and squeezed with everything I had.

The Klanner struggled and we fell backwards. He dropped his weapon and began clawing at my arms and neck. His swastika was fresh. I could smell the burnt flesh.

"Nia?"

No answer. I assumed she might be grabbing the first Klanner's gun.

I squeezed. The second Klanner gasped and abandoned trying to loosen my grip. He began punching back at me, trying to land a solid blow. I heard a rustling around our feet.

The Klanner was still swinging, but with less force. Nia rose up on her knees just in front of us, but something was wrong. She was pale and one eyelid was half-shut. She was holding the side her neck with one hand and it was covered with blood.

"Nia!"

I squeezed my arms around the Klanner's neck so hard that my biceps began to cramp, and he finally stopped struggling. When I was sure he was gone, I released him and pushed him away. Then, I crawled over to Nia.

Nia had dispatched the first Klanner with her second blow. The *Atlas* spine was splashed in blood. The pinch I'd felt in my abdomen, however, hadn't been a pinch. It was a bullet ripping through my side. It had apparently exited cleanly, striking Nia's neck, nicking her jugular.

Her eyes stayed with mine as I gently pried her hand away from the wound to check it. A jetting spurt of blood sprayed across my face. Nia re-clutched the wound and tears began streaming down her cheeks.

I straddled Nia on my hands and knees with my face just above hers. She placed her free hand on the nape of my neck. I stared into her eyes, realizing they were lighter than I'd originally thought. I took her free hand and kissed it, and then held it to my cheek.

Nia blinked repeatedly and took a deep breath. I kissed her lips. She tried to say something.

I turned my head to listen, my ear to her lips; but she couldn't get anything out. I pulled away and stared into her eyes again. They started to roll back.

The hand over her wound was slipping, releasing more blood.

"No!" I said.

Her eyes refocused and I held them. I eased her slipping hand away from the wound, transitioning mine to where hers had been. Her hand slipped to her side.

"Baby, I said. "*Please*. No. Nia. Please, *please*."

Her eyelids started to fall.

"Nia." I started to kiss her and she responded. I could feel her lips. We kissed.

I kissed her and then she was gone.

I raised my head.

Her eyes stared. She didn't even seem surprised.

My eyes filled with tears. I closed her eyelids with bloody fingers and kissed them, licking my lips, kissing the blood away.

A little more adversity.

Nia, Terry, Shen, Rudy, Mrs. Burgess.

When the Marines found us, they transported us to a temporary HQ near Ballinger. I was later told that Shen and Terry volunteered for the rebuilding effort. I wound up in the Corps.

They had found me in bad shape, barely alive. I still don't remember everything.

When the rest of the Klanners came, they saw me laying on the floor with Nia in my arms. They told me to get up, but I wouldn't. They tried to pull Nia away from me, but I clung to her more tightly.

"Let go uh that nigger," the leader said. "Act your race, brother. Stand up. Drop that nigger whore, now."

I refused to answer or even look at him.

"You hear him, son?" another inquired.

I ignored them both.

I closed my eyes, smelling Nia's hair, her skin. Her blood. I kissed her cheek.

"You're a fucking disgrace." the leader said. "A waste of white, corrupting yourself with that animal. Let her go and get up. And I'll make sure none uh your brothers violate her filthy corpse."

I opened my eyes. "Don't touch her," I said. *"Don't you fucking touch her!"*

One of my glaring "brothers" grinned.

I started to cry. "Don't fucking—"

Through my tears I saw a rifle butt come down on Nia's head. I heard the sickening crack of her skull and started to scream, trying to cover the wound with one of my hands. I screamed and raged. One Klanner slapped me in the side of my face with the butt of his shotgun, knocking out two of my teeth. They tried to pull Nia's body away, but I wouldn't let go.

And that's the last thing I remember.

I'm told that the Klanners smashed my head up pretty badly before the Marines arrived and put them down. Initially, they didn't think I was going to make it.

Nia, Terry, Shen, Rudy, Mrs. Burgess.

When I recovered from my injuries, I was a perfect candidate for what the U.S. military was calling the Tactical Defense System Renewal Operation. At first, the brass was hesitant to clear me for service. They were concerned about my wounds and the trauma I suffered. But the situation demanded all hands on deck. The civil war was mostly over, but they still needed to win the peace.

The accelerated course of basic training was strange, at first. All the things I might have hated about it before, repetition, drills, marches, morning reveille—the mechanics of it all—they came easily. I enjoyed the regimen, maybe even taking refuge in it. I fell in as if it were second nature. I was moved to active duty in less than four weeks.

I was surprised and amazed and then entirely pleased by my new composure; and it showed in my combat proficiency. Under fire, I cut down every hostile shadow along the horizon. In the trenches, I cracked every Klanner skull within reach.

I felt no remorse or pity. I cut through the enemy with machine-like stealth, no sadness, no hatred and no hesitation. Compassion was a pre-war luxury.

Six months into the campaign, the Klanners, who in the beginning had outnumbered us, were on the run. After the last of the Bible Belt Battalions surrendered in Alabama, the civil war, on any broad scale, was over.

The brass promoted me. I think it was an incentive to get me to stay. But I wouldn't have left anyway. I couldn't. Civilian life held nothing for me. I climbed the walls even on short R&Rs. I had found my rightful place in this new world. I had changed too much.

There were still active Klanner cells, groups that needed to be put down. And after everything I'd been through, patrol assignments were about the only thing that made peacetime bearable. War does that.

But still, sometimes I wondered if I would ever be able to switch it off or compartmentalize it. Surely, I'd have to eventually.

Occasionally, I considered what Nia would think if she saw me now; but I never dwelt on that speculation for very long. Nia no longer existed and I was pretty certain I was no longer the sort of man she could love.

Nia, Terry, Shen, Rudy, Mrs. Burgess.

I rose from my squat and stepped over the scooter. No doubt, this was where the 2-4 hostiles were hiding. Time to go to work. I reexamined the dilapidated cityscape and then disengaged the safety on my weapon. It was getting late.

In the building where our Intelligence indicated hostile operations, I detected an extranormal light source shining through a second-floor window. A careful scan of the perimeter revealed no snipers, so I crossed the street silently and slipped into the building through a broken first-floor window. The inside of the structure was lit only by the dwindling ambient light.

I stopped, listening.

I made out two distinct male voices and the whimpering of one male or female, possibly injured. I proceeded cautiously to the stairwell. The stairs were solid and I propped the door open to have more light. In a matter of seconds, I was outside the door of the apartment where I'd spotted the light through the exterior second-floor window.

I stood motionless outside the door for a long moment. The whimpering had stopped and there was a fourth voice, but it was low. I couldn't make out gender or disposition.

I kicked in the door and fired on three Klanners before they even had time to turn around. A young girl, whom the men had been standing over, darted under a table before the Klanners' bodies hit the floor.

A thirty-something year-old woman came charging out a side room, firing a Baby Browning or small Luger. I neutralized her as well. She collapsed next to the men, two of which had huge, fresh, square-shaped scars on their foreheads.

We'd been seeing a lot of this. Renegade Klanners attempting to assimilate, some earnestly, some to perpetrate a ruse. They cut or scraped the Klanner brand off. It was a crude procedure, and it made the skinhead variety of reformed Klanners look like jittery golems. The scars on their foreheads left no doubt they'd once been committed Klanners. The brass' take on it was that it was best to neutralize anyone with a scar on the forehead. It wasn't my job to welcome former Klanners into the new government, even if they'd had a change of heart.

Intelligence was convinced that most of them were not abandoning the Klanner cause so much as trying to infiltrate the new U.S. government's scattered co-ops and communes to create havoc. So We typically just shot them all to be sure.

The young girl never ventured from her spot under the table, but I could tell she was watching me. I asked her if she was injured.

She didn't answer.

"I'm not here to hurt you," I said. "I just want to make sure you're okay."

For a moment there was no response.

"You killed peepaw," the girl replied.

"Your father?"

"No. Peepaw."

"Your grandfather?"

"No. *Peepaw*."

I knelt down and slid to my knees to get a better look at the little girl. It was darker under the table, but I could tell she was six or seven and had curly blonde hair and bright eyes.

"Are you hurt?"

The little girl studied me noncommittally.

"Are you hurt?" I repeated. "I can help you."

The little girl looked in the direction of the fallen bodies, one of whom was Peepaw. "He was trying to fix it," she said.

"Have you been hurt? Were they trying to hurt you?"

"I have a sore tooth. Peepaw was gonna fix it."

"What is your name?"

"He was tryin' to pull my tooth."

"What is your name?"

The little girl looked like she was going into shock. I holstered my weapon and made a concerted effort to soften my voice. "Why don't you come out from under the table?"

The little girl raised her right hand like she was going to use the bottom of the table for leverage to slide out. I smiled and leaned in.

"My name . . ." she said, hesitating—but her right hand wasn't reaching for leverage. There was a makeshift sheath on the bottom of the table, concealing a machete. By the time I realized what was happening, she had swung the blade.

I jerked my head back too late.

I felt the tip of the machete split my scalp open, but I automatically seized it, blade first, and smashed the little girl in the forehead with the hilt. She scrambled backwards and I rose, flinging the table from my path with one arm.

Blood poured down my forehead. I wiped it away.

The little girl was helpless—in the back of my mind I knew this—but I didn't stop.

Before my actions even registered, I seized the little girl by her throat and began jabbing the hilt of the machete into her horrified face. I couldn't even hear her screams.

First, I collapsed the bridge of her nose. Then her eye sockets. I didn't stop till I had cratered her face and sunk the hilt all the way to the back of her skull.

Nia, Terry, Shen, Rudy. Mrs. Burgess.
Nia.

I knew exactly how she'd judge what I'd just done to that little girl.

Something in me snapped. I dropped the little girl's body and stepped backwards, tripping over a broken table leg. My stumble turned into an awkward jog and then a run.

I screamed and tore at my clothes. I bolted through the hall and down the stairwell. I tumbled out a side entrance on the first floor and found myself lying in a drift of ashes. They were floating again, all around me.

When I sat up, I heard a strange, repetitive whir.

Gathering myself, I unholstered my weapon and took cover. I surveyed the vicinity and discovered nothing. I scanned the rooftops—more nothing.

I considered the possibility that it might be a copter some distance out, but HQ had precious few choppers and rarely risked sending them into the city.

Nia, Terry, Chen, Rudy—Rudy.

I crouched and listened closely.

The whir was coming from directly above me.

Mrs. Burgess.

When I turned, the noise seemed to mimic my movement.

Nia, Terry. Chen.

I rolled instantly and fired three shots straight up.

Nothing.

I spun and fired three shots into the window of the Klanner apartment.

After the gunshots, the whir continued.

Nia. Terry.

I froze for several moments, focusing completely on the sound. Then, I raised my free hand to my right temple to concentrate. But I couldn't. I was completely rattled, my thoughts jumbled.

Nia, Nia. Terry.

I slid my fingers over to the top of my head, following the whir—and there it was.

Nia. Nia.

The little girl had done more than split my hairline.

Nia.

A portion of the upper left side of my head was gone.

Nia.

I scrambled to a large plate glass window in the side of the building to catch my reflection in the fading daylight.

Nia.

Where that part of my frontal lobe had been, there was now only crackling wires, sparking circuitry and some sort of hydraulic mechanism.

Nia.
They'd saved my life, but at what cost?
Was I even human?

Nia ...

Nia ...

Nia ...

E. R. Bills, award-winning author and editor, is known primarily for his nonfiction writing, but he has also published fiction and poetry. He co-edited *Road Kill: Texas Horror by Texas Writers, Vols. I & II*, with author Bret McCormick, and he was the sole editor of *Road Kill: Texas Horror by Texas Writers, Vol. III*. His upcoming horror collection, *Pendulum Grim*, will be released later this year.

Harvey
James H Longmore

Josh Regan stared open-mouthed into the dried-out, hollow eye sockets of the corpse. An involuntary scream got itself well and truly stuck in the back of his throat, and he gagged on the acid tang of bile that rose up from his guts.

Staggering backwards, Josh felt the darkness of the old house close in around him, smothering his senses, making his head spin. Blind panic soon took over his racing mind, and Josh turned on his heels to run. Although desperate to be away from the ghoulish sight of the withered body, he was painfully unfamiliar with the layout of the home he'd just burglarized. As a consequence, he managed to bark his shins against the unforgiving rim of the low, mahogany coffee table hidden amongst the inky shadows.

"Ow!" As white-hot shards of pain darted through his legs, Josh found his voice. *"Sonofabitch!"* In pain, truly panicking now, he

was utterly desperate to flee from the desiccated cadaver sitting there, nonchalant as you like, in the overstuffed armchair in front of the dark, silent TV. Josh fumbled his way across the unlit living room, where his confused brain thought it remembered the front door to be. Josh stumbled against the crowd of dust-laden furniture, his straining heart thumped hard and fast in his chest—its overbearing, rhythmic sound pounding in his ears like crashing waves on a stormy beach.

Fumbling in the inky darkness, Josh caught a whiff of the sharp stink of his own fear-sweat, reeking like a vile spirit, and he felt the pits and the back of his grey U of H hoodie sodden and clinging to his back like a rotting, second skin. It didn't occur to him at the time, but it was cool in the house—even though there was no tell-tale thrum of air conditioning—yet sweat oozed from Josh's pores, making his face slick, dripping into his eyes. The thought occurred that maybe his nerves were too shot for the burglary game now. More likely, the copious perspiration was because it had been two days since his last fix.

Finally, and with a shrill cry of utter relief, Josh found himself outside the dreadful house. He staggered out, the flimsy bug screen clattering behind him. And, because this was a typical small town in Texas, every house light in the street blazed on, and the residents were out on their respective porches brandishing their constitutionally mandated firearms. Somehow, the diverse catalogue of weaponry he found trained on him seemed a little less terrifying than the mummified thing he'd discovered in the house

*

The cops arrived, finding Josh on his knees in the dead center of the street, hands on head, surrounded by a half dozen pyjama-clad folk, pointing everything from 38 calibre handguns to twelve-gauge shotguns at the submissive man. Considering that Josh Regan had been caught red-handed burglarizing the Delaforce house and was looking at a considerable custodial stretch, The police were confused as to why he actually appeared to be relieved to be out of the place.

"There's a body in there," Josh informed the fat cop who took delight in squeezing the metal cuffs tight onto his damp wrists. Stale breath wheezed from the cop's overtaxed lungs like air from a busted tyre.

"Then you're in more trouble than you can handle, asshole," Police Chief, Stanley R. Goodfellow growled as he manhandled his catch toward the dusty black-and-white. The obese cop wrinkled his nose at the sour, sweat-soaked stench wafting from the kid like the stink from a cracked sewer pipe. Though prone to perspiration himself, the Chief had never known a skinny perp to sweat like this one. That included the fucked-up deadbeats who loved to destroy their bodies with cheap, home-made Meth' and Bath Salts.

"It wasn't me," Josh protested. "Dude's been dead a fuckin' long time!"

"We'll be the judge of who's dead, and for how long," Chief Goodfellow grunted. The exertion of bundling the kid into the back seat of the cop car was almost too much for his corpulent frame. "Hey, Curly, go check that out, would ya?" he barked.

The younger cop mooching around the small crowd of townsfolk enjoying a slice of free night time entertainment, was himself snatching a sneaky look-see through the ladies' nightwear, rendered translucent by the police car's headlights.

"Yessir," Curly – Deputy Charles Henstridge to those who offered him any modicum of respect – replied. Begrudgingly, he made his way towards the house from which Josh Regan had fled in abject terror not half an hour before.

*

The police tape flapped in the morning breeze; its noise akin to a cascade of unruly bats frantically fleeing a belfry. The Police Chief slurped on his already tepid double-shot coffee and cast a glance at the handful of idle, shivering cops. With disdain, he eyed Henstridge. Officer Henstridge had tried to claim a sick day for his supposed trauma at finding the shrivelled-up corpse. The kid claimed it had given him PTSD or some such. Goodfellow, a veteran of the second Desert Storm, had advised the young officer to quit being such a pussy and get his lazy ass to the crime scene by sun up. The official assumption was that the mummy in the overstuffed chair was Henry Delaforce.

Henstridge was gulping his fourth bottle of water so far that morning, the Chief noted. Ten-to-four odds he'd need to go pee the minute he was asked to go back inside the house. Not that the man needed an actual excuse to slack off. The other deputies, Smith, Dupeux, Lambert, and Balbino milled around the periphery of the thin, plastic barrier; between them they made up the majority of the town's police force.

Banham Falls was a small town of just five thousand or so mostly law-abiding and particularly God-fearing souls. It was a fairly close-knit community of proudly maintained, white-sided houses, a couple of schools, and a modestly sized oil refinery. It was the refinery that provided the most employment in the town, as well as undrinkable water and the tangy, chemical aroma that hung over the place. Goodfellow had been born and raised in Banham Falls. Most likely he'd die and be buried there, too. He figured he'd seen everything a small south Texas town had to offer up; but the sight of poor old Henry Delaforce's mummified body, sitting in that armchair as if he was just waiting for the ballgame to come on, was something the cop had never figured on.

They'd left the body *in situ* at the behest of the Medical Examiner, who'd promised to be along later that morning. Evidently, he had something better to do than poke and prod a dried-up dead person in the late hours of Friday night. In truth, it wasn't as if Mr. Delaforce was going anywhere, now was he?

Goodfellow snorted and took a huge swig of his coffee, gulping it down with little satisfaction. He peered up at the house he and Deputy Henstridge had so diligently surrounded by tape the night before. With curiosity, he eyed the brown, crisp lawn and the shrivelled flowers that bore more than a passing resemblance to their deceased owner. Of late, the weather had been as dry as a nun's tit, with nary a drop of rain in near-on two months. So far as Goodfellow could see, today was not going to be an exception. The morning skies were a clean, crisp blue, not marred by so much as a wisp of cloud. Most likely, Delaforce's sprinkler system had packed in at some point after poor old Henry passed on. Goodfellow mused that dead folk do have a tendency to neglect such things.

The withered foliage bothered the cop. He knew the neighborhood well, knew the whole damn town like the back of his hand. It puzzled him that the Nazis at the Home Owner's Association hadn't descended in their usual heavy-handed fashion. Normally, they'd have insisted Delaforce put his yard to rights, post haste. Goodfellow knew all too well that the HOAs in Banham Falls were aggressive to a fault when it came to the maintaining of the town's cutesy, small town 'merica look. He'd fallen foul of them himself, a couple of times in the past, when his front lawn strayed a quarter-inch above the regulation height.

Whatever the reason, they'd seen fit to ignore the neglected state of the Delaforce yard. Perhaps, if they'd actually done their job, Henry's body would have been found sooner. He'd still be quite dead, of course. The thought of the guy withering in his armchair, for what had to have been months, while the world went on without him, gave Goodfellow the heebie-jeebies.

Noticing a lanky, bald-headed guy across the street, Goodfellow hollered, "Pardon me, sir!"

The man squinting at the goings-on at the Delaforce house was not a member of the armed posse who'd captured Josh Regan the night before. How the heck had the man slept through all of that kerfuffle? The tall guy blinked over at Goodfellow and pointed at himself with a quizzical look on his bestubbled features.

"Yes, sir, you." Chief Goodfellow didn't hide his annoyance. Nobody else was around at this ungodly hour, so who the fuck else did the shiny headed freak think he was talking to?

"Can I help you, officer?" He meandered over. He rubbed the crusted sleep from the corners of his eyes, positioning himself to better gaze in puzzlement at the handful of cops and the tape that cordoned his neighbor's house. "What happened here?" he asked.

"Your neighbors apprehended a burglar last night. You didn't hear the commotion?"

"Heavy sleeper." The guy peered down at the cop and offered an embarrassed grin. "You'd be surprised what I can sleep through."

"You lived here long, Mr. –?" Goodfellow asked.

"About thirteen years now," the tall man replied. "It's Dave – Dave Brubaker." He offered a hand for the cop to shake.

Glancing down at the man's hand, Goodfellow was surprised at how long and slender the guy's fingers were – almost like a woman's. He ignored the offer. "How well did you know the Delaforces?" he said.

"As well as anybody knows their neighbors these days, I guess," Brubaker told the cop. "Pretty much kept to himself, after his old lady up and left on him. Sheesh, it's been ten years now."

"Mr. Delaforce lived alone?"

"Yeah, his missus took that goddamned fuck-up of a kid with her." Brubaker blanched. "Pardon my French, officer."

Goodfellow shook his head. He'd never understand how come folks felt the need to apologize for cussing in front of law enforcement. Wasn't like they were men of the cloth or anything. "Did the wife and kid ever come back? To visit, I mean."

"No, sir," Brubaker replied. "And good riddance too, as far as we were concerned."

"We?" Goodfellow said.

"All of us," Brubaker added, "the whole goddamned street. That kid was a bad'un through and through."

Officer Goodfellow's interest was piqued by this, and he figured – a tad too late now – that he really ought to be writing all of this down. He allowed the silence between them to ask the next question.

"It was funny how the cats and dogs quit going missing when Kathy took that horrible boy away," Brubaker continued. "There was a time you could barely see the street lamps and tree trunks around here for missing pet posters. We all suspected it was the Delaforce kid, but none of us had any proof. He was as smart as he was despicable."

"You think he was doing something to the neighborhood pets?"

"We *knew*, officer." Brubaker's face flushed with remembered frustration. "We just couldn't *prove* it."

"So, when was the last time you saw Mr. Delaforce?"

"Erm –" Brubaker fidgeted on the spot as he thought, as if the idea was uncomfortable for him. "It must have been Wednesday – yeah, it was definitely Wednesday. I caught him at his mail box to ask him about his basement. Ours was letting in a little water and I wanted to know if his was, too."

"Wednesday?" Goodfellow was nonplussed, to say the least. "You say you saw Mr. Delaforce *two* days ago?"

"Yessir."

"Are you sure about that, Mr. Brubaker?"

"Absolutely, officer." Brubaker squinted at the cop with an expression akin to amusement. "Why do you ask?"

"I can't comment on the specifics of an on-going investigation, sir, but we have reason to believe Mr. Delaforce has been dead for quite some time." Goodfellow figured he'd be okay to give that much away without compromising what was turning into an interesting case.

"Well, he was looking alive and well when I spoke to him the day before yesterday, officer." Brubaker eyed the cop with suspicion now. "And come to think of it, so did his garden. Me and the rest of the Resident's Committee had Henry in the running for Yard of the Month – there's a trophy and a book token up for grabs – what the heck did you people do to his yard?" The bald guy assessed Henry Delaforce's crisp, brown grass and withered, desiccated flora, with disdain. His nose wrinkled as if he'd caught whiff of an especially noxious stink.

"Thank you for your time, Mr. Brubaker." Goodfellow ignored the question. He had very little desire to be drawn into the minutiae of Brubaker's petty suburban life. "I'll send a deputy over later to take your statement; please don't go anywhere." And with that, the cop turned on his heels, walked back toward the Delaforce house, leaving Brubaker scratching his shiny head in the center of the street.

"Deputy Henstridge!" Goodfellow called to Curly who was staring vacantly at the police tape as if it were hypnotizing him. "Curly!" Goodfellow yelled a little louder. This time, his deputy spun around, almost dropping his half-empty water bottle as he did so. "Take Lambert. Go check out the house again – there's a basement."

Henstridge paled. "We already looked, sir," he mumbled as Goodfellow approached.

"Did you specifically look for a *basement*, Deputy Henstridge?"

"Er... no, sir," the young cop replied. His eyes flicked across the dead lawn to the house; the memory of his first meeting with Henry Delaforce still vivid and painfully raw in his mind. "But –"

"Yeah, I didn't think these houses had them, either," Goodfellow pre-empted his deputy's excuse. Basements were a rarity in this part of low-lying Texas. If the Delaforce house had one, and his men had not found it, that suggested to the Chief perhaps someone didn't want it to be found. This thought triggered a niggling voice at the back of Goodfellow's ever-inquisitive cop mind, and he simply had to find out *why*.

"Okay, sir," Deputy Henstridge said with reluctance edging his tone, "but I gotta go pee first."

*

It was Deputy Lambert who found the trapdoor to the Delaforce basement. It was a roughly put together thing concealed beneath the cheap Ikea rug in the dining room. Mercifully, it was out of sight of the dried-up Henry Delaforce. *When was the*

Medical Examiner coming to cart that disgusting thing away? The crude trapdoor sported a single, metal hoop handle.

"I guess we should take a look-see," Lambert said as he mopped away the beads of sweat accumulating on his brow despite the tepid temperature inside the house.

"The Chief said *look* for a basement," Henstridge, ever the obstinate one, replied, "and we looked."

Lambert cast a wry smile at the deputy. He could see the kid was uncomfortable; he had a damp sheen of sweat across his sickly face and pit stains from hell spreading down his uniform shirt. "I do think we're supposed to check it out, Curly," Lambert said with firmness in his voice. Dealing with Henstridge was like training an unruly puppy – it was all in the tone of the voice.

The young deputy huffed and rolled his eyes. Nonetheless, he helped Lambert heave the trapdoor open. A sweat stain grew on his pants, making him seem to have peed in them.

The two cops stared down into the dark silence that greeted them; neither knew what they were looking for. Lambert pulled a flashlight from his belt, clicked it on.

"What are you doing?" Henstridge appeared shocked at this turn of events.

"We're not climbing down there in the dark," Lambert replied. His patience was quite frayed at Curly's laziness. "And I do mean *we*."

Defeated, Henstridge thumbed the button on his own flashlight and pointed it down into the square hole. The stark, yellow light revealed steep, wooden stairs leading into the basement. He popped the snap on his holster, too, freeing his gun, just in case. Deputy Henstridge may have been one lazy sonofabitch, but he wasn't stupid.

At the bottom of the steps there was a door. It was a thick, wooden affair with a half dozen fat, steel bolts securing it. A weak thread of light struggled around the periphery of the door, as if it was a smidge too small for its frame.

"Looks like somebody does have something to hide," Henstridge commented as he slid the first of the bolts from its catch. His curiosity was aroused now.

"Or something they don't want to get out," Lambert replied. "These bolts are all on the outside, and there's no locks."

"Oh yeah." Henstridge seemed undeterred by his own misjudgement. "Ya think old man Delaforce had some kind of Ariel Castro thing going on down here?"

"Could be," Lambert grunted as he crouched down to release the last of the bolts. His knees popped like distant firecrackers. "Maybe we're gonna find Mrs. Delaforce and a whole bunch of secret kids." He flashed his colleague a sardonic grin as he stood back up. "Or maybe it's just Henry's weed farm."

"Now, that, I could do with." Henstridge laughed. He followed Lambert into the dimly lit, claustrophobic basement room.

"That and a goddamn drink; I'm freakin' parched," Lambert said. He stooped his head to avoid the low ceiling. "I'm sweating it all out down here." Even in the feeble light from the solitary bulb hanging overhead, the cop could see his regulation shirt was soaked through; it was a losing battle to keep the perspiration from stinging his eyes.

"What in tarnation is that?" Henstridge pointed his flashlight at the far corner of the basement room. There, next to another heavy, wooden door – as over-bolted as the first – sat a small camping stove. Scattered around it were a handful of discarded propane canisters and an array of empty food cans. "Odd place to go camping," the cop commented. He picked out the labels on the cans. All appeared to be varieties of condensed soup.

"Takes all sorts, I guess." Lambert cast his flashlight's eerie glow about the room; his free hand hovered over the gun, heavy against his sweat-sodden hip. *"Oh, sweet Jesus!"* the cop cried out. His flashlight dropped to the dirt floor with a muffled *thump,* sending up a plume of fine dust to dance around his feet.

"What the fuck, Gerry?!" Henstridge was spooked by his colleague's sudden outburst. "What the hell is wrong with you?"

"W-what *is* that?" Lambert composed himself just enough to pluck his flashlight from the dry, dust-laden floor and aim it at the corner opposite the stove.

"Oh, sweet mother of god." Now it was Henstridge's turn. "Not another one." Just when he figured he'd seen enough withered-up corpses for one lifetime, Deputy Curly Henstridge found himself staring into the empty eye sockets of another.

The body was that of a woman, that much was evident. It was, however, impossible to tell how old she'd been when death caught up with her. Judging by her attire – tweed skirt, white, button-up blouse and sensible, low-heeled shoes -- Henstridge took an educated guess at the deceased being middle-aged when she quit breathing. Taking a tentative step toward the corpse, pausing only to wipe an errant droplet of sweat from his eyebrow, he directed his flashlight at the dead woman's face.

"Jesus, Curly," Lambert whimpered. His stomach churned at the sight of the stretched, parchment skin surrounding the rictus grin of the skull. The eyes had shrunken away to nothing a long time ago. The woman's hair had shifted to one side when her scalp shrank away from the yellowed, knitted bones of her skull, creating the somewhat comical appearance of an ill-fitting wig.

"Looks like she's been down here awhile," Henstridge said, more to break the eerie silence in the basement than to inform Lambert. "Perhaps Mrs. Delaforce didn't run off after all." He stepped away from the body and his attention turned to the bolted door near the dead woman. "And maybe Mr. Delaforce was hiding something before he wound up in the same state as his wife?" Henstridge began sliding the bolts open. His mind was still thinking *weed farm* as Lambert joined in. Both cops were keen to discover what lay on the other side of that massive door.

Bolts undone; Lambert trained his flashlight upon the door while Henstridge tugged at its handle; his hand was slick with his own sweat upon the cool metal.

"C'mon, ya bastard." Henstridge grunted with exertion. The door felt jammed into its frame, like the wood was warped and swollen. Both hands. Another hard tug. The door jerked open. Henstridge staggered back as something warm, damp, and intangible *whooshed* by him with enough force to ruffle his hair and snatch the breath from his throat. "What the –?" the cop gasped. A fresh wave of sweat broke out along his spine, soaking the back of his shirt through.

The room beyond the door was lit by a series of strip lights – five in all – which thrummed like a hive of annoyed insects along the low-slung beams of that second basement room. The stark, flickering light illuminated the entirety of the spacious room, including the emaciated frame of a naked young man chained up at the farthest corner.

Henstridge drew his gun; Lambert quickly followed suit, and the pair stepped into the chamber. Lambert clicked off his flashlight and slipped it back into his belt. All the while, he directed his weapon on the nude guy standing motionless by the wall.

"Stay where you are, sir," Henstridge instructed. At once he felt foolish – it was painfully obvious, with the shackles and thick chains coiled at the young man's feet, he was not going anywhere at all. The man stood stock-still, staring at the cops, surrounded by clear puddles of water that shimmered in the cold, iridescent light and steadfastly refused to soak into the dirt floor. The guy's body was pale and angular, his ribs and hipbones prominent against his light-starved, translucent skin. His eyes were sallow and sunken. He watched the cops with nervous suspicion, yet didn't move a muscle as they approached with guns drawn.

Purposeful, cautious, Henstridge made his way toward the frail man. The cop gave a hasty glance around the room, noting that it appeared relatively new compared to the first room; as if it had been more recently carved out under the Delaforce house. Also, he wondered why the periphery of the room was piled high with literally thousands of tiny silica gel packets. They were the kind you find in new shoes, lady's purses, electronics – myriad things that need to be kept safe from the ravages of moisture. And here they were, absurdly out of place, in the stark, flickering light of Henry Delaforce's basement, stacked up in huge, cascading mounds all the way up to the wooden joists.

"What's your name, sir?" Henstridge's voice was dulled in the dank atmosphere of the room. "Can you tell me your name?" The cop edged ever closer.

"Harvey." The young man strained to form the word. "I'm Harvey Delaforce."

"Shit," Lambert muttered beneath his breath.

"Don't you worry, Mr. Delaforce – Harvey – we'll have you out of here in no time," Henstridge assured as he reached for his radio – they were going to need bolt cutters.

"You can't do that, officer," the young man replied. He took a step forward. His naked body glistened in the cool light.

Henstridge stopped dead in his tracks. He was three, maybe four strides away from the guy, and now he was worrying about booby-traps. "Why can't we do that, sir?" he questioned, "are there *bombs* down here?"

Harvey Delaforce laughed lightly; the sound so terribly out of place down there in the grimy confines of the basement. "There are no bombs or bear traps, officer," he said with a sardonic grin, "only me." And as he spoke, the puddles of crisp, clear water surrounding him began to move.

Henstridge and Lambert stood, mouths agape, as the small pools rose into columns – some small and squat, others almost to the bare sheetrock of the ceiling. As the cops looked on, sweat running down their backs, under their arms, and along the insides of their pants, the water columns took on a variety of shapes.

There were dogs, cats, what appeared to be squirrels, birds and rabbits, a pony, and a bunch of people, all faithfully sculpted by the shimmering water – right down to the wrinkles and creases of their faces.

"Henry," Henstridge gasped, recognising one of the faces from a photograph he'd seen displayed over the Delaforce fireplace. His gut told him that the female shape – as naked as the day she'd been born – was Mrs. Delaforce; Harvey's mother. "What the hell did you do to them?" the cop asked.

"*Hydrokinesis*," Harvey replied, as if that one word would explain everything. "Dad made up the word – I think the old fart thought he was being clever." His voice sounded cheerless; his mind plagued by memories of happier times.

Henstridge plucked his radio from his belt. The thing felt unpleasantly damp from resting against his sweat-soaked trousers. He clicked it on. "This is Deputy Henstridge. Requesting backup, copy?"

"You guys okay down there?" crackled the reply.

"Yeah, that's why we need back up," Henstridge growled. "We need bolt cutters and –"

"I said *no*," Harvey Delaforce snapped. His strained voice resounded about the room. "You can't do that, officer, I need to stay here." The water sculptures rippled, influenced by the young man's irritation; their eerie, transparent faces displayed something akin to anger. Henstridge thought he'd heard panic in the guy's voice.

"You can't –"

Deputy Lambert collapsed to his knees. The dull thud of his gun hitting the floor startled Henstridge. Lowering his gun, he twisted to see what the hell was going on behind him.

"I don't feel so good, Curly." Lambert's voice was parched and rasping, though he drooled strings of saliva onto his chest. Sweat poured from his face, and his tear-filled eyes appeared to shrink, even as Henstridge watched. The deputy's clothes were drenched, his hair plastered to his scalp, and his body trembled as if painfully cold. Then, as Henstridge looked on in disbelief, the cop's bladder let go and a dark pee stain spread across the front of his department-issued pants. As the pool of sweat, tears, drool and urine dripped to the basement floor, it made its way in a skinny, meandering rivulet – slowly, unerringly – toward Harvey Delaforce.

"Can you hear me?" Henstridge barked once more into his radio. All he heard was static. Face red with rage, he turned his attention to Harvey, his raised voice wavering in terror. "What the hell are you doing to him?"

"I can't help it, officer," Harvey replied. "I have tried to control it – believe me, I've tried – but *it* controls *me*." He sounded apologetic. "And every day it gets a little stronger, it even got to Dad in the end – did you *know* the human body is over sixty percent water?" He glanced at the bizarre, liquid statues gathered around him like ghoulish friends.

Henstridge's mind spun back to his first encounter with the tragically dehydrated Henry Delaforce, a grim reminder of how Lambert – who now lay twitching on the basement floor, his eyes rolled back in sunken sockets – would look once all of the water departed his body.

"I'm guessing it's reached outside the house already," Harvey said with sadness. "And who knows how far it'll go now you've opened the goddamned door?"

Henstridge took a step back. Slick droplets of sweat oozed from his every pore, his eyes streamed with uncontrollable tears, and his mouth filled with saliva that dribbled from the corners of his cracked lips. The cop then felt his bladder release; the warm sensation in his crotch was unmistakable, as was the sharp, acrid tang of ammonia assaulting his nostrils. Only this wasn't like peeing. To Deputy Charles – *Curly* – Henstridge, it felt as if the stuff was *crawling* out of his bladder of its own accord, like it had a mind of its own and he had no control over it. The cop looked down through the haze of his tear-filled eyes and saw a thin stream of yellow water snaking its way from between his feet toward Harvey Delaforce.

Fixing his blurred stare at the young man, Henstridge let the radio fall from his hand, and with every ounce of waning strength he could muster, he raised his Glock and aimed at where he figured the scrawny, naked guy's head should be.

Outside he heard the unmistakable *pitter-patter* sound of fat, raindrops pounding the parched ground. The noise echoed in the cool, bone-dry air of the Delaforce basement.

James H. Longmore, James hails originally from Yorkshire, England having relocated with his family to Houston, Texas in 2010. He has an honors degree in Zoology and a background in sales, marketing and business. His writing style and storytelling has already been compared to James Herbert, Richard Laymon, Stephen King, Dan Brown and Robert Ludlum. An Affiliate Member of the Horror Writer's Association, and founder of HellBound Books Publishing LLC, James has to date five novels published, plus his definitive short story collection, all in addition to three novellas and a whole bunch of short stories dotted about in myriad anthologies.

www.jameslongmore.com

www.hellboundbookspublishing.com

You Can Outrun The Devil
if You Try
William Jensen

I turned thirteen the summer the murders stopped. For the preceding decade a body was found every year, usually in July or August when the heat scorched Texas to a dead, gunmetal gray and sunsets hemorrhaged in the west. You felt the tension as we moved out of spring. Women refused to leave home after dark. Teenagers whispered legends and half-truths about the crimes. That year LBJ gave his "Great Society" speech, and in Houston the Colt .45s became the Astros and moved into their new, beautiful dome. The Dallas Cowboys had the best season they'd ever known. But in my home of Anson, Texas, the reign of the Rice County Ripper was about to end.

My daddy was the sheriff, and he took a lot of grief for not being able to catch the killer. People said he needed to call in the Rangers, but Daddy couldn't let it go. Every summer, as the cicadas snarled through the dusk, my father became stoic and stern. He stayed up late looking at photographs, muttering about the victims. From my room, I'd listen to him pace, his boots scuffing the dining room floor as the season dragged on. I thought my father was obsessed.

The Ripper killed women, all young and usually runaways; none of them were from Anson. That year they found two dead girls. The first was a nineteen-year-old from San Antonio. She'd been left off Farm Road 1126.

Daddy and his deputy came home late the night she'd been discovered. I'd been on the couch watching *Attack of the Giant Leeches* on TV and trying not to think about the terrible heat outside. Daddy's deputy was named Lewis and had worn the badge for less than a year. He looked pale and starved as he trailed my old man inside.

"There's some leftover brisket in the ice-box," I said.

"I don't think I could eat a bite," said Lewis. "It was just awful. I didn't know anyone—"

"Cut it out, Lewis."

"Sorry, boss."

"What happened?" I said, twisted around on the couch and facing them. Lewis stood slouched and pale. He was lanky like an oak branch, and his cheeks and nose stayed in a near constant blush. Daddy poured two glasses of whiskey and set them on the table. He motioned for Lewis to sit. He sat. Lewis held his glass with both hands.

"You should go to bed," said Daddy.

"There was another one, wasn't there?"

"The bastard cut her in half, Mason. Her legs were on one side of the road, her head and arms on the other. I don't know how anyone could—"

"Lewis, you keep talking and I'll ask you to leave."

"I'm sorry, I'm just pretty gone rattled."

"Mason," said Daddy, "go to bed. We'll talk in the morning."

I grunted, turned off the Zenith, and marched upstairs. I opened and closed my door loud enough for Daddy to hear, and I sat on the landing, holding my breath. I listened to Daddy and Lewis talk, their voices solemn, low, and shaky at times. It was almost as if by just discussing what they'd seen, they might condemn themselves to a similar fate.

"Drink your drink," said Daddy.

I heard the deputy struggle to swallow his liquor. I leaned forward so I could see them. Lewis slammed his glass down and gasped. He squinted and ran his tongue over his teeth. Daddy lit a cigarette and watched him. Daddy was practically the opposite of Lewis—muscular, tall, and handsome with dark hair. He leaned forward and rested his arms on the table. He smoked.

"I don't know if I can do this," said Lewis. "The job, I mean."

"You'll be fine."

"Seeing something like that... it tests my faith, Rusk."

"Want another?"

"No. I need to get home. God, he's sick, whoever he is," said Lewis. He almost wept as he spoke. "The bastard took her eyes."

"Here," said Daddy, "have another. You're part of the club now."

"There wasn't any blood, Rusk."

"He moves the bodies."

"I just got married. How am I supposed to go home to my bride and …?"

"You'll figure that out."

"The guy is a skillet full of rattlesnakes, ain't he?"

Daddy poured two more. Lewis and my father spoke a bit longer, but eventually Lewis left. Daddy stayed up and kept drinking. He cursed, mumbled, and sighed. I leaned back to stay out of sight, and I listened with a nervous curiosity, bunched up and trying to remain mute. I always eavesdropped. I wanted to hear the truth about the bodies, the gore. Daddy never spoke to me about the ripper. He said I wasn't old enough. He told me it was police business and not Jr. High gossip. I'd grown up with stories about the Ripper, and the tales about him floated around the schoolyard to the point he grew to mythical status. My friends always thought I knew more than I let on, because Daddy was the sheriff. And I suspect that is even more of a reason why Daddy didn't tell me anything about the investigations.

Daddy and I lived alone at the family farmhouse at the end of a long gravel road the color of bone. Neither the house nor the barn are still standing. They burned down years ago. It had long since ceased to be an operational farm. It was just a dwelling with low property taxes. We were surrounded by cedar and mesquite. Cliffs of limestone stood in the north that blocked the winds from the upper plains. Everyone else in our family had died. I never knew any of them. My mother passed away when I was two. I don't have any memories of her. Daddy liked to say she was in Heaven watching me, but I never believed that. I never believed in an afterlife.

A few weeks later, for my thirteenth birthday, Daddy took me into San Antonio to watch *Von Ryan's Express*, which I thought was the best movie I'd seen up to that point. On the drive home through the hill country, back toward Anson, he asked me if I had given any thought to my future.

"My future?" I said.

"Yes, you're basically a man now, Mason. You're going to have many new responsibilities."

"You mean like a job or college?"

"More like what traits you want to have. What type of man you want to be."

My father steered with one hand, guiding the truck around the curves and bends with confidence. The man smelled of aftershave and cigarettes. "Ribbon of Darkness" by Marty Robbins played on the radio. Daddy kept his eye on the road. He waited for me to speak.

"I guess I want people to like me. To trust me. Like they do with you."

Daddy smiled.

"Even if that means doing something you wouldn't enjoy? Or what if it is something you don't believe in? Do you have any idea how many times you're going to have to make unpopular decisions?"

"Well, no," I said.

"Would you rather stand by your ideals? Even if that means everyone would hate you?"

"Yes," I said, "at least I think so. I don't know."

"It's fine," he said with a smile. "It isn't supposed to be easy."

Daddy drove on. He told me I was becoming a fine young man, and he was proud of me. It was a rare compliment. My father didn't often express his feelings. Hearing him say something like that meant the world to me. We rode with the windows down; the hot wind whipped and washed us clean and dry.

No major clues were found with the dismembered woman on Farm Road 1126. Since the Rice County Ripper struck once a year, everyone figured the terror was finished for the season. But then, in August, when the heat was at its worse, he struck again.

That evening I was out with friends at the Dairy Queen. We discussed two topics: girls and the Ripper. Some of my friends believed he'd never be caught. Others said he wasn't even a man; he was a vampire or a skinwalker.

"Texas is older than you think," said one boy. "A lot of bad mojo happened long before the Alamo."

"What are you saying?"

"Just that there's things we don't understand. And sometimes the past catches up to you."

"You are so full of crap," I said as I finished my milkshake and got up to leave. My friends laughed and warned me to watch out for the Rice County Ripper on my walk home. I laughed, too. I don't know why I thought it was so funny. I suppose, without consciously thinking it, I considered myself impervious.

I didn't see any monsters along Farm Road 1126, but as the sun went down, I kept thinking about how much bloodshed my corner of the map had seen. Maybe there was something about the land and a curse. I walked against traffic. The headlights of oncoming cars came white as ghosts and vanished just as quickly.

At the end of the dusty road, I saw the outline of my house, but not a single light was on inside. I saw my father's truck and police cruiser, so I knew he had to be home. I figured he was asleep. When I came inside and went into the dining room, I saw someone sitting at the head of the table. It wasn't my father. It was just a figure, no one I recognized. I froze for a second and let my eyes adjust to the dark. I wasn't sure how to approach or even if I should.

Something else was different. The house was lit by only a few candles scattered around the table, and they cast crooked shadows and a soft, golden glow. I didn't see my father. My eyes slowly focused. The person at the table was a young woman; she was older than me but not by much, maybe five or six years. She had short, blond hair, bobbed like a flapper's from the '20s. Sweat made her face glisten. The girl trembled without noise.

My brain tried to fill in the details and make sense of what I saw—a co-worker, an old family friend, a relative I'd forgotten—but I knew she was a stranger. She wore denim shorts and a man's undershirt. The girl didn't look at me as I approached. She was crying but without tears, as if she'd run out of them.

"Daddy?" I said but heard no response. The girl flinched in her chair. She stared at me. She grimaced.

"Kid," she said, "you got to help me. Untie me."

I stepped forward and saw that her wrists and ankles were bound to the chair. A bit of blood and a bruise smeared around the corner of her mouth. I stood there dumb, sucking in hot, still air.

"What? Who are you?"

"He pulled us over. We thought he was going to bust us. My friend got away. This guy is going to kill me. He's crazy."

My father suddenly appeared and stood about ten feet behind the girl. He had his shirt off, and his eyes were wild. He held one hand behind his back. He stood still, barely visible by the candlelight. His belly moved in and out as he breathed. I stayed by the girl, unsure what to do or where to look. He stepped forward but remained behind the girl who twitched her head trying to see him. I heard him sigh. Cicadas hummed outside. The girl in the chair panted and grunted as she tried to break free.

"Daddy?" I said, not knowing what else to say or do.

"Hot outside, isn't it, Mason? I think it gets worse every year."

"Please, kid. He's crazy. I don't want to die."

Daddy placed his left hand on the girl's shoulder. He spoke, but he didn't look at me. He looked through me.

"I learned a long time ago that the world works in a type of give and take. You've got to put in if you want to receive. When your mama died on us, I realized I needed to give more to the world. The summer she died, the heat was so bad it would drive a man mad. Nobody could stand it. I keep trying to make it better, Mason. A man can't stand this type of heat."

I tried to stay calm. I chose my words carefully.

"Daddy, I'm going to untie this lady and we can—"

His right hand came around from behind his back. He held his hunting knife neither tightly nor loosely. I focused on the blade. Dad's sight drifted off into some nothing in the distance. The girl began to sob.

"No," he said. "I learned how to stop it, Mason. After your mama died, the heat started to cool. All it took was a sacrifice."

"You asshole," said the girl. "Do you even know how insane you are?"

"It has to be done, Mason. I don't know how or why it works. But this is what it takes. You have to trust me."

"Shelly got away, you freak. She's going to find the cops, the real cops, and you're going to jail."

"Daddy, you can't do this. You don't want to hurt anyone, and I know…" My voice disappeared. I couldn't speak, and my insides melted. Everything started to snap into place with a screech. Somehow it had never crossed my mind, but how could it? Those nights Daddy stayed up with the photographs hadn't been about solving the case as much as it had been about reliving the experience and avoiding being caught. He'd never called in the Rangers, not because of pride, but for his own survival. I reflected on all the behavior changes in the summer and realized how sick he was, but I couldn't force myself to do anything. Part of me refused to believe it. Nowhere did I imagine Daddy to be capable of any of this. I wished I had never learned any of it. I wanted to close my eyes and have it go away.

"The bigger the sacrifice, the more elaborate it is, the better. Sometimes the first one doesn't take. But you're thirteen now. It's time you learned."

Daddy snatched the girl's hair and pulled her head back. She clenched her jaw and bared her teeth. Daddy extended his arm and held the knife toward me.

"Take it," he said, his voice calm and flat.

Daddy gestured the knife at me again. The girl whimpered.

"Don't leave me, kid. Don't let me die. Not like this. I want to go to college and have a family. I want to go home. I want to see my parents. I want my mom. Please don't let him—"

Daddy yanked her hair again. The girl yelped and went silent. Daddy closed his eyes and sighed. A vein in the girl's neck pumped and throbbed. She was drenched with sweat.

"Mason, they're going to come for me. Her friend did get away. It's just a matter of time now. But someone has to do this. Someone needs to end this horrible, miserable heat. It has to be done."

We looked at each other. I didn't take the knife. Daddy shook his head with disappointment. He nodded a little as if listening to cynical instructions and muttered something. The girl began to pray but not for long.

Daddy let out a howl as he slid the blade across the girl's throat, just below her chin. The girl's eyes went wide, and the blood kept coming and pouring and coming. She gurgled and gasped and coughed. Daddy let go of her hair and stepped back. The girl's shirt turned red and wet. She trembled a little as her eyes went blank, and she turned limp and still.

I couldn't move. It all happened so quickly that I didn't understand what was occurring until the girl was dead. It felt like a vulgar magic trick, a disturbing illusion or some joke that didn't make sense. Blood dripped onto the floor. Blood puddled by the girl's feet. Daddy told me to come forward. I shook my head. I lost the ability to speak. I couldn't tell him no.

"Mason, it's okay. Come here. You need to learn. Someone must carry on the tradition. I don't have much time."

I started to cry, but noiselessly, and I stood outside myself as my brain and soul iced over and shattered into a million shards and splinters. I wanted to scream, but I couldn't. I wanted to run, but I couldn't. I wanted to do anything but stand there looking at the girl, her eyes zeros and void, her front stained merlot. She wasn't going to college. She would never have a family or travel or see her friends again. She sat there in a lump, just organs and skin.

Daddy reached around and placed a hand on her chest. His palm and fingers were covered with blood when he pulled it back. He ran his hand down his front from his sternum to his belt, leaving a crimson streak along his center. He closed his eyes. He let out a long breath before he looked at me.

"Your turn," he said.

I stepped backwards. I started shuffling away. Daddy lunged and grabbed my arm. His hand was still wet with the girl's warm blood. He pulled me to her body. He held me in place before her. Daddy stood behind me with his hands on my shoulders. He leaned in and put his mouth close to my ear.

"This is for you," he whispered.

He put a hand on the back of my skull and slowly, almost gently, pushed my head toward the girl and pressed my face between her breasts where the blood soaked her shirt dark, her sacrifice unwilling and afraid. Blood smeared my cheeks, my brow. Her blood ran over my lips and into my mouth. She tasted of metal and salt, thick without sweetness. I choked and gagged, but Daddy pressed harder.

"Yes," he said. "Suck her inside and absorb her. Claim your heritage."

I began to bawl, not just crying but loud wailing with heavy tears as I squirmed under my father's strength. He kept chanting, "This is your birthright, so take it."

I shrieked and slid out from his hold. I fell to the floor, my face half stained maroon. Daddy stepped toward me. Electricity burned through my bones. I got up and ran. I don't remember those first steps or even how I got through the front door. It was like I bolted outside in a snap, and I was suddenly in the dark heat with dust floating up from the road and the humidity clawing at my skin. I could barely breathe. You heard the cicadas in the distance and smelled the cedar and mesquite baking in the night. I didn't know where to go. Daddy appeared in the doorway, tall and black in silhouette. But then there was light. It grew from the other side of the hill and along the gravel driveway, beams of pale phantoms with motes floating in and out of their glow. Trucks came to the crest and rolled forward, clouds of dirt billowing around their tires. The engines growled and revved.

"It's time, Mason," shouted my father. His chest was caked with blood. He held the knife by his side. "It's up to you."

Daddy's eyes stayed calm and blue, and his voice sounded both sad yet loving. The trucks drove closer. Daddy walked forward. I shot to my left and across a field of rock and weeds and toward the grove of cedar before the limestone and the wilderness. I didn't think. I only ran. At first everything was a blur: speed and darkness without thought or reason. But when I was cloaked by the cedar, thick and rich and sweet like gin, I stopped and tried to breathe. I turned and watched. Three trucks sped to the front of the house and circled Daddy. Men stood in the back of the trucks. Headlights shined out in jagged streaks. I heard a woman holler.

"That's him! He took Jenny. He tried to kill me."

That was the night they caught the Rice County Ripper. There wasn't a trial. No one was arrested. The men in the trucks took my father to the center of town and hanged him from an oak in front of the courthouse. The man they'd put their faith in to protect them, Rusk Samuel Stein, wouldn't harm another woman or man.

They never found me.

I knew I'd be a pariah. No one would believe I didn't know anything, that I wasn't a part of it. I disappeared. First to San Antonio, then to Oklahoma, and eventually west to El Paso and Phoenix. I've never gone back to that little town, and I doubt anyone would recognize this old man as the son of the Rice County Ripper, and what would they say if they did?

It seems like each summer is hotter than the last. Heat waves swelter through the cities and the valleys, and fires burn through brush and chaparral. Young people say it's global warming. I hope that's the case. At night, when I try to sleep, I can't help but wonder if my father knew something,

something unspeakable and vile but nonetheless true. Demons or madness, I don't know, but I can't bear the heat anymore. I've resisted my nature and my bloodline all my life. Tonight, I hope my blood is sacrifice enough.

William Jensen is the author of the novel *Cities of Men*. His short fiction has appeared in *North Dakota Quarterly*, *The Texas Review*, *Tinge Magazine*, and elsewhere. He has received multiple Pushcart nominations. Mr. Jensen now lives in Austin, Texas.

From These Muddy Waters
Patrick C. Harrison III

"Friend o' mine had three fingers bit off by a alligator gar one time," Pap said, wiping sweat from his creased forehead and replacing the weathered Stetson on his balding crown. He stroked his long, gray beard, an action of habit rather than an attempt to corral the wild hairs, and peered across the gentle ripples of lake water.

The boy, Joe, wondered what those old eyes were seeing. Not the lake—the lake of the present, that is—of that he was certain. Joe knew if he kept silent and didn't distract his grandfather's mind with rubbish, then soon enough his mouth would tell what his eyes were seeing. Leaning to one side of the two-seater, single engine jon boat (the 'smack' according to Pap, even though the little boat looked nothing like a traditional smack), Joe checked his fishing pole, reeling in the line until it was taut. There was no fish yet.

Pap lit a cigarette and coughed out the first inhalation. "Don't ever pick up smoking, Joe," he said, looking disgustedly at the thing before placing it back between his lips. "Don't do it."

"I won't," Joe said.

"Your daddy never smoked, that I'm aware. I was always proud of him for that."

Joe lowered his head, looking uncomfortably at his sneakers. The conversation from here would either lead to sad stories of Joe's father and tears and regret, or—

"Them alligator gar, Joe, they're real bastards."

Joe silently sighed relief. But that's how Pap was—as the dementia progressed, sometimes a memory took hold and he would spill an hour-long yarn, and sometimes he would bounce from one topic to the next and back again.

"I couldn't been no older than thirteen or fourteen—bout your age, I reckon—when my friend Bill Sharp lost his fingers. Lake Tawakoni wasn't but twenty or thirty years old at that point. The dam was still nice and perty and there wasn't but a handful of houses on its banks, and those was all Caddo Indian families who believed they had some kinda claim to the land.

"Anyway, my daddy, your great grandpappy, used to drive his ol' Ford into Greenville to work the cotton gins there. So, when there weren't no school, my friends and me would pile in the back of that rusty machine and he'd dump us off at this winding road of black dirt that led to the lake. We all carried our poles, of course. And someone would usually bring a shovel so we could dig up some fat nightcrawlers, unless the grasshoppers were out and easy to catch. Some years the grasshoppers were thick as curdled milk when you walked through the tall grass. You took too deep a breath, hell, you'd be coughing their yella wings and legs into your hand for the next hour."

Pap stopped and sucked on his cigarette, eyeing his pole and the boy's too. He scanned the murky, brown waters, the sun hammering down on his shirtless, withering body. Joe tested his line again, knowing already that no catfish had so much as sniffed at his bait yet. He waited.

"Where's all the fish, Joe?" Pap asked

Joe shrugged.

"Well, they'll find us eventually. Always do. 'Cept this one year, the fish seemed to disappear all at once. Nobody caught nuthin for damn near a month. That was back in 1964, I think. It was the damnedest thing. It was like they all dropped dead. 'Cept they couldn't a dropped dead cuz weren't none of 'em floating on the water or washing up on the beach. Was like they disappeared, I suppose. And then all at once, they was back, and we was catching 'em like you ain't never seen. Yessir, that was 1964. 'No score in sixty-four,' Harold Donaldson said after about two weeks of no fish. All sorts of rumors spun about, of course. Everything from government testing atomic weapons below the lake to Indian curses to goddamn aliens stealing our fish. Pardon my language, Joe. I reckon it was just one of those once-in-a-century type things, where creatures ya think ya know everything about, up and start doing something else for a change. Like grasshoppers or locusts, ya see. I seen in the National Geographic about plagues of those bastards wiping out entire farms of wheat and even corn in the 1800s, like they just came out of nowheres. All them fish—bass and catfish and crappie—maybe they was all just takin a siesta in a ravine somewhere. I don't know."

Pap took one last drag on his cigarette and tossed the butt into the water. "They just disappeared," he said, almost a whisper, his eyes glazing over again.

Joe smiled and nodded, watching his grandfather's frail, tanned body. How many summer days had he spent on these waters? How many fish had he pulled from its depths? How many adventures had his body endured that his diseased mind would never be able to tell? Not only was dementia eating away at his memories (mainly the short-term ones), but emphysema was quickly sucking life from his body. It was only a matter of time before Pap's tales were lost to the endless well of history.

"Pappy?" Joe said, absently scratching at his cheek the way Pap stroked his beard.

The old man looked up, his eyes wide. It was as if he had forgotten the boy was even there.

"What about the gar, Pappy?"

"The gar?" Pap said, his face momentarily twisting into a look of confusion. "Oh, you mean the alligator gar don't ya, Joe?"

Joe nodded.

"You know that damn thing bit off three of Bill Sharp's fingers. We was all walking down to the lake—me and Bill and Derek Underhill and Otto Franklin, who would commit suicide a few years later jumping into the lake with cinder blocks tied to his legs. His mamma reckoned it was over a girl. But truth be told, I don't think Otto was ever all that interested in the ladies.

"Anyway, we all had our poles. Derek, Otto, and myself had cane poles. We'd wade out up to our waist and reach our canes out where we thought them fish were. But ol' Bill, he'd got hisself a new Penn rod and reel for his birthday a month or two prior. Boy, he was proud of that sucker. He'd chuck that bait out there and the reel would go to screaming like a wild eagle. We was all thoroughly impressed. I remember when he first got that Penn and he went to throw out his bait—he was all proud as a doggy under the table on Thanksgiving—and he heaved that pole over his head like he was trying to hit plum over to the other side, and that ol' boy fired his bait strait into the water right in front of him. Ha! We laughed and gave him hell. I reckon I'd still give him hell about it, were he alive to take it.

"But on that day, his cast was true. He tossed that line about as far as I ever seen a man cast. And it weren't no time at all that his rod was jumping, and we all knew he had a fish; the only question was how big. We all thought it was big mudcat or a blue, ya know, on account of it was so heavy for him to reel. I remember Otto saying it was probably a small fish, but the line was caught around a log or a bucket or something, cuz the thing didn't seem to be putting up no fight. You know, Joe, if you're sneaky enough, you can tie someone's fishing line to a bucket when they ain't lookin' and they'll think they're reeling in one hell of a fish.

"Well, it turned out to be a alligator gar. Big ol' bastard too. If you ain't never seen one, they look plum prehistoric with their long jaws and big teeth and scales. I thought Derek Underhill was gonna wet hisself, he was so scared. When Bill finally got it up on shore, with our help, we talked Otto into laying beside it so we could get an idea of how big it was. We reckoned it was about five goddamn feet long. Pardon my language, Joe.

"We all told Bill to forget about that damn hook. 'Just cut the line,' I told him. But he was adamant, he wanted his dern hook back. God only knows why. In his defense, the gar looked dead. It was laid on the beach not doing a thing. So, he told me and Derek to open its jaws, which we did reluctantly."

Pap held his hand open in the air, demonstrating the mouth of an alligator gar. He snapped it closed. "Steel trap," he said. "Weren't shit we could do to stop it." He laughed and shook his head and pulled out another cigarette. "Don't ever start smoking, Joe."

Joe laughed and shook his head like his grandfather. A gentle breeze slithered across the lake, but it did little to quell the summer heat. Joe reached over the side of the jon boat and tossed a handful of water in his face and another over his bare shoulders. He brought his line taut again and held his hands gingerly over the pole to feel for even the slightest movement. No fish.

"Ya hot?" Pap said with his bushy eyebrows raised.

"Yes, sir."

"Here, lean ya head forward. This old fart knows an ol' trick to fix that."

"Um, okay," Joe said, cautiously leaning forward.

Pap removed his Stetson cowboy hat, dunked it into the water, and dumped it over Joe's head, leaving the hat where it sat.

Joe gasped and looked up laughing, the hat sitting askew on his head. The gentle summer breeze now produced gooseflesh across his body.

"Reckon that cools ya a bit," Pap said.

"Yeah," Joe chuckled.

Pap nodded and said, "Caught a bluegill like that one time, just reached into the water with my hat and came up with him. Was with your grammy when I did that."

"Should we rebait the hooks, Pappy?" Joe asked.

"Nah." Pap waved his hand. "The waters are easy today. There's still good bait on there. The fish will come. Ya know, Joe, once you've been fishing enough, you can tell what you got on the end of your line just by the way it hits the hook and how it fights when you reel 'er in."

"Really?"

"You bet. Bass are fighters. They'll hit hard and jerk on the line and twist and so. A lot of smaller fish, like bluegill and perch do that too, but on a smaller level. Catfish, they more pull on your line than fight it, ya see? Some of the smaller ones will still fight pretty good, like small channel cats or bulls, but they still have a heavier feel to them than a scaly fish. Unless you snag a carp, or buffalo some people call 'em. You get one of them bastards, you got a fight on your hands.

"Everything fights a little different. Ya get turtles sometimes, especially if you're fishing with shrimp or dog food. Ya get snakes. Other...other things." His voice trailed off. "I've seen some strange things pulled from these muddy waters, Joe."

"Strange?" Joe said, his curiosity peaked. "Like what?"

But Pap was distant now, his eyes staring at the floor of the smack, his hands folded loosely in his lap with the cigarette nestled in his fingers. To Joe, the old man's face looked more creased than ever, like someone had taken a chisel and gouged out large portions of previously smooth flesh. And were those tears welling in his eyes? Joe thought they were. This could be another instance of dementia taking control of his emotions. It happened before. Pap had gotten angry and thrown a cup of coffee when he couldn't find his car keys. He started crying one morning when he went to wake Grammy up for breakfast, forgetting that she now lived in a nursing home on Wellington Street in Greenville. So maybe...

"Is everything alright, Pa-"

"Ya daddy didn't drown, Joe."

"What?"

"It...it just shows up. You never really know when. Kinda like them fish disappearing, then reappearing all at once, seemingly outa nowhere."

"Pappy, what do you mean my dad didn't drown? Everybody knows he did." Joe said this last part with no conviction at all. Already he believed Pap, that his father had not drowned while trying to pull in a trot line. It was a likely enough story, sure. Many men had gotten tangled in fishing line and trot lines, making their last breath two lungs-full of murky water from some fishing hole. It seemed fitting for a lifetime fisherman to die where he lived doing the thing he loved. And yet, hadn't that been what made it seem so odd to Joe? How could a man who, like Pap, spent his entire life on Lake Tawakoni, be so foolish as to let himself get hung-up in a trot line, and then not have a knife or some means of getting himself loose. It made no sense. Four or five years after the incident, Joe overheard the deacon's wife saying that his old man had probably been drunk when he drowned. But according to his mom and Pap, his father had never taken to beer or liquor of any sort. So, again, it made no sense.

"What do you mean he didn't drown, Pappy?" Joe asked again.

"Just…just hush a minute, Joe. I ain't scolding ya, I just need to gather my thoughts. Your ol' Pap will tell ya everything."

Joe, as best he could, waited patiently while Pap finished his cigarette, his sad, wet eyes staring out at the waters or at the floor of the smack or at his thin hands; never looking up at Joe. And then, with his cigarette spent and its butt tossed to the fish, Pap started.

"I been around this lake my entire sad life, Joe. My earliest memory is of catching snakes and turtles and toads over where Wind Point Park sits now. I remember my momma chasing your great Uncle Frank and me out the house with a broom when we brought home a whole pail of reptiles."

The old man stroked his beard, smiled briefly, and continued.

"Every lake has its legends, I reckon. Tawakoni ain't no different. The Caddo have a name for it: Caddaja. What Cherokee there were 'round these parts, called it Uktena. The Mexicans have a name for it that I ain't even gonna try to pronounce. And my daddy, he told me he used to pal around with a fella from Cross Plains that swore up and down it was some ancient god type thing called Cthulhu.

"Now, I don't know about all that shit, Joe. But what I do know, is that every legend is born of a nugget of truth. And this here legend—I knew this even before I seen what I seen—has a hefty helping of truth to it. Momma used to tell me and Frank, 'Watch out for the Caddaja!' every time we took two or three steps in the direction of the lake, which was damn near a mile from our back porch. She always hollered it in a lighthearted manner, and we reckoned it was just her way of saying don't get in no trouble. Lord knows we did anyway. Someone told ol' Frank that the best way to catch a catfish was with chicken livers. While that may be true, I don't imagine that was advising Frank to whop out his Case pocket knife and carve up four of Dick Anderson's fattest chickens just to get their livers. Goddamned if that didn't get us in a heap of trouble. You'd a thunk ol' Frank had gone and porked Anderson's daughter and then lopped off her head as a souvenir. God almighty, Joe, pardon my language!

"Anyway, what I'm tryin to say is, it was common occurrence for parents and elder folks to tell young'uns to watch-out for the Caddaja or Uktena or what-have-ya. Ya don't hear it so much anymore, on account of the city folk moving in and the country folk moving out. But some old-timers, like yours truly, still know the word *Caddaja*. Your daddy, he knew it too.

"The legend, so far as we knew as kids, was that the Caddaja was a reptilian creature that dined on small animals and, naturally, misbehaving children. Some said it walked upright like you and me and others said it slithered through the grass and swam in the lake and down the Sabine River and such.

But it was ol' Dick Anderson, a good number of years before Frank carved up his chickens, that I first heard talking about the Caddaja like it was a real flesh and blood…animal or…or something."

Pap looked out across the lake, the breeze stiffening a little now, making his beard dance. Retrieving another cigarette, he hid its tip in his palms and lit it on the fluttering flame of a struck match. "Don't ever start smoking," he reminded Joe, then on he went.

"Ya see, like everyone else who lives round here, Anderson was a fisherman. He was more fond of the trot line than the ol' rod and reel; a *wade line* is what he called it, on account of he never went no further out than he could wade. He'd have fifty or so hooks on a line and he'd bait it up with dog food or grasshoppers or nightcrawlers or—hell—chicken livers for all I know. And Anderson—he was a old bastard like I am now—he'd drag his Boston Terrier—Marty I think his name was—he'd drag Marty out there in the water to help him retrieve whatever fish he got. Anderson would put all his fish in a basket and they'd haul em ashore. I don't reckon a little Boston Terrier helped much, but that's what he done.

"Well this time, Anderson was collecting his fish off the line, wading in water just over his belly, and ol' Marty was swimming alongside him. According to Anderson, it felt like there was a Sherman tank somewhere down that trot line, and he was already fantasizing about the fish fry he'd be having that coming Sunday. But as he moved along, not coming up with many fish, he reckoned that his line was probably wrapped around a log or some such thing.

"And that was when—as he was kicking hisself for not having all the fish he'd hoped for—that the Caddaja came out of the water and took Marty. The trot line was wrapped around the thing, he said. But that didn't keep it from dragging poor Marty to his death. Dick Anderson told my folks that it took Marty so fast that he didn't even have time to yelp. He was swimming along one moment, gone in a cloud of blood the next."

Pap stuck the cigarette in his mouth, but didn't inhale, just letting it sit there. Looking at Joe with an awkward smile, he plucked the cowboy hat off the boy's head and put it on his own. "That's better," he said.

"Did Mr. Anderson say what the Caddaja looked like?" Joe asked.

"Course he did," Pap said. "He didn't see much of it, but he hollered from the rooftops what he seen. I'll get to that, though." The old man took a deep breath and continued.

"Ya remember me telling ya about my ol' buddy Otto Franklin, the fella that jumped off the bridge? Well, he done that when he was seventeen, four or so months before we was all gonna graduate from Hawk Cove High School; all eight of us in the class, that is. See, ol' Otto lived south of Hawk Cove, across a part of the lake called Kitsee Inlet. There was a bridge he crossed—it's been replaced by another now—that was about half a mile long. On occasion, his folks would bring him to school in whatever junker they had, if it was running. There was other times Otto would ride his papa's horse to school. But more often than not, he'd just walk.

"Well, in the days leading up to his suicide, Otto got to telling me and Derek and Bill Sharp—the fella who had his fingers bit off by the gar—that he'd seen the Caddaja on his walks to school in the morning. He said it was swimming around down there below the bridge, watching him. Of course, we all laughed and gave him a good joshing over it. Ya know how boys are. I remember Derek Underhill saying, 'Otto, you wouldn't know the difference between a Caddaja and your grandmother's cooter.' Pardon my language, Joe, but that's what he said.

"But all laughs aside, Otto was serious about what he seen. Two days before he took the plunge, he came to me and said not only was he seeing the Caddaja, but it was talking to him. He said at first, it was just saying his name, real slow and like a whisper: *'Ot-to, Ot-to, Ot-to.'* But then he said it starting telling him to come swimming and jump in and such."

Pap paused, his hands trembling and causing the cigarette to lose its ash, and said "Come test the waters Otto, it feels fine. Don't let me go rotto, Otto, I'll make it worth your time."

"What…what does that mean?" Joe said, shivering despite the heat of the setting sun.

"That's what Otto said the Caddaja told him. Chilled me to the spine when he said it, like it did you just now. Then…then Otto said that on that very morning, the Caddaja had threatened him. He said the Caddaja told him that if he didn't jump into the lake then it was going to tell the world his big secret. I knew Otto's secret of course, but by then I didn't care; he was my friend, ya see. But he was deathly afraid of it getting out.

"I tried to reason with the fella, of course. I told him he was imagining things and sleep walking and whatever I could think. It was ridiculous. I remember saying, 'Fish monsters aren't real and they certainly don't recite poetry and threaten people with secrets.' That was the last time I spoke to Otto Franklin. He stomped off all flustered with me. I reckon he wanted to wallop me, bloody my nose. I guess I wish he had. He jumped on a Saturday. They pulled him outta the water on Sunday. Half his body was gone, eaten away by…fish they supposed"

They sat silent for a bit as the air slowly cooled with the diminishing sun and increasing wind. Pap smoked another cigarette and checked his pole. Joe checked his own pole and pulled on his t-shirt. He was beginning to think that Pap had forgotten all about the stories he was telling, when the old man started up again.

"There was other incidents, of course. Like I say, it just seemed to show up at times. A lady by the name of Doris Lightfoot, an ol' flame of your Uncle Frank's, said that the Caddaja took her whole stringer of perch and bluegill right out of her hand. Said it woulda taken her whole arm if she hadn't jerked it back so quick. There was three sisters—the Aguila sisters—went missing in seventy-four. Their father blamed the Caddaja, saying they was playing in the water before they vanished. Though, most people reckoned he done something to 'em himself. There was three other people committed suicide jumping off that bridge before it was torn down in favor of the new one. I don't recall no one jumping off the new one, but who knows. In the mid-nineties there was a whole flurry of sightings," (Pap made quotation marks with his fingers as he said this, emphasizing their perceived believability) "and that set off a stampede of folks coming in from Dallas and Texarkana and God knows where else, trying to catch the bastard on their rod and reels. Nobody ever caught nuthin but a few big catfish, though."

Pap sighed and looked his grandson in the eyes. "You was only a baby, Joe. Not even two years old yet. We never shoulda taken you on that boat."

"What?" Joe said, his eyes widening with sudden realization. "I was there?"

Pap wiped tears from his eyes and sniffled. "You was there, Joe. God forgive me, you was there."

This revelation hit Joe like a mule kick in the gut. He had always been told that he was at home with his mother when his dad drowned. Obviously, if the drowning part was fictional, it stood to reason that more of it was too. But had he *really* been there? Even as a toddler, surely, he would remember his father's death, if he had been there.

"Your momma—God love her—tried to keep ya at home. But we was insistent on taking ya. 'A boy's never too young to go fishin!' I remember saying. And your dad agreed, of course. He was plum tickled to be bringing ya along. And on a night adventure at that! In the summertime, that's when ya want to go, ya see, at night. Just pray the mosquitos don't carry ya away.

"Your daddy had a little smack weren't no bigger than this one. No engine on it neither; just paddles. We bundled up a sleeping bag between our seats and sat ya in the center of it, and then we set out to rowing with a flashlight duct taped to the bow of our little boat like some half-assed searchlight.

"We had a little electric lantern too, but damn how the darkness engulfed us once we was out on the water. It was like the whole world disappeared, and weren't nuthin left but us on that little smack, floating along on muddy water. Even all the mosquitos and deer flies vanished once we got a hundred feet or so offshore. Joe, you was just so interested in everything. Ya kept standing up and looking all about and your daddy had to keep setting ya back down. I figured you was wanting to play in the water, so I hefted you up—and you was a fat little baby, Joe—and I leaned ya over the side and let ya slap at the water and laugh. Finally, your daddy made me quit, saying if he took ya home with a soaking wet jumper on then your momma was gonna be filleting us for dinner instead of fish.

"Anyway, we gave up rowing after about thirty or forty minutes, figuring we was at least close to the center of the lake. Like I say, we couldn't see no land-markers. Only a few lights along the shore, here and there. It was a cloudy night, I reckon, cause weren't no stars or moon to speak of. It was plum spooky, I must admit. But we wasn't gonna show it. We baited our hooks and tossed our rod and reels in opposite directions. We ridiculed each other on our casts like always, and claimed to be better fishermen than the other. Your daddy said if ya shit your diaper, we oughta roll a sponge in it and throw it on a hook and see what the catfish thought. I laughed so hard at that, that I dropped my cigarette over the side of the smack, I remember that.

"We'd been there an hour or so and all we had to show for it was a little pound or two channel cat that I snagged. It was barely big enough to slice fillets off of, but I threw it the basket anyhow. Your daddy was still confident, saying any minute he was gonna land that big sucker. You seemed to have lost interest in the lake and had taken to playing with a mound of colorful rubber worms that your daddy had taken outta his tackle box. We was having a good time.

"And then your daddy's fishing pole bent over— all the sudden like—like something heavy jumped on it real quick without even testing the bait. The pole was damn near jerked from his hands. If it had been…well, maybe things woulda turned out different."

Pap paused now, looking at his pole and then at Joe's, each of them wedged beneath the seats they sat on. "Maybe we should call it a day and reel in our lines," he said. "It looks like I was wrong about the fish biting today. We can motor over to that little bait shop by Wind Point and get you a snow cone before it closes. Whaddaya think, Joe?"

Joe considered, looking around at the still waters and setting sun. "Can you finish telling me about my dad first, Pappy? I really want to know what happened."

Pap sighed, a grief-stricken sigh. "Of course, ya do, Joe. And you deserve to hear it. It's just…it's just difficult, ya understand?"

Joe nodded and Pap nodded in return.

"Your daddy," Pap said, "like I told ya, nearly lost that pole. But his hands gripped it tight and he hollered *'Whoa!'* and he said *'Goddamn, it's a big one!'* And I could tell it was too. He had a nice sturdy rod—a Berkley or Ugly Stick or something, I don't know—but I was afraid, the way that thing was bent over, that it was gonna snap and all would be lost. So, I set my own rod and reel aside and went to your father and held the lantern and told him if he needed me to hold the rod or grab the line or net, then I was there to help. Slowly but surely, he started reeling in his catch.

"It was dark as the bottom of the sea, like I said, but I hefted that lantern up high as I could get it, and we had a little circle of light around the smack. And as your daddy drew his catch in closer, I could see how muddy the surface waters was, on account of how the fish—or what I thought was a fish—was fighting. I figured it was a big ol' carp or maybe an extra feisty alligator gar. Maybe even an actual alligator. I knew it weren't no catfish. Matter fact, I never seen any fresh water fish fight like that. Your daddy was gruntin' and heaving his arms back, his skin all turning red and veins juttin' outa his arms and neck. He was struggling, and I thought I might need to take over. I weren't quite as frail back then, Joe. No emphysema." Pap tapped at his chest and continued.

"About six feet or so from the side of the boat, what your daddy had hold of came to the surface. Well, part of it came to the surface, I should say. His hook had snagged what looked to us to be a large snake. But it wasn't scaly like a snake and we couldn't see no head, but we could see what we thought was the tail. It was greenish-brown to my eyes in the limited light and about as big around as a man's wrist, and it was thrashing like ya expected an injured snake to do. *'What is that?'* I remember your daddy saying.

"I don't know what made me turn around. I don't remember hearing anything or seeing anything in my peripheral. But I turned around right as your father was getting that thing up close to the boat, and that's when I saw the rest of what he had snagged. And…and it had hold of you, Joe."

"It had *me?*" Joe said, his heart thundering. "Like, it was trying to take me?"

"Yes, Joe, it was taking ya. Getting ready to eat ya, is what it was doing."

"Oh my god. And…what did it look like, Pappy?"

"Well, have you seen pictures of eels, Joe? It was mean and ugly looking in the face like an eel. Greenish-brown, like I said. Slick looking. But on its head was two horns. They weren't sticking straight up like ya think of the devil having, they was laying back kinda like a Billy goat. What your daddy had hooked turned out to be a type of tentacle. All around the thing's head, growing out from its neck, were long, snake-like tentacles, all slithering and splashing. They didn't have suction cups, like an octopus, they was just slick. I remember that. And back behind the mess of a hundred tentacles or more was the rest of it. Even in the lowlight I could see it moving in the water. It was like an eel and thick as tree trunk and twenty or thirty feet long, I'm sure of it.

"It had ya wrapped in five or six of its tentacles, Joe. And its head was at the edge of the boat with a mouthful of sharp teeth. Very sharp teeth…

"*'It's got the baby!'* I yelled and dived across the boat at the thing—the Caddaja, I reckon I should call it what it is. I dived at the Caddaja and started wailing on its tentacles with the lantern and trying to pull you lose. Your daddy was right behind me doing the same thing. Whatever interest he had in the fishing pole was long gone. You was almost completely covered in tentacles. All I could see was the crown of your head and one pudgy arm that stuck out between the slithering bastards.

"The Caddaja hissed at us when we started attacking and other tentacles started wrapping around us and trying to pull us away. I reckon it didn't want much to do with us, cuz we was too big for its mouth. But it could make a quick meal of a child. Tentacles went around my arms and legs and waist, even my neck. It was applying pressure to where I couldn't breathe. Everything was turning dark and fuzzy. But once I lost the strength to fight, it let loose of me and crumpled atop your sleeping bag like a soggy sand bag. I was dizzy and nauseated and my whole body felt like it was being stuck with needles. I just…couldn't do shit to help, Joe.

"As my eyes cleared, I saw your daddy had took out his knife and was sawing his way through an army of those fuckers. They had him all wrapped up, just like they did me, but he was cutting through 'em one at a time, spraying that monster's black blood all over the goddamned place. The Caddaja was screeching and your dad was yelling. They was in a fight to the death. The more tentacles your daddy severed, the more seemed to wrap around him. They was squeezing him and he was turning beet red in the face. I could see that, even in the little light the lantern was still putting out. But, Joe, your daddy kept fightin'. He weren't gonna stop for nuthin'.

"With the Caddaja having to use more and more tentacles to fight your daddy, it started letting loose of you. One slipped away and I could see your feet. Another slid off and I could see your belly and your other arm. Two more let go of you and only one was left. Using what strength I still had, I crawled forward and grabbed hold of you, at the same time biting down on that one last tentacle. My teeth went through its flesh and it tasted just like mud from the bottom of the lake—dank and gritty and nasty. It relinquished at last and I fell back with you in my arms. *'I got him, Jacob!'* I hollered. *'I got Joe, now get loose of that thing!'*

"He turned his head just a little when I said that, his eyes all bloodshot and blood pouring from his mouth and nose. He turned just enough to see that I had ya. He kept fighting, but the tentacles were around him like a cloud now, all of 'em focused on your daddy. The Caddaja had forgotten all about the baby it had been after. It was fighting for survival now.

"Your daddy swung and slashed and cut and sawed. But it was too much for him, Joe. The knife eventually fell from his hand and his body went limp. I screamed and hollered and tried to fight at the beast with one hand, while clinging onto ya. The Caddaja had perched its head on the side of the smack and it just sat there for a second. It was wore plum out, I reckon. But it still held tight to my poor Jacob. It was afraid, I think, that if it let go of your daddy, he would kill its stinking ass. Even as the Caddaja slipped off the edge and began descending into the lake, it still held him. I cried for it to let go. I pounded on those descending tentacles. But over the edge your daddy went. Over the edge my Jacob went."

Pap was crying steadily now and so was Joe. They each brushed at their eyes, sobbing. "He," Joe started, then stopped with a fresh outburst of tears. "He...he saved me."

"Yes, he certainly did," Pap said. "I don't know how long I laid in that boat crying with you in my arms, Joe. There were thirty-two severed tentacles in the boat with us, some of 'em still slithering around. I remember counting the fucking things the next morning. Pardon my language, Joe. I'm just…a bit upset, I guess."

"It's okay, Pappy," Joe sobbed. "I'm glad you told me."

They sat silently for a bit. Pap lit-up the last of his cigarette's and told Joe never to start smoking. The breeze eventually dried their tears, and the moon and the stars came out and shone brightly upon the lake, making the muddy waters sparkle with rejuvenated beauty.

"Reckon we should head in, Pappy," Joe said. The word *reckon* felt odd coming out of his mouth, but it felt good too.

"I reckon so," Pap said, turning to start the motor.

"Wait, we got to reel in our poles."

"Oh, right you are, Joe. This old man is losing his marbles."

Joe laughed, picking up his rod and reeling it in high and fast the way Pap had taught him. High and fast to keep it from getting—

But then the line jerked and pulled, and the rod bent over like a horseshoe, nearly pulling itself free from Joe's hands.

"Pass me that rod, Joe," Pap said calmly, his face blank and creased and dark in the moonlight, his hand outstretched and open. "Come on, Joe, give it here."

Patrick C. Harrison III (PC3, if you prefer) is an author of horror, erotica, splatterpunk, and bizarro fiction. To date, he has published a novel, a collection, and short stories in various anthologies, with more to come in the near future. Patrick is also the editor-in-chief and co-owner of Death's Head Press, a publisher of dark fiction. He resides on the outskirts of Greenville, Texas with his wife and children.

Buzzard Luck
W. H. Gilbert

My pa always said we were cursed with "buzzard luck" but I never saw it quite that way. Sure, times were tough, as they say, and they never much seemed to get any better, but I guess I always rather'd look on the upside of clarity. I'm a glass half full of American beer kind of guy. Yeah, Dolly up and left me for that hat salesman up in Fort Polk, but that just meant I had the kids all to myself. They were a handful—and that's the apt word for the matter—but the Good Lord saw to it I'd never have to work again and all it cost me in the smash up at Halliburton was my right arm. But, again, to my good fortune I scrawl my John Hancock and touch my pecker left-handed; though the kids didn't give me much time for writing, nor peckering, much anyhow. All that to say, things ain't as bad as my pa made them out to be, and besides at least I had my head, which is more than anyone could say for Mr. Twain.

He was the peculiar sort. A writer from up North, I remember the first time I laid eyes on the man when he took the old Victorian at the end of the block nestled behind the willows and pecan trees. It was a dreadful-old thing, all grey and brown and burnt red, and looked as if it wore its skeleton on the outside--what they call "Stick style". Nobody had lived in that thing since I had been a tot myself, but it fit the writer from up North just fine. He couldn't have been any older than fifty years, but you wouldn't know it by the way he carried himself. Tall, gaunt, frail and bent-over, it looked like his clothes, all black, were too heavy for him and sunk him further toward the earth.

I told my kids to come greet the man but they were too afraid. From the window in our little kitchen, they could see him standing at the end of his short, rocky driveway, admiring the high-vaulted crest of his new home above the cover of its tall trees. The kids, Lorelei, Shebelle, and Augustus, said that he looked like a skeleton-man.

"A Skeleton-Man for the Skeleton House," Augustus whispered with his hands over his eyes.

"Aw heck, there's nothing to be afraid of," I insisted and told them to watch while I welcomed the new neighbor.

Out the door and down the road, I looked over my shoulder and saw three little sets of eyes peeking just above the bottom frame of our kitchen window.

When I reached the man all in black, he turned to me and looked rather like a vulture. Withered yellow eyes pocked in the surface of his ashy face, and he stretched out his hand to shake mine. It didn't strike me funny until much later that he didn't hesitate in going for a left-handed shake before even noticing I lacked the right. His hand felt small, clammy, and, well, wrong; it was smooth the way a baby's hand is, I don't mean any offense in the way of South and North, nor man of money or man of the land kind of talk. If I could've made my living at a desk or inside, you bet your sweet ass I would've taken that way, and I ain't got much pride in me for a rough hand. But his was smooth like something never been touched.

I tried my damndest to hide my revulsion to such a loathsome touch as his and managed to cough out my name. He answered with his.

"Aleister Twain," he said.

Now, take me for a fool all you want, for anything you'd like, but I knew then and there it weren't the title given to him at birth, on account of it sounding a tad womanly and also on account of it being the name of that Satan-lover across the pond.

"That accent ain't from around here, and I'm guessing since you own it neither are you," I said to him.

"You would be correct," he said. And it was then I noticed he looked ancient, not only in posture but in his eyes.

"Well, what brings you here to our little Hollow?"

"I'm a writer," he said, and then he made a little clicking gesture with his fingers. "And the subjects of my writing have all but dried up in the city. I've come to the country for the inspiration of the common folk."

"Writer, huh?" I said looking for conversation. "What kinds of things you write about?"

"The only things that matter, I suppose."

I nodded and chewed the inside of my cheek.

"I've never been much of a reader, myself," I said.

"You don't say?" he said with a smile.

I hid my resentment rather well, as my wife used to say.

"But my kids like to read. Especially my youngest, Shebelle," I said, "Reads more than any seven-year-old that I know."

"You know very many?" he asked.

The dark man smiled at me and I didn't like it. He thought me an idiot, but better to be underestimated than over, so I just gave him a smile back and laid on the extra cheese.

"Well shucks, Mister, didn't know we had a celebrity in our midst. I'll inform the neighborhood next time we have us a shindig," I turned to commence my retreat when I said to him over my empty shoulder, "The inspiration is nice, but be sure to enjoy the air and company out here in the sticks. Don't take it for granted."

And he said, "I shan't."

I got back home and hurried the kids from the window and lied to them saying our new neighbor wasn't anything to be afraid of. Even still, I made them promise to never leave the house alone and never to go over to the Skeleton House without myself.

It was a fair enough warning, but we didn't see hide nor hair of Mr. Aleister Twain, the grey man in black, all summer. Summers in Texas, even back in those days, were hotter than most everywhere else and with the humidity from the Gulf, you didn't even want to be outside most days. But the writer from up North brought a certain chill with him.

Many nights I would find the children missing from their beds and peeking out the kitchen window toward the dark house hidden from them by the night and the trees. When I made them go play, they wouldn't get any further than the curb in the direction of the Skeleton House and that would have given me comfort had I not seen the way my girls and boy stood transfixed by something I could not describe. Oftentimes they would just stand there, in a line staring without word whispered to one another, before I hollered at them and broke them of their mystification. I was worried the strange man from the North Country might find them loitering and get on to them for their curiosity, but those fears were not answered in those months of summer. No, sir.

Neither the kids nor I saw him again until October.

Not until right before Halloween, as a matter of fact.

Scary man or not, come fall season the kids'—especially Shebelle—favorite thing to do was pick the pecans that fell from the tree in front of the house at the end of the road. We didn't have much in the way of money when I was working and even less now that I depended on the payout from Halliburton and odd jobs around town, but we—I'd be lying if I said it was only the kids—loved to go all out for the holidays. What we had done since the little ones were small was pick the pecans around the street, shell them, and sell them. In the last few years Lorelei had even taken up baking them into little pies to sell at the church outside of town. We used the money to buy materials to make our own decorations like pumpkin patches or scarecrows and mannequins and painted wooden figures to adorn the house and lawn come Halloween and Christmas. It got us all in higher spirits and the kids still liked to fiddle with the stuff so I figured best to keep it up while they still enjoyed my company.

I grabbed a handful of bags and, after some time assuring them nothing untoward would happen with myself there, walked with my girls and boy down the street toward the Skeleton House. I whistled a tune to loosen them up, but I don't think it did much good because, it being the time of year it was, I believe I whistled "Monster Mash". It had always been their favorite, but not that day.

"I'm going to let him know we're out here so he doesn't get any wrong idea," I told them.

"Daddy, please," Shebelle said.

I waited for her to continue but she only silently mouthed the word "No."

I bent down and gave her a peck on the forehead and swatted her behind playfully with the bag.

"You kids start picking. Only the biggest and best, now; we wanna beat the squirrels to them," I said and gave them a wink.

They simply stood clustered together and did not move, except for Shebelle who grabbed for her brother's hand.

I approached the door, the planks of the porch bowing and creaking, angry under my feet. I paused at the door and held my breath, expecting to hear the man from up North waiting patiently right on the other side of the wood for the rattle of my knock. I didn't hear anything, so I rapped my knuckles against the stern door. There was a hollow echo on the other side, but no sound of approaching footsteps or movement.

I peeked around into a window but saw nothing. I waited a bit longer before answering my own knock with another but when I did, still nothing. I turned to the kids.

"Guess he's not home."

"I saw him walking around upstairs this morning!" Augustus said.

"Didn't see him leave this morning," Lorelei said with her eyes wide.

"I've never seen him leave," Shebelle said from behind them.

"It's okay," I told them again. "In a few days, we'll leave him a pie as payment."

I held the pecan broom in my hand, rolling its mesh cage along the ground to gather the nuts fallen into the matted green grass. Augustus played along, bobbing his head to a tune only he could hear, but still wary of getting too close to the house that sat in odd stoic silence. Lorelei had filled her bag already and was now stuffing even more of our bounty into the pockets of her jeans. Shebelle stood, stiff-legged, staring up at the top of the house.

"You want the picker-upper, darling?" I asked.

She motioned me over with a finger and pulled on my shirt until my ear was at her level.

"He's been up there watching us, daddy," she whispered.

I looked back to the higher level of the house where it looked like her eyes were fixed and saw only a dusty, grey window with no man behind it. The windows of the old place seemed to let in very little light as a thick shadow clung to every nook and cranny of the home. There in the window overlooking the front yard lurked only the darkness of the house itself.

"I don't see anything, baby," I said.

She held her breath and did not blink. It looked as though she was in a staring contest, or afraid of losing sight of what she was seeing if she looked away even for only a second.

"Do you want to leave, Belle?" I asked.

Finally, she nodded.

I turned to the window and waved. Still, I saw nothing.

"I think that's enough for us to handle for a while, don't you kids?"

They breathed sighs of relief and hauled the bags over their shoulders.

As we walked home, I was very glad that I had called it early. I could not shake the feeling that there had been something strange back there that I hadn't noticed. Until later.

Shebelle hadn't been looking at the second-floor windows.

She had been looking at the top of the trees.

A few days had gone by and we had shelled all the pecans and baked several small pies with them. Those that we did not use went into the freezer until we sold them at the church. I decided, against my better judgment, now might be a fine time to deliver one of the pies unto the man from who's yard we absconded with the key ingredient. While the kids drew pictures of what they wanted to be for Halloween, I wrapped the largest of the small pies in two layers of plastic and walked out the front door.

The first cool wind of October greeted me as I walked across our lawn and I began thinking up what ghosts and ghouls we might construct in that coming week. It had become a tradition for our house and, such is the way of things in small towns, it became an anticipated event for the other kids in the neighborhood and others on our side of the highway to come and ogle this time of year. I have never been a perfectionist, one hand or not, so I will not lie and say that the yard ever looked like something you'd see in a movie or magazine, but for what it was, it always turned out better than I foresaw, no doubt because of the enthusiasm and creativity of my kids. I've never been very imaginative, let alone an artist, so all of the crazy ideas came from Gus, Belle, and Lei.

The first year we had constructed traditional scarecrows, using hardware store-bought skeletons as our base and dressing them up with straw and raggedy clothes, and laid pumpkins strewn about. But Lorelei had the idea to make it look like one of the scarecrows had massacred the others, what with their arms and legs hither and thither and hay littered all over in place of blood.

A year later, spurred on by some movie he had just seen, Gus wanted the theme to be "aliens," so we set about, dressing our existing scarecrow from the year before as a farmer, and painted our pumpkins and turnips and the like all otherworldly colors of purple and bright green. But the kicker was the UFO he had made out of an old dish and hubcaps he had found on the side of the road and suspended from our oak tree with some wire. I put an old light we had from the chicken coop in the center of it and he controlled it from the porch.

This year we had promised creative control to little Shebelle, and I hoped to God it would bring her out of the funk she had been in since the new neighbor had moved in.

I approached the Skeleton House with some trepidation, examining its trees and top floor and finding nothing out of the ordinary. The ordinary, of course, being a house so old and decrepit you found its relatives on the cover of any spooky storybook for children.

Mounting the stairs once again, I felt that familiar give as I took it step by step, all the way up to the front door. I paused and listened, once again expecting to hear steady breathing on the other side. Once again there was instead, nothing. I gave it a knock and waited for footfalls to answer. When none did I knocked again, louder still.

My patience wearing thin, I peeked through one of the windows that looked into the living room and nearly bowled over backwards when I saw him.

There, half-in, half-out of the shadows from the hall at the far end of the living room, I saw the man's legs kicked stiff at an awkward angle.

I forgot the pie and fumbled for the doorknob. The pie in its tin slid down the door and splattered at my feet on the frame. I wrenched as hard as I could both ways but the door was locked. I stiffened my shoulder and slammed against the door. It held fast and I felt the shock go through my body and up through the hairs on my head. I shook off the sudden dizziness and threw myself at the door again. It budged slightly. The wood was old and would give if I were persistent, so I was. I threw myself at it again. And again. And again.

The door rocked against its hinges. I winced away the sharp pain that was shooting through my body like lightning and gave it all I had one last time, and nearly tumbled over myself when the door gave way. I caught myself and regained my balance, slipping once in the pie at my feet, but steadied inside the doorframe with one of my knees, sending another knife of pain through my leg.

I wished to God to run over and help the poor man out, believe me I did. Don't think me crude or childish when I say, the smell stopped me dead. Well, that's a poor but apt choice of words. A smell unlike anything I've ever been exposed to in my life, even when living on a farm as a young'un, met me in the doorway like a wall made of bricks. It was the smell of death, all right, but of death that had been locked away to stew during a summer in Texas.

After I had blown the chunks of everything I had eaten the day before, I ran home on rubbery legs and called the police.

The cop that arrived first could have walked out of one of the shows on TV: he looked like he could knock a tough a good one and probably had. His hair was thinning on top and he sported a reddish mustache. I had never seen him around town, so I figured he was from the county. Wasn't sure why one of our local boys couldn't handle a stiff, at first.

"You sure this is the man who introduced himself to you as Aleister Twain?" the officer said.

Several investigators had scoped out the area and were taking pictures where I thought they must have been seeing something I couldn't. I looked past them at the bloated body. I had left the door open on my exit and luckily the worst of the smell had wafted away in the early-season breeze, but the aroma still clung to everything like a disease with no cure. And, amid it all, lay the corpse of my late neighbor whom I'd met only once, months before. He was missing what would have been anyone's most distinguishing feature, but it was he, all right.

"He ain't got a head," I said, "but that's him."

The officer turned and looked at the body. The head was gone but there was no trace of blood where the head would have been. He turned back to me after a moment.

"You're certain?"

"I only met the guy once, but I am one hundred percent on it. You don't really mistake this kinda man for any other, is my point."

The officer nodded in understanding and leaned into me.

"You're more right than you know," he whispered under his breath.

"What do you mean? You know this guy?"

The officer was biting back something.

"We've heard some things; things from up north where he's from. He was into some bad business. Had a lot of people looking for him."

"You think this could be some kind of a hit?"

The officer shook his head.

"Nothing to be concerned about at this time, sir. But we're going to be looking into it."

"Keep me in the know, if you can," I said.

He asked me a few more questions and I gave him a few more answers, all straight and no bullshit. I never made a habit out of bullshitting the law. Never went too well for the bullshitter.

As I began to make my way out the door, I turned back to the officer with the mustache.

"Say," I said, "You have any idea how long he's been there dead?"

"Too early to tell, really," he said.

I nodded but before I could turn to leave, I saw him begin to say more.

"But by the state of decomposition, I'd say he's been here for a while."

I hung in the doorway just long enough for him to say it.

"A few months, I would say."

Believe me, I ask myself every day why I hadn't called to report the lack of movement around the place. But to be honest, when we get right down to it, he was a strange man. He may have been a recluse or hermit, for all I had known. He sure hadn't seemed the type to invite the neighbors over for a BBQ.

I had tried to keep the gory details of the way I found Mr. Twain from my kids, but something in the back of my mind told me the other kids from the subdivision down the street had probably said one thing or another to them. They were back in school now and there wasn't much to talk about in our little hamlet, so a story like this grew with very little water or sunlight and spread fast. From the way they whispered to each other with grave looks on their faces, they must have heard. Whether or not the other children knew what had happened or not, they talked and probably embellished. And that was natural. All kids have a morbid curiosity.

Little Shebelle had yet to come out of her funk, so I encouraged her to draw out how she might want to decorate the lawn. She agreed with a sigh and went about with her pencils and sketchpad.

I sat with her in front of the dead tube TV in the living room while she sketched, sitting on the floor. I had a cold one in my hand, something I usually saved for special occasions but I had felt the old familiar thirst from my younger days.

She had been at it for about half an hour, making odd little noises to herself and scratching away in wide, wild strokes with one pencil until its lead broke. She would grab another and continue in the manner until she had to grab one more. When I peeked over her shoulder, Shebelle looked embarrassed and tried to stash her drawing away.

"Aw, don't do that, girl," I said, "Let me see what you got there."

Reluctantly, she handed the sketchpad over.

I don't have a great memory, never did, and like I've said before I've never had much of an imagination, but I'm keenly aware that the mind of a seven-year-old is surely a scary one; especially my little Shebelle. Her nightmares were filled with things straight from, what I've heard called, the id. Unshaped by the grinding stone of time, her little brain had cooked up some doosies that gave even myself goose-skin. But what I saw on that sketchpad were obscenities no child should know.

"Darling," I said and tried to find the words but couldn't.

She held her hands to her eyes and said her sorries until they became whispers through drooling lips. She was crying.

"You ain't in any kind of trouble, girl," I said and took her under my arm.

"I think I am, daddy. I think I am."

"Why would you say something like that?"

Shebelle didn't answer. She only threw her arms around me and held me tight.

The page had been cast aside and now looked back at me from where it lay on the floor. The things crawling from the charcoal muck seemed to be laughing at the indignities they were inflicting on the stick-people that looked an awful lot like myself and her brother and sister. I nudged the sketchpad closed with my boot and kissed the top of her trembling head.

"Belle," I said, "can you tell me what made you think of something like this?"

"From his stories, daddy."

My heart sank to the pit of my stomach and threatened to fall further.

"Whose stories, baby?" I feared I knew the answer to that question.

"The Skeleton Man."

"Darling," I said, trying to hide that my mouth had suddenly become dry. "That's impossible. Mr. Twain has been gone for a while now."

She took me by the hand and led me through the house. When we passed the kitchen I could hear Augustus and Lorelei playing outside on their bikes, and I wished very badly that I had asked Shebelle to do likewise. She led me to her room and showed me, under her bed, a stack of pages. They looked like they had been scrawled with ink from the tips of fingers rather than a pen or typewriter. It was scratch more than words, but what I could make out sent spider-hairs of ice through my veins.

For the umpteenth time that day, my mind and mouth failed to make language.

But I didn't need to ask the question.

"He leaves them outside for me," she said. "There."

Her head hung low, Shebelle simply pointed with one tiny hand toward the window by her bed.

From far away I heard the front door open and shut; Lorelei and Augustus were asking what was for lunch. Absent-mindedly, I made them something to eat, although I can't recall what it was.

The rest of that day was a blur.

Shebelle didn't want to take part in the decorating this year. Had it been any other time I would have tried to turn her around on it, but I did not. Lorelei and Augustus wanted to help and did, but mainly just to keep up cred with their friends and neighbors. In light of what had happened down the street, I opted for a more traditional display. Scarecrows and pumpkins were the reason for the season this year. I hoped any of the other kids looking forward to it understood.

The early day was overcast, but didn't rain. The air reflected steely silver and buzzed with electricity, so everything said *rain*. But rain did not come. While the kids were in school, I was dressing the life-size but cheap, plastic skeletons up in their scarecrow duds. Flannel shirts and straw hats and overalls and sackcloth masks to go over their heads. I stuffed the oversized clothes with bales of hay that I had bought from Dale Guidry for two pecan pies.

As I piddled about dressing up the display, I felt the strange sensation one gets when walking in the woods alone. It was that feeling of being watched by something impossible to see for the dense thicket. I looked back to the Skeleton House, its attic window peering at me above the trees like a leering eye, and felt a shudder creep up my back. I didn't like having my back to the place.

The house had always been creepy, even when I was a young boy. We always told stories of a witch who'd lived there, one that ate up little boys brave enough to go up and knock on the front door. Of course we used the word 'brave' and not 'stupid' so that we could convince any new kid to run up and do it. We would run away giggling and laughing after it was done, but any time someone went missing in our little town, we knew without saying the house had something to do with it.

When Dolly and I had first married she said she'd like to own the place and fix it up, but when I took her to look at it up close she changed her mind. That talk had turned to burning the place down when she had started to feel trapped in a little house down the road from this great nightmare of a home. I often wonder if that was part of what drove her away, but I don't think about it too hard. Best not to.

While looking up at the empty attic, I thought, for the briefest measurement of time, I had seen a flicker of light. Not a flash, but some weird shade of color wave in and out like a ribbon, twirling and then gone. I rubbed my eyes and looked again but if it had been there the light left no trace. The only thing staring back at me was that deep blackness of the house with no light.

I felt a cold bead of sweat beginning to roll down the right side of my head and went to wipe it away, but I didn't feel my hand where it should be. I realized I didn't have my right arm. It was gone like it had been for nearly seven years. I hadn't made a mistake like that for a long time.

The bead of sweat ran down from my hair and into my eye. It stung but I winced until it didn't anymore and went back to work.

It wasn't until Halloween night when I finally met with the dead man.

We had returned from trick 'r treating and came back to our house, the small dark thing barely alive with the few props out-front. It was a sorry example of what we had become known for in our little corner of the planet. It was something I had taken pride and joy in during those latter years, spending the time with my kids and getting them to think up all kinds of horrors to scare others. It was a peculiar way of learning more about the ones closest to you. A morbid way, sure, but a way nonetheless. And now our little display was little more than a few scarecrows littered about with pumpkins at their feet. It wasn't my finest work, and I was ashamed.

But I bit back that regret as we came up the path, Lorelei and Shebelle grasping my left hand and Augustus at my other side. Their bags were heavy and full of the full-size chocolate bars and suckers and fruit-flavored gummies given away at the houses in the newer subdivision down the road, and as we walked, Shebelle's sack of sweets rhythmically bumped against my leg.

Closer to our house now, the Skeleton House had come into view at the end of the block. Shebelle clutched my hand with righteous intent. She squeezed so hard my fingers popped.

"Ouch!" I yelped.

"Daddy, I don't like it," she said.

"I don't either, dad," Lorelei spoke up. "It gives me the creeps."

"It don't scare me, none," Augustus said. But his voice trembled and I saw that he refused to turn his eyes on the house.

"Something tells me you kids won't think much of it come tomorrow and it'll all be over until this time next year," I said. "Ain't nothing to be afraid of, it's just an old house!"

"Dad, you used to say ghosts lived in it," Lorelei said.

I gave her a look to say, *Eh tu, Lei?* I thought we was friends.

"I just told you those stories to spook you," I said.

"Yeah, well it worked," Lorelei said.

Shebelle rested her face into the side of my jeans and hugged me around the waist.

"Let's get you kids in bed," I said.

We went inside and as they took their baths one at a time, I took some Hershey's from their bags and toasted marshmallows over the light on the stove and made a plate of hot s'mores. Once I got them into bed, I tucked them in well in their blankets and read a story to Shebelle. It didn't have any monsters or ghosts.

When I rinsed off the plate in the kitchen sink, I passed by the window and, against my better judgment, I looked toward the Skeleton House. I had told myself not to, that I didn't have to prove anything to myself. What was known in life? One of buzzard luck? Sure, I told myself every day to look at the world through a glass half full of domestic, but that optimism never left any room for magic. On that, my pa had been surely right. The world was a stranger to such, and if it had ever known the touch of the Divine it was long gone in the days of Old. So, knowing this, why did I feel the need to tell myself not to look? It was that curiosity that never died. And I saw it, and when I did I felt void. All the air in me went out like a basketball punctured with scissors. And I felt hollow. I felt empty.

In the window of the Skeleton House was the bobbing visage of a skull like you might see in a storefront window on the thirty-first night in October. It was grinning, all teeth and bone, and the whole round thing glowed neon green against the phantom shadowed black of the attic. It floated in that darkness, its jaw opening and closing as if mouthing some unheard riddle, but in my head, I heard it calling me.

Come, it sang, *Come and see.*

My feet moved on their own. My legs carried me through the house, out the door, across the lawn, down the road, through the trees, and up to the house. There, the door was opened to me.

I crossed that doorway into the other world and the smell of the man's body was long-gone, replaced instead by a smell of something sweet and inviting. Like a grandma's kitchen the day she bakes goods of cinnamon and nutmeg for the church.

Waiting for me at the foot of the stairs was the skull, now pulsating at a heartbeat's pace, flickering between bright green and purple and pink and sickly blue. I reached for it and when I did, I saw now that my arm glowed in a similar manner. It was my right arm, and it pulsed a vibrant color I had never seen before. I felt the air breathe against it and felt it move through the space between us. I realized my arm had never left and I had finally found it once again.

In a blink the skull was gone and I heard the rattling of things in the walls. It was a thousand little bones falling into place around me, scuttling to find one another in the dark.

A strong and gentle breeze closed the door with a firm ease.

I went to the window and it was like moving through a marsh. The air was now thick and resisted my motion.

I looked through the window as the last trick 'r treaters and their mothers and fathers found their ways home. A few of the younger children, all dressed in costumes of the night, dragged their tired and weary parents by the cuffs of their normal-day wear to "come and see! come and see!"

It was then I saw the small gathering collecting at the edge of my lawn. The crowd was staring toward my house. The elders were confused and impatient and the young were filled with wonder.

And I watched as the scarecrow in the flannel began to move. It glowed with a pulsing light of many colors from a heart under its straw, and as it stumbled forward on its plastic skeleton legs the crowd made a sound of amazement.

It took up the ax at its side and commenced to chopping.

W. H. Gilbert, born in southeast Texas, is a returning writer to the Road Kill series, the second volume of which contains his first published short story. He tries to live every week like it is the week of Halloween, but finds that an increasingly difficult task to accomplish in the Lone Star State. He has another recent story that can be found in the anthology collection The Toilet Zone, also available from HellBound Books.

The Dark Rift

Jeremy Hepler

9:57 PM

Kate Brussard hadn't thought about the Dark Rift for almost an hour when she stepped onto her front porch smiling so big it took up half her long face. She *did* feel different. Her friend Caroline had been right. Having sex with David had made her feel happy in a way that she'd never felt happy before. Confident happy. Stupid happy. She spun around and watched David pedal into, through, and out of a streetlight's glow at the end of the block and shook her head.

David Burchalter was eighty percent arms and legs, clumsy, and seemed to be color blind when he dressed. But Kate felt a special connection to him that had nothing to do with his looks. He always seemed to know exactly what she wanted to hear, and exactly what she wanted him to do. Tonight he'd taken her to a house on Yale Street, abandoned months ago, like many others in the small central

Texas town of Clifton. Before they'd arrived, he'd placed two pillows, a blanket, an electric lantern, and two Dr. Peppers in the center of the vacant living room. He made love to her and then snuggled with her afterward. His long arms wrapped around her slender body, he told her he'd been dreaming of this night for years. Then he told her how their future together would be long and exciting, and how all the chaos going on in the world would change for the better. He said everything she wanted to hear. As usual.

A few seconds after David was out of sight, Kate glanced down at the empty Dr. Pepper bottle in her hand and an unexpected giggle shot out of her mouth. David had traded his iPod to get her the DP. He knew it was her favorite. The only thing she'd asked for and didn't get on her sixteenth birthday, two months earlier, because most of the local stores had been looted. But David had found not one, but two. He loved her. He really did. This bottle proved it. She wanted to hold it up and scream it to the world. But with the urge came the realization that her mother was probably watching through the peephole.

After straightening her yellow tank and jean shorts, and drawing in a deep, smile-stifling breath, Kate began pounding on the door to the beat of the opening saxophone in *Summer Breeze,* her father's favorite song, their family's secret knock.

The door opened almost instantly and her mother grabbed her by the forearm. "Get in here. Where have you been? You were supposed to be home hours ago."

"I was with David. You know that."

"And you promised you'd be home before dark. You know it's dangerous to be out at night."

Another unexpected giggle seeped out of Kate's mouth that had nothing to do with her mother.

"What? You think it's funny, Kate? People are getting killed and robbed and raped all over the place. Even small towns like ours aren't safe anymore. After what happened to Jake, I thought you understood that." Her mother closed the door. "Here." She handed Kate a key ring fat with keys. "Lock it, and then make sure the back door is locked, too."

Kate glanced at the dry erase board hanging on the wall in the foyer as her mother walked away. Her mother used to write dates and reminders on the board to keep the family coordinated, but now, ever since her mother had begun receiving messages from God shortly after the first attack on the United States, it served as a platform for end-of-the-world warnings. A week earlier a quote from Revelations had been replaced by Nostradamus's Quatrain 2:91.

At sunrise one will see a great fire
Noise and light extending towards the north
Within the earth death and cries are heard
Death awaiting them through weapons, fire, and famine

Kate didn't read the entire message. She already had it memorized. Her mother had been shoving it down her throat all week. She locked the front door, made sure the back was locked, then dropped the keys on the dining room table and went to the bathroom to wash up.

After wiping down her body with a damp towel, she realized that she didn't have any more rinse-less shampoo. She threw on a T-shirt and her blue robe and headed for her parents' bathroom to grab another bottle from the closet where her mom stored the extras.

Her little sister Melanie was playing in the hall near the stairs, holding a stuffed Dora in one hand, a stuffed Boots in the other. Kate crouched down behind her and tickled Dora's stomach. "What are you doing, Dora?"

Melanie answered in her get-with-the-program voice. "We're going to rescue the rainbow fish trapped in the sea monster's cave."

Kate kissed the back of Melanie's head. "Cool. Good luck."

Melanie raised Boots up above her head and groaned as Kate started walking away.

"Good luck to you, too, Boots," Kate added.

Melanie jiggled Boots happily, and then met eyes with Kate. "You're going to sleep with me tonight again, right? You promised."

"Of course," Kate said. Melanie had been having nightmares for months, almost every night since Jake's death. "My tickle toes might try to get you when I fall asleep though. Are you sure you can protect yourself?"

Melanie giggled. "Yes."

"I hope so."

Kate continued toward her parents' room with an unbreakable smile on her face.

10:17 PM

Kate's parent's door was slightly ajar and the light was on. She could hear her mother whispering somewhere inside. Her mother had been doing that more and more lately – talking to herself, to ghosts. To God. Most of the time Kate couldn't make out what her mother was saying, and her mother wouldn't address it when Kate had asked. Kate inched quietly toward the door and peeked inside.

Her mother stood in front of her giant dresser. Jake's senior picture was propped up against the wall in front of her, behind four glasses of pink Kool-Aid.

Jake was three and a half years older than Kate at the time of his death six months earlier. The only boy, the oldest, Jake had always been Mother's favorite. "Her Angel." His death had not only killed a large part of her, but had also warped the part that was left behind. He'd gone out with his buddies in search of food and gas a few days after the riots started and never came back. One of his friends, Harold, or maybe it was Tony, Kate couldn't remember, had brought his bloody jacket to the house the next morning, saying Jake had been shot over in the Pucket Plaza Bakery parking lot. The only other information Kate remembered the boy giving was that Jake had died instantly, painlessly.

Kate's father and one of his friends had gone back to the lot and searched for the body to no avail. They held a makeshift memorial in the backyard two weeks later. Shortly after that, Kate's mother went from receiving occasional messages from God to receiving them daily, and her paranoid, wild-eyed rants spiraled out of control, lasting longer and longer, delivered with more passion, greater conviction. She boarded up the windows, and added multiple locks on the doors. They started conserving water, hoarding food. Kate was only allowed to leave the house when the sun was bright and for no more than an hour, and she could only go as far away as two blocks, and only if David or her friend Caroline went with her. Melanie wasn't allowed out of the house at all. The only local information the girls received was from David or their father when he ventured out to trade for goods and food. National news occasionally came across from the few Austin television stations still on air and sporadic NPR broadcasts. Kate dreaded the day when there would be no more electricity. And based on conversations she'd overheard between her mother and father, she feared that would be sooner than later.

As Kate stared through the cracked-open door at the same picture her mother's eyes were locked on, thoughts of Jake began racing through her mind: his body slamming her on the trampoline, taking her water skiing at Lake Waco, letting her win at Connect Four, teaching her how to play Tetris, how to ride a bike. When the images stopped, Kate's mother was still staring, still whispering the same word over and over. It sounded like, "Soon, soon, soon." And she was spooning powder into the four glasses, staring at the picture of Jake.

It took only a moment for something inside Kate's head to click – The Dark Rift, four cups, *"soon, soon, soon,"* the picture, the powder, her mother's behavior. Memories of a History Channel special on Jim Jones she'd watched with Jake a few years back sprung to the forefront of her mind. A bubble of anger materialized inside her chest, ballooned and burst, all in a matter of seconds. She raised her hand and shoved the door open. "What are you doing?"

Startled, her mother dropped the spoon on the dresser and cut her eyes toward the door.

"What are you putting in those glasses?"

"Didn't we teach you how to knock?"

Kate marched into the room. "That's not sugar, is it? You're going to kill us. Four glasses. Four of us."

When her mother didn't respond, any lingering doubts about the accusation Kate had made vanished. "You bitch! What gives you the right?"

"Kate. Shut it. You don't want Mel to get scared."

Kate shook her head. David had always assured her that her mother would get better, that the world would get better, that they just needed to be patient, but he was wrong. "You can't do this."

"Kate. You don't understand. You're too young. There's too much...I –"

Kate pointed at her mother, cutting her off. "You're crazy," she said, then ran out of the room. She made her way downstairs and grabbed the keys off the dining room table as she called out for Melanie. Melanie yelled back from her bedroom and Kate trotted off in that direction. When she turned the kitchen corner, her mother was standing directly in front of her, blocking the hallway.

"Give me the keys, Kate. Now."

"No."

"Don't make me take them from you. We've raised you better than this."

"What? You expect me to just let you do this?" She pointed her finger at her mother's chest. "You've lost it."

"Keep your voice down. If you upset Mel, you'll never forgive yourself."

Kate tried to shove past her mother but couldn't. Her mother was almost a foot taller, thirty pounds heavier. She had been an All-State softball player at Baylor University, had run track, but Kate never would've anticipated that she was *this* strong. She wrapped her arms around Kate, lifted her off the ground, and easily carried her into the kitchen, slammed her down on a chair, and jerked the keys out of her hand.

Kate's mouth fell open in dismay. "Kate, if you scream or yell and upset Mel, I swear I'll never forgive you, either. Now calm down."

Kate stood, straightened her robe, and peered into her mother's eyes, trying to see some hint of her *old* mother, her *real* mother. She was looking for the funny woman who played tea party and Barbie with her for hours every afternoon when she was little. The caring woman who didn't leave her bedside, or bathe, or eat, for almost five straight days when complications arose after Kate's tonsils were removed. The cool woman who taught her how to apply just enough make-up to get Bobby Clawson's attention in math class when she was thirteen. There was no sign of *that* woman. That woman was dead.

"Come to my room and let's talk like women, not fight like beasts," her mother said.

Kate nodded. As she followed her mother upstairs, she could see the butt of her father's pistol shifting around in her mother's baggy pant pocket.

10:28 PM

Kate sat down on the corner of her parents' bed, the corner nearest the closed door. Her mother sat in her grandmother's old rocker in the corner by a boarded up window, in shadow.

"The world's coming to an end soon, Kate, you know that."

Kate stared at the shadowed chair as it gently rocked. "I don't know that, Mother. And you don't either. No one knows exactly when the world will end."

"Oh, yes, we do, Kate. It's obvious. Just open your eyes and look. Almost all of the world's economies have crashed. Wars are raging all over the planet. Most of the police forces and hospitals are overwhelmed, unable to help anyone. Then there's the rapid advancement of global warming and coastal flooding. We're running out of energy and food and –"

Kate cut her mother off. She'd heard this speech too many times. "I know, I know, I know. Species depletion. Fresh water crisis. Human Survival Chaos Theory. Earthquakes. Volcanoes. Tsunamis. No one fears God anymore. And on and on and on...." Kate's voice quaked a bit. Her mouth felt like sandpaper. "But kill us? Your own family?"

"It's all coming to a climax tonight, Kate. I received the final message this afternoon."

Kate didn't respond. She glanced at the pictures of herself, Melanie and Jake dotting the walls. She thought about the gun in her mother's pocket. A shiver ran up her spine. The rocking of the shadowed chair became quicker, with a creak now.

"Do you know what the term tipping point means, Kate?"

Kate nodded.

"Well, tonight's humanity's tipping point. God has warned us about this over and over and over. The Bible predicted it. So did the I Ching. So did the Egyptians. The Mayans. After tonight, the world will spiral downward into a miserable, desolate place that not one good soul will want to live in."

"I know *you* believe that, Mother, but I don't. You don't know what tomorrow will bring."

Her mother continued like she hadn't heard a word Kate had said. "Whether we receive a super solar wave, or the magnetic poles reverse, or giant earthquakes and volcanoes obliterate the earth, or if we all become zombies for God's sake, we don't want to be around tomorrow to see it. We don't want to go through that level of pain and suffering. Things are bad enough already. We can all die together. In each other's arms. At home. Painlessly. Peacefully."

"You're doing this because of him." Kate pointed at Jake's senior picture on the dresser behind the four glasses. "You just can't handle the fact that he's dead, and you're using this Dark Rift crap to justify ending your own pain. I miss him, too, but killing all of us because he died isn't fair. It's not right. Even if something terrible does happen, what if God wants us to survive?"

The rocking stopped and Kate's mother pushed out a long breath. "In the end, there'll be no survivors. Besides, look at yourself. Do you think that a young girl who doesn't have the slightest clue about real responsibility can survive something of this magnitude? You would never be able to take care of yourself, defend yourself. Your father and I have always done everything for you."

"I'm not that young. I'm not helpless."

"Reading James Patterson paperbacks and watching R-rated films doesn't make you smart or mature, Kate. Neither does sex."

Kate forced the lump in her throat down with a dry swallow.

"You have it written all over your face. I saw the way you watched David pedal off. I wasn't born yesterday. Besides, your pants were unzipped when came inside. And your hair was a mess."

Kate thought she'd checked her pants on the porch. Was this a mother-trick, a ploy to get her to confess?

"I'm not mad because you did it, Kate. I'm actually kind of glad you got to experience it. But it won't make you any more equipped to handle the Dark Rift."

Kate's stomach started to cramp. Following a long pause she said, "Melanie's only five years old. What about her experiences?"

"I thank God every day that she's only five. This will be easier on her than anyone else. She'll go to sleep peacefully, snuggled up next you, her favorite, and then wake up in a better place, a perfectly safe place, with the rest of us. To her it won't be death. It will be magic."

Tears began to stream down Kate's face. She turned away from her mother. "Father will never let you do this to us."

"Well, he'll be home soon, and you can talk to him then."

Kate stood up.

"I'm actually glad we had this talk," her mother said, rising too. She walked over to the dresser and picked up two of the glasses. "There's no need to be upset. Everything will be all right. We'll all be together. Jake will be back. We'll be happy again. I promise."

Kate didn't know what to say. She didn't know what to do.

"Carry the other two glasses down to the table for me? We need to go check on Mel."

Kate shook her head.

"Don't do this, Kate. Don't make me force you."

Kate thought of the gun in her mother's pocket. She had never felt more afraid of anyone than she did her own mother in that moment. "Take these," her mother said, holding out the two cups in her hands, glaring at Kate the way she'd stared at their dog after he'd had chewed up the couch cushions. Kate remembered her mother beating the dog with a spatula.

Kate took the cups, and as she followed her mother downstairs, she didn't take her eyes off the pistol in her mother's pocket.

10:50 PM

Kate was sitting on her bed, wearing a pair of white pajamas covered with red hearts. They were a birthday present from her father. She took her eyes off the empty Dr. Pepper bottle in her hands and scanned her room. The radio, TV, posters, pictures, sketches she'd drawn. Was this really the last time she'd ever see them? Was there really nothing she could do? Would her mother *really* shoot her? She felt nauseated and alone. She wished her father would get home. She wished Jake were still alive. She wished David were here to hold her. She wished that she could stop crying. Outside her door, she could hear Melanie laughing and her mother moving furniture around in the living room. A few seconds later, her door eased open and Melanie's little head poked in.

"Mom says we get to sleep in the living room tonight. All of us together on the same mattress. Like a slumber party."

"Awesome," Kate somehow managed.

Melanie nodded and giggled and left, too young and too excited to notice Kate's bleary eyes.

When the door clicked shut, Kate walked over to the mirror above her dresser. She hated to admit it, but she did look young, and scared, and a little pathetic. She was seeing what her mother saw: a little girl with tear-streaked cheeks and swollen eyes, wearing kiddie heart pajamas and holding an empty plastic bottle in her hands for comfort. She didn't want to be that little girl. And more importantly, she didn't want her mother to think she was that little girl. She wanted to prove her mother wrong, so she wiped the tears off her face, put on a little make-up, changed into a blouse and jeans, and hid the bottle in the top of her closet. She was walking toward the door when it swung open and her father smiled at her.

"Hey, honey."

"Daddy." Kate wrapped her arms around him. She held on a little longer than usual. "Dad, Mom…Mom's going…she wants to….she's got your gun and…"

Her father nudged the door closed, then placed the tips of his fingers on her lips. "I know, Kate. She told me."

"Told you what? That she wants to kill us? Because she said that –"

"I'm dying, Kate. I have cancer. I've it had it for a while now."

"What?" Kate stumbled back and crumpled down on her bed. She felt dizzy. "What?" That was the only word she seemed to be able to find. "What?"

"I'm not going to be around to protect you guys anymore. Or to feed you. And to be honest, it's getting harder and harder to find people willing to trade food and water anyway." Kate felt nothing as her father combed his fingers through her hair. "I'm not sure if this is the end of the world forever like Mom says, but I do believe something catastrophic is on the horizon. And I know that three girls left alone with no protection or source of food will either starve to death or be discovered and raped and beaten and abused by what's left of humanity. You'd be chewed up and spit out so fast your head would spin. There would be nothing but pain and suffering for you, and I can't die knowing that. I know it's hard, but we'll all go to the other side together. As one. I honestly believe that's best for us as a family."

Kate found another word. "David…David…"

"David's only sixteen. He can't be expected to take care of you guys. He wouldn't know how. Besides, he has his own family to help out with. I know you care about him, but that's ridiculous. These are drastic times, honey, and we have to take drastic measures."

Kate didn't know what to say. Not unlike her mother, she felt like a part of her had just been killed. The part that gave her permission to fight for survival.

"Everything and everyone you love will be with you forever after tonight. I don't believe in much, but I believe in that, honey."

Kate didn't feel any lips on her forehead, but saw her father kiss her. And she saw the knife in his left hand.

"Come on, let's go eat some grilled cheese sandwiches with Mom and Mel before bed."

11:32 PM

Kate didn't eat any of her grilled cheese. Her parents ate and chatted a little, but they didn't try to talk to her at all.

Melanie didn't talk much either. She hadn't eaten since breakfast, and she wolfed down her entire sandwich in a matter of minutes. When she looked longingly at Kate's plate, Kate winked and pushed her sandwich across the table.

After everyone was finished, Kate's mother brought the four cups of Kool-Aid from the counter to the table and then raised her cup high as if about to toast a newlywed couple. "Here's to our family. God loves us all and will always guide us."

Kate paused when her fingers wrapped around her cup. This really was happening. And if she tried to do anything about it, her mother would probably shoot her. And what would that do to Mel? She could feel both her mother's and father's eyes on her. She looked their direction. They both were both smiling, and her mother's hand was on top of her father's hand. The one holding the knife he'd used to cut the sandwiches. She took in a deep breath and watched her father and Melanie drink every last drop of their Kool-Aid. When Melanie tipped her cup upside down, glanced at Kate and let out a loud, "Ahhh," Kate tilted her cup and let the liquid race down her throat.

Once Kate's cup was empty, her mother announced, "All right girls, it's time for bed."

"Yay," Melanie said, running and jumping onto the mattress they'd pulled into the living room. "I want Mommy to sleep in front of me, and Kate behind me, okay?"

"All right dear. But you need to calm down. We need to be asleep by midnight so we'll get plenty of rest."

Without a saying a word, Kate, her mother, and father all lay down exactly where Melanie told them to lay.

"Kate, Kate, Kate," Melanie pleaded after they were all situated. "Will you tell me about the time you saw Santa Claus? He's going to be here in few months, you know?"

"Su–" The word caught in Kate's throat. She cleared it. "Sure."

Kate's father placed his hand on her back. She heard a thump when her mother dropped the gun on the floor at the head of the mattress as she began to tell Melanie the Santa story.

"When I was five years old, the same age you are now," Kate said, "I heard something on the roof on Christmas Eve. You know what it sounds like in the fall when the fat squirrels are running across the roof?"

"Yes."

"It sounded like that, but a hundred times louder. When I came downstairs I heard another noise by the fireplace…"

As Kate mindlessly recited the story about the night she met Santa, her thoughts drifted elsewhere.

She wondered where David was right now. What he was doing. If he was thinking about her. What he would say if he were here. Then, she wondered what his reaction would be when he found out about her family. She figured he'd probably be the one to find them. No one else came to visit anymore. She tried to imagine the look on his face after he broke in and saw her lying there pale and cold. She pictured him heart broken and bursting into tears and falling to his knees. And even though she knew it was wrong and morbid, the fact that he might find it hard to go on without her made her feel something like relief.

Then her thoughts went to Jake. Sweet Jake. She did believe in Heaven, a permanent good place for good people, and thought that if God was as good as her grandma had always claimed, that Jake had gone there and would be waiting for them. It would be nice to see him again. To hear him make some sarcastic remark about dying just before he lifts her off the ground and gives her a giant bear hug and spins so many times that she feels like she's going to puke. She thought about the joyous look her mother would have etched on her face at such a sight. Ah, it would be nice to have Mother go back to being Mother. To look at her and give her a real hug. And it would be nice to not have to live like a prisoner anymore. To be able to go where she wanted, when she wanted, and not to constantly look over her shoulder. No more fearing that the next thug hoping to take advantage of someone hadn't chosen her. The longer she thought about it, the more part of her *was* ready to get off this roller coaster. The tracks did seem to be crumbling beneath her as the ride accelerated. And if everything turned out like she hoped, maybe it would be better on the other side. Maybe it would. Maybe...

Two minutes before the grandfather clock in the corner of the living room chimed midnight, all four members of the Brussard family were fast asleep.

8:33 AM

Kate woke with a start and sat upright. Panicked, she scanned the room. Her mother, father, and Melanie were all heaped together, lying chest to back, their arms draped over one another. Kate reached out and touched Melanie's arm. It was cold and stiff and slightly blue.

"No...no..."

She quickly stood and hopped off the mattress. She checked her mother and father. They were both cold, stiff, blue. Dead.

Her thoughts raced. What was going on? Why was she alive? She should be dead. In Heaven with them. Or...maybe she *was* she dead? Maybe there was no Heaven. Or...maybe she was dreaming. Yes, she had to be dreaming. But why–

And then a thought hit her, out of nowhere, like a lightning strike on a clear blue day. When she'd burst into her parents' room the previous night, her mother had been spooning the poison into the cups but had immediately set down the spoon. She must not have put a proper dose in the last cup—the cup Kate drank from after dinner. That had to be it. But…but…

Kate's hands and knees trembled as her eyes slid across her lifeless family. Tears streamed down her cheeks. Her heart jackhammered against her sternum. "I have to get out of here," she whispered over and over, bouncing from one foot to the other.

Trying her best to avoid looking at their face, she fished the keys out her father's pocket and scooped the gun up off the floor. Then she fumbled into her shoes in the foyer, unlocked the front door, and sprinted out into the bright, red-tinted Texas morning sunshine, heading for David's house.

9:04 AM

Bug-eyed and out of breath, Kate stumbled across her lawn and up to her front door. Her shirt was gone, her jeans torn. Blood was splattered across most of her body. The sunlight was even redder now, thicker, scorching. Unwelcoming. Not normal. She was glad she hadn't locked the door when she left because she didn't have the keys anymore. Or the gun.

David followed right behind her, limping. His leg was broken, his clothes torn, and he, too, was splattered in blood. He had a horrified look on his face.

"Come on," Kate yelled. "Hurry." She held the door for him. After he was safe inside, she slammed it closed, glanced at her dead family on the floor, then met David's terrified eyes.

"Where is it?" he asked.

"I saw her putting it in our cups when she was in her room. It's got to be up there somewhere."

Kate grabbed David's hand and helped him hobble up the stairs. "What if there's not enough for both of us?" he asked.

"Then we'll use a knife. We have plenty of those."

Jeremy Hepler is the Bram Stoker-nominated author of CRICKET HUNTERS, THE BOULEVARD MONSTER, and numerous short stories and nonfiction articles. He received the Texas Panhandle Professional Writer's Short Story Award in 2014, and his debut novel was a Bram Stoker Award finalist in the Superior Achievement in a First Novel category in 2017. He lives in central Texas with his wife and son and is currently working on his next novel. For more information, you can follow him on Twitter, Facebook, Instagram, Goodreads, and Amazon.

Hometown Hero
Dan Fields

I woke up running again last night. Once I get started on something it's hard for me to quit, whether what I'm doing is good for me or not. Almost every night my toothbrush comes away pink with blood on the bristles. The day before school let out, I jerked off too hard and couldn't touch myself again for a week. Running hurt so bad that week I nearly pissed my track shorts. I couldn't sit at the dinner table, just ate in my room. My mom and dad seemed okay with that.

Coach Bellamy says I'm something special. He ain't ever seen anything like me. Coach is a tough ol' bastard. What he thinks matters to me, but I know he's lying.

Last June, after school let out, I broke the 400-meter hurdles record. Not just my school record but the record at the county track and field meet. Hell of a day for the Adams Creek Panthers.

Our football team, the other Adams Creek Panthers, every season they show up and do just okay. For a Texas high school that's a black eye, but I know some of the players and I reckon they do their best. Them big bastards could snap a track runner like me in half, if they could catch me. A couple have tried. People say Coach Mack who's in charge of the football is a drunk, can't make them any better at scoring touchdowns than he found them. He's brothers-in-law with Principal Garrett, so that's that.

Coach Bellamy, now, he's the real deal. Set some records for himself back in the sixties. Hammer throw, long jump. He's getting old, don't have the speed he used to. His two assistant coaches run and fetch for him and pace the track team on our endurance runs. He still cusses and coaches louder and better than anybody I ever saw. Always checking up on me, muttering in my ear to stay focused. I'm scholarship good, that much I know, because he tells me twice a day. Claps me on the shoulder too hard, says I'm one of a kind, but talks like a man who dreamed a bad storm and is anxious to get it over with. Coming from him any praise ought to mean something. It does, but it would mean more if it was true. Thing is, Coach Bellamy ain't allowed to talk about Lone Star Leighton. Nobody is, even though every eye in Adams Creek is on me to be some kind of second coming.

Talent was never something I thought much about. I'm a runner. Blessed or gifted or born to it, depends who you ask. Pastor Kelly at Varsity Christian Athletes tells me to "lift it up to God." So I do, I guess. When I push hard on a long run, my head fizzes. I see Lone Star Leighton ahead of me like a ghost. Harder I kick, the tighter a big fist crushes my heart 'til I have to stop and puke. Pastor Kelly did a sermon once on apostles getting stoned to death in the Bible. Most of them saw visions and got lifted up to God. I wonder sometimes if what I feel is anything like that.

I don't see Lone Star at daytime practice or in meets. He shows up on my night runs, twenty yards ahead of me. I cry hot water, my knees wobble and I can't close the gap, but I don't puke on my night runs. I may dry heave and cough up the taste of pocket change, but that's only my body and brain jacking with me.

I work like hell for my stats. Coach Bellamy still calls me on weeknights, hollering for me to keep my shit together. I run everywhere every day of summer while my teammates are off having vacation. I do my night runs. And I reckon some folks do what they can to show they appreciate me. I ain't had to pay for a pizza or much else I wanted in six months. Used to bribe people's older brothers to buy me beer. Now any high school teacher would steal me some if I asked. I get treated better at school than Charlie Mausbacher, the quarterback. I know that ain't usual, or fair. He's no slacker, and why else would you sign up to be a quarterback except to be the Mayor of Swinging Dickville? I heard he said some shit about me, but ain't nobody repeating it much. Must be a lonesome feeling wanting to talk trash and nobody listens. I got real life to worry about.

At the end of April, I came down with an awful cold that was maybe gonna turn out flu. I asked about taking a couple weeks off practice. Coach's whole face jumped and he said this time of year was crucial. I had to keep my act together, get some sleep and gut it out. In school, Coach had to tone his language down. He backed me into Principal Garrett's office, where the two of them told me real carefully how important it is to set my goals early. I was fixing to apply for college, and I'd need as much to show for myself as I could. "Still need to get those long-distance runtimes down," said Principal Garrett, kinda nervous-friendly. I knew we were talking about Lone Star Leighton, even though nobody talks about him. If I was sick, they said of course we'd re-examine my plans, but heading into senior year I needed to make sure I had the time and dedication to achieve everything needed achieving. Shit like that. "Eyes on the finish line." The door was behind me but I couldn't shake the feeling Coach and the principal were muscling me up against a brick wall. So, I said nevermind, it was fine, I'd take some vitamins and sleep more. After that I noticed Principal Garrett came out to watch afternoon practices. And Mrs. Stevens, my biology teacher. And Señora Villalobos, who teaches Spanish. And Señor Cruz, who cleans the halls and bathrooms. And Constable Jacobs. My mom and dad showed up sometimes, even though they both work. I thought they'd say I was training too hard, but they seemed okay with it.

I started my night runs because I needed some time with nobody watching me. I go three nights a week minimum, whether or not Coach calls me after dinner for a pep talk. First time was after I woke up in the middle of the night, sure that my phone was ringing even though it quit as soon as my eyes opened. I got my gear and headed to practice, running in the dark for a mile and a half toward school 'til I realized the sun wouldn't be up for hours. I'd had some kind of dream it was dawn already. Then my phone rang. I couldn't see a callback number, or maybe my sleeping brain couldn't unscramble it. But the voice was Coach Bellamy's or near enough to it, and it cackled at me, "Keep runnin' anyway. You're a by-God miracle." I figured it was as good a time as any for a run.

Now I wake up running. Last night wasn't the first time.

I did get special treatment once. Back in pre-season training I sprained my ankle real good. They carried me around like the prince of Egypt, to and from the sports clinic. Coach and the principal told my folks not to sweat a dollar of it. Only the best for the school's finest. Mom and dad seemed okay with that. I reckon Coach knows when to push me and when to let up on me. Look how the county meet turned out.

The record book, and my name in it, is what all the hollering's about. Once I get my shit that much more together and cut my middle-distance times down, I'll be the champ for a long time. All the talk about one-of-a-kind-by-God miracles is making me feel like one.

Soon as I become the best, my school can get rid of two records that have stood over forty years. Bobby Roy Leighton's records, him who'd be called Lone Star later on. Adams Creek is itching to cross out them tainted numbers and move on. There's no picture of Bobby Roy in the trophy case. Everybody knows why, so nobody has to mention it. Sumbitch has me beat by four-tenths on the 3K and a tenth of a second, one slim nut hair I can't shave off, on the 1500 meters. I came close to breaking that one back in April, the week I poured snot from both nostrils and possibly out my ears. Afterwards I lay on my side in the grass hacking phlegm for two hours. Coach, looking gloomy, said it was a dang good effort, I could sleep in and skip next practice if I wanted to. My mom and dad seemed okay with that. People coming off the bleachers practically stepped over me, muttering it was a pretty good run. Almost good enough, they meant.

Since then I've run myself so hard it's all I can do to shut my eyes and sleep. I'm a whittled-down hickory limb. My soles are hardened up so thick I could kick a big dog's head in.

Couple weeks ago, feeling low, I ran into Coach Bellamy outside the drugstore. He whomped me on the back, asked how ol' King Panther was running. I snapped, told him to lay off, I was keeping to my workouts and he didn't need to be calling me up at night to remind me. He looked at me funny, asked what the hell did I mean. His phone's been broke for a month, and he knew better than to worry about me. "Unique damn talent," he said. I saw his eyes pucker down like he wouldn't forget I mouthed off at him. Maybe he'll spread the word. I get another pat on the shoulder like Coach and half of Adams Creek gives me, I'll break somebody's arm.

Here's some history for you:

May 17th through 18th, 1975: Bobby Roy Leighton of Adams Creek High School (Adams Creek, Texas) added two middle-distance running records to a top-notch track and field career. Folks believed he was headed for greatness. Treated him like a hero just shy of Jesus and Lefty Frizzell.

After graduation, Bobby Roy and two pals went road tripping to Arizona and southern California. His family and teachers expected him back to train for freshman season at Texas Christian in Fort Worth. Full scholarship. None of the three boys would set foot back in Adams Creek. One surfaced nine months later, passing out flyers for a rock club in San Diego. He wouldn't come home or discuss his former buddies. Nobody saw the second friend again, ever. Only a pair of dirty postcards from Nevada hotels, both in Bobby Roy's handwriting, came back to Texas. One went to the Admissions dean of TCU, one to the Leighton family home.

August 28th, 1977: an old man was found half-buried under big rocks in Deseret City Cemetery outside Delta, Utah. Naked, beat and bled nearly to death, he was treated at the community hospital and described several young people who'd robbed and roughed him up. He went comatose and stayed that way.

August 29th, 1977: the sheriff's department of Millard County, Utah, and as many state patrols as they could wrangle, raided an illegal encampment in a limestone cave near Howell Peak. They arrested nine people for possessing drugs found at the scene. Five of them nine went up on murder charges. A year before the old man, someone had slaughtered a vacationing family at a highway rest stop, including a teenager, a toddler and a pregnant mother. Most of the blame fell on Bobby Roy "Lone Star" Leighton, pride of the '74-'75 Adams Creek Running Panthers. Leighton claimed under questioning that he and his female accomplice, Miss Jeanetta "Jupiter Genie" van Kempel, had been high on angel dust at the time and were "just looking for a ride home."

They figured the cave dwellers were a religious cult, supporting themselves with violent crime. Leighton was some kind of leader figure, one of the brainy ones preaching the gospel of hard drugs and group sex to the dumb ones. In court they showed infected tattoos of cosmic symbols they'd put on themselves. The judge couldn't make them stop singing. Leighton and others made the mostly Mormon jury sweat, giving fake names under oath like "Joseph Smith" and "Angelic Starsucker Moroni."

Four, including Leighton and van Kempel, were handed death sentences, but just then Utah was all boogered up about replacing the state firing squad with lethal injections. Only two got put to death. Leighton and van Kempel got their sentences commuted to life without parole. Their lawyer wrote a dirty bestseller book and retired.

Nobody in my hometown told me this about Lone Star Leighton. They only said Bobby Roy was a bright young man turned his back on God and home. Fine, but you'd reckon parents and church folks would give a kid some hints about what makes a boy go bad, how to keep from doing it. I put the story together at the county library over in Olmer. Lorna Jacobs helped me, the constable's daughter. I didn't mention her yet. We're sort of going together.

We kissed for the first time at a Varsity Christian Athletes dance, right after I broke the hurdle record. Lorna's not on a team but she volunteers. Her folks make her. I'd been dancing with Greta Mahler who followed me to the bathroom. She had rum breath and let me feel up on her, but that was all. Charlie Mausbacher says Greta jerked him off at Methodist youth camp. I don't believe everything he says, but I wasn't really up to go further with her. I went and talked to Lorna instead. She'd gone to smoke a cigarette by the trash bins behind the community center, where her dad and Pastor Kelly wouldn't see. She offered me one and I said better not. Then I took a drag and she kissed me. Her dad's chummy with me on account of he's a big sports booster, reckons I'm a solid citizen and safe around his daughter. Don't seem suspicious about how much time Lorna and I spend doing homework together, when I'm not sleeping or night-running. My mom and dad seem okay with it too. By July I was feeling up on Lorna plenty, but only Lorna. And myself, of course.

Lone Star's always there on my night runs, trotting just ahead of me. He's got perfect technique, not breaking form a half dozen ways like I do if I don't concentrate. He chants to me, sort of teasing but also hyping me up like a soldier. Sometimes I see the finish line ahead, but it moves away at the same speed I run. Lone Star's the only one who ever crosses it.

I was born a long time after Lone Star and his freaky pals got locked up. Most of them are dead. His girlfriend or cosmic wife or whatever, Jupiter Girl, croaked a few weeks ago from a stroke or brain cancer or something. I wonder how hard they tried to save her life. Must be a lonesome feeling to go down hurt or dying when the world knows what mean awful things you did.

One article says when they raided that Utah cave with them killers inside, Lone Star took off on foot.

Even jacked on drugs and dehydrated, he bolted so fast nobody could catch him. Kept going 'til some deputy thought of knocking him down with a car.

I've heard Lone Star Leighton's real voice, just once. Lorna found it for me, a news clip of some serial killer website. She's not into the whole Lone Star thing like I am, but she don't dodge the topic like everybody else. Long as I'm nice to her and make out with her some, she don't mind what we talk about. I try and read stories that she writes, but I ain't that good a reader. I'd rather she text me things. Our texts get pretty hot, and I can keep up because all the words we use are short. I bet our English teacher would fall down dead. Lorna don't seem worried about how much I run, or that I space out. But if I stopped running, said to hell with it, I think she'd be the only one in town wouldn't mind.

The news clip was from '78, when the Utah bunch went to trial. A pack of cops was dragging Leighton up the court steps. He looked pretty worked over, like they'd hit him with a few more cop cars. A ring of news people surrounded the police and Lone Star looked into a camera and growled, "How fast is fast enough?" and spit blood in the face of a cop jostling his shoulder that was hurt. The other cops jumped on him, whipped him good while reporters and everybody watched. It set the trial back two weeks.

Jupiter Girl was in the footage, too, looking kinda proud of her man for acting a freak. Call me crazy, she looks a little bit like Lorna. I didn't tell Lorna that. But maybe if Lone Star and Jupiter had met up in high school, not out on some desert, they'd have been okay.

Lorna's into art and stuff, real cute in a way the sporty girls aren't. Not hot and toned but sweet and mysterious with these, like, little curves on her. The day before school let out, I saw her and wanted to kiss her. Instead I got a boner that wouldn't go away. I had a hell of a time getting rid of it before practice.

I saw Coach Bellamy again last week, out front of the liquor store. He ain't phoned me up since I lit into him, but he gave me the thumbs-up and said, "Keep it sharp for the fall, son. Big year comin'." He still wouldn't own up to hassling me with midnight calls. I stared at the ground, had a sudden urge to make him own up. Grab that thumb and snap the bone. But when I looked up, he'd already gone.

Next day when I came home from swimming with Lorna, Principal Garrett called the house. Told me how excited everyone was about my senior season. I said sure, me too. He sorta downshifted his voice to say no matter what, I could expect full honors as the school's all-time greatest runner. Months away from the season even starting, the shithead was already betting short on me. If I didn't set them last two records, let the school wipe Lone Star Leighton off their books fair and square, they'd do it anyway and put me down as official champ. I might as well piss up a tree as show up to compete. Adams Creek could live with my name in the record book, I realized, even with a little star next to it. Whether they wrote one in or not, that star would be there. Future teams would go after my records, not Lone Star's because those wouldn't exist no more. Every generation after me thinking they were chasing a champ, when they'd really be trying to outrun second-place dogshit.

I'd put together a plate of leftovers while I listened to Principal Garrett. Swimming with Lorna had got me hungry, feeling almost human. When I got his drift, I chucked a pile of cold meatloaf, spuds and gravy straight at the wall. Busted the plate, stained the flower-print wallpaper. Walked straight out for a run without cleaning up. When I got back, the kitchen was clean and nobody said a word about it. Could've been a test to see how I'd act. I ain't heard since about fixed-up records or phony-ass awards. Principal Garrett and my folks let the whole thing go. They seemed okay with it.

August came hotter than Hell's buttcrack. Especially at night, since it ain't supposed to feel so hot when it's dark. I went farther and faster every run, almost had my own cross-country program going. One night I was walking down Live Oak Lane, getting my heart rate back to normal. Headlights turned the corner and a siren whooped. Constable Jacobs. I thought he'd bust me for being out after curfew. Instead he waved hello. "My God, it's true. The Alpha Panther out for his run." He insisted on driving me home. I still figured I was in trouble for something, but what could I do? Turns out trouble couldn't touch me. The constable was all stoked seeing me keep fit. "Discipline, just plain damn discipline," he said. "Never seen the like."

He told me Lorna thought I was nice, asking her to dance at the varsity dinner when she wasn't even on a team, buying her ice cream after school. I don't know where Lorna came up with that, but I appreciated her talking me up. Constable said they'd be glad to have me for supper one night. I remembered my "yes sirs," complimented Lorna for being smartest in class. He liked that. Didn't give me no watchful daddy business about dating his girl. I realized he was flattered to be giving me a ride. Upset my guts a little.

He got serious for a minute, stopping outside my house. Said I oughta watch myself running around so late. He admired me training but nighttime was dangerous. "You know ol' Pete Garrett, the principal, told me he's seen footprints a time or two in his flowerbed. Probably schoolkids making plans to throw shit-paper on the lawn, but still. Just a block east of where I picked you up. Not friends of yours, was they?" He winked, but went on to say bad things tended to happen after dark. "Don't go messing around with any of that... well, you know that business at the drive-in."

Sure I did, and I thanked him as I stepped out of the car. He pumped his brake lights at the stop sign before speeding away. I reckon that was to say, "So long, champ! Keep it between the ditches."

That "business" at the drive-in was major news for a week or two, before it became one of them things polite people don't discuss. Adams Creek people are experts at not discussing what everyone's talking about. Some people say it would be funny if it weren't so awful. I reckon some people can't tell the difference.

Just over the bridge toward New Dunbar is a big flat lot that's been the drive-in theater for something like sixty years. People from big cities don't believe we still have one out here. About the 20th of July, whenever the Friday was, a call came in anonymous to Constable Jacobs. They found Charlie Mausbacher's car parked in the pines behind the drive-in, while they were changing reels between the Friday Family Feature and the Midnight Monster Massacre. Charlie and Greta Mahler had picked up a bunch of Frostee Freeze, probably to sneak into the horror show after they'd got a little busy. Charlie wouldn't usually go off the team diet like that, but they'd smoked a bunch of weed and got hungry. Still couldn't wait to bone, I guess. The way Constable Jacobs figured it, Greta passed out after the sex, maybe during. Too much pot for a skinny pep squad gal. The constable got her covered up before her parents came for her. She cried lots, but didn't remember nothing.

Charlie lay across the seat with his junk still out. He was alive, just barely. No marks on him that didn't look like football bruises. They thought he'd had a blood clot or a bust vessel, like in some weepy sports movie. Folks have got romantic souls about young athletes. Doctors couldn't find no clots, but he'd lost so much oxygen to the brain they decided some cannabis allergy must have closed off his airway. Anybody with sense would say it looked like somebody throttled him. But when it comes to drugs, people in my town will believe any wild thing.

There were wrapped burgers and the smell of French fries in the car, even half a milkshake leaking on the floorboard, but no plastic takeaway bag. Nobody thought that was funny, even though the Frostee Freeze gives 'em out like nobody ever heard of saving the planet.

Mr. Crenshaw, who runs the drive-in, made a big deal out of Charlie's car being parked in the woods, off his property. He's got his business to look after, I reckon. The newspaper quoted him, "I keep my premises secure. I'm not the county reefer patrol, and thank God for that."

Greta's gone to stay with cousins in Lubbock. So far Charlie still can't talk. If he learns to walk again, he won't be setting no passing records. Good-hearted volunteers wheel him around school for now. Reckon they'll dedicate half of the next Christian Varsity banquet to giving him some courage award. No skin off me. Hope it makes him feel better. When I heard how they'd found him, I was amazed he lived.

You'd think a good Christian town like Adams Creek would come to a halt, mourning a promising sophomore quarterback cut down by tragedy. But there's no evidence of nothing but a shameful accident. Around here we believe we're given our trials for a reason, including the Mausbachers. Pastor Kelly says lift it up in prayer, and we do what he says.

I'm not gonna beat Lone Star. He's already beat me in my head. Does it four nights a week now. Nobody minds me looking like a knotty fence post with raccoon eyes painted on. They call me focused. Nobody sees I'm whipped. Lone Star is known for two things, and the more I chase him the more I think the only record of his I stand a chance of beating ain't his athletic record. I think maybe I've started training for something different.

Dad let me borrow the car tonight. Mom was at church bingo, but I bet she'd be okay with it too. Dad tried to make a joke, wouldn't I rather run? Neither of us laughed. I said I wanted to take Lorna to the drive-in. Instead we went for a burger and a slice of pie and never made it to the movie. Lorna said she was pretty sure about hearing back from

UPenn and UCLA. She applied early. Her folks made her apply to Texas too, but she wants to do art someplace else. "How 'bout the desert?" I asked and she laughed, but it didn't mean nothing to her. I said I didn't know where to apply, but if they wouldn't give me money to run, they wouldn't want me. We parked out by the creek, the real Adams Creek. The water looked like black volcano glass. I had something in mind I felt like doing, and she felt like it too. She don't mind how rough and wire-skinny I've gotten. Says it's kinda sexy, which nobody ever said to me before and gave my brain a good fizz. I like how she is, too.

We ain't been going together long, just the summer, but I feel like me and Lorna have gotten to know each other pretty well. Especially in the last hour. Especially nine minutes of that hour. I don't feel bad about it, whatever Pastor Kelly or our folks might say. I'd do it again if she let me. Right after, when we were both hot and damp from each other, feeling the breeze cool our sweaty parts, I know she felt good about it. I'm sure of that. Then she asked what was on my mind. Like a dumb shithead I opened up my mouth and told her. Not everything, but enough. I saw her sweet freckled face change while I talked. Maybe I thought it would turn her on, me being dark and edgy. But her knees pushed together and her feet curled up under her. Her body hunched away like a dying plant. Even in my passenger seat with nothing on, she wanted to hide from me. Whatever good thing she felt while we'd been doing it dried up fast. Her cigarette went out. I reckon she'd take herself back from me if she could. I can't blame her, feeling that way after I mentioned the drive-in. I know that's one thing I went on about, my trips to the woods outside the drive-in, watching people come and go to see how patient and quiet I could wait. Nobody asked me when I last saw Charlie before his trip to paradise with Greta Mahler. People know about my night runs, but a guy'd have to be a damn lunatic to run halfway to New Dunbar and back in a night.

Lorna knows more about me now than she wants to. I was her I wouldn't want to give it up, not even handjobs, to a guy with my imagination. I'd feel like I was feeding something ought to be starved right out of the world. Amazing how clear a guy can think after getting off, but never before.

Maybe I should have confessed more, but I'm glad I didn't mention the last day of school. How I went to the girls' locker room to borrow back some lane markers for the track. Lorna was alone, taking her time between gym and last period. She was smart enough nobody hassled her about being late to class, and it was only study hall. I almost hollered from the equipment closet, give her a heads-up, but I hung back where I could see her in a changing mirror. Back then I'd never seen her naked, not even in a bathing suit. Barely ever talked to her before. By the time I felt bad about watching, wasn't nothing I could do but stay quiet. I liked how she was, kicking off sweaty shorts with her little painted toes. She's a cutie, not so much a hottie, but she had more going on than any girl who'd let me feel up on her.

I did real damage finishing myself off, trying to be fast but also still and quiet. Had to bite down on a lost-and-found softball mitt. Afterward my piece looked like I fell off a skateboard on it. Tonight, while we did it, that sweet raw pain came back to me in 3-D. I made a funny sound when I came. But since the end of school I've had more practice. When I stop to look in windows on the way home from night-running, I can get my business done quick and easy. My favorite window is on Magnolia just past Live Oak Lane. Principal Garrett's house. No, I don't go to look at the principal. Him and his wife have separate bedrooms, and he ain't home most nights anyway. Mrs. Garrett's nice, works in the doctor's office, and stays up late reading without much on, drinking wine. I wonder lots of things outside her window. Longer that reading lamp stays on, the more I feel invited to take my time. I wonder what she'd say if she knew I was there. Wonder how much noise the window latch makes, how far I could get into the room without any noise. Wonder what Mrs. Garrett would have to say then.

If I ever talked myself into going in that window, and why the hell not, I could get away quick anytime I needed to. I'm faster than anybody in the county. Faster than anybody who's lived here lately.

I hope Lorna goes and tells somebody what I told her – my folks, her old man, Coach Bellamy, Principal Garrett. Hell, Coach Mack the drunk. She must understand I'm too chickenshit to step up and tell them I'm going to pieces. Lord knows I've had time to. Now it's even too late to tell Lorna I was kidding. I don't think she'd do me again, even if she believed I was kidding. She ain't dumb and she's no slut either. Anyone finds out she let me bone her in a car, they better not say nothing like that.

I could've asked her to drive away with me and see what kind of world we found out there together.

The more I stew on it the more I guess I hoped she'd want to. She's got more reason than me to stick around, better places to go than nowhere special. If it came down to cutting and running from trouble, maybe she ain't fast enough to keep up with me and Lone Star.

Lorna's gone now. Threw on her clothes, made me drop her off. Wouldn't kiss me goodnight. If she goes quick to warn folks about me, I'll let her. By the time I feel different it'll be too late. They'll have me, everybody will be safe. Just another run at something I couldn't finish. But once I get started on something, it's hard for me to quit on my own. I've got this picture in my mind of Lorna as something special, better than what she comes from. But even if she don't want to be around me, would she have the guts to tell a whole town what it doesn't want to hear?

I've waited ten minutes to find out, and that's plenty. Could be Lorna's just like the rest of Adams Creek, and if she is I'm better off. I'm done with this place. Almost done. I've got some of my energy back and feel like I could go again. One for the road. Lorna's out, so I figure I'll take a drive by Magnolia Street and see what Mrs. Garrett's up to. If the constable's there waiting for me, I 'll know Lorna spoke up. If not, I'll have to hit the road anyway after what I got in mind. *Buenas noches,* Mrs. Garrett, *adios* Adams Creek. My dad's car is low on gas but once the tank runs out, I can get a pretty long way on foot.

One more corner now, and I'm on Magnolia. Just past Live Oak Lane. There's a window across the street. For a minute it's all I see, before I look for lights on in the house, cars in the driveway, headlights coming up toward me. Coach says before you inspect a route for obstacles, concentrate on the finish line. I'm relaxed as I step out of the car. Twenty, thirty more paces and something's gonna happen. Something.

"Big year comin'," Coach told me. No joke.

I don't smile much, but right now I can't help it. At least I have my answer.

Dan Fields absconded with a film degree from Northwestern University in 2006. He has recently published fiction with *Sanitarium Magazine,* Tell-Tale Press, Harbinger Press, and the Jolly Horror anthology *Don't Cry To Mama*. He lives in Houston, Texas, with his wife and children. See more at www.danfieldswrites.com

His Death Offers No Respite
Thomas Kearnes

ishop Medical resembles a big beige cereal box. Sunlight hits the building at a slant. The main entrance, its row of moving glass doors, buzzes in shadow. Would-be patients rush inside on two feet, but the discharged creep out in wheelchairs. Some won't survive. That's the nature of a hospital: no one can guarantee escape. I'm reasonably sure, myself, entering, I will be lucky. Bishop Medical will not claim me today.

I drove two hundred miles to see him. Two hundred miles to watch him wither. Two hundred miles to bid him good night. Stomach cancer. Terminal.

He's not dead yet.

There is time. There is this afternoon. There is the matter dangling from the tiny canister on my keychain. There is the box cutter snug and secure in my pocket.

He told me his room number when I called from the interstate. 'I look really different,' he warned. I kept tabs on his Facebook page. It's how I knew he was in the hospital. We aren't friends, but he agreed to a visit. I was halfway to Dallas before I called. I was stunned to learn that he must have, at some point, unblocked me.

I approach the help desk. Caden Quaid, I tell the lady. I tell her I'm visiting. I'm an old friend.

It's been a while since I've stepped inside a hospital. Dell didn't need a hospital. When the ambulance ferried him away, the driver didn't engage his siren. No need for flashing lights. It was too late for Dell O'Dowd.

Getting that apartment in Houston suddenly seemed deeply naïve.

The oblivious old woman behind the desk gives me the information I already possess. I never have problems accessing the forbidden. I appear meek and pleasant. Strangers often strike up conversations. No one considers me a threat. No one bothers to speculate about damage I might do.

I don't expect Caden to be alone. In almost all the Facebook photos of his quickly dwindling frame, his best friend poses beside him. Ken is balls-out queer, one of those middle-aged gym rats so common in gay circles: the two-day scruff, biceps showcased beneath short sleeves, shirttail tucked to leave no doubt his waist is trim. I'd let Ken fuck me on one condition: photographic evidence for Caden. I'd savor his reaction to me pissing on his favorite hydrant.

The elevator deposits me on the fifth floor. Going up, an old man, scabs covering his bald head, attempts conversation. When I make no reply, the chunky woman behind me volunteers. I am not being cruel, simply too focused on the box cutter tucked in my jeans. My timing has to be precise. Walking the fifth floor, browsing room numbers until I spy 534, I rehearse in my mind the moment I'll press the blade against Caden's throat.

"Knock, knock."

My Converses squeak as I enter the room. It's bigger than I expected, private: the walls and linoleum floor are each the same soothing gray. The stiff cream-colored curtain is drawn back, but the sun nears the opposite horizon. Caden must enjoy the dawn each day. At rehab, he was always up before sunrise, crossing the courtyard while I had my nightcap cigarette.

"I knew you'd come." There's a slight tremor to his voice, but it brims still with mischief. "I told Ken—I said, don't worry, Avery will absolutely be here."

"And on time, too." I smile.

The clock's minute hand stands a few ticks shy of twelve.

Caden laughs. The sound dies in his throat. "Actually, a little early."

He's a neglected prune, the last in the box. Were we not acquainted, I'd peg his age at sixty, maybe even sixty-five. In truth, he hovers well within his mid-forties. His face, once round and plump, has collapsed. Sunken cheeks and eyes, his hair now gray and perilously thin. Stringy tendons articulate themselves down his neck. I make a point of landscaping that throat. He was once overweight— not much, and the extra pounds perched agreeably atop his hips. Now he might top out at 130 pounds, that sparse mass stretched over his six-foot frame.

His arms and legs had shed all their meat—they're sticks, twigs, the brittle kindling used to nurse a new flame.

He's not dead yet.

The box cutter, still in pocket, presses against my thigh. I carried my keys loose while searching for his room. It's an old habit. I like the dull jingle. But I don't want him to make note of the tiny canister dangling from the keyring. At rehab, I once mentioned it's where I kept my tweak. It was a precaution, jamming my keys into my other pocket just before I entered his room.

Ken glares at me. I respect his frank disapproval. I'll soon confirm his worst suspicions.

"When did you finally get clean?"

"Caden says you're in recovery yourself."

"And gratefully so. How long, Avery?"

He's a tenacious muscle mutt. During that exchange, Caden has eased himself from bed into his wheelchair. An IV pole stands at the ready, but no tube connects the hanging bag of solution to his arm. Will he soon be released? No one wants to die in a hospital, though that's often the point. Had I waited just one day more, I might've missed him. Caden groans as he settles into the chair.

Ken rests his elbows atop the bed's metal rail, arms folded. He can foil my little plan, insist I conduct my visit under his eye. Caden is in no position to protest—assuming he would.

"About eight months," I make sure Ken knows it means nothing to me. "Give or take."

"You don't know your sober date?"

"Careful there, Caden. You can't be king without a throne." I cross the room. He smiles and weakly raises an open hand. I reach for his shoulder, but my hand retreats to my side. I'll need to do more than touch him, soon, but not this moment. "What does it matter if I stayed clean last summer?" I counter. "I stayed clean today."

Caden's friend grunts. "He said you were a pragmatist."

I laugh. "Caden doesn't know that word."

Stricken, Ken's eyes pop.

Caden bats my hip, laughing himself. "Still a snob, aren't you, asswipe?"

"Still a philistine, huh, Prom King?"

Back at rehab, Dell and I liked to peer over the balcony as Caden sauntered across the courtyard. So confident, so satisfied with himself. His steps fell upon the grass like kisses, he blessed with a smile all who passed. 'He's scrumptious,' I muttered. 'I wanna suck his dick,' Dell replied. It always came down to sex for him, that dear man. I smirked. 'All hail the Prom King,' I proclaimed. 'The birds sang of love. The mosquitoes hunted flesh.'

Caden and I laugh. I push his wheelchair toward the doorway. Visitors and nurses skitter up and down the hall. Over the loudspeaker, a doctor named Killingsworth receives marching orders: Trauma Room Three, STAT.

"I'm gonna jump in the shower after this show ends," Ken declares. Glancing over my shoulder, I catch him reclining upon Caden's unmade bed. The intimacy of this transition both sickens and stirs me. "Back in thirty?"

Caden gives the affirmative. Thirty minutes, I think. Should be enough time. I imagine the click as the box cutter's blade snaps into place. The hall teems with fated life. It will soon be Thanksgiving.

I know this because turkeys and pilgrims cut from construction paper loiter upon the corridor walls. I'm waiting for Caden to resume the conversation.

The wheels on his chair smack upon the sticky linoleum, sounding like a hungry child's lips. My Converses squeak. We exist, Caden Quaid and I. Our tired, mundane noises fill this tired, mundane world. It doesn't register with me that I've slipped my keys from my pocket, not till I hear their jangle. That tiny metal canister complicates the melody.

"I wanted to wait until…" His breath leaves him. He hasn't craned his neck to look back. His bony shoulders hitch as he inhales. "Ken doesn't need to hear this."

"It's just us now, Caden. Prom King and the Geek."

"I'm serious, Avery."

We've lost velocity. I'm looking for an empty room. A room-number placard denied cut-out Turkey Day tokens. An agreeable male nurse passes us, scrubs a bit too snug, haircut a bit too precise. This time, Caden does turn his head. At least until it snaps back, accompanied by a wince.

I smirk. "He's far too young for us. For *you*." I don't break stride. I don't turn to linger on the twitch of his ass as he hurries past. Dell has been gone eight months. I've toured a few bedrooms since his broken heart ceased its beat, but these trysts soothe nothing, solve nothing. I fuck men for the same reason dogs bark—and have just as little to show for it.

The box cutter lies in wait. I've never before threatened a man's life.

"I meant to call you. After you…after *we* lost Dell. I meant to. I swear." He gasps. I'm not sure how to interpret this candor. "I unblocked your number. I don't know what stopped me." He turns back, twists his face toward mine. His hazel eyes have lost none of their salesman shimmer. "Why didn't you call me...?"

Because I imagined every explanation you might offer, and each only nursed my rage. It did not abate. I did not acquit you. I say none of these things.

"You blocked me after our last fight," I remind him. "Right before his overdose. I had to message Ken on fucking Facebook."

"You never tried me."

"You wouldn't have liked what I said."

Caden chuckles. I can't see his expression, but hear the weak, low sound. "I would've listened. I needed to talk, too..."

Room 517. No Thanksgiving kitsch! No placard stamped with a patient's name. Waning afternoon sun fills the room. I swivel Caden's chair a neat ninety degrees. So excited to spring my trap. I lost all hope of an afterlife after turning five, but I can't help—almost forty years later—indulging juvenile fantasies of Dell. He might spy me from the heavens, overjoyed to know vengeance may travel slowly, but it does make the station. I nudge the door shut with my foot.

"If you wanted somewhere private..." He takes a breath, loses it before it can fill his lungs. He takes another. "There's a solarium on the first floor."

"I dare you to define that word." I've stopped pretending we're friends, and so has my voice.

He turns back. Fear pulses across his gaze. "What do you want, Avery?" I wish he'd *yield* to me: hands held aloft to protect his face, a quaking voice, maybe even a startled cry. I must proceed. No doubt Ken counts the minutes.

He's not dead yet.

I maneuver myself before him. I've rehearsed this moment for months. I've never liked speaking in a formal setting. It requires charisma and poise. Dell enjoyed an abundance of both. When he confessed his heart to Caden, he didn't stammer once. I know because I listened, unseen, from the doorway. One day, a man might speak to me so plainly. Dell might have been that man, had heartbreak not hobbled his spirit. I left the doorway before they finished.

"I don't feel good, Avery. I need to—"

"You remember Dell had a sister, don't you? Only relative who was worth a damn."

I drop to my knees before his chair, my hands folded atop his knobby knees. I shudder to imagine his bare legs. "Imagine calling Eden to say her baby brother has died. Imagine telling her he *wanted* to die."

Caden flinches. He hiccups for air. I watch him struggle. I should've started filming the moment I shut the door. "Avery, I'm sorry. I knew how you felt about Dell. I knew—"

"You *knew* how he felt about *you*."

Beads of sweat flee his forehead.

"And you erased him. From your phone, from Facebook. You erased *me* when I asked why."

His tone sharpens. "I let you keep tabs on me. I'm sure you kept Dell informed."

"I told him you were terminal."

Caden grunts. His eyes brim with tears. I need him to reclaim his composure before I start recording. If Eden pities him, I'll have no one to indulge my forest-blaze rage. It will devour me, like Caden's cancer devours him. "That's why he overdosed..." His face clenches with indignation. "Why did you fucking tell him that, Avery?"

Dell and I spent our first month in rehab, before Caden's arrival, constructing a universe made for two. Brick by brick, confidence by confidence, the bond refusing to sever no matter how brazenly Dell later consumed Caden's each step across the courtyard. We knew each other over three years, and I never lied to him, not once.

"You and your fucking rehab romance," he spits.

I've explained enough. Ken awaits our return. I whip out my iPhone. I will record him confessing his guilt to Eden. His refusal to love Dell cast him into an abyss so deep, he might never—even in death—reach its stone-strewn bottom. No one else will see it. At least his sister will know I loved him enough to obtain his killer's confession.

"Fuck you, Avery." He swivels his chair toward the door. "I'll wheel myself back."

I stride across the room. My keys and the canister jangle still. Somehow, as I advance toward him, the box cutter finds itself in my grip. I make note of the emerging blade's click. I force the blade against Caden's withered throat. He doesn't scream or call for help. I'm not sure how to interpret this toneless moment—the threat of violence shouldn't seem so banal.

"This won't bring Dell back."

"I'm more deeply aware of this than you can fathom."

"I'm so goddamn sorry. I don't—"

"Ready to party, Prom King?"

With my thumb, I flip open the lid of my keyring canister. I instruct him to wheel himself into the bathroom. I follow, box cutter blade wavering at the stretch of shoulder left bare by his gown.

The mirror, a dour rectangle bolted above a gleaming sink, is positioned too high to reflect the seated Caden. But I find myself, trapped inside smudged glass, all too visible. I've filled out since rehab. I think of myself as slender, but my belly flattens only with effort. I'm shorter than the men I pursue, taller than the ones I dismiss. My eyeglasses came cheap, the dark frames defiantly thick and graceless. With my coal-black eyes, cheekbones set at too high a slant and pointed jaw, I am no one's idea of handsome. I used to fret about keeping a lover. I made him laugh, Dell liked to tell me. I found this reassuring, sometimes.

I dump the canister's contents on the counter. Three clear shards, all of modest size—enough for a thick, healthy line once crushed and scraped for snorting. I, however, don't plan to partake.

"You crazy son of a bitch..." His jaw hangs open, he looks at me like he *knows* me. It's an expression I've never seen. For a passing moment, guilt blips on my radar. I congratulate myself: there it is, proof that grief and rage have not eroded my humanity in full.

I return the box cutter to his throat. A single drop of blood hugs its lethal edge. I could hurt him. I could end both his suffering, and mine, with a clean cut.

He looks ashen. "There are tumors in my stomach, Avery." His voice breaks, he brushes his knuckles against his eyes. I hadn't expected him to cry. The Prom King has no reason to weep. "Snorting that shit might kill me."

I crush the shards beneath my bathhouse membership card. "You're terminal, Caden." The card scrapes the counter as a dazzling white line of speed takes shape. "You have a choice: you can die or you can die happy."

"What the fuck will this prove?"

I crouch down, my head level with his. I whisper, like a lullaby for a child already asleep, "If you tattle, I'll demand the doctor test your piss. What would Ken think?" I rise to my feet. "Now finish your dessert like a good faggot. We have to start filming soon."

"Not here, man. Take me to the solarium."

Again, with the wheels smacking the sticky corridor floor. Again, with the abstractionist pilgrims convened around the placards outside each patient's room. Everyone fleet of foot, so many places to reach, so little time to reach them. There's no plausible way to keep the box cutter at his neck. An orderly or nurse might glimpse the weapon. Getting him spun was my only way to assure his cooperation. It tickles me, though, my lover's killer must endure an unwanted high—and all the urges no doubt ignited in its wake.

Caden pants as I push. He twists and fidgets. He complains of cramps. He's afraid he might die. I hiss one warning after another: can the theatrics. We have less than twenty minutes, and the solarium is five floors below.

He refused to confess in Room 517. He's convinced I'll slash his throat once we're done. Caden assures me the outdoor deck adjoining the solarium boasts privacy and adequate light.

Patients, visitors and staff, however, will be within shouting distance. I suppose I could've forced the issue—after all, I have the box cutter. Parading down the hall, knowing he is the Prom King, and this is my coup...well, why not enjoy every one of the thirty minutes afforded me?

As we travel, a trim Latina nurse approaches. Pausing, she tilts slightly forward, her face brightening. I stop pushing. Whether Caden is clever enough to signal her, or anyone we encounter, I'll soon know. She places her hand, tender and graceful, on his shoulder. He won't meet her gaze. He clutches his armrests to tame his tremors. I do not wish him to know kindness.

"Hey there, handsome. Heard you discharge tomorrow."

His torso spasms, head jerking in response. They are now face to face. Still, he does not reply. She rises to full height, perhaps eager to address me. I bend forward and kiss Caden's temple. Whispering, but loud enough to assure she hears, I promise him a few minutes in the cool breeze while we watch the sun surrender to the horizon. He grunts.

He's not dead yet.

"Will you stay with him?" she asks.

"For however long he needs me."

Caden's breathing has grown labored but he finds the fortitude to dazzle her, that same smile beneath which my Dell capsized. She waves and continues down the corridor.

I roll him the opposite direction. One more turn, another corridor and we'll reach the elevators.

"I used to hate hearing I was handsome."

I refuse to engage. The tweak has made him chatty. He requires a witness. Unless another man watches as you bare your soul, it hardly seems worth the toil. The wheels shriek in protest as we take the corner.

"I was other things, too. Besides handsome."

Perhaps fortune will smile upon me, and our car will carry others, strangers. Surely, Caden won't insist they rubber-stamp his humanity as he hopes I might. I punch the down button, and we wait. He won't stop squirming. He moans as if pained.

"Suck it up, Prom King."

"Please, I need…I need to find a bathroom."

"No, sir. The elevator will be here any second."

He chuckles, but it's a bitter sound. "Don't worry, we'll make your fucking movie."

After the ding, the elevator doors slide open. To my delight, we're at no loss for companions. A black, overweight orderly stands at the front of the car, facing the corner. A frazzled woman in her thirties wearing too much eye shadow holds two grade-school girls, one by each hand. The girls' rude stares trouble no one. Finally, an older woman wrapped in an ankle-length corduroy coat stands beside me. I feel her gaze. She wishes to speak. The doors slide shut. She has mere moments to overcome her trepidation.

"Is it cancer?" Her smile flickers. "I'm about to see my husband. Should be done with the chemo by now."

Caden moans. I press a firm hand upon his shoulder.

"My husband's been sick over a year." This answer surprises me, too. I stretch my back, shoulders rotating with affected fatigue. "Whatever time we have left, I want to spend it together."

Her lips part, but she does not speak. Caden's head and shoulders jitter. Why claim Caden as my own? Perhaps it's humiliation. Perhaps it's to force-feed him the toxic tableau of a life spent sharing one bed. He was so unwilling to grant that wish to Dell but now has no choice—he must indulge my perversion of it.

Clutching his abdomen, Caden moans, a deep and primal eruption, then doubles over. This time, everyone reacts: the orderly, the frazzled woman, those impudent girls. Even in sickness, the Prom King has no trouble drawing a crowd.

"Stop the elevator," he pleads. "I need to—" I shush him, crouch down to whisper whatever threat seems plausible. Before I begin, however, he butts his head against mine. "Now, Avery!" My ears ring, and it takes a few moments to remember that I'm a kidnapper, but my hostage refuses to obey.

The older woman reaches for the panel of lighted number beside the sliding doors. She promises Caden that "we" would find him a bathroom. *No!* That simple directive blots out all other thoughts. I'm running out of time. Desperate, I reach out to grab her hand, but the *ding* distracts her. She refrains and, like the rest of us, waits.

The doors slide open. We're on the third floor.

Caden calls out for someone to hold the door. An elderly couple shuffles forward, perplexed, perhaps sensing a discord clumsily tamed for their benefit. They step aside, the husband extending his delicate, spotted hand over the groove into which one of the sliding doors retreated.

We have to go, Caden and I. Delays, delays, delays. Surely less than fifteen minutes now. Still, I've yet to give his wheelchair that bon-voyage push, the force needed to turn the wheels. It's those wheels that Caden, himself, vainly tries to turn, but I clutch the handgrips with brute force. We can't leave this elevator without a plan.

"Sir, your partner's in great pain, it seems." The older woman must have problems with the word *husband*. "Do you need some help?"

The elderly man outside the passenger car flops his open hand against the sliding door each time it tries to emerge. Ignoring the older woman, I push Caden into the lobby. There are six elevators surrounding us. The third floor looks just like the fifth. Even the brazen aroma of antiseptic has been replicated to perfection. Two parallel corridors sandwich the bank of elevators.

Caden whines and curses. "It doesn't matter which way. Just keep going till we find…" He gasps, head thrown back with such force, he lifts from his seat for a moment. "An empty room." He stabs his pointed finger at the left corridor. "Find me an empty room."

Nurses, visitors, they risk leery glances at our two-man revue.

"Fine, Caden. But let's make the potty pitstop a quick one."

We're already in motion.

"You'll get your fucking video, Geek."

Down the corridor, football helmets cut from construction paper festoon the placards bearing patients' names. I wonder who decided the themes for each floor. Helmets seem a mite bland compared to the rosy-cheeked pilgrims two floors above.

Caden's breath turns shallow and harsh, as if he were in labor. The sheen of perspiration coating his face reflects the corridor lights. His hair is drenched. Eyelids clenched shut, he trusts me to find an untaken toilet.

More visitors, more nurses. Orderlies. Even a few doctors. We've passed at least twenty rooms, both sides of the corridor considered. The corridor, itself, opens not far ahead. A nurses' station, probably. If even one indulges her curiosity, filming might be (again) delayed, or worse. Ken won't hesitate to unleash the hounds if I fail to return Caden unharmed. I will not disappoint Dell, however, no matter how formidable the forces against me. I never did our three years together, and his death brings no respite.

"Avery, turn left! Right here! Room 323!"

I instruct him to deep-six the high decibels. If no one looked before, they damn sure might look now. Once we've entered the empty room, we'll fortunately be forgotten.

Caden sobs, insisting the pain intensifies with each breath. The bathroom door catches against the wheelchair's footrest. I strain my shoulder jerking back the chair, allowing the door to swing wide and admit him. He rolls to a stop beside the toilet, and I dare entertain relief. He's too weak, he cries, to lift himself from the chair to the commode. Hurry, he begs. My belly is about to explode! Just then, a wretched odor fills the bathroom. Caden's bowels, it seems, believe Room 323 needs a fragrance both fecal and fierce. I'm holding his skeletal form upright, by its armpits. I try shifting him to the toilet, but his wheelchair stymies my every move. I refuse to panic. I knew Caden was sick before I hit the road, and sick people have volatile relationships with toilets. Just ten more seconds, and I'll recover my wits—just ten seconds!

Caden Quaid doesn't have ten seconds to spare.

His unplanned bowel movement announces itself with a fanfare loud, wet and lingering. Fortunately, Caden wears gray Nike athletic shorts beneath his papery gown, but the good news stops there. He neglected to slip on briefs beneath those shorts. The runny fecal follies stream down his bony legs and pool upon the linoleum. Moments later, a smattering of foul-smelling chunks, too unformed and moist to bear the label of *turd*, form dainty little heaps upon that same linoleum. The stench is so pervasive, so intense, I wouldn't blame anyone who might doubt one man alone could spawn such epic nasty.

It's humiliating and no shilling of shame could meet the expense. I still hold Caden upright, my hands cupped beneath his armpits. I look him dead in the eye. I don't offer compassion. Did he show any compassion to my sweet Dell? How will the Prom King handle shitting himself while tweaked and trapped with a man ready to mock his misfortune? If filming must wait, only a distraction this delectable will satisfy. Caden simply stares ahead, blankly, through me, as if this bathroom were measured in acres, not inches.

"No one's calling you handsome now."

"I'm fine with that. Actually, I prefer they call me Caden."

I'm stumped at his refusal to trot no matter which carrot I dangle before him. Whatever abdominal pain he was suffering seems vanquished, but he's no doubt still tweaking. I may have trouble keeping his bitch mouth shut.

He's not dead yet.

"You can put me down, Avery." I drop him abruptly, but his balance does not deny him. "I need a shower. You're not rolling me down the hall while I simmer in my own shit."

I can't argue with his logic. Reeking of turds would draw first the noses, then the nosiness of all who crossed our path. Still, at most, ten minutes remain before Caden's chair reverts back into a pumpkin. I instruct him to hurry. He asks me to excuse myself to the main room. Forget it, I reply. The bathroom door locks from the inside, and fuck him for thinking I haven't noticed. Irritated, he slips off his paper gown and steps into the shower. He hasn't the strength to stand for the entire ordeal, but a wide-topped stool awaits in the stall. I watch as the spray wets his desiccated form. I'm thankful Dell never has to witness his dream lover's decay. He wouldn't allow himself the perspective necessary to enjoy it.

"That tweak you forced up my nose was bunk, by the way." The bathroom is so small and the spray so weak, Caden's voice carries. I'm in no mood for banter so let the remark sink beneath the silence. "Bet you saved the good shit for yourself, huh?" Tweak makes Caden bitchy. He doesn't bother to look my way. "I bet you're spun right now. This very fucking moment."

For the record, I've been sober since Dell's suicide. Eight months—I was telling that pissant Ken the truth. I know tweaking will spur illusory multi-hour conversations with him. Such seductive fantasies, and most would forgive me if I succumbed—but there are boys quite alive who need me more. I work overnights for a gay hotline in Houston. I field everything from coming-out trauma to suicide threats. I stay sober. Indeed, after I record Caden's confession, I must make haste down the interstate, Dallas receding in my rearview. The hotline expects me at midnight.

"Fine," I say, my voice toneless. "I did a couple of bumps in the parking lot. Vindicated?"

Caden shuts off the water. "I'm not judging you. I should, but I won't." He dons his paper gown, perhaps not noticing the dried shit spattered along its hem, then drops into his wheelchair. Its creaks and rattles bemoan the blunt impact of his bones. Clearly, he's exhausted.

"Forget the solarium," he says. "Let's get this fucker over with right here and now."

"What convinced you I won't slash your throat?"

"All those assholes we traumatized in the elevator—they're my witnesses, Geek."

Besides, he adds, his Nike shorts are ruined so he's totally nude beneath his paper gown. While we're outside at the solarium, there might be a gust of wind. If not that, the gowns themselves are more than a little transparent, particularly under harsh fluorescents, hard to avoid at Bishop Medical. Please, he says, I've played along with this. I could've stopped this farce at any time.

Caden has a point. But I have a box cutter, and he's high on crystal meth.

"The solarium seems a reachable goal. We still have time. But we have to scoot."

As we return to the elevators, the squeaks and smacks of the wheelchair form a sort of tune, one played on crude instruments. Caden takes deliberate breaths, his chest and head rippling, adding a kinesthetic component to the wheels' meager music. He hadn't bothered to articulate his disappointment, in expression or with words, when I insisted our adventure end with the solarium. Slumped upon his throne, he muttered capitulation, ready for me to push.

At the elevators, the waiting nurses and suited gentleman pay us no mind. We lumber into the open car. When the doors open to the ground floor, I allow myself to sample the ripe satisfaction promised me the moment Caden's confession ends. I must discipline myself. He silently lifts a leaden hand, pointing this way or that. We're approaching the lobby. Those sliding glass doors shift left to right, right to left. A half-hour earlier, they admitted me—with my box cutter and bit of crystal. I should recall the scratched twang that calls out from what I only now recognize as the help desk. When I glance her way, though, nothing stirs my memory.

"Yoohoo! Over here! Hey, handsome." She laughs. Being ignored must delight her. "You didn't come flirt with me today."

Caden smiles, lifts an open hand with more vigor than I would expect, signaling me to stop. We're down to mere minutes, and my only advantage beyond Ken's deadline is that the gym rat has no idea where we are. Our potty break, however, resulted in witnesses, as Caden took pains to mention. As he flirts with the help desk hussy, I speculate whether further booby traps await.

A harried husband barges his way to the help desk. His wife was brought here. Reba Blakely? I wheel Caden away, grateful for the distraction. Moments later, he announces our arrival.

I expect a solarium to be more heavily beset by plant life. Instead, palm leaves and intimidating ferns line three of the walls, rubber-cushioned sofas and chairs positioned before them. It feels like the waiting room at a clinic in a bedroom community, one where several doctors split the steep rent. The only things missing are back issues of *People* and *US Weekly*. Caden slaps my chest with the back of his hand. "There," he mutters, "that door takes us outside."

Despite the aggressive greenery obscuring the glass walls, I glimpse enough of the sky for my skin to prickle: such maroons and deep oranges appear only at dusk. I extend my arm to push open the hydraulic door, allowing Caden the latitude to wheel himself outside.

"Gentlemen, the observation deck closes at sunset."

Caden pauses upon the threshold. We turn our heads to greet the latest in a ceaseless series of roadblocks. She's a stout woman, her middle years soon ending. Too much foundation showcases instead of conceals her jowls. A badge offering her name and mugshot rests above her left breast. Maybe she's too incompetent to handle any other Bishop Medical domain.

"Please, ma'am." I smile and furrow my brow to simulate sincerity. "It's the first time in weeks my husband's felt well enough to leave his room." Caden places a loose hand atop mine, and I stutter. I don't want a partner in crime, I want justice for Dell. "After the sun sets—we'll come back, I swear."

The stout woman fingers a strand of pearls not there. "Your *husband,* is that right?"

Caden smiles, and it occurs to me, like a bulb's dying flash: he has an agenda, too, and maybe I've been foolish. Still, Dell is counting on me. Caden thanks our hostess and urges me, in an affable tone the tweak seemed to silence, to wheel him outside.

The deck is comprised of shapeless slabs of burgundy stone, bits of sprouting grass, twigs and acorns shed by the massive oaks, their drooping lank limbs. A squat brick wall, hardly high enough to meet the knee, lines the perimeter. The air has chilled. Errant gusts flirt beneath Caden's gown, its hem ballooning one moment, dropping the next. "You see," he snipes, "fucking wind." He insists I wheel him to one of several patio tables stationed in front of the solarium's windowed wall. You can sit across from me, he adds.

"You don't have to pretend we're married anymore," I snap. He keeps forgetting who has the box cutter. Across from him, I tap and slide until my iPhone is ready to record.

"Give me another rundown. I'm not confessing more than once."

"It's simple," I remind him. "Tell my lover's sister your name, how you met Dell, how you learned of his love and how you dismissed it." I glance over my shoulder. That molten orange orb will kiss the horizon in mere moments. If only we'd found an empty room sooner, if only Caden respected the dynamic I forged between us. I double-check the viewfinder. I tell him we're recording.

"Hello, Eden. I'm Caden Quaid. I'm forty-four years old and live in Dallas. I met your brother three years ago at a rehab in Houston." He pauses, gulps air. "As I'm sure you know, Avery was there, too. He's making this little motion picture. You deserve to know what happened to your brother. So do you, Avery."

My shoulders tense. I worry Caden may have fallen from the frame. But we're running out of light and Ken must surely be worried by now. Still, why address me? More disconcerting, I detect no remorse or shame. He speaks like a suburban dad as he delivers punishment to his toddler. He whips through our history as a threesome: Dell, Caden and Avery—the Three Faggoteers. This may interest Eden, but I'm waiting to hear his misdeeds after we left, after Dell and I found a shitty apartment in a shitty neighborhood, and he returned to Dallas. What precisely did he say to Dell that night over the phone, inducing such anguish I could listen no more?

"We were on the phone. I told him I had cancer. He started crying. He said he loved me too much to lose me. I didn't return your brother's feelings. He knew that. He didn't care."

Dell O'Dowd needed *me*. Dell O'Dowd loved *me*. Dell O'Dowd chose *me*.

"He volunteered to drop everything and move to Dallas. He said he'd nurse me through, no matter how long it took." His eyes dim, and he appears unnerved. "I asked about Avery. What would he think if your brother left him in the dust? All that bastard could manage was some lame-ass promise that Avery would find a way." His breathing becomes labored once more, but it's the anger, nothing else. A vitality besieges him. The Prom King never wastes the spotlight. "I told him I was about to hang up. He and I? We were strangers now. Any man who would shit on some dude so devoted to him had bigger problems than dope. We never spoke again."

I'm looking elsewhere. I'm looking anywhere. Over my shoulder, I glimpse the last of the sun slip behind the horizon. It's good he's nearing the end. Eden needs to see his face. Wait, why is it quiet? Just crickets and white noise from the nearby interstate. I must've zoned out. I can't remember what Caden last said. My eyes dart to my iPhone, wrist resting on the table. No way Caden remains in the frame.

Caden snatches the device from my hand and slams it on the table. His eyes burn with a fury that's my due, not his. He holds my gaze. His breath slows. That stout woman who believes we're married must wonder why we broke our promise.

"Fuck his sister. I'm talking to you. The day I heard Dell died, I had one thought: what will Avery do with his freedom?" He gasps for air. The adrenaline must be wearing off. Dell will be so disappointed in me. "Loyalty should be earned, Avery. You see what Ken and I have? You deserve that, too." He must need what little stamina remains after our half-hour adventure to deliver this pep talk. "I'd be happy to cash in my chips, but I stay alive. My best friend needs me."

I can accept failure. I can accept defeat. I'm the Geek. Our tribe rarely ascends the winners' podium. I leave Caden as he hunches over the tabletop, too desperate for oxygen to notice that I'm almost to the solarium door. He calls my name. He whines that he's too weak to roll himself back to his room. The Prom King needs me.

"I hope your death is both painful and pitiful." I don't wait for his reaction.

The stout woman asks what happened to my husband. She needs to close and lock that door, it's security protocol. I don't break my stride. She's too much of a creampuff to accost me. Back in the corridor, I pause. Which way to the lobby? I must go to work. I'm welcome there.

Except, I dart off in the opposite direction, deeper into the hospital. Except, I find the elevators. Except, I wait patiently, my head bereft of thoughts, as I ascend five stories. Except, I hustle down the corridor until I see Caden's name and that perky pilgrim. The door to Room 534 stands ajar.

That night, after Caden hung up on Dell, he flopped onto the bed we shared and sobbed. Did he need to talk? He didn't tell me, not then, that Caden had discarded him. Instead, his small, timid voice insisted he didn't deserve me. Life is chaos, I told him. Be thankful someone wants to hold your hand while the world burns. I don't deserve you, he repeated. Later, as Dell dozed, he slung his arm over me. One day, I was certain, he'd open his eyes and truly *see* me for the first time.

Someone, presumably Ken, is taking a shower. It seems he isn't as vigilant as I feared. I slip into the bathroom. I close the door; wince as the lock clicks after giving it a twist. He's nude, of course. Rather impressive rear end. He hasn't noticed me. No one bothers to speculate the damage I might do. The box cutter finds its way into my grip. The blade emerges with a quick nudge from my thumb.

I'm standing close enough to touch him. Instead, I slash his bare back.

I stay alive. My best friend needs me.

He gasps and whips around, stumbling, to find me brandishing my box cutter. He was right about me. He demands to know what I did with Caden. I answer by slashing his face, the gash running from ear to chin. I've prepared for bloodshed. "Please," he begs, "Caden needs me." I nod. At last, we agree on something.

He struggles, at first, but won't scream. He begs me to stop, but I cannot. He's not dead yet.

Thomas Kearnes graduated from the University of Texas at Austin with an MA in film writing. His fiction has appeared in Hobart, Gertrude, A cappella Zoo, Split Lip Magazine, Cutthroat, Litro, Berkeley Fiction Review, PANK, BULL: Men's Fiction, Gulf Stream Magazine, Wraparound South, Night Train, 3:AM Magazine, Word Riot, Storyglossia, Driftwood Press, Adroit Journal, The Matador Review, Pseudopod, the Best Gay Stories series, Mary: A Journal of New Writing, wigleaf, SmokeLong Quarterly, Pidgeonholes, Sundog Lit, The Citron Review, and elsewhere. He is a three-time Pushcart Prize nominee. Originally from East Texas, he now lives near Houston and works as an English tutor at a local community college. His debut collection of short fiction, "Texas Crude" is now available at Lethe Press, Amazon and Barnes & Noble.

Lights Out
Sylvia Ney

Rhonda sighed and leaned back against the wall. Town socials could be a lot of fun, but they could also be exhausting. Her momma and a few friends sat next to her, and she let her eyes drift closed as they began trading gossip.

"That's him," Margaret whispered.

"Who?" Betty whispered in return.

"The guy I was telling you about yesterday."

"The one who just moved here with his parents?"

"His name is Leon. His family moved to Texas just after the war."

"But he just moved here last week?"

"Yes, and he's single."

"You didn't tell me he was so, so…"

"Seeing is believing."

Rhonda smiled. It was impossible *not* to notice a new addition to their neighborhood, especially a handsome one. She opened her eyes and followed the gaze of her friends.

Her heart tripped immediately. She tried her best not to stare at the striking man in uniform, but she found it difficult.

"Don't you think so?"

It took Rhonda a moment to look back and realize the women sitting around her were all wearing the same knowing smile.

"I'm sorry," she felt herself blush. "What did you say?"

Margaret could only laugh, but Betty answered, "We were just saying that he must be one of the most attractive men we've ever seen."

Rhonda couldn't help looking back toward Leon who stood across the room with the preacher. His eyes met hers and Leon smiled. She quit breathing.

A moment later he had disappeared. She strove not to seem overly anxious as she scanned the guests. He was so tall, she should be able to see him, even in this crowd.

She stood up, trying to get a better look. Rhonda was only vaguely aware of the conversations and activities that continued around her. There was her cousin Zora, flirting with a group of men, Mary served punch from a beautifully decorated bowl, and Dorothy was fighting with her husband as usual.

"Would you like to dance?"

Rhonda startled at the deep timber of his voice. How had he managed to sneak up on her? She stared mutely at him. In truth, words escaped her for what seemed an eternity. His dark eyes held her captive. It took her a moment to realize he held sunny blossoms out to her.

"Yellow is my favorite color."

"Mine is red."

"I love honeysuckle."

"Does this mean 'yes' to the dance?"

She only vaguely recalled passing the flowers to her mother for safe keeping. However, Rhonda would never forget the feel of his hands as he guided her across the floor. Or the way he smelled when she took a steadying breath; like soap and the forest.

"I'm Leon."

"Rhonda."

"My brother and I just moved here with my parents. I guess you can tell I've been in the military."

"Oh, yes." She'd mumbled stupidly.

"What do you do?"

"I clean houses, and cook."

"Nothing better than a woman who knows how to run a home." She blushed in reaction, immediately imagining being in charge of his home. "Now that the war is over, I hope to get a job working with my hands. A home and family of my own would be a dream come true."

He smiled broadly. She was too overwhelmed to add much to their conversation, but Leon didn't seem to mind.

When the dance ended, he immediately asked if she'd like two more. After her shy nod, he spent time telling her about traveling during his term of service. Leon even mentioned how he had met and shaken hands with Harry S. Truman after the soon-to-be-president had given a speech on the importance of Civil Rights. After the second dance, she finally got up enough courage to ask questions of her own.

"So, what do you think of our town of Breaux Bridge?"

"I love it so far. Everyone has been very nice, and the food is the best. My brother hopes to get a job at the sugar mill."

"Will it be hard for y'all to live in such a small town after seeing so much of the world?"

"Nah, as I mentioned before, I'm hoping to settle down soon. I saw too much during the war. Small town life with friends and loved ones seems like my idea of heaven."

The faster paced song ended, and *When the Lights Go on Again* began to play.

"I love this song." Leon said, immediately moving closer to accommodate for the slower style dance.

"It's one of my favorites too."

Now she loved it for a whole new reason. Rhonda hung on his every word, memorizing every movement he made. She would always remember the feel of his smooth ebony hand against hers. The warmth of his other hand at her back as they moved together, searing the memory there forever.

As the third dance came to an end, Zora cut in to introduce herself. *No, God, please no. Don't let that horrid creature corrupt him.* Yet, all Rhonda could do was watch in agony as her cousin spent the next dance hanging on Leon's arm.

Rhonda returned to her seat near momma by the wall. *Please God, let him come back to me after this song.* She was devastated, but not really surprised when Leon's attentions turned to her cousin. Rhonda tried to be happy for him. He genuinely seemed to fall in love with her miserable relative, and they disappeared together four songs later. She never saw them again that night.

That next Sunday, Zora sat with him in church. By the end of that month, Leon had a new job in construction and they were married.

A week after the ceremony, Zora confided to Rhonda that she had married Leon because, even though white men liked her in their beds, they did not want to marry her. She claimed Leon served a purpose; which meant he provided a paycheck, a home, and left town often.

Rhonda now hated Zora as much as any human could hate another. As children the two girls often played together. Rhonda had loved her cousin Zora. It was only when they became teenagers that she realized Zora was twisted. The girl thought she was better than everyone else because of her looks. She'd been fathered by a white sugar mill owner. Her momma, Rhonda's aunt, had been one of his servants. As a result, Zora had beautiful golden skin that caught the eye of many men, black and white alike. Now in her twenties, she put those looks to work for her so she didn't need a job. At least not one any respectable woman would have.

A lot of men called Zora beautiful. Her large eyes and long flowing hair made her appear like an angel, but Rhonda knew she was just a slimy dusty butt who deserved to be in hell.

Rhonda reached up to tug at her own short locks. She might not be anywhere near as pretty as Zora, but she would be smarter. She would get what she deserved.

When they first married, Rhonda had hoped Zora might actually fall in love with her husband. It was clear he adored her.

After months of watching them together, Rhonda knew Zora was incapable of love. Leon treated his wife like the princess she thought she was, and in return she made a fool out of him every time he left town on a construction job. Rhonda felt sure he must know. He must have some idea by now what she was really like. *He's just too honorable to leave her; no matter what she does.*

Even Leon's own brother, George, was paying her visits.

Rhonda stood across the street from the house that should be hers. She tightened her grip on her new possession and waited. The gun had belonged to Daddy, but now that he was gone it empowered Rhonda. She meant to put it to good use. It all came down to timing.

Zora doesn't deserve Leon. I would never cheat on him.

Rhonda let the gun fall to the bottom of her purse. Her own job of cooking and cleaning for the Blythe's kept her busy. Tuesday was her only day off, and she intended to make the most of it. She stood waiting to catch the beast alone.

The smell of honeysuckle drifted in the air around Rhonda, reminding her of the day she met Leon at the town picnic. She wiped the sweat from her brow, closed her eyes, and let the memory wash over her. *Leon's eyes staring at her, his hands on her as they danced, his scent...*

Rhonda spun and slapped at the offending honeysuckle growing so rudely to remind her of what she had lost. *Why should Zora have Leon and the blossoms?*

She ground her teeth as she watched George strut away from the little white house with the flaking paint. Bile rose up in the back of her throat. *His own brother! I have to save Leon from her.* Rhonda listened to George whistling and waited until he was around the corner before approaching the front door. The rusty screen squeaked and Rhonda flinched before she knocked.

"Did you forget something, honey?" Zora's sultry voice called from the back of the house.

"It's me, Rhonda."

"Oh, come on in, sugar."

Rhonda took a deep breath. It cost her pride to pretend to like the slut, but it had been the only way she could spend time near Leon. Hopefully, one day very soon, he would notice she was worth more than his miserable wife.

"Good morning," Rhonda mumbled.

"Yes, it is."

"George spent the whole night again?" she asked, watching Zora rummaging through her closet for something to wear.

"No, I was out with Frank last night. George came by early this morning."

Zora had no shame. It was a point of pride for her to brag about her time with men and what she got from them.

"I don't know how you find the energy."

"Yes, well, I deserve the best and the men just love to give me the best," Zora said. She paused a moment before pulling out some new clothes and jewelry to show off.

"You definitely got the best." Rhonda replied, thinking of Leon. *He doesn't deserve the crap this tramp is dishing. He's too trusting. If I told him about her, would he be able to forgive me? He might think I had condoned her behavior. No, I don't need to mention that I know. After today, it won't matter.*

"What shall we do today? I need to know what to wear."

"I thought we might go shopping in Beaumont."

"Perfect. Jimmy left me some cash and his car yesterday."

Rhonda rolled her eyes. Jimmy was one of the white men enjoying Zora. She was totally out of control.

"When will Leon be back?"

"I don't know. I hope not for a while, but it could be any day now."

Rhonda sighed. She missed Leon so much. He was always decent, kind, and trustworthy. He was also really good at his job. Unfortunately, this meant he traveled a lot with the construction crew. She hoped he would return soon. For now, she had to conceal her real feelings and remain friendly with Zora. *It won't be long now.*

"We should stop for lunch on the way. I'm in the mood for some crawfish, corn, potatoes…oh, and a coke."

Rhonda's stomach growled at the thought of food. Leon loved spicy crawfish and sweet corn. *Leon.* She was so hungry. She hadn't eaten yet today because she was anxious to get started. Rhonda's stomach growled again. *I'll eat after…*

"I'll drive. I need to stop on the way."

"Where do you need to stop?" Zora asked, slipping on a jade dress that was too small for her. The fabric between the top buttons pulled apart, showing more of her skin than the plunging neckline already revealed.

"I need to get some cash from my man." Rhonda smiled at the lie and then frowned down at her own garment. She should have worn something more sensible than the pale blue dress her momma had made for her birthday.

"Sugar, you been holding out on me? Tell me all about him."

Rhonda shrugged, and glanced back to Zora before brushing her dark hair back behind her ear. "Ain't much to tell. He lives in that swampy area before you get to town."

"How exciting. Here I been thinking you were a little bit dullsville and you've had this big secret."

"Yes, I have a big secret," Rhonda agreed.

Rhonda wrinkled her nose as Zora applied too much perfume and lipstick. *What a waste!*

"Is it love?" Zora asked as they climbed into the car.

"Yes."

"Tell me everything."

Rhonda thought about Leon. How do you describe a man to his wife? Zora would never understand her feelings for Leon. She thought her husband was so safe and boring.

"I don't know what to say. I've liked him for a long time, but I think he has only recently started to really notice me."

"What's his name?"

"Lee." Rhonda held her breath as she put the car in drive. It wasn't necessary. The similarity was lost on Zora. The woman never had seemed to notice, or care, about the interest Rhonda showed in Leon.

"Can he give you much?"

"Everything I need."

"I can't wait to meet him. Sounds like Jimmy…"

Zora rambled on and on about how she had Jimmy panting after her. Rhonda tightened her hold on the steering wheel in an effort to keep from reaching over to slap her cousin. *I have to be patient… wait until we reach our destination.*

An hour later she slowed to weave the car around the swampy land to the area she had scouted out in advance.

Rhonda parked and got out.

"Sugar, where's the house? Where are we?" Zora asked, opening the door to plop her shiny red high-heels into the black mud.

"We have to go the rest of the way on foot," Rhonda replied. "We're not far."

"Maybe I should wait here," Zora frowned over the damage to her shoes.

Rhonda didn't wait for her to follow. She knew Zora's curiosity wouldn't allow her to miss anything she could gossip about later. Rhonda led her all the way to the edge of the brown, mosquito-infested swamp water. She stared at the green algae hugging the sides of the bank. Downed trees emerged from the water as if they were dark angels looming up from the abyss in order to grab your soul and drag you back to hell with them. Buzzing insects, croaking frogs, and chirping cicadas surrounded them. Their eerie and mournful music was perfect.

"Are we taking a boat?" Zora asked, coming up beside her to look out at the slimy water.

"No," Rhonda said. She pulled the gun from her purse. "I'm taking the car back and you're finally getting what you deserve."

The blast from the gun caused Rhonda to simultaneously cringe and stumble back. She had never fired a weapon before. She had never even seen her daddy use it.

A dark stain appeared on the front of the jade fabric. The look of shock on Zora's face as she fell back into the water must have mirrored Rhonda's own. Rhonda stood there for an immeasurable time, the smell of gun powder, fish, and wet soil wafting in the air.

The water was too shallow to hide Zora's body, but the blood attracted a nearby alligator. As soon as the feast began, Rhonda spun around and ran back to the car.

I can't stop to think about what just happened. She had to get Jimmy's car back to the house. Someone might track it or her. Rhonda gripped the wheel and tried not to speed home.

Everyone would assume Zora had run off with some other man. They knew her reputation. Rhonda would, of course, offer Leon the consolation he deserved. No one would ever know. Zora's body would never be found.

She smiled when she pulled up to the house. Zora was gone and Leon would soon be hers. She would go in to leave the keys on the dresser where she knew Zora often kept them.

Rhonda had planned everything perfectly; everything, except the fact that Jimmy was waiting in the bedroom.

"Where's Zora? I heard my car," Jimmy slurred. Clearly, he had been drinking. She did not like the way he looked at her. Experience taught her that men often assumed her relationship with Zora made her an available playmate as well.

"We … we … went for a drive," Rhonda sputtered. "Here are your keys."

"Where is she? I got one hour till I gotta be back at the mill."

"She's not here."

"Well, maybe *you* can accommodate me," he said, shuffling forward. Before she could understand what was happening, he threw her on the bed and followed her down.

"Stop!" she wailed in panic. Rhonda fought to free her hands so she might push him back.

"I got a whole hour." He groaned in a puff of alcohol-scented breath before falling to the floor.

"I ain't interested." She scrambled up and moved toward the door.

"Well, I am." He grabbed her ankle.

Rhonda hit her head on the bedpost on her way down. She landed on her hands and knees only to be yanked back by her hair.

"Stop!" she yelled again, tears coming to her eyes as he pushed her to the floor. Somehow, he already had his pants undone.

She flailed out as he tried to push her dress up. Her hand landed on her purse which must have fallen during the struggle. She tried to push Jimmy back with one hand while she sought her cold, hard savior with the other. His ruffled blond hair hung in his eyes. His face was flush from drink and exertion. Strange what you noticed when you were scared.

At last!

Without giving him time to realize what she held or what might happen, she fired the gun. The look of shock on his face reminded her of Zora. Rhonda laid there immobile until his dead wait collapsed on her. She struggled to roll out from under him.

Once she gained her feet, Rhonda dropped the gun, picked up her purse, and ran for the door. Tears were streaming down her face now. She raced into the woods behind the house. She ran as fast as she could, as far as she could. Nothing made sense to her anymore. She ran until she stumbled and fell in the dirt. She stayed down.

Sticks and rocks cut into her skin. It didn't matter.

Rolling to her side, Rhonda curled into a ball. She lay in the dirt crying and shaking for so long she began to lose feeling in her left side. Unfortunately, the rest of her body was not so lucky. Her head was pounding, and she could feel the lump where she had struck it on the bed. Her palms and knees burned from slamming to the floor, and then again on the ground where she lay now.

She had no idea what time it was when she calmed down enough to wonder. She wasn't entirely sure where she was either. Slowly sitting up, Rhonda realized it was dark now. *It's pitch black. No light.* There wasn't even any moonlight filtering through the trees to shine down on the fallen leaves and twigs.

She rose to her feet and stumbled along, feeling her way, until she found the road heading north. There was the gas station. *The lights are out.* It too was dark, closed for the evening. She was about two miles from Zora's house now, and one mile from her own.

Rhonda took a deep breath and compulsively tried to straighten her hair and clothes. On the chance that someone might drive by and see her, she decided to stay hidden in the trees as she made her way home.

Finally stumbling to her door, she entered the house and headed straight for the bathroom. Momma was staying in Port Arthur with her sister this week and would not be home until Sunday. Rhonda would not have to answer to anyone tonight.

She took a long bath. Leaving her stained clothes discarded in the hall, she let the steaming water burn into her. The phone rang several times, but she just remained in the tub and let the moisture soothe her torn flesh. She lost count of how many times the phone rang. Rhonda barely registered that someone kept trying to call. She didn't want to talk to anyone now.

Long after the water had grown cold, she emerged from the tub and dried off. She put on her robe and stood in the center of her room, staring at nothing in particular. The phone rang again. She almost ignored it, but figured the person wasn't going to give up.

"Hello?"

"Rhonda? Where have you been? It's two in the morning. Have you heard the news yet?"

"Dee?" *Why is Zora's neighbor calling me?*

"Rhonda, have you heard?"

"Heard about what?"

"Leon. He killed Jimmy Donovan."

"What?" Rhonda nearly shouted.

"I guess he came home and caught Zora with him. He must have lost his mind and shot Jimmy with his pants still down. No one knows where Zora is. Someone heard the shot and called the sheriff. They caught Leon still standing over the body with the gun."

"Oh, God," Rhonda sank to the floor. "What happened?"

"Rhonda, it was terrible. Jimmy's family, and friends… There was a mob… you know… because he killed a white man. The sheriff didn't do anything." She could hear Dee crying over the phone. "Rhonda, they hung him. Leon's dead."

Rhonda lowered the needle on her favorite record. She began to sing along as she lowered herself back into the tub. *When the lights go on again all over the world…*

She laid her head back and enjoyed her favorite memory. Strong ebony arms embracing her, his deep voice singing along to their favorite song: *When the lights go on again all over the world, And the ships will sail again all over the world, Then we'll have time for things like wedding rings and free hearts will sing, When the lights go on again all over the world…*

Goosebumps rose along her flesh. It didn't matter that the water was so cold. She wouldn't feel it for long. *I love Leon so much. Now we will finally be together.*

She opened her eyes to look down at her arms submerged in the water. Rhonda watched the red swirl away from her wrists.

Red is Leon's favorite color.

Sylvia Ney serves as an Adjunct Professor for the University of Texas at Austin as well as a High School English teacher. She has published newspaper and magazine articles, photography, poetry, and short stories.

Sylvia has served as a Board Member of both the *Texas Gulf Coast Writers* and *Bayou Writers Group* in Louisiana. She enjoys encouraging other writers by sharing her love of Journalism, Fiction, Photography, and Poetry. To learn more, visit her at: https://www.sylviacney.com/

The Year Walk
Mark A. Nobles

Elwanda had been locked in the root cellar of her family's farm for almost 24 hours. She sat still and silent, breathing shallow, slow, and in rhythm with her heartbeat. Her eyes had long since adjusted to the pitch blackness of the cellar, which did not mean she could see, but that her mind had become adjusted to the blindness. Over the hours she had learned to discern and differentiate between the gobs of layered smells and even identify the direction from which each smell emanated.

She could smell the dirt floor. To Elwanda the smell of brown dirt was the smell of home. She could smell the three burlap sacks of potatoes piled in the southwest corner of the cellar. There was a bushel of beets on the south wall. Next to the beets was another burlap bag of yellow onions. Along the west wall were five rows of shelves which held a row of canned peaches, the peach orchard had been especially productive last year, and half a row of canned tomatoes, and half a row of pickled okra. The okra patch had been slight.

The dearth of okra made Elwanda sad. Each time a jar of pickled okra was opened she would loudly declare 'I can eat my weight in okra,' and she would promptly set about proving it. This year she had tried to hold back her hunger for okra in order to make them last through the winter. This plan was not working as it only left more okra for the others, especially Little Joe, her younger brother, who professed a love for okra as strong as Elwanda's. She had spent a goodly amount of time meditating on the wisdom of this tack.

The third row held jars of pickled beets, chow-chow, and pickled cucumbers. The fourth row held pickled peppers, carrots, and pearl onions, sweet pickles, and pickled pears, which Elwanda thought should have been stored closer to the peaches. The fifth row was all canned tomatoes, cabbage and peas.

The stone stairs leading down from the kitchen were located in the northwest corner of the root cellar. Along the remaining north wall were burlap bags of corn, corn meal, and purple onions. Lots and lots of purple onions. If the musky smell of brown dirt was the smell of home, the smell of purple onions frying in an iron skillet was the smell of comfort. Elwanda's mother chopped and fried purple onions with every meal. Every meal. Breakfast, lunch and dinner. When Elwanda left the house, she could smell the scent of purple onions on her dress. It was an omnipresent redolence in the Stasey home.

Elwanda La Vonne Stasey was born January 10, 1922 in Desdemona, Texas. When she was but two, her family moved from Desdemona to western Oklahoma. Her father was an oil field worker and the Desdemona fields were pretty near dry by 1924, so the Stasey's picked up and headed to the next muddy, oil boom town where her father, Clyde, could find work. Elwanda's granddaddy died in 1930 and her father uprooted the family and returned to Texas. He traded his oil field hard hat and roughneck for a dirt farmer's straw hat and redneck. Elwanda's grandmother, Gramma Gunda was Norwegian and refused to part with the ways of the old country. Gramma Gunda scared Elwanda's mother, Juanita, who did not like to be alone with her. This would prove to be an untenable situation when they returned to the family farm in Chalk Mountain, because Clyde was in the field from sunup to sundown and the children were always outside doing chores or chasing chickens through the mesquite thicket.

On the bitter cold day in January when Elwanda was born, Gunda took one look at the red faced babe and declared she was a child of grace and power.

"Elskede," Gramma Gunda would say, "will go on her first year walk on the winter solstice of her eighteenth year. She is special, we will learn much from her."

Elskede was Norwegian for 'beloved one,' Gramma Gunda never called Elwanda, 'Elwanda,' it was always Elskede. Every time she did, it pushed Juanita closer to the edge. When Clyde castrated a bull or one of the buck goats, Elwanda always ran up Chalk mountain to escape the wail of the animal. If Juanita could have, she would have run up Chalk mountain herself every time Gramma Gunda called Elwanda, 'Elskede.'

Gramma Gunda always spoke to Elwanda using a mixture of Norwegian and English. Her already heavy accent grew thick as molasses when speaking to her Elskede. Juanita often complained to Clyde that Gramma Gunda and Elwanda had developed a language of their own, part Norwegian, mostly English, but still difficult for Juanita to follow. Clyde thought it wonderful Gramma Gunda passed along the family's mixed heritage; Juanita disapproved, and even refused to teach Elwanda Spanish, her own mother tongue.

Juanita wanted her children accepted as white. She was light skinned and always introduced herself as Nita, but everyone knew she was Mexican. While the other women of Chalk Mountain never avoided Juanita, they rarely included her in their sewing bees or basket socials. She did not want her children to suffer the same prejudice she had lived with all her life, but she was most concerned about Elwanda's soul.

Juanita believed this Year Walk business was pure witchcraft and she believed it right down to the marrow of her Baptist and Catholic soul. Juanita had been raised in the Catholic church and had been richly reverent but when she fell in love with Clyde, she gave up *The Church* and agreed to be washed in the blood of that old-time religion. Her family had not spoken to her since. At Elwanda's birth, Juanita was briefly torn between her old and new religious faith, when Gramma Gunda insisted Elwanda be christened, but Clyde refused. Baptists are dunked when old enough to make the decision themselves, not as babies. Gramma Gunda was fierce in her insistence Elwanda be christened, but Clyde held steadfast, and Juanita reluctantly sided with Clyde. When Little Joe was born a few years later, the argument erupted again, and again, Clyde prevailed. Neither of the Stasey children were christened at birth. Elwanda had been baptized at 13, Little Joe was still not quite old enough to make the decision.

To prepare for the Årsgång the walker must remain alone in a closed, dark space from sunup to midnight on the winter solstice, Christmas, or New Year's Eve. They must not speak or eat and must remain seated. Elwanda had dutifully fulfilled these requirements. She had sat motionless on a three-legged milk stool and not tested her vocal cords at all. She could feel her blood flow from heart to feet to head and back to heart. She understood how snakes smell with their tongue. Through the hair on her forearms, she could feel Little Joe walking in his bedroom which was directly above the root cellar.

She had no idea how long she had been sitting on the three-legged milk stool in the root cellar. She was. Time was. It all was.

She cocked her head toward the door to the root cellar just before the rope handle tugged and pulled up the slat. Light from the kitchen streamed down the steps and into the room. Gramma Gunda walked three stone steps down the stairs. "It is time for your walk, Elskede," she spoke.

Elwanda rose and followed Gramma Gunda up the stairs to the kitchen. The smell of the oil lamp was pungent and unctuous. Gramma Gunda walked to the back door and opened it to the night. As Elwanda walked to the open door, Clyde came behind her and placed a woolen shawl about her shoulders. She wrapped it about her and silently walked into the night.

Elwanda had been well prepared by Gramma Gunda for her first Year Walk.

No talking. Ever.

Walk directly through the woods to the church. Do not be distracted. No matter what she saw or who she met.

Walk counterclockwise around the church three times, go to a window, peer inside. Remember what she saw.

Walk back to the house, again. Let nothing distract her or tempt her off the path.

Reenter the house through the same door from which she left.

Gramma Gunda never told Elwanda who or what she might meet in the woods or what exactly she would see in the church windows, but she had told her countless stories and fairytales about mythical and fantastic beasts and that the Year Walk would reveal portends. It was said that on the Winter Solstice, the night Gramma Gunda had chosen for Elwanda's Year Walk, spirits from the otherworld cross over and roam the lonely, dark places.

Gramma Gunda told Elwanda tales of the bäckahäst or brook horse, a beautiful gray mare that invited children to ride on her back. The bäckahäst could carry as many children as she liked, as her back would elongate to accommodate any number of children. When the bäckahäst felt she had enough children riding, she would jump into a brook, river or any body of water, drown her riders, and turn their souls into trinkets with which she adorned herself.

The Huldra was a denizen of the woods who was especially haunting to Elwanda. Gramma Gunda said she was a beguiling, beautiful woman who lured victims to her home deep in the forest to either marry or kill. Huldra took the shape of an ordinary young woman, but from her back the roots of the forest grew. Long, twisted roots sprung from her nape to the curve of her back, reaching out to the trees and brush of the woods. Huldra was a guardian of the forest, a nurturing, necessary being, but her loneliness pushed her to seek companionship.

The Nøkken, a male water sprite, was the most terrifying creature one might encounter on the Year Walk. The Nøkken was a shape shifter and could appear as anyone but most often approached the Year Walker as either a boy, young man, or old man. He never strayed far from water and had the ability to play any instrument, often a fiddle. The Nøkken charmed and disarmed his prey with hypnotizing melodies.

Clyde and Gramma Gunda watched Elwanda fade into the darkness before closing the kitchen door. When they turned, Juanita stood in the doorway of the living room, arms folded, her face wearing a disapproving, furrowed brow. She turned and went back to bed, Clyde followed. Gramma Gunda put a kettle on to boil and sat down at the kitchen table.

Completely alone, Elwanda tied her shawl loosely around her shoulders as she walked. Clearing the yard and gate, she was embraced by the woods. She seemed to glide along the path, taking sure, silent footsteps, breaking no twigs and barely bending the grass beneath her feet. Her way was lit by a falling last quarter moon but Elwanda guided herself with all her senses. Shards of moonlight pierced the darkness and shadowed the forest floor. The very air seemed to part before Elwanda. No breeze touched her cheek or stirred her black hair.

"Are you lost, child?" came a voice more inside her head than out.

Elwanda did not speak nor pause upon her journey. She must not speak, or her Year Walk was finished.

"Come and sit with me," continued the voice, lilting and feminine.

A few steps later, Elwanda entered a small clearing. A beautiful young woman, with hair blacker than Elwanda's, sat on a flat stone next to a fire that Elwanda had, but moments ago, mistaken for moonlight.

"You must not know what night it is or you would not be out walking so alone." The woman smiled at Elwanda, but Elwanda moved across the clearing without pause and disappeared back into the woods. The woman, beautiful beyond compare, let loose a laugh that sounded as if she had never cared a whit and had never known one iota of trouble.

Elwanda blinked and her next step snapped a twig, but she persisted. Regaining her composure, Elwanda forged ahead towards Chalk Mountain Primitive Baptist Church. On her eleventh step past the clearing she shook the voice from her head, on her thirteenth step she reentered, what seemed to be, the exact same clearing. The same beautiful woman, sitting on the same flat stone by a fire, wearing a cloak of powder blue stretching out behind her some five feet. This time the woman looked at Elwanda. "Join me," she beckoned. "Alight and be mine."

Elwanda hunkered, shielding herself like a turtle and kept moving. The woman stood. As she rose, dirt flew from the buried roots extending out her back and into the ground. The trees creaked. She spoke words into existence, "I am the medicine you will seek."

Elwanda was sure now, the woman was Huldra. Elwanda's heart beat faster. Until now she thought Gramma Gunda's stories were just that, only stories, handed down from the old world. But now, the stories had become flesh. She had no time to think. Keeping silent, she pressed on, though a gasp did escape her throat. In seven steps, she was across the clearing and back into the woods.

She counted her steps and on the thirteenth, she again entered the clearing. The woman was once again seated, the dirt behind her undisturbed. "Come," she beckoned, "what harm ever came from warming by a fire?"

Elwanda cocked her head and kept her pace. On her sixth step her shawl ripped from her shoulders, but on the seventh she was through the clearing. The sounds of the dark woods were loud now, mice stampeded through the underbrush, an owl screeched for its mate, and for the first time she heard water flowing over smooth rocks.

Elwanda was approaching the old wooden bridge that spanned Rough Creek when she noticed a new sound, unnatural but sweet, braiding its way through the chill night air. Someone was playing a violin lilt. The melody was high, swirling, and effortless. As belonging to the woods as the bullfrog's croak, and the cicada's buzz.

Elwanda crossed the small bridge in only three broad steps. The violin ceased after six steps on the other side. Behind her she heard boots hit the planks, but she did not crick her neck to look back.

"But, miss, spare a moment. Just a brief moment, miss."

With the knowledge that Gramma Gunda's stories were real, Elwanda knew the violin, boots, and voice belonged to Nøkken, the water sprite. Elwanda wanted nothing to do with him and felt relieved she had passed him so quickly and easily, until she remembered she had no choice but to return home by the same path.

In no time Elwanda was approaching the old Baptist church. She left the tree line and approached from the east. The church faced west with the old graveyard on the north. She had no idea of the hour but had walked to the church most every Sunday of her life. The journey was most always a fifteen minute walk, however, on this night she had no idea if time ticked in the usual increments.

She walked to within five yards of the whitewashed building and stopped. She faced south and began walking backwards, counter clockwise around the church. When Gramma Gunda delivered her instructions Elwanda had always thought this would be the most difficult part of the Year Walk, circling three times around the church backwards and counter clockwise. She knew she would trip, especially while walking through the graveyard. But after what she had seen and heard in the woods, she knew she was truly in a different world and trusted her footing.

Once around.

Twice around.

Three times around safely.

Back where she started, Elwanda faced the church. The back door and two windows on either side gazed back. A blueish light, that had not been there before, shone through the two windows.

"Courage up," she thought, but not a word or sound passed her lips.

"Approach a window after you have thrice circled the church, and gaze inside to learn the portends of the coming year." This was what Gramma Gunda had told Elwanda to do. She was determined to do it. This is what Elwanda did.

She approached the window to the south of the back door, stood on tippy-toes and peered inside. The entire congregation was in attendance, sitting precisely where they sat each and every Sunday. Preacher Bonds stood behind the pulpit, mouth agape, right arm outstretched, pointing accusingly, mouth open in sermon.

Elwanda's hamstrings ached, she relaxed, went flatfooted, let them recover, and stood tippy-toed again to peer through the window. Her eyes immediately went to the third row and scanned for her own family. There they sat. Father with restless eyes, as usual, mother raptured, also usual, and Little Joe, headless, nestled between them.

Headless. Why was Little Joe only a headless body?

Elwanda pushed back from the sill and went flatfooted again. She tucked her chin to her chest and furrowed her brow. A chill went down her spine. Gramma Gunda had not told Elwanda how to interpret what she would see through the windows. Taking the stories to be more myths than reality, she had never thought this through. Never really thought to ask what she would see. She never thought she would actually be here, on the Year Walk, at the church, Nøkken and Huldra at her back, waiting for her in the woods.

She tippy-toed up for one more look through the window. She wanted to be sure she had committed to memory all she had seen. Little Joe was still headless, and as she swept the pews it seemed Mr. Parker had a slight blueish tint to his face and hands, and Mrs. Tishler had a purple birthmark peeking up past the collar of her dress that was not there last Sunday. She almost did not notice Old Joe Fenoglio, who always sat alone in the back, was also headless, like Little Joe. Elwanda felt sick. Old Joe, sitting in his Sunday suit, fiddling with his hat, for which he now had no head, was a widower with no family left in the county. He always sat in the back, hoping that after the service, someone would invite him to their home for Sunday dinner.

Elwanda tiptoed, backwards, away from the window. She repeated in her mind: Blue Mr. Parker, purple birthmark Mrs. Tishler, Headless Old Joe, blue Mr. Parker, purple birthmark Mrs. Tishler, headless Old Joe.

She did not have to commit to memory headless Little Joe.

Sure she had missed nothing and positive she remembered what she had seen, Elwanda went flat footed, turned and strode north towards the cemetery. Surrounded by a wrought iron fence this was not just the oldest cemetery in Chalk Mountain, it was the *only* cemetery in Chalk Mountain. The oldest burial marker is that of Abigail Davis, who died in 1874. Elwanda was no stranger to this hallowed ground, as she and the other children were charged with weeding and caring for the cemetery after church service. Mrs. Bonds oversaw the children and would tell tales on the dead as the children weeded and hoed.

As Elwanda opened and stepped through the gate, she heard a horse whinny in the woods. She stopped and stared into the blackness of night. The trees, barely discernible, in the thickness of the blue-black night, seemed to beckon her. Their outstretched blanches called to her like fingers slowly folding over palm, rhythmically, over and over.

Elwanda knew exactly to which grave she was headed. It was two plots over and one row back of Abigail. It was plaintively marked 'Three infants of Mel and Gillie Dykes.' There were no dates and curiously, no markers for either Mel or Gillie.

When Elwanda reached the plot and marker for the three Dyke infants, she knelt, reached out with her left hand and clawed a handful of dirt from the foot of the grave. She stood and examined closely the dirt in her hand. Carefully, with her right hand, she picked out a pebble, a half dozen or more blades of grass, and a small twig, and tossed them all, one by one, over her left shoulder. When she was certain she had nothing left but dirt, she placed her clenched left hand in her pocket and deposited the dirt.

She walked backwards out of the cemetery, never taking her eyes off the Infant Dykes grave. Elwanda left the cemetery in this manner not because it was how Gramma Gunda instructed. She backed out because the pit of her stomach told her this was the safest way. Her time in the root cellar had taught her to hear more than just the sounds around her, it had taught her to listen to her own instincts.

Exiting the cemetery, Elwanda made straight for the woods. She did not take the path from whence she came. She reentered through the thicket twenty yards up from the mouth of the trail. She hoped staying off the beaten path would shield her from Nøkken and Huldra. Her gut told her it would not, but had put forth that it couldn't hurt.

Hoofbeats trembled the ground, quickly followed by a horse whinny. Bäckahäst, she whispered in her mind. Ducking branches, and unsuccessfully attempting to avoid briars, Elwanda made her way towards home. Avoiding the path would take longer but hopefully be less contentious.

Elwanda's pace picked up as she calmed and focused on returning home. She seemed to sense branches and briars and anticipated the clearest path through the brambles. She could see the path, now just ten to thirteen yards to her right, it shone in the moonlight like a zoopraxiscope flickering at three-quarter speed. The hoof beats started low, but grew in intensity from behind her. The brook horse snorted as it neared, and this time Elwanda heard the laughter of children. She turned and saw a white horse with three children on its back, the horse was full of vinegar, and the children laughed in unadulterated glee. The bäckahäst was heading for Rough Creek.

When the brook horse had passed, she bade to hurry and perhaps arrive at Rough Creek in time to save the children. As she turned, she ran headlong into the chest of a man. The force of the collision knocked Elwanda off her feet. Groggily, she looked up and saw a nicely dressed man in a tailored suit. The suit was of the finest materials and of a style she had seen in pictures of her grandfather in his Sunday best. The man held a fiddle in his right hand and a bow in his left.

"Beg pardon, ma'am," he said. "I wandered from the path, and yon horse caught my attention. You move so quietly that I did not see nor hear your approach until we had collided." He put the bow in his right hand and reached out with his left to offer Elwanda a hand up. She declined and rose up on her own two feet.

The dandy smiled and took back the bow in his left hand. "Again, my apologies," he gave a slight bow. Elwanda nodded and attempted to bypass the man but he turned and matched her pace through the brambles. "Would that happen to be your horse and children? You look too young to be mother of three." He did not seem to draw breath between words but never ran out of breath to say more. "I see the horse and children quite often." He paused to give Elwanda a chance to reply. He smiled when she did not. "Of course, you're not their mother, that mare and those children have been running from church yard to creek for decades, and you are just a child."

Elwanda remembered the Infant Dykes and cut a look at the man. When their eyes met, his attempted to dance with hers. Before her next step, Elwanda heard a long whinny and a crystal burst of childish laughter, quickly followed by a splash. Three steps later she was at the banks of Rough Creek.

The water flowed lazily, clear and inviting. Elwanda heard the footsteps of the dandy approaching from behind. "I can teach you a tune that will tame the horse," he said. His tone was relaxing and made her feel enclosed and comforted. The dandy's voice had the lilt of peace.

Elwanda looked up and down the bank. There were no ripples from the horse and children leaping into Rough Creek. The footbridge spanning the creek was no more than thirty yards to her left. She knew she had to keep moving or she would never leave. The water was too inviting and the dandy's voice too embracing. She lit like a flash for the bridge and was across before she was conscious of her progress. Firmly on the home side of Rough Creek she heard the fiddle playing a laconic tune that somehow emanated from above, not behind her as it should.

She locked her pace to a slower gait and pondered whether to remain on the path or head back to the brambles. She knew Huldra was somewhere between her present location and home. She was not so sure she would be allowed to pass through the clearing so easily as before. She decided to remain on the path, but closed her eyes and walked guided by her mind's eye.

She stepped into the clearing occupied by her home in what seemed to be half the time it should have taken. Unrealized by her she had passed through Huldra's clearing and fire three times. On the first passage Huldra was dumbfounded, the second she threw pebbles at Elwanda, and on the third she cursed her in a language older than Chalk Mountain.

Just as she was about to lose all sense of balance her father opened and ran out the back door and grabbed her up in his arms. Gramma Gunda stood in the doorway and motioned them inside. Clyde picked Elwanda up in his arms and carried her in the house and to her bed. She slept for 33 hours. Juanita took Elwanda's chair from the dinner table and sat next to her bed until she awoke.

Elwanda opened her eyes and saw her mother. "Mama."

"My baby," said Juanita. She reached out and stroked Elwanda's hair.

"I'm powerful hungry."

Juanita laughed. "I have to pee like a plow horse, but after that, I'll make you whatever you want."

When Elwanda dressed, cleaned up a little and went into the kitchen, her mother already had bacon frying in the skillet. Gramma Gunda sat at the table. She looked up and smiled at Elwanda.

"Put on your shawl, and we'll go for a walk and talk."

"I lost my shawl in the woods last night."

"This is your shawl, now," said Gramma Gunda. She reached into the seat of the chair next to her and raised a purple woolen shawl and offered it to Elwanda. It had been Gramma Gunda's when she was a girl in Norway.

"Oh, Gramma Gunda," Elwanda said with glee. "That is your finest shawl. It is not meant for me. Not to wear as an everyday cover."

"It is yours now, to wear whenever you wish."

Elwanda took the shawl from Gramma Gunda and wrapped it around her shoulders. It was the softest, warmest garment she had ever draped.

Gramma Gunda smiled. Juanita tensed, flipped the bacon, and commenced to scrambling eggs. "If y'all are going outside, might as well feed the chickens."

Outside, Gramma Gunda and Elwanda slowly walked to the coop. "I was not sure you would make the Year Walk, but I know you did," said Gramma Gunda. "What did you see, Elskede?"

"It seems like a dream, Gramma. I'm not sure I saw anything."

"It was no dream and you know it. You must tell me."

"In the forest…" Elwanda hesitated.

Gramma Gunda took the lid off the barrel holding the chicken feed, took out the scoop and filled the bucket kept next to the barrel. "Never mind the forest for now. You made it to the church and back. Tell me what you saw through the windows. Start at the church."

Elwanda closed her eyes to remembered what she had seen and memorized, "Blue Mr. Parker, purple birthmark on Mrs. Tishler's neck, and headless Old Joe Fenoglio"

"Anything else?"

Elwanda did not want to mention Little Joe's headless body. She did not want to face it. "That is all." She took the bucket from Gramma Gunda and entered the coop, some chickens scattered, and others came running for the feed.

"And the medicine?"

Elwanda nodded. "I took it from my pocket, wrapped it in a kerchief, and hid it in my room. You know mama finds dirt anywhere in the house and sweeps it out lickety split."

"Wise girl," said Gramma Gunda. "Where in your room did you hide the medicine?"

"A girl needs some secrets, Gramma Gunda."

"Aye, aye, aye," said Gramma Gunda, wagging her finger and smiling. She had been telling Elwanda that 'a girl needs secrets' since Elwanda was five. "See now? Like I told you," said Gramma Gunda. She stopped smiling and pointed her finger squarely at Elwanda. "But you will bring the medicine to me after supper."

"Yes ma'am." Deep in thought, Elwanda rotely scattered the feed to the ground. "What does it all mean, Gramma?"

"Mainly it means we have healing to do."

"Can we heal Old Joe?"

"Mr. Fenoglio, to you, child, but no, headless means death, as you likely have guessed. And a death not by sickness or disease, but by calamity such as accident or murder, God forbid, or plain old age," Gramma Gunda shook her head plaintively, "Isn't any medicine for those things. Like as not it is just Old Joe's time to go."

This is not what Elwanda wanted to hear. It chilled her to think of Little Joe's headless corpse.

Gramma Gunda reached into her apron pouch and pulled out her silver snuff box, opened it, and took a pinch. "But we ought to be able to fix up Mr. Parker and Mrs. Tishler right as rain." She snorted the pinch of snuff up her right nostril, coughed, snorted, and replaced the snuff box in her apron. "I'll take the medicine and mix in into a poultice for Mr. Parker and Mrs. Tishler."

"But it is just dirt."

"It was dirt, now it is medicine."

"How do we know it is the right medicine?"

"Don't know, don't care. The medicine you fetched will cure what ails you." Gramma Gunda could see Elwanda was not quite swallowing this explanation. "Elskede, how do we know the sun will rise tomorrow in the east?"

Elwanda shrugs.

"Because it always has, and it always will. At least for our time and a great while past our time."

Juanita came to the back door and hollered, "Food is on the table."

Elwanda scattered the remains of the bucket in the coop yard and left, latching the gate behind her. "I could eat my weight," she said, placing the bucket back by the barrel.

"Good, you'll need your strength, we still have work to do." Gramma Gunda and Elwanda headed for the kitchen.

A few days later, the Stacey house was back to normal. Clyde and Juanita rose well before daylight, Clyde gulped a cup of coffee and Juanita started the stove and began preparing breakfast. Elwanda and Little Joe rose about the time breakfast was on the table. The family shared breakfast, then Little Joe headed for the schoolhouse, Clyde to the field, and Elwanda helped Juanita with the chores. Gramma Gunda rose when she awakened and did what she pleased. Sometimes she 'helped' Juanita, much to Juanita's irritation, sometimes she rocked on the porch, sometimes she knitted. On this day she went to the kitchen, stoked the wood burning stove, and set to sorting herbs and powders that were of unknown origin to Elwanda and Juanita.

"How long will you be taking space at the table and stove, Gramma Gunda?" inquired Juanita.

"No longer than I need," said Gramma Gunda, in a voice sweet as mustang grapes.

After the noon meal, Gramma Gunda walked out of the house and called to Elwanda. When she walked up, Gramma Gunda said, "I'm taking this poultice over to the Parker place, he had the sickness in his eyes last Sunday, might as well give him the cure before it takes hold to strong."

"Want me to call daddy in to drive you?"

"No, Elskede, it is not far, and the walk will do a body good," and off she went in the direction of the Parker homestead, not half a mile away.

The afternoon passed without merit. When the late winter yellow light began to dim, Juanita stuck her head out the back door. "Elwanda," she shouted.

Elwanda came out of the barn, "Yes, mama."

"Your brother should have been home half an hour ago, walk the path and fetch him."

Elwanda shivered. She had almost managed to put the image of headless Little Joe out of her mind, but now the thought of Little Joe, lost or dead in the woods, seemed all too real. "Yes, mama," she said, and hurried down the same path she had taken on the Year Walk. The school was no more than a quarter mile past the church.

Once in the woods Elwanda slowed her pace and peered into the brush looking and listening for Little Joe. It was not uncommon for him to be late from school. Clyde often said the boy would go through twice the trouble to avoid doing half the chores. But the headless vision of Little Joe pulsed through her brain like blood through her temples. She kept eyes and ears tuned for Huldra and the Nøkken. Once seen, they can be encountered again at any time.

She prayed she did not see Little Joe riding the back of the bäckahäst.

Elwanda was in the woods for over an hour. She did not see Huldra, Nøkken, the bäckahäst, or Little Joe. Tired and scratched up from the bull nettles and bramble, Elwanda made her way back to the house. She heard her mother screaming her name while still fifty yards out. The panic and worry in Juanita's voice was an extra weight on her already trouble soul.

"Oh, child," Juanita exhaled when Elwanda emerged from the woods. "I was starting to worry about you as well as your brother."

Clyde exited the chicken yard and walked towards Elwanda. "I take it no sign of Little Joe?"

Elwanda shook her head in the negative.

Clyde's voice was calm, but his eyes betrayed worry. He turned to Juanita, "Take the truck and fetch some neighbors, we need as many men in the woods as we can muster before nightfall," he said. "I'm heading in, straight up the path until I pick up his tracks from school." Juanita nodded in acknowledgment. "Bring the men here and have them fan out and start walking the woods." With that Clyde turned and disappeared down the path.

Juanita stood a few feet outside the back door, her right hand clenched and covering her mouth, her left hand balling up her apron. Elwanda walked past her and up the steps to the back door. "Where are you going, Elwanda?"

"To fetch the keys," she said, stepping through the door. In less time than it took for Juanita to wipe a falling tear, Elwanda was walking back out the door, letting the screen slam and the latch hook rattle. "Let's go, Mama," she said.

"Oh, child, you know I can barely drive, and with my nerves…"

Elwanda cut her off. "Daddy's been teaching me for over a year," she said. "I can drive fine."

Juanita was startled, but relieved. She followed her daughter to the driveway and they climbed in the truck, Elwanda behind the wheel. The ignition fired on the old 32 Ford and Elwanda threw the stick in reverse, she let out the clutch and checked her rear view and saw Gramma Gunda turning into the driveway. She eased back and Gramma Gunda made for the yard.

"Will wonders never cease, Elskede. Nita, what are you doing letting this child behind the wheel?"

"No time to waste, Gramma," said Elwanda. "Daddy's gone out looking for Little Joe and we're to fetch more men folk to join him before nightfall."

Gramma Gunda could see the worry in Elwanda's eyes. "That is a lot of commotion." She wrinkled her brow.

"I'm worried sick, Gunda, Joe has never been this late, something has happened." Juanita's voice was high and strained.

Gramma Gunda looked straight and deep into Elwanda's eyes. "Surely, we have no worries in this house," she said. "Not this year."

Elwanda broke away from Gramma Gunda's gaze, cricked her heck and engaged reverse. "We have to go, Gramma. Daddy said."

The men searched for Little Joe deep into the night. They found nothing. They were back in the woods at break of day. They found nothing. The search continued for nine more days. The number of men showing up started to dwindle after day six.

By day nine it was only Clyde and two of his closest friends.

They found nothing.

Elwanda stood inside the chicken wire sowing corn to the hens. Gramma Gunda came out the kitchen door, walked down the steps, crossed the yard, and stood outside the gate. The two women stood in the moment for a long while, letting emotions settle.

Finally, "Why didn't you tell me, Elskede?"

"I didn't think it would come true."

"The truth does not care what you think, Elskede." Gramma Gunda flapped her apron. "If we had known beforehand…" her voice trailed off.

"You said there was nothing to be done about the headless."

"There is balm in trying," Gramma Gunda said. "And sometimes death can be cheated. Not often. I've never seen it happen, but there are stories."

"There are always stories, Gramma," shouted Elwanda. "I am tired of the stories. I see no benefit to the stories."

"Mr. Parker benefited. Mrs. Tishler will benefit. Her poultice is ready."

The two women spoke to each other only with their eyes for a long, long time.

Sheriff Carl W. Turnbow turned his vehicle into the Stacey driveway a little fast, tossing dirt and gravel into the yard. When he hit the brakes, the car slid to a halt. Cutting the ignition, Sheriff Turnbow was out of the car before the engine had died. He did not bother shutting the car door. "Where's Clyde," he shouted.

"In the field, I reckon," answered Gramma Gunda.

Juanita came at a trot out the back door with eyes as big as moon pies and no color in her cheeks. Her mouth was open, but she dared not speak.

"Go fetch your daddy, Elwanda," said Sheriff Turnbow. Turning to Juanita he hurriedly spoke. "We ain't found Little Joe, Nita, so calm down."

"That makes it worse, Carl." Juanita started to cry. "I just want to know."

"Let's go inside, Nita," Sheriff Turnbow wrapped his arm around Juanita and gently turned her towards the backdoor.

Gramma Gunda just stood and took it all in. Elwanda exited the coop, put the bucket by the barrel, and headed at a trot toward the back field. As Turnbow and Juanita entered the house and Elwanda disappeared into the field, Gramma Gunda interlocked her fingers in prayer and began to whisper in Norwegian. The screen door slammed.

Fifteen minutes later Clyde and Elwanda entered the kitchen. "What did you find, Carl?" Clyde was half a tick below shouting.

Juanita stood at the stove, pouring one of two cups of coffee. Sheriff Turnbow looked at Clyde, then cut his eyes to Elwanda.

"I figure she is old enough to know," states Clyde.

"Sure enough," said Sheriff Turnbow. "Well, Hugh Underwood was out rabbit hunting and ran across a body about a mile north of the Rough Creek walk bridge."

Juanita covered her mouth and stifled a gasp.

The sheriff continued, "We got up there and it looks like it is Joe Fenoglio."

"God rest his soul," prayed Clyde.

"Appears he was mauled bad by a bear."

Clyde raised his eyebrows and cocked his head.

"You are thinking right, Clyde," the sheriff said. "Black Bears don't generally want nothing to do with a person, unless the person intrudes upon their business or their babies. Old Joe was out there with only a pistol and .20 gauge. No way he would have riled up that bear on purpose."

"Rabid?"

"That is what we think. I've had reports of two rabid skunks and a raccoon in the last month and I got a cousin over in Duffau that put down two rabid coyotes last week." The Sheriff swirled his coffee and seemed to be lingering. No one was eager to speak. Everyone was thinking of the rabid bear and Little Joe.

Eventually, Clyde roused from the stupor. "I'll walk you to your car, Carl."

The sheriff stood and handed his cup to Juanita, "Thank you for brewing the coffee, Nita. You needn't have gone to the trouble, but I'm obliged." The sheriff walked out the backdoor and Clyde followed. Halfway down the drive the sheriff spoke, "I hate to say it Clyde, but is has gone on near two weeks."

"I know."

"If that bear took him... well, there weren't much left of Old Joe and he's more than twice the size of Little Joe."

"I know."

"And if we didn't come across him as quick as we did Old Joe, the coyotes have likely scattered..."

Clyde cut him off, "I know, Carl."

"It is time. That is all I'm saying."

"It is easier said, Carl."

The two men stood by the cruiser. Carl with his left hand on the top of the car, his right fumbling with his keys. He looked off into the fields. Clyde, hands in his pockets, both fists clenched, stared at his boots.

"I'll see you Sunday," said Carl as he opened the door to the cruiser and climbed inside. Clyde withdrew his right hand and slapped the hood three times. "See you Sunday. Give Molly my best."

Late that night after Clyde and Juanita had gone to bed, Elwanda sat on the backdoor steps, peering into the darkness. Gramma Gunda opened the screen door and walked out, reaching to steady herself by grabbing Elwanda's left shoulder. Stepping down on the dirt of the backyard she pulled one of the old wooden, straight backed chairs Juanita kept by the door so she could sit and shuck corn or snap peas or beans. She kept two chairs by the door, but no one ever sat with her except Little Joe or Elwanda, and then only if they were made to. Shucking corn and snapping peas or beans is a lonely endeavor.

"I guess you seen the purple creeping up Mrs. Tishler's neck last Sunday," she said as she fell into the chair.

"I did, yes ma'am."

"I have her poultice ready." Gramma Gunda reached into her apron pocket and pulled out her snuff. "I suppose you should take it over to her."

"Yes, ma'am. I'll go first thing in the morning."

"Take it tonight child, I don't know she should wait."

"It is awful late, to be calling on someone."

"What ails Mrs. Tishler is something powerful. She needs to apply the poultice at midnight while the moon is waning." Gramma Gunda snorted a pinch of snuff into each nostril. "And that would be tonight." She inhaled deeply. "I do not trust that woman to follow my instructions, so I did not give her the medicine." She shifted in her chair. "She will leave a light in the window. She knows you are coming. You will take the road."

"Yes, ma'am."

"Be careful on the road. Stay clear of the woods."

"I know, Gramma."

"Once seen…"

"I know, Gramma." Elwanda stood up on the steps. "Where is the medicine?"

"On the table." Elwanda turned to step inside. "I told your father to baptize you both, right after you were born," said Gramma Gunda.

"I know, I've heard the story and remember y'all fighting about Little Joe."

"A baby is not safe unless they're baptized."

"I don't think being baptized would have saved Little Joe, Gramma."

"It would not have saved him from dying, but it would have saved him from what he has now become." Gramma Gunda's voice was shaky and she sounded old, worse, she sounded frail. "I did not mean for this to happen, Elskede. I swear, please believe me. I did not mean for this to happen. I would never have sent you on the Year Walk had I known. Had I the slightest foretelling."

"Nothing would have changed," said Elwanda going inside.

Gramma Gunda sat in the straight-backed chair and stared into the woods. "I would not have lost you both." She took two pinches of snuff and snorted one up each nostril.

Elwanda came out of the house with the poultice, kissed Gramma Gunda on the cheek and headed around the back of the house to the driveway.

"There are more dangers in the woods than you know, Elskede." Gramma Gunda had sternness in her voice but fear in her eyes. "I mean it. Stay on the road."

Elwanda nodded to Gramma Gunda and traipsed up the driveway toward the road.

The Tishler's owned the mercantile and lived in town about three blocks from Chalk Mountain Primitive Baptist Church. Everything in Chalk Mountain was three blocks or less from the church. Taking the road to town, instead of the path through the woods, more than tripled the distance. Elwanda knew the dangers of running the woods but felt if the Year Walk had not prepared her, then what was the point? Once she was out of sight from the house, she cut across the Brickmeyer's fallow field and entered the woods.

As soon as Elwanda entered the tree line she felt as if she were being watched and tracked. The brambles and vines were so thick she walked in a permanent stoop and pulled the clutched poultice up from her belly to her chest. The moonlight cut through the branches and diffused like fog. Nothing felt real. She, herself, felt fake and foreign. Only whatever it was tracking her felt solid, all else shifted and shimmered. The air was thin. Too thin to carry sound. It was not quiet, or even silent, sound did not seem possible, except for the sound of the thing keeping pace parallel with Elwanda.

Keeping pace but not parallel. The thing was angling slightly towards her. The world through Elwanda's eyes seemed refracted. Nothing was where it really was, like looking at a stick half in the water.

She persisted. She stepped where she sensed level ground, not where level ground appeared to be, causing her gait to be heavy, as if stomping. This distortion of sound and vision was meant to distract Elwanda and she knew it. She slowed her heart, regulated her breath, and kept a finger hold on reality. She had to serpentine her way through the brambles and vines, the undergrowth too thick for a beeline. She could not judge whether or not she would first meet the path or the thing stalking her. Holding her direction towards the path was difficult.

Music, stroked from a violin, wafted through the forest. Elwanda felt the notes against her skin and heard them as if she was listening underwater. The thing tracking her stammered and jerked when the music began. The brambles and vines before her thinned, disappearing into the dirt, easing her path and turning her winding progress more pointed. The brambles quit tugging Elwanda and instead steadied and pushed her along.

Inside her body she heard a moan and knew it came from the thing.

As if waking from a dream, Elwanda stood in the middle of the path. She knew how she got there but did not know when. She stood facing the direction of home. When she turned facing the church, she realized she was only yards away from the mouth of the path. To her right and behind, she heard the sound of roots tearing and smelled the scent of freshly turned soil. She ran for the mouth of the path. The ground pushed her like a wave and spit her out of the forest.

Elwanda walked without incident to the Tishler's home. She was a bit worried when she saw no light in the window as Gramma Gunda had said there would be. As she walked closer, she could make out the silhouette of Mrs. Tishler standing on the front porch. Coming up the walk Mrs. Tishler uttered a quiet greeting. Elwanda was relieved that it actually *was* Mrs. Tishler.

"Thank you, child," said Mrs. Tishler when Elwanda handed over the poultice. "You are quite welcome, ma'am," replied Elwanda. "Did Gramma Gunda…"

Mrs. Tishler interrupted, "Yes, I know what to do," and with that, she turned and scurried into the house. "This is the devil's work, I know, but Lord help me, I do not want to die," she said, slamming the door behind her.

Elwanda stood in the yard, not sure what to do next. She turned and headed down the street. She had no gumption for walking home through the woods. She was tired, thirsty and ready to be home in her bed. Even so, she decided to take the long way and stick to the roads.

Reaching the edge of town, Elwanda turned on the Farm to Market leading out to the Stasey homestead. Wide open fields of cotton, wheat, and hay ran parallel to the road on either side. There were three farms between Elwanda and home. Each field ran more than one hundred yards wide before hitting the tree line of the forest. She walked at a steady, decent pace, head down, eyes focused on the dirt and pea gravel road. She was comforted by the sound of the occasional hoot owl hidden by the trees.

Less than three quarters of a mile down the road the world went silent. The air turned thick as cotton and the hair on Elwanda's forearms bristled. She cocked her head to the right, towards the forest.

She halted. She was being tracked again. Something was pacing her and she felt it wanted to come out of the thicket towards her. There was a barrier, thin, but real, encasing the forest. The barrier confused Elwanda, moreover, it confused and frustrated the thing straining against it to get at her. She began walking again, but at a faster clip.

The thing had moved slightly ahead of Elwanda and she could feel the barrier bulging more and more with each step. She began to trot, then broke into a run. She tried to calculate if the thing might break the barrier before she reached home, which was still more than three quarters of a mile away. She had no idea when the barrier would break, until it did. The unseen barrier snapped, making the sound of a dried log crackling in an orange fire.

The thing tracking Elwanda hurled out of the forest. It was the color and consistency of mucous and dried blood and held its form by a thin film with the texture and look of a translucent scab. "Llaaawoh," it screamed, even though it had no mouth.

The thing was on Elwanda's back in a moment's fraction. It beat and kicked her like a cowboy breaking a bronc. It forced her in the direction of the tree line. Elwanda relented and moved in that direction. The beating eased but did not stop the closer she moved to the forest.

Elwanda and the thing on her back moved drunkenly ever closer to the forest. The thing shouting "Llaaawoh," unceasingly, accompanied by Elwanda's sobbing cry. Upon entering the forest, the branches and brambles tugged and tore at the thing, but it held firm to Elwanda's back. When they reached the path, Elwanda attempted to turn towards home but a grapevine wrapped her right elbow and tugged her towards the church.

Vines and branches snapped and whipped at the thing, but it clung to Elwanda's shoulders and kicked her ribs. She was not certain if she heard violin music in her ears or in her mind, but she did not care. It comforted her to know that Huldra and Nøkken were present and helping. For what reason and to what end? She did not understand.

"Llaaawoh."

"Llaaawoh."

"Llaaawoh," the thing screamed in a tone equal parts rage and lament.

Elwanda's heart slowed and a thought edged its way into her mind, squeezing out a bit of the terror there.

"I told your father to baptize you both, right after you were born."

"A baby is not safe unless they're baptized."

Elwanda remembered Gramma Gunda telling her the story of the Myling on her thirteenth birthday, right after Elwanda's baptism at Chalk Mountain Primitive Baptist Church.

"The Myling is an unbaptized child who has died in such a manner that it is not buried in hallowed ground. It is cursed to wander the woods and lonely roads, looking for lone travelers at night. Finding such, the Myling jumps on the traveler's back and beats them, demanding to be carried to the graveyard, so they can rest and find peace in sacred ground. Mylings are huge and grow ever larger as the traveler trudges towards the graveyard. The myling grows so enormous and heavy that even the strongest sink into the soil. If the traveler cannot deliver the myling to the graveyard the Myling becomes so enraged, it will beat the traveler to death."

The thing on her back was Little Joe, demanding to be taken to and buried in the graveyard of the church. Elwanda stopped fighting and began to purposefully march down the path to the church. With each step the Myling grew larger and beat her more fiercely. Vines and branches whipped at the Myling, one swept and caressed Elwanda's cheek.

She marched towards the church.

The thing cried, "Llaaawoh, Llaaawoh," repeatedly, and beat and kicked Elwanda, and grew larger the farther down the path they traveled.

With each step Elwanda's feet sank into the dirt.

Ankle deep.

Calf deep.

Knee deep.

Eventually, Elwanda fell to all fours and crawled, and clawed her way forward. She could now see the mouth of the path. Tombstones peeking in the distance. As she paused to catch her breath, a vine sprang from past the end of the path, wrapped around her right wrist and began to pull Elwanda. Still she made slower and slower progress.

Head bent, Elwanda closed her eyes and tried to focus on the music in her head and work with the vines and branches. She was only feet from the mouth of the path but still yards from the graveyard.

Crying, she felt the last of her strength give way and collapsed into the ground. Before passing out, Elwanda heard the whinny of a horse, opened her eyes and saw the bäckahäst enter the path, bend her neck to the ground, pick up the vine in her mouth, turn and stomp towards the graveyard, dragging Elwanda down the path. She had not the strength to crawl forward, but managed to call up the power to hang on.

She felt and tasted the dirt in her mouth as she was pulled along. "Llaaawoh, Llaaawoh, Llaaawoh," the Myling cried, but now it was not a wail of rage but joy.

Before passing into unconsciousness, Elwanda thought she heard the voice of Little Joe call her name.

The whole world sparkled, the air so crisp and clean the day they buried Little Joe. Juanita had felt faint and several of the women took her to the fellowship hall to sit and rest as they went about setting the tables with fried chicken, potato salad, baked beans, and all the assorted fixings that go with an after-funeral meal. It goes without saying there were gallons of sweet tea and enough banana pudding chilling in the fridge to feed the county.

Pastor Bonds and the men folk milled around outside the fellowship hall, smoking and making small talk. They had long since run out of 'polite' things to say to the Stasey's about the loss of their two children and were more than happy to let Juanita rest inside with the women. Clyde and Gramma Gunda lingered down by the fresh grave of Little Joe.

"She's gone, isn't she," said Clyde.

"Not like you mean, son," said Gramma Gunda. "She is gone, not gone like Little Joe, but she won't be home for dinner."

Mrs. Tishler stuck her head out the door of the fellowship hall and told the men food was on the table. Everyone thought it best to wait and let Clyde and Gramma Gunda come up on their own accord. When the stomach growling started to sound like a herd of swine, Preacher Bonds walked down to the gravesite and brought Clyde and Gramma Gunda up to supper.

After a month of Sundays life settled into a new routine. That is what life does. No matter how often or how much life changes, eventually, it takes the change and transforms it to routine. Water finds the lowest point and life turns chaos into routine.

The evening Elwanda took the poultice to Mrs. Tishler, Gramma Gunda stood all night in the backyard, looking into the woods, issuing prayers of protection. The next morning Preacher Bonds found Little Joe's bones scattered about just inside the graveyard. They were broken, exhibited gnaw marks, and were not all accounted for, but enough to determine they were what remained of Little Joe. There was no sign of Elwanda. The ground leading from the forest to the graveyard looked as if a plow had come from about thirty yards down the path and stopped at the gate. It had been overturned and furrowed. No one knew what to make of this. Everyone was puzzled and bandied wild conjectures. Everyone save Gramma Gunda, who had stayed uncharacteristically silent throughout the ordeal. Everyone thought it odd when she scooped up a handful of dirt from the furrow and placed it in her pocket. However, as everyone considered

Gramma Gunda odd to begin with, this did not raise many eyebrows.

The men folk scoured the county for Elwanda. After a few weeks the search was called off and a small service was held for Elwanda at the church. A marker was placed in the graveyard next to Little Joe. Some in Chalk Mountain were convinced Elwanda was not dead but had run off to Fort Worth or Dallas. Young people did that sort of thing with regularity in Erath County. Preacher Bonds thought there was no harm in giving peace to Clyde and Juanita. Gramma Gunda seemed indifferent and did not attend the service.

On solstice nights Gramma Gunda can be found standing in the Stasey backyard facing the forest path. She seems to be listening intently and if approached can be heard humming a quiet tune.

Mark A. Nobles is a sixth generation Texan. Born on Fort Worth's infamous Jacksboro Highway, Mark proudly claims blood and kinship with Thunder Road's gamblers, outlaws, and wastrels. His work has appeared in Cowboy Jamboree, Sleeping Panther Review, Crimson Streets, Cleaver Magazine, Curating Alexandria, The Dead Mule School of Southern Literature, Haunted MTL, and other publications. He has produced and/or directed three feature documentaries and several short, experimental films. Mark lives in Fort Worth but hopes to die in the desert. He loves his two dogs, two daughters, and Texas, but not necessarily in that order. He can be found and followed on Facebook @ Flyin' Shoes Films.

Smile for the Camera
Russell C. Connor

When the alarm went off, Dan fumbled for his phone on the nightstand, wincing at the brightness of the screen in the dark motel room.

Today's route instructions were waiting for him in an email from the Söka corporate office, same as every morning. He scanned for the name of the forgotten Texas town they were sending him to, then opened the Söka Maps app and plugged it in. The GPS told him his destination lay just under an hour away in current traffic conditions.

The first golden rays of morning were just washing over the motel's parking lot like spilled paint he stepped outside. His Söka-issued Dodge Stratus—what executives in the company jokingly referred to as a 'Terra Firmer'—sat in the parking space outside his room. It was covered in garish purple and neon orange stripes, the company colors, so bright it almost glowed. Mounted to the top was a criss-crossing network of black metal struts that looked like a luggage rack on steroids: a tripod rig to support the huge, rotating camera in the middle. The heavy box sported a fisheye lens as big as Dan's fist and could telescope to a height of ten feet above the vehicle's roof.

Dan had found the job listing for a 'Map Driver' discreetly buried on Craigslist. At first glance, Söka appeared to be nothing more than another cheap Google knockoff. But Dan did some research on the Swedish company before accepting the position and found that they had some serious buzz in the tech industry.

He tossed his bag in the Terra Firmer's trunk and then walked to the motel office. Never turn down a free continental breakfast; one of the helpful hints from Söka's Map Driver training manual. The office was empty aside from a half-asleep clerk and a burly guy in a flannel shirt sitting at one of the tables in the small dining area, reading the paper.

Dan grabbed a plate and heaped it full of runny scrambled eggs. As he sat down at a table, he noticed the guy in the flannel shirt glance up with a raised eyebrow. Dan ignored him, tucked into the grub, and pulled out his phone to study the day's route again.

The town was called Bajo Cruce, and that name was probably the only Spanish thing about it. Söka could pinpoint its approximate position within the state, but when he tried to zoom in closer to see the roads within it, he got a message that said, 'Map Forthcoming.' Of course, it was; the information he provided today would be used to create it. All these backwater Texas towns were the same anyway: a few sad streets of doublewide trailers and ramshackle houses…a non-chain convenience store, usually with the word 'Lucky' somewhere in the name…maybe a local post office, if the population was big enough. The kind of place that people only move *out* of, never into.

A hand slammed down on the table beside him, startling Dan so much he dropped his phone into his eggs.

"Zat your car out there?" The man in the flannel shirt stood beside him now, leaning over Dan's breakfast. His face was lean and leathery, with a scraggly beard clinging to the underside of his jaw. He jabbed a calloused finger at the motel office's front window to punctuate his question. "Purple and orange thing?"

"Uh, yeah," Dan answered, picking up his phone to wipe yoke from the case.

"You're with that…that *Goggle*, ain't ya?" the man demanded.

"Well, not exactly. It's a separate company that—"

But the guy was already nodding as if Dan had confirmed it. "Yeah, I'll bet. One of them goll-damn internet places goin' around, takin pitchers of people's property!"

Dan sighed. He should've known. Street View programs were very unpopular with a certain demographic who believed it to be an invasion of privacy. That subset of the population grew the further south you went, and you couldn't get much more south than Texas. Söka and Google had both been served with multiple lawsuits and injunctions, and entire towns had even banded together to form human chains to prevent drivers from entering their streets. Just last month, Söka had sent out a warning email after a mapper had been pulled from their vehicle and severely beaten.

In a world obsessed with selfies and Snapchat, it seemed that no one really liked having their picture taken when they weren't in full control of the camera. Hell, Dan's ex had required an hour's notice and full makeup application before he was allowed to so much as point his phone in her direction.

Flannel Shirt wagged the same finger in Dan's face. "You best not be takin any pitchers of *me*. I don't wanna be on any goll-damn internet."

"I wouldn't dream of it, sir," Dan assured him with a friendly smile.

"Good." Instead of going away, Flannel Shirt slid into the chair beside him and leaned in conspiratorially close. "You know what they do with all them pitchers, don't ya?"

"Yes. They make maps."

The man threw back his head and groaned at the ceiling. "Oh, wake up, son! The government's usin' 'em to keep tabs on us! Gettin' the layout of all our homes! They got special infrared that can tell how many guns we got, so that way, when they outlaw firearms, they'll know exactly how many to conf'scate!"

"All right, well, I have to go now." Dan slid out of his chair, leaving the rest of his breakfast as he walked quickly toward the door.

"Stay off that goll-damn internet!" Flannel Shirt's words chased him into the parking lot. Dan couldn't help wondering if the man thought 'goll-damn internet' was an accepted euphemism for the web. "They're readin' yore mind on there!"

Dan waved over his shoulder, then hurried to the

Terra Firmer and sped out of the parking lot.

Forty-five minutes later, he watched as a GPS dot representing his phone moved smoothly along the digital version of the highway. According to Söka Maps, the outskirts of Bajo Cruce lay somewhere just ahead. However, through his windshield, Dan saw nothing but flat Texas prairieland smashing against blue sky, broken only by a gargantuan outcrop of rock in the distance off to his right.

On his phone, the road he needed to take was quickly approaching. Dan squinted ahead into the morning sunlight, searching for an exit sign, and almost missed the turnoff when it appeared from nowhere. He slammed the Terra Firmer's brakes, laying down twin trails of smoking rubber on the blacktop.

Two narrow concrete lanes met the highway at a stiff right angle. They snaked across the scrubland, disappearing into the bright horizon. There was no street sign or marking of any kind; Dan only knew it was County Road 116 because Söka Maps told him, but even their information ended after a few hundred yards.

He could see something in the distance, though. Some sort of blocky structure that straddled the road. After rechecking his route instructions, Dan turned and cruised down the narrow two-lane road toward it.

Five minutes later, the highway was lost behind him, but he could make out the structure ahead now, a decorative archway made of reddish stones. He could see nothing beyond that point, not even the road, although he couldn't be more than a half mile from this Bajo Cruce. The desolation might've been creepy, if his first stop wasn't also visible, just a hundred yards ahead.

A dark-bricked house sat all by itself on the roadside, like a pebble washed up on some lonely shore. Just the sight of something manmade—evidence of civilization—made Dan feel better, at least until he pulled to a stop in front of it.

It wasn't very big, surely no more than a single bedroom, and constructed like something from the 50's. The windows were curtained, and a dust-covered black pickup sat in the driveway that branched off the road. The place even seemed cheerful: eaves freshly painted, the scrub grass that served as a lawn neatly mowed, shingles new and shimmering.

So why did his continental breakfast start squirming in the pit of his stomach as he studied it?

Söka wanted a picture here for the route. Dan booted up the computer installed in the dash that controlled the camera equipment. The Söka logo appeared, then the user menu. He touched the button to raise the camera. Above his head came a low hum and a series of clicks as the rig on the roof rose into the air like a periscope and began taking the 360-degree panoramic photo. Dan watched the live feed in the readout.

The empty road in front of him appeared, along with that far away shelf of rock that rose above the flat landscape like a giant hand clawing its way out of the earth. The angle, taken from twelve feet in the air, made the image seem strange, even alien, like the pictures NASA released from the rover on Mars.

Then the camera swiveled, the fisheye lens taking in the prairie to his right. As it hummed and clicked above his head, the curtains in one of the house windows twitched. A face stared out at him for a half second before disappearing again.

"C'mon, c'mon," Dan muttered. The camera continued to swivel.

The front door of the house swung open. A burly man dressed in black jeans, a matching black dress shirt, and a black ball cap emerged. He was big enough to tear Dan in half, and he didn't look happy as he raised a hand and shouted, "Hey! What're you doing?"

"Shit, not another one," Dan mumbled.

He squeezed the rim of the steering wheel. The camera was only halfway through its circuit, taking in the road behind the car. Dan wanted to floor it, but one of the hard and fast rules Söka put to their mappers was that driving with the camera in the extended position was an automatic termination.

The guy started toward the Terra Firmer just as the camera faced him. On the dashboard screen, a tinier version stomped across the lawn. This meant he would show up in the final image, forever captured in a bullish charge for goll-damn internet users to look up and laugh at, like that naked woman in the infamous Google Street View address.

Dan only glanced at the screen as the camera moved away from the man, completing its rotation, but he could've sworn that…for just a moment…the guy appeared to have the face of a gleaming white skull beneath the brim of his ball cap, with two dark, empty sockets where his eyes should be.

The camera finished retracting when the man was only a few steps from the vehicle. Dan threw the car into gear and stomped the gas pedal as soon as it finished. As he accelerated away, he heard the man yell, "Wait! Hold on, damn it!"

Dan sped up. In the rearview mirror, he watched as the man ran to the black truck in the driveway, backed into the road, and roared after him.

"No, no, no," he groaned.

The imposing stone archway lay dead ahead, a curve like half a McDonald's M that rose thirty feet above the earth. Its red-hued bricks were as big as car tires and stacked in a way that seemed to defy physics. On the other side, the road disappeared into the long shadow thrown by that mammoth rock outcropping, which took up the entire horizon. Dan drove even faster, the needle hovering near seventy, but the black truck was catching up to him. Sunlight winked off its grill, making it look like a row of needle-thin teeth. Dan heard its horn blasting a continuous bass note.

Then he sped through the archway and momentarily lost himself in the view on the other side.

Beyond the stone bow, the land sloped sharply downward; that's why the road had seemed to disappear. A narrow crevasse opened before him, one bounded by sandy cliff walls that widened into an entire valley far below. Dan could see houses and streets down there, sitting within the deep well of darkness created by that jutting rock shelf.

The descent was so steep and sudden, his speed caused the Terra Firmer to go airborne. Only the seatbelt saved him from bouncing off the steering wheel when the tires reconnected with the pavement. His phone flew off the passenger seat and smashed against the dash, spraying pieces in all directions. He fought to keep the car on the road as he plunged into the crack in the earth, the valley walls rising on either side of him. Once he had the vehicle under control, Dan looked in the rearview mirror.

The black truck braked hard, skidding to a stop just short of the archway. Dan saw the driver get out and stand in the middle of the road, waving his arms over his head, like a drowning swimmer.

He breathed a sigh of relief and kept driving.

Rather than a Spanish mission or old west border town, Bajo Cruce reminded Dan of some quaint, seaside New England village. For starters, it was much larger than the depressing scraps of civilization he usually went to. It looked to be eleven or twelve blocks long and five wide, a collection of tidy houses and mom-and-pop businesses. The buildings were painted bright colors and terraced along streets that ran languidly through them. From this high vantage before the road descended, he could see a playground and even a structure that appeared to be a school.

It all belonged on a postcard, except for one thing.

The entire town existed in a strange, perpetual twilight created by the high cliff walls and the rock shelf, which hung over the valley like a lid on a jar.

Dan entered the shadow just after the black truck gave up pursuit. The difference in illumination was so stark, he had to flip on the headlights until his eyes adjusted. With that slab of granite overhead, blocking out the sky, it felt more like he'd driven into a cave. He pulled off the road at the first stop-sign intersection so his pounding heart could slow down.

Further on, he could see a barbershop, a salon, a café, and a host of other shops. What he didn't see were other cars, or so much as a single human being. Despite that every building in Bajo Cruce looked brand new, the place was silent and empty.

Well, whatever. Having no one around made his job easier. He just needed to get it done before the guy in the black truck decided to hunt him down after all.

Dan reached around under the passenger seat for a full minute before he found his phone. A shard of glass jabbed at his finger. He fished the device out and cursed when he saw the shattered screen. The damn thing wouldn't even power back on.

Since he couldn't access the route directions in his email, he would just have to get pictures of every major intersection and let Söka sort it out.

Dan pulled the Terra Firmer into a good position in the middle of the street and extended the camera. He hoped there was enough light for it to work; these things weren't designed to take pictures at night. For the first time, he noticed there weren't even streetlights along any of the avenues. This place must be pitch black at night.

When the image resolved, it was grainy, dark and washed out. Oh well, not his fault. Dan tapped his leg impatiently, waiting as the camera rotated toward the buildings…

A gasp escaped him.

On the screen, the storefronts no longer looked cheerful and quaint. They were ugly, bombed-out shells, made of crumbling brick and covered in dark, weeping stains. Windows were shattered; potholes pitted the perfect sidewalks. The image was more like something from a war-torn ghetto. Dan gawked at the screen, then looked out the window and back again, over and over, trying to account for the difference between what the camera was recording and the images his eyes were seeing.

It had to be wrong. Some trick of the weak light. Or maybe someone had hacked the camera. Shoot, they had apps that did stuff like this to your videos, put random explosions and falling meteors over your loved ones' faces. Couldn't be too hard to overlay an entire fake town on top of what the camera recorded, right?

Dan didn't like how these excuses sounded frantic in his own head.

For the first time, he recalled how the man in the black pickup had appeared for a moment to be a skull.

He refused to give in to fear. This town already owed him a cell phone; it was damn sure going to smile for the camera. He turned left, following the new street past an old-fashioned ice cream parlor, a playground with slides and a seesaw, and a one-screen movie theater, until he came to a cross street controlled by an honest-to-goodness stoplight. He checked for non-existent traffic, pulled into the intersection, and let the camera work.

Again, the image of the surrounding structures defied what his eyes told him. Through the camera, the whole town looked ancient and dilapidated. Several of the businesses were nothing more than collapsing façades hiding burnt-out interiors. Beads of sweat broke out across Dan's forehead as he studied them.

Then he saw movement.

Dan paused the camera and watched the screen, leaning forward until his nose practically touched the glass. In the ruins of the movie theater, a face swam out of the eternal dusk. It wasn't a skull, like the man at the house, but more of a glowing visage whose only features were shapeless black eyes and a gaping mouth. A suggestion of a body hung below it, a ragged, incorporeal form that hovered above the ground. As the specter floated through the wreckage toward the street, a sound reached Dan's ears, one that he could hear even inside the Terra Firmer with the windows up.

A low, angry groan.

On the screen, the phantom reached the shattered front door of the building, where it was joined by a second, and then a third, all of them fading into view like a developing Polaroid. They crowded together, moving toward the car, their wailing voices joining the first.

"Fuck this," Dan whispered. He cancelled the picture and brought the camera down, thankful to be rid of the horrible image. Their moans, however, were getting closer. He put the car in reverse, intending to speed back out of this town, and had to slam on the brakes to avoid ramming into the shoe store that now sat behind him.

Dan twisted around in the seat to look through the back window. The road he'd come from was gone. He now sat in a three-way intersection, the line of stores behind him unbroken. His mind reeled at the impossibility.

Outside the car, the moans grew louder. Something scraped against the passenger door. Dan cried out in terror and slammed the car into drive, then pushed the pedal all the way to the floor. For the next few minutes, he sped down the friendly, shadow-laden streets of Bajo Cruce, taking turns at random. The town's layout had looked straightforward from above, but now the avenues seemed more like a maze, the turns forcing him away from the direction his mind insisted the exit must be.

And outside the vehicle, the somehow indignant groans continued, multiplying into a nightmarish chorus.

He slowed down just enough to take another turn and then slammed on the brakes.

The street was a dead end.

Dan sat helplessly, fear choking him. The angry muttering was so loud, invading his head, making it impossible to think. And the fact that he couldn't see the forms that made that noise, didn't know how far away they were, somehow made it worse.

Then again, he *could* see them, if he wanted…

Dan jabbed at buttons on the console until the camera mounted to the roof extended and began swiveling.

Those ghostly forms were *everywhere*, hundreds of them lining the busted sidewalks to his left and right like the crowd at a parade. They watched him with their blank eyes as they groaned. Dan felt his sanity scrabbling for something to hold on to, a scream building in his chest that might never stop. But then the camera faced forward again, and he noticed something that made him hit the button to halt its movement.

The screen showed the same buildings to either side of the car that he could see when he looked out the windows, but the road in front was open and clear.

There was no dead-end.

But which was real? What his eyes saw, or what the camera recorded?

Against Söka regulations, Dan drove forward cautiously with the camera still up. When the Terra Firmer's bumper touched the building in front of him, it swirled away like smoke, revealing the same stretch of road he could see through the camera.

It was all just a mirage.

"All right, I got your number now." Dan grinned and drove on.

This time he watched the screen in the dash instead of the road. Crumbling hovels flowed past. The camera revealed the true arrangement of the streets, opening new turns that he eagerly took, but it also showed the endless line of groaning spirits as they drifted into the road. Their formless arms reached for him. A whimper issued from deep in Dan's throat as he shot between them in the ever-narrowing confines.

Then, through the windshield, he caught sight of the main road on the other side of the buildings to his left. It stretched up and out, ascending toward the crack of sunlight visible beyond the canyon walls. Dan drove through an antique store that dissipated around him and then braked to keep the car from rolling over as he careened around the corner.

His heart sank.

This was definitely the road back out. But on the screen, his path was blocked by a massive swarm of wraiths that filled the street. Their caterwauls created a deafening wall of sound.

And behind them, where the road ascended

sharply, a lone figure stood in the middle of the pavement. Dan recognized the man from the house, still dressed in his black t-shirt and matching jeans.

Through the camera, however...he wore a dark hooded robe, and a face made of gleaming bone looked out from the cowl.

Before Dan could accelerate, the ghostly forms surged toward the vehicle, surrounding him. Even though they looked about as tangible as fog, they swamped his forward momentum and brought the Terra Firmer to a halt.

His door was yanked open. Unseen hands grasped his arms and legs and hauled him from the car. Their irate keening assaulted him, made his ears ache. He felt himself get hoisted into the air and carried aloft toward the nearest building.

And, just before they dragged him into the darkness, Dan thought he understood.

In the boondocks down south, even the dead didn't like having their picture taken.

Russell C. Connor has been writing horror since the age of five, and is the author of two short story collections and eleven novels. His books have won two Independent Publisher Awards and a Readers' Favorite Award, while his short fiction has been featured in multiple publications including the *Stupefying Stories Showcase* and the anthology *Strange Afterlives*.

Two Nuns Walk into a Bar
Elliott Baxter

"Two Nuns Walk into a Bar!" Chick screamed.

"Come again?" I replied.

"Two Nuns Walk into a Bar, you just passed it. Turn around!"

I looked in the rear view and saw a wooden sign, the kind you see hanging over English pubs. It had a large black silhouette of a duck head in the center and in white Old English lettering written around the edge it read, 'Two Nuns Walk into a Bar.'

"What the hell?" I said.

"I mean it, turn around."

"We don't have time, Chick. We kind of have things to do, remember?" Chick remembered; he just didn't give a shit.

"I know the situation," said Chick. "I just don't give a shit."

I sighed, there was no use arguing with Chick when he was in need of a drink. The Econoline was the only vehicle on the road, so I slowed down, made a U-ie, and headed back to the pub. The place was a nondescript wooden shack with more bare wood than paint. The boards warped and undulated such that the building resembled a reflection in a fun house mirror. Two metal signs nailed to either side of the door boasted Jax and Pearl beers. Both signs had multiple bullet holes scattered over them. The door looked depressed and sad.

I parked the Econoline next to a mint, coal-black, 1964 Lincoln Continental.

"You sure you want to park here?" From the tone of Chick's voice, I knew he did not want me to park there.

"Why not?"

"The lot is empty. Plenty of room. Why crowd whoever drives that Lincoln? Bar parking lot etiquette is similar to urinal etiquette, Buster. You should know that."

"Hell, you talking about?"

Chick sighs, like I'm an idiot. "You walk into a bathroom and there are three urinals, and a guy pissing on, say, the one on the far right."

"Of course, you go to the one on the far left."

"Correct. You never crowd a man at the urinals. Same with a bar parking lot, you never crowd a man's car in a bar parking lot. He may need a lotta room backing out." Chick slapped his thighs with both hands. "That's all I'm saying."

"Fuck it," I said, as I threw the Econoline into park. "We're here. Just don't scratch the damn Lincoln getting out." I killed the engine, removed the keys from the ignition, opened the door and slid to the ground. My shoes made a crunching noise when they hit the gravel, not unlike the sound of walking on dry leaves in the fall, but a tad more melancholy. Chick opened his door, careful not to hit the Lincoln, and dropped to the ground. "Don't that beat all?" he said.

Chick's surprise was well-founded. The Lincoln was idling. Just running with no place to go.

"Dumb som' bitch is asking to have his ride stolen," I said.

"More likely that Lincoln belongs to the baddest son of a bitch in the county and everybody knows whose it is." Chick looked at me before heading away from the van. "Seems to me like another reason not to park right next to it, in a completely empty parking lot." Chick raised his hands and spun around to emphasize his point.

"I have gotten far in this life by pleading ignorance," I said. "We'll be fine. Let's wet the whistle and get on with our rat killing."

"Bad juju," muttered Chick, but he shut his door and headed toward the bar.

Walking to the entrance seemed to take longer than it should. The stars overhead shone bright, twinkling some sort of manic Morse code. Not to sound cliché, but it was quiet, almost too quiet. I got to the sad door first and when I reached out my hand, I was momentarily confused. The door was a cheap, pressed wood interior door, not made to stand duty in the weather. The knob had long since been abused beyond working and had been replaced with a brass handle. For a second, I didn't know whether to grab the knob or handle. I guessed handle. I guessed correct. The handle swung the door open. Being left handed, I'm never right, but I'm often correct.

I walked inside, with Chick following close behind. He had a habit of playing a game where he slips inside a door someone else opens, without touching the door himself. Chick has a lot of oddball habits and superstitions. You either get used to them or beat the shit out of him. As soon as we were inside, we both stopped to adjust to this new environment. Every bar's got its own atmosphere.

The place smelled like wet cigarettes and forced laughter. Chick smacked his lips in anticipation of a whiskey close at hand. A jukebox sat in the front corner to the left of the entrance. ZZ Top's 'Jesus Just Left Chicago' was playing. The volume was soft, but clearly audible.

Chick let out a breathy, hushed, "No way."

I turned in his direction. He was standing perfectly still. Something had captivated him, so that even his alchy tremors had stopped. He was staring at the jukebox, mouth agape. I swear his eyes twinkled.

"She's a beaut, is she not?" said a voice out in the recesses of the bar dark.

I squinted to see where the voice originated. There was a small table along the back left corner of the room. If I slanted my eyes and held my mouth right, I could barely make out the silhouette of a man seated with his back to the corner.

"That's the finest reproduction of a Gabel Kuro I have ever seen," Chick spoke like an old woman in church, muted and reverent.

The silhouette snorted, "We do not do reproductions at *Two Nuns Walked into A Bar*, do we Waddle?"

"No, sir. No need."

I hadn't had the opportunity to fully check out my surroundings. There was a bartender standing behind the bar, doing what bartenders always do when not pouring drinks, polishing glasses with a white rag. The man was squatty, dressed like an old timey western bartender, white shirt with black armbands, a western ribbon tie, and black pants. He sported a thick, dark mustache, curled with wax.

"That cannot be a real Gabel Kuro," said Chick. "There are only six of those in the world and I know where every single one of them reside." Chick managed to get his feet un-plastered from the floor and began to walk slowly toward the jukebox. "This jukebox, if it is real, was made in 1940, it was designed by Clifford Brooks Stevens, it was the last juke made by the John Gabel Company. It only plays 78s." Reaching the jukebox, Chick caressed it gently.

The man struck a match on the tabletop and lifted it to his lips to light a cigarillo. In the yellowy, orange glow I saw no outstanding features save a pencil thin mustache. He wore a shirt so black I wasn't sure it was really there, and sported a lavender beret rakishly tilted atop his head.

"That which you are so lovingly touching is the first, the very first, Gabel Kuro ever produced." The man shook out the match as he inhaled the first drag off the cigarillo and disappeared back into darkness. "A prototype, hand made by Brooky Stevens his own self." The man exhaled a long, slow breath of smoke.

"Uh-unh," said Chick, not taking his eyes off the machine.

"*Uh-huh*," said the man.

"I need a whiskey," said Chick, as if shaken out of a dream. He pulled away from the juke and turned to the bar. "Four fingers, top shelf, and a draft."

"Coming up," said Waddle, the bartender.

"Waddle," said the man in the corner. "Put that man's drinks on my tab."

Waddle nodded.

I followed Chick to the bar. "That's okay, Mr. Waddle," I said as I reached into my front pocket to pull my wallet. "We can pay. I'd also like a whiskey with a beer chaser, please."

Waddle the bartender looked to the corner for instructions.

"The offer is much appreciated, sir," I hastily added, "but if it is all the same to you, we can pay, in cash." I felt uneasy turning down the drinks from the stranger in the corner. But the thought of being in his debt gave me a queasy feeling. As my eyes adjusted to the dusk of the bar, more objects, as well as the man in the corner, began to stand out. Apart from the beautiful, art deco jukebox in the corner, the entire bar was decorated in forgettable, nondescript, milquetoast, mid-70's Naugahyde, low rent furniture. It was the type of place you forgot two steps out the door. I had the feeling this was purposeful.

I could now see the man in the corner was lithe and lanky. The table at which he sat was barren save what may have been a tequila sunrise and a leather gaming dice cup. A pair of white dice sat next to the tan leather cup. 'Jesus Just Left Chicago' ended and was followed by 'Beer Drinkers and Hell Raisers.' I wondered if the 'Tres Hombres' album was being played in sequence and where the hell they'd found a 78rpm disc of *any* ZZ Top music.

The lanky man gave no discernible signal to Waddle, who proceeded to pour two shots of top shelf whiskey and draw two beers from an unmarked tap. Chick smacked his lips again when the whiskey and beer were set before him. As soon as he picked up the whiskey he turned and looked lustfully back at the jukebox. I pulled a Grant out of my wallet and set it on the bar. "That juke really that rare?" I asked Chick.

Chick snorted, "They call the Gabel Kuro 'the last jukebox,' because it is the last jukebox Kuro ever made, but for me, it is the last jukebox because it is pure perfection. Every other juke pales by comparison. Falls short. Not worthy. It is the best of the best. Look at the lines, colors, wood. Listen to the sound, my god man, it is high art!"

"It's a juke box that only takes nickels." Okay, I admit it *was* a beautiful machine and I only said that to rile Chick.

"Sometimes you really get my goat, Buster."

From the corner table came the sound of the dice being dropped into the leather cup. I tried to ignore it. My head involuntarily turned to look at the lanky man in the corner. He was already staring at me when I met his gaze. He picked up the leather cup in his left hand, holding it only with his thumb and middle finger, and gently rattled the dice in a circular motion.

The color drained from every object in the room. Granted, the only colors were monkey shit brown and oxblood pleather, but still, the room went monochrome. I couldn't hear the dice careening and colliding, but I seemed to feel them churning in a clockwise circle across my chest and back, as if the interior of the leather cup was my own skin. I don't mind saying I had a big old case of the willies.

"Maybe we ought to drain these drinks and leave," muttered Chick. In all the time I had known Chick he had never left a bar of his own free will. Especially, after only one round.

"No one leaves *Two Nuns Walked into A Bar* without throwing the bones," said the man in the corner.

"We just came in on a lark," I said.

The lean man in the corner rose to his feet. The chair scraping the wooden floor, as it slid back, sounded like a demon's belch.

"No one comes into *Two Nuns Walk into a Bar* on a lark." The lean man walked toward us, all the time twirling the dice in the cup. "Do they, Waddle?"

Waddle continued to wash and dry glasses as he spoke. "There are no larks, whimsies, or japes within a hundred and twenty-three miles of *Two Nuns Walk into a Bar*," he said.

Chick sat at the bar, head hung low, gripping his beer mug with his right hand. He must have figured we weren't going anywhere soon, because he flipped his right index finger straight out and back, quick as a whip, a clear signal for another round to an experienced bartender like Waddle.

The lean man's footsteps clanked across the wooden pier-and-beam floor as he approached the bar. Waddle had already poured Chick his second whiskey and was drawing his second beer when he shot me a glance over the tap. I raised my eyebrows and gave a quick, subtle shoulder shrug indicating '*yes.*' If I was going to die or suffer worse, may as well have another drink in my innards.

"I've never met a stranger, but I do not know your names."

There was something odd about the way the lean man spoke. His words sounded thin, like they didn't move through the air so much as they were *in the air*, and revealed themselves when needed.

"My name is Ch-Chick."

I had never heard Chick stutter. He was more scared than I was. This realization near doubled my fear.

The lean man stepped between us and dramatically raised the leather cup in the air, threw it open side down, on the bar.

"Nice to meet you, Chick."

He then turned to me and said, "And your name, sir?"

"Buster," I said with the steadiest voice I could muster. "Buster Brown."

"Well, I'll be damned. That isn't saying much, but I'll say it again." He drew a deep breath and exhaled the words, "I'll be damned."

The lean man then proceeded to sing the Buster Brown Shoes jingle:

"Does your shoe have a boy inside? What a funny place for a boy to hide.

Does your shoe have a dog there too? A boy and a dog and a foot in a shoe.

Well the boy is Buster Brown."

The lean man just stood. Staring me in the eye. Grinning. His left hand still on the leather cup turned mouth down on the bar. It occurred to me he was waiting for me to applaud. I slow-clapped, mainly because I didn't know what else to do.

The lean man cut me off. "Are you a gambling man, Mister Buster Brown?"

He drew my name out in three long breaths.

"No, sir. I'm a poor man who spends what little money I have on booze. And when I'm flush, maybe a little cocaine, but I'm rarely flush."

The lean man furrowed his brow. "I don't believe you, Buster Brown." He turned to Chick, "Does our friend, Mister Buster Brown, gamble, Chick?"

"Well," Chick's eyes were wider than dinner plates. Beads of sweat appeared on his forehead. "Once he bet me a dollar he could shit on command."

The lean man burst out laughing. "Shit on command! That's a good one!" When he caught his breath, he continued, "I simply have to know. Can Mister Buster Brown shit on command?"

"Turns out he c-could," Chick stuttered again.

"Well, there you have it. Seems you *are* a betting man."

"Well, it was only a dollar, and I already knew I can shit whenever I want, so it isn't really a bet when you already know the outcome."

The lean man smiled. "Well, the value of my wager is less than a dollar."

He smiled and I swear his coal black eyes twinkled.

"And I know the outcome. Seems the same to me." He raised the leather cup from the bar to reveal double sixes.

"Beat it."

It was more a command than a request. He scooped up the dice, dropped them in the cup, gave it a shake and held it out to my chest.

I took the cup from his boney hand. Stared down into it. There was nothing but darkness. I swirled the leather cup and heard the dice rattle around the sides. I placed my right hand over the top of the cup to shake it up and down, but it felt like hot flames licked my palm. I winced, removed my hand, looked down into the cup to see a pair of red eyes, just before they blinked out.

"Oh, don't do that," said the lean man. "I should have told you. My apologies."

I swirled the cup in circles, trying to stall. Looking into the eyes of the lean man, I could see he had all the time in the world and was in no particular hurry for me to cast the dice. Chick stared at the back of the bar, thinking if he pretended he wasn't paying attention, he wouldn't be affected by the outcome of this bizarre game of chance. Who was I kidding? This was no game of chance.

I drew a deep breath and slapped the leather cup mouth down on the scarred oak bar. The leather cup landed with a 'whump' but I could neither hear, nor feel, the dice hit and bounce.

I held my hand on the cup for several seconds.

"Let's see what you rolled," said the lean man. He pulled back his thin lips revealing a pearly grin.

I slowly pulled my hand away from the cup, leaving it mouth down on the bar. I could not take my eyes off the lean man.

He looked from the cup to me.

"You have to pick it up."

I stood at the bar. Hands at my side.

"Are you deaf? You have to pick it up."

There seemed to be a sense of urgency in his voice. When I pulled my hand from the cup, I simply didn't want to see what would happen next.

I figured I was dead or worse, so no sense rushing it on myself.

"Pick up the cup, Buster."

The bartender stopped drying pilsner glasses.

The lean man blinked rapidly.

I began to slowly back away.

Slamming his fist on the bar the lean man commanded, "Pick up the damning cup!"

"Let's go, Chick."

Chick, turning away so as not to look at the lean man, walked away from the bar.

The room drew flush with oxygen and grew hotter than holy hell. The lean man's eyes burned with anger, but his words were calm.

"Hold on, Buster. I understand the problem here."

He smiled, "You don't know what you win when you lose. Let me explain."

I had been backing up in what I hoped was the direction of the door. I almost shit my pants with relief when I hit it and it opened. I stepped outside and held the door until Chick walked through. The night air was cool, almost crisp.

"Well I'll be a son of a bitch, that has never…"

I let go the door and it shut before the lean man finished his sentence.

Elliott Baxter was born in Texas but spent his formative years growing up on naval bases across the country and the world. A confirmed bachelor, though not by choice, Baxter now lives on a Farm to Market road in rural Texas with his dogs and enough goats to maintain his Ag exemption.

The Fear All Women Have
Ralph Robert Moore

Dan in darkness.

Unable to see.

Bending forward, searching his right hand down. Fingers playing piano across cool smooth porcelain. Tapping his fingertips further down. Locating the metal lever. Pressing it into a downward slant. Hearing water underneath the lowered toilet lid erupt, swirl. Holding down the slanted lever, because the toilet was old, and you had to wait until the spiral of water was gulped into the square hole at the back of the bowl before letting the lever up.

Once the tank started refilling, he shuffled around in the after-midnight dark. Stretched his right arm out, left arm out. This was the scary part each middle of the night. Having to take two or three steps forward in utter blindness, bare feet shuffling across the cold travertine tiles. Nervous hands swinging side to side, seeing nothing, fingers feeling for their brush against the opposite wall of the black bathroom. And he found it. Reassuring. Chances were, he wasn't going to fall over in the dark. Both hands to the left, he felt his way along that opposite wall, its solidness like his mother's hand, until he reached the doorway of the bathroom. Now another leap of faith. He had to pass through the doorway without being able to see it, left hand swaying down, clawing scary open air, until it touched the edge of his night table. Swing, feeling nothing. Swing, nothing. Swing, swing. Nothing. Feeling weak in the knees. Swing, fingernails skating across the surface of the night table, plowing—but gently, he had learned from past mistakes—against his small digital clock. Okay. Doing all right. Left hand gripping the night table, he stepped forward into the unknown, elbows tense, aiming his right hand down, groping in the darkness for the soft edge of his mattress. Found it! Almost there. Right hand holding onto the mattress, released his left hand from the unseen night table, holding his breath, maneuvered his left hand over to the edge of the mattress as well. Both hands on the mattress! Almost there. Even more so. Lifted his right knee up onto the mattress. Pulled up his left knee. Palms finding his pillow, for some reason always difficult to do in darkness, always farther away than expected. His wife murmured in the black air. It sounded like she said, 'Pepperoni'. Didn't want to wake her. Stretched his long legs down the length of the bed. Pulled the top sheet, blanket, bed cover over his body. Settled on his side facing his wife in the warmth of their bed, repositioning the pillow under his profile, repositioning it once again, for greater comfort, and again, closing his eyes, trying not to think of anything, just fall naturally back asleep, where we all want to be at three a.m., repositioning his elbows, his pillow.

Silence.

Stillness.

Breathing.

A pile of tomatoes, and he had to slice the redness of all of them for wedding reception sandwiches. Good. Starting to dream.

Feathery run across forearm hairs.

Lifted his head.

Did that actually happen?

Brushed his right fingers across his left forearm.

Nothing.

Felt like a cockroach's race across his skin.

Is there a cockroach in the dark bed with them?

Fuck.

Fully awake now, right palm sliding left, right, across the flat sheet, trying to find a cockroach that may or may not exist.

Is it possible it was his wife's long blonde hair? Lifting in the breeze from the ceiling fan, floating across his forearm?

Fuck!

How am I supposed to fall asleep if there might be a cockroach crawling over me?

Got up on his left elbow, unhappy, not happy, right palm swirling everywhere across the sheet to resolve the issue so he could fall back asleep.

Wife lifting her head in darkness. "What you doing?"

"Nothing."

"Making noise!"

"Go back to sleep, hon. I'm just rolling over."

"Wha?" Grogginess. "Time to get up."

Dan looked at his digital clock. Four-thirty. They don't get up until five. "Another half-hour."

"Four-thirty!" Fumbled a small hand to her edge of the bed, fingers searching in blackness, he could hear them, barging against the Kleenex box and bottled pills on her night table, finding the lamp on her night table. Clicking.

Yellow!

Everywhere.

Eyes squinting, he quickly checked to see if he could anywhere spot the dark skittering retreat of a cockroach, on the sheets, the headboard, the white walls, ceiling. None in sight. "Go back to sleep! We have another half hour!" Turned around to glare at her.

A woman he had never seen before.

Brunette, and younger.

Rubbed her nose with the side of her index finger, looking right at him. "It's four-thirty!"

He didn't know what to say.

Waited for her, looking at him, to be as startled as he was, but…she wasn't.

With her feet she kicked down the bed cover, blue blanket, white top sheet off their bodies, exposing her shapely bare legs. "I can't afford to be late again. You know that. Not after Angela's warning last week, and confusing pastrami and corned beef."

Stared at her, shocked, not knowing what was going on. What happened during the night that he was suddenly in the same white bed with this unknown woman? Why didn't she see he wasn't her husband?

She noticed the front top of his blue and white striped pajama pants lifting away from his belly. Voice of a sleepy wife. Surprised, and kind of interested. Dark eyes thinking private thoughts. "Did you want to fool around?"

"I…"

Pulled her pajama shorts down her bare legs with a wife's casualness, spreading her thighs, brown pubic hair lifting above her cunt.

Slid her unfamiliar, girl next door eyes sideways toward him. "It's been a while! Okay if I don't come?" Scrunched her face, scratching above her left ear.

He had always been faithful to his wife. They still had sex, but not that often. And when they did, at this point it was a little bit like making a shopping list. But still. His marriage vows. Those were sacred.

He slid up inside her warmth, him hard, her wet, and he hadn't felt that wonderful differentness since he married fourteen years ago, finding out how his cock fit inside a new woman's cunt, how tight it would be, how her hips would move in an unpredictable way under his hips, how her skin would smell, where her hands would land on his body.

She snaked her right forearm behind his neck, lifting her chin under his eyes. Choked voice. "It's been a long time since you've been this passionate!"

To her, it was getting fucked by her husband for the three-hundredth time, but to him, it was fucking this beautiful young brunette for the first time ever.

Face pressed against his chest, small hands holding onto the backs of his big shoulders, her lips burst apart, hips lifting obediently, legs wrapping possessively around his waist as he had his own explosion.

After, they rest in each other's arms a few minutes, bellies breathing against each other, Dan still stunned he got to fuck her, he rolls off, she stands up shakily by her side of the bed. Hair mussed. Reaches down, strokes his bare knee, lifting her brown eyebrows. Look of girlish admiration. "That…that was nice. It's been a while. Thanks."

They both pad out from the master bedroom into the bright eyes of the kitchen. Him wearing blue and white striped pajama pants, her a Wajeco Forever t-shirt, and just by the arrangement of the stainless-steel appliances, the black granite counters, he realizes this is not his house. But she doesn't seem to notice any difference. Sometime in the night was he transported into her life? But she doesn't realize she has a different husband now?

On the tiled kitchen floor, a blue bowl with brown food nuggets in it. So, they have a cat? Or a dog? Impossible to tell dog food from cat food.

He keeps hoping she'll mention her name, or his name, so he'll get some more information, but of course married couples don't use each other's names that often.

"Will you get breakfast going, babe?"

Dan nods. "Absolutely." Walks over to the tall side-by-side, although of course he has no idea what she expects him to cook, he's just bluffing at this point. Swings the tall right door open. Inside, the almost empty illuminated shelves. No eggs, no butter, no bacon. Just almond milk, tofu, edamame.

Asks her, before he can catch himself, "Are we vegan?"

"Huh?" Walks over, puzzled eyes smiling at him. "Cereal? You're getting senile in your old age." Raises her right hand to the top of his head, affectionately ruffles his hair.

A small blond-haired boy toddles out into the kitchen. "I'm hungry."

His wife leans forward in her bare feet, palms on her knees, looking down at their son. "Hey, Sweetie! Want some orange juice?"

The boy nods. Draws in a big breath. "I had to pee last night and Chandler had to pee too so I opened the door to let him go out. But then when I came back from peeing, he didn't come inside."

Dan, lifting boxes of cereal off a pantry shelf, saw the look of horror on his wife's face.

"You let him go outside, Sweetie? He's been outside all night?" Glances at Dan, fear in her eyes.

He's arranging the tall boxes of cereal on the breakfast nook table thinking, *Is Chandler another son of theirs? A dog? A cat?*

He clears his throat. "What door did you let him out?"

The boy points to the back door, small face registering he did something stupid.

Not cool to leave a sibling or a pet out all night, but at least in this warm Southern California climate, there shouldn't be any serious consequences.

He leaves the boxes of cereal on the table so his wife can choose, probably a smart decision anyway. Looks at the son whose name he doesn't know. "Let's go find Chandler."

Unlocks the back door, swings it inwards.

Outside, white snow drifts, cold wind blowing.

Steps back across the kitchen floor, stunned.

Where are we?

"Babe, you can't go out like that. Did you forget? North Texas had a freak snowstorm last night."

I'm in Texas?

"Of course. Let me put on a shirt, get a jacket and some shoes." Leans over his son. "You need to bundle up too. Maybe mommy can help you select something appropriate to wear."

When he came back from the bedroom, his son, name still unknown, was zipped up in a heavy jacket, fake-fur hood over his head. The little guy looked like he was having trouble walking in his astronaut outfit.

"Okay!" Gave his wife a kiss. "Let's go looking for Chandler, then we'll have some cereal!"

"Babe, you want some gloves?"

"No, I'll be fine."

Outside, backdoor closed behind them, he realized he should have dressed more warmly. *Fuck it.*

Took his son's gloved hand in his bare hand, led him out past the chest-high evergreen hedges bordering the backyard's cement patio.

Raised his voice to be heard over the white wind. "You know, I don't want you to feel like it was dumb of you to let Chandler outside last night to pee."

The boy looked relieved. "It was okay, Dad?"

Crunched across the white snow with his son to a stand of bushes. "Absolutely, sport. For instance, did you know a lot of boys your age don't know their own name, yet?"

"Yeah? I know my name."

"Exactly! Your name is…"

Pride on his red-cheeked face. "Brandon!"

"That's right! Brandon. And what's my name?"

Brandon was enjoying this quiz. "Daddy!"

"Right again! And what's my first name?"

"Raymond!"

"That's my boy! And what's mommy's name?"

"Tania!"

"Okay. You did good!"

The little boy bumped his shoulder against Dan's thigh. "Thanks, Dad." Small features silently working on something. Finally, he looked up. Scared. "Are you proud of me?"

Dan stopped walking through the snow. "What? Yeah! Of course, I'm proud of you!"

Fear still in this little kid's blue eyes. Starting to tear up. "So, the other night, when you said you were ashamed to have me as a son, that's not true now?"

Dan went down on his haunches, looking into the child's face. "That's not true. Daddy was upset. But I love you. I'm proud of you."

"Yeah?"

"Fuck, yeah."

Brandon burst into tears, rubbed his small face against the front of Dan's jacket, like a dog. "Thank you, Daddy!"

They trod on through the snow of the backyard. "Let me test your intelligence some more, okay Brandon? Is Chandler a dog, a cat, your brother, or something else?"

Brandon snorting. "He's a puppy! That was easy, Dad."

"Good for you!" It was below freezing, and probably was the whole night. Didn't look good for Chandler.

Near the back of the yard, by the property fence, a wide shed probably used for lawn maintenance. "Let's check out the tool shed. You doing okay, Brandon?"

"Absolutely!" Proud little boy, showing off for his Dad's approval.

They trudged toward it, lifting their feet up and out of the snow, burying their shoes back in the snow, lengthening their parallel tracks in the snow toward the shed.

Once they reached it, Dan went up the three steps of the wooden staircase, twisting the door knob.

Darkness inside. Should have brought a flashlight. But in the dawn light it looked like a lawn mower, hedge clippers, shovels, trowels, buckets, wheel barrel.

"I found him! I found him, Daddy! Hey, Chandler! Good doggy!"

Dan clomped outside the shed to the top of the three steps. Stomped down the wood.

Brandon lying on the icy white ground on his stomach, looking underneath the stairs. "Hey, boy! I love you!"

Reaching his right hand underneath the steps, big grin on his face. He found Chandler!

Dan got down on his knees in the cold snow next to the boy, lowered his upper body until he was lying next to Brandon, looking under the steps.

A small dog underneath the stairs, huddled in a back corner, trying to find warmth through a long, cold night.

Brandon wiggling his small thumb between his index and middle finger, that old human trick of trying to intrigue a dog.

Chandler on his side, lying stiff at the back corner under the wooden steps, face frozen above his paws.

"Hey, boy! Are you hungry, Chandler?"

"Brandon?"

"I found him. I'm pretty smart, right Dad? You're not ashamed of me, right Dad?"

"I'm sure not. You're a wonderful son."

"Can you reach under there and get him, Daddy? So we can give him some food?"

Dan wasn't a father. Had no idea what that was like. But in this moment, he put his hand on the back of Brandon's head, stroked the back of the boy's fake-fur hoodie. "We have to go back inside."

"Yeah! Pull Chandler out so we can feed him!"

"Chandler's dead. He froze during the night."

"No, he didn't!"

Dan reached his right hand under the stairs, stretched his arm deep into that dark space. Grabbed onto Chandler's frozen corpse, dragged its curved stiffness out from under the steps. "Look at him. He's dead. He froze to death during the night."

Brandon, trying to talk to the stiff corpse, little voice rising, eyes crying.

"It's okay. It happens. Don't worry about it."

"He had to pee, so I let him out!"

"You did the right thing! At least he got to pee before he died. Don't worry about it. It happens."

Back in their breakfast nook, the three of them ate their cereal at the black table, not talking much.

After they spooned up the last of the milky residue, which to Dan's taste was a bit over-sweet, Brandon climbed up on his father's lap. "Did I kill Chandler?"

It was weird having a child in his lap, like having a cat curl up. "No. Chandler died because he didn't pick a warm enough place to spend the night. That was his mistake." He stroked the boy's blonde hair, and realized he really liked being able to guide a small child toward adulthood.

Tania smoothed her brunette hair away from her young face. Lit a cigarette. "We should bring Wheezer back from the nursing home. I really miss having a dog in the house, and I know Brandon does, too. Maybe even you?"

Dan lowered his eyes, still stuck in this situation where he had to pretend to be Raymond, husband and father. But as he lowered his eyes, he realized he was starting to enjoy this new life. A beautiful wife, a young son. "Chandler was special. Yeah, let's get Wheezer back."

Tania squeezed the top of his hand. "Will you take care of that, Raymond?"

Dan nodded. "Absolutely." So Wheezer, who was probably a dog, was in a nursing home. Why? Was he really old? "Brandon! Let's test your intelligence again. What nursing home is Wheezer in?"

His son looked up from his praying hands. Small voice. "I don't know, Daddy."

Fuck.

"You know, it'll probably help if when I go to this nursing home, I have any documents that were drawn up at the time we placed Wheezer in this home."

Tania sat up in her kitchen chair. "Smart! Let me get them."

While she was away from the table, Dan glanced over at his son. "How are you doing in school?"

Guilty look. "Okay. I guess. I don't like chemistry."

"I didn't like it either. Too much memorization."

Tania came back with a sheet of paper. "This is what they gave us."

Dan read the signed agreement. Perfect. All the information he needed. Silver Bird Retirement Home. Located at 1323 Redemption Drive, Desoto, Texas 75115. PET OWNER and RESIDENCE understand and agree PET loaned as therapy pet to RESIDENCE will be returned to PET OWNER on the same date as PET OWNER's request for such return.

"Let me get this done, and then we can have a great day together, you, me, Brandon, Wheezer. Maybe I'll order some Chinese spare ribs for home delivery, and we can have a family meal together."

Tania reached across the kitchen table, grabbed Dan's hand. "It feels like maybe we're getting back on track as a family, Raymond? Yeah? Maybe all that ugly anger is going to go away finally? Please?"

Dan stared into her young eyes. "It's going to be different from now on. Our family is going to be a loving family, supporting each other, and you and I are going to get back in touch with the reason we got close to each other in the first place." He was conscious Brandon was listening, so he had to be circumspect. "Our bed is going to be happy again."

She reared up her brunette face. "Do that for me baby, for our family, and I'll let you do anything you want. You understand what I'm saying? Even that thing with the mangoes."

He nodded.

Before he left, he went back to the bedroom, its bathroom, pissed in the toilet.

On a hunch, just pushed down on the lever to flush, lifting his right index finger off the metal slant afterwards, didn't hold it down until the flush finished.

And the toilet flushed fine.

So, yeah, he was somewhere else.

Outside, wearing Raymond's coat, he stepped carefully across the frozen driveway to the red car, soles of his shoes sliding downward, but not so much he couldn't correct the drift, his hands grasping the security of the car's hood.

He had the keys. That was easy. Rising from the kitchen table, patting his pockets. "Where did I put those damn car keys?"

Tania with a wife's smirk. "Maybe behind you, on the bookcase, next to the stapler? Where you always put them?"

Unlocked the driver's side door. Swung it open. Glanced inside the interior, illuminated by the small yellow light in the car's ceiling.

Shit!

It had a manual transmission. He didn't know how to drive a stick.

Folded himself inside. Put the key in the ignition. Twisted the key clockwise. Engine erupting, thrumming.

Shut the driver's side door.

Slid the dashboard temperature control to HEAT.

Looked at the stick shift between the driver's seat and front passenger seat.

How do I do this?

Fortunately, Tania and Brandon were inside the house, so they didn't see his hesitation.

Left foot lifting, he pressed that shoe down on the clutch.

The stick was numbered 1 to 4, with an added R.

R for reverse?

He slid the stick towards R. Lifted his foot off the clutch.

The red car rocketed backwards down the driveway, skidding across the ice of the side street, hitting the opposite curb. His right foot stomping down on the brake, causing the car to slide sideways.

Came to a stop.

He looked out his driver's window at the house. 1349. Okay. Remember that.

Slid the stick into the 1 position, drove with a loud engine noise to the end of the block. Looked up at the green street sign. Hooper Street. He lived at 1349 Hooper Street.

Took out Raymond's phone, found the GPS directions to get from 1349 Hooper Street to 1323 Redemption Drive. Turned left onto Oleo Boulevard.

Driving down Oleo Boulevard, the car lurched and jerked as he tried to learn the stick shift's different gears, and how to coordinate a shift change with his left foot stepping down on the clutch pedal. He cruised down Walter T. Galwoon Avenue with very few grinding noises, and by the time he turned right onto Redemption Drive, it was like he had driven a stick all his life.

He was a quick learner.

Dan pulled into the wide parking lot of the Silver Bird Retirement Home. One-story sprawl of windows and corners and brick walls.

Walked through the glass doors of the front entrance into the reception area. No one behind the counter. Mural across the tall side wall of the lobby, blue and red and yellow paint, old people's faces, white, black, Asian, looking upwards, happy.

Music from the ceiling. Recognized it. *We've Only Just Begun* by The Carpenters.

Rang the bell on the reception counter.

The door at the rear of the reception area opened. An overweight woman with blonde hair strode closer and closer, eyeglasses glinting. "Are you delivery? You have to use the side entrance."

"I'm not delivery. I'm Raymond Evans. My family loaned you our dog Wheezer to use as a therapy dog for your residents, but now we're going to have to take our dog back. We've had a family tragedy."

The woman reared her face, inspecting him through her eyeglasses. "I remember you! Is there any way you'd reconsider pulling him out of the therapy program? Our residents love Wheezer, and he clearly loves spending time with them."

Dan put both palms on the receptionist counter. "I'm sorry. But we just lost our only other dog. My son is heart-broken. He wants Wheezer back."

Lowered her head. "Understood. It's hard when anyone loses a pet. But when it's a child? Let me buzz you through, Mr. Evans."

Moved her hand below the white counter.

The door to the right of the receptionist counter buzzed.

Dan twisted the knob, looked back at her. Small smile. "Thanks for understanding."

Went through, into a large area with old people in a far corner watching a game show on TV, lots of sound effects, a number of doorways, and in an opposite corner, an unattended piano.

Saw a black man in light blue shirt and pants who looked like he was staff. "Hi. Excuse me. My name's Raymond Evans. Our family let Silver Bird use our dog Wheezer as a therapy dog here, but now we need to take him back. Can you help me?"

The black man raised his head. "Yeah! Wheezer. The residents sure do love him. Why don't you come with me?"

Dan followed the black man down a hallway decorated with inspirational posters about the joys of old age, lots of old people smiling, lights glinting in their eyes, into a cafeteria area, round tables filling the space.

A blonde cocker spaniel was sitting on its haunches by an old woman's chair. She was lowering pinched-off chunks of her cheeseburger into his mouth.

The orderly grinned. "Ms. Angie? This here's the owner of Wheezer. He's come to take him back."

White-haired Angie looked up from her lowering fingers. "Oh, no. Really?"

Dan smiled sympathetically at her. "I am sorry, Ma'am. But just this morning we've lost our only other dog, and my boy is heart-broken. He wants his Wheezer back."

"Well, he is a wonderful dog." Got sentimental. "He's the most intelligent, playful dog I've ever known in my long life."

"I'll be sure to tell my boy that."

Moved closer to the dog, saw there was a leather leash on his collar he could use to walk Wheezer outside.

But Wheezer, sweeping his black nostrils forward across the floor of the cafeteria, taking some tentative sniffs up the front of Dan's pants, backed up on his paws, growling. Didn't recognize Dan's smell.

Dan bent forward. "Here you go, Wheezer. I'm taking you home!" Held his hand out so the dog could sniff it.

Wheezer backed up some more. Barking.

Fuck.

"Where is your politeness?"

Dan turned around.

An old, white-haired man, indignant. Rising up in self-righteousness. "The lady told you she didn't want to part with the dog. So, who are you to decide you have the right to take her therapy dog away from her? When she's so close to death. Have you no shame?"

"This has nothing to do with you. Ma'am, would you hand me the leash, please?"

"I asked you a question!"

"Ma'am?"

"What makes you think you can come in here, la-di-da, and wrench this poor dog from the people who have spent all this time loving him? And what are you going to do if you get him back?" Clenched his teeth. "Cut him up for a Korean barbeque? Eat him with chopsticks over a bed of rice?"

"Ma'am?"

The old guy, wearing a loose-fitting white jacket, stomped over, standing between Dan and Wheezer. Sneered. "Oh, so it's okay to rape women, right? According to you. It's okay to call proud African-Americans trying to get ahead in life 'niggers.' That's okay with you, right?"

"Ma'am, hand me the leash, please."

Wheezer tapped away on his black paws from Dan, nostrils sniffing.

"Ma'am?"

"And if you fuck a twelve-year-old girl because she's wearing clothes you consider too 'sexy', I guess that's okay too, right? It's her fault? This small child was 'asking' for it? Is that your mindset?"

Angie handed Dan Wheezer's leash.

"Thank you."

Wheezer, at the end of the leash, scrabbled his back paws away from Dan's hold on the leash, snarling.

The old white-haired guy in a loose-fitting jacket rolled his head back, so his voice could be heard everywhere in the facility. "Calling all wheels! Calling all wheels!"

Dan yanked on the leash, dragging the reluctant Wheezer, black nails on his four paws sliding across the floor. "We're going home, boy. Time to be reunited with Brandon. This is a good day."

"Calling on wheels! Calling all wheels!"

The double back doors at the far side of the large room pushed open, female and male seniors confined to wheelchairs rolling through, heading toward Dan.

The old, white-haired guy, snarling, reared his head, pointing at Dan. "There's our target. He's stealing our dog! He's been convicted of rape, racism, and child molestation! Kill him! Kill him!"

The wheelchairs rolled with determination toward Dan, old faces set in anger.

Dan yanked on Wheezer's leash, pulling his paw-sliding reluctance out of the room, down the wide hall with the inspirational posters, into the front lobby.

The wheelchairs crowded through the door after him, dozens and dozens of sneering mouths.

Using his right shoulder, pushed the glass front doors open, dragging Wheezer outside, into the cold white air, bending his knees, scooping Wheezer's protest up in his arms, the dog's black paws scrabbling painfully against his chest, mouth lifting repeatedly, trying to bite Dan's pulled-away face, as he raced with Wheezer in his arms across the parking lot, to Raymond's car.

Wheelchairs bursting through the front doors, most of them rolling toward him. Some headed in the opposite direction, to block the exit to the parking lot.

Dan stomped to the driver's door of Raymond's car, beeped the door open. Wheezer rearing up his head, fangs snapping below Dan's right ear.

Opened the door. Threw the cocker spaniel inside. Blocked it from running out.

Slid in behind the steering wheel. Locked all the doors.

Wheelchairs rolling behind Raymond's car, squeaks, squeaks, squeaks, to prevent it from backing up.

Started up the car.

Wheezer nipping the air by his right shoulder.

Dan puts the car in first gear. Drives up over the cement curb in front of the car onto the grass.

Jostles across the green grass, elbows vibrating, leaving tire tracks. Steering around tree trunks. Bumps down onto the hard road surface.

Switches into second gear. Third gear. Looking up into the rearview mirror.

Drives home, left hand on the wheel, right palm shoving Wheezer back each time the cocker spaniel lunges at him with his fangs.

Curves into the driveway.

Handbrake up. Engine off.

Opens the driver's side door.

Pulls on the leash, dragging Wheezer out of the car against the dog's will, paws scrabbling sideways across the passenger seat, stick shift, driver's seat, landing down on the concrete of the driveway.

Yanks the protesting Wheezer up to the top of the driveway, down the walk to the front door, ringing the bell, side-kicking Wheezer's lunges away from his calf, Tania opening the front door, brunette and young and lovely, Dan announcing, "Here he is!" Letting Wheezer off his leash so he can scamper joyfully across the white carpet to Brandon, who's standing up from the sofa by the back windows.

The cocker spaniel jumping up, jumping up, as only a dog can do, front paws hitting Brandon's belt, hitting Brandon's plaid shirt, tail flicking sideways furiously in excitement.

After Wheezer got over the ecstasy of reconnecting with Brandon, he sniffed Tania, just as enthusiastically, then trailed back to Dan, not jumping up on him quite as much, but at least not trying to bite him anymore, thankful Dan had brought him home.

Later that evening Dan and Tania sit around their kitchen table with Brandon, the family together, inside, and playing a game of Monopoly.

Black and white dice tumbling, corner over corner over corner, in the quiet peace of their low-lit kitchen, across the colorful squares of the game board. At one point, Dan drew the Go Directly to Jail, Do Not Pass Go, Do Not Collect $200 card. Brandon bobbed up and down on his seat, flirting with disobedience. "Go to jail, daddy! You've been bad!" Tania winked at her husband.

When Brandon's pewter dog landed on Park Place, pale eyebrows shooting up with a little boy's surprise at his good fortune, and desire to maximize this advantage, Dan helped him organize his red and blue Monopoly currency in order to buy the property, taking the slips of paper from his short fingers, adding it to the bank, handing him the stiff cardboard square for Park Place, and in that moment, that transfer of paper for cardboard, he felt such a tremendous surge of love for his son who was not his son.

In his real life, his before life, he had never had another version of himself.

Like most Monopoly games, the rolls of dice, the acquisitions of property around the board, and railroads and utilities, the counting out of small bills, the lifting up of Chance or Community Chest cards went on deep into the evening, wide window behind them darkening. After all these hours, no one had yet landed on the Boardwalk square, not that unheard of. Brandon, propping the side of his right jaw against his right palm, that elbow anchored against the table top, was clearly losing interest (despite owning Park Place).

Tania's turn to roll. She hid the two die in the cup of her knuckled hands. Looked across the table at Dan. "Do you remember that day at the laundromat? Soon after we first got together?"

Dan, of course, had no idea what she was talking about.

Closed his eyes. "Of course."

"We were doing our laundry, it was like twenty minutes before the cycle would end, we went to the back of the laundromat, the restroom, we both snuck inside, locked the door behind us, you lifted me up onto the sink, pulled me forward to where I was sitting on the edge of the sink, I was wearing a dress, you pulled my mmm down and off, and lowered your mmm and mmm, and slid your mmm into my mmm, and we did it." She reached across the table, the Monopoly board, the rows of small colorful fake currency, the different player icons, fingers stroking the top of his right hand. "That was the day I fell in love with you. Truly fell in love with you. Even though I had said, I love you, before that. That sense of adventure you brought into my life. The sense that we were different, that we could do anything we wanted." Sad brown eyes looking at him, trying to see if that Raymond still existed. "I used to think about that good time over all the years afterwards, when things weren't so good. As we all do." Squeezed the top of his hand even tighter.

"I do remember that day." He started tearing up, because of course he didn't remember that day. That was another man's time spent with Tania. Not him. And his face scrunched even more, warm tears flowing, once he realized he had never had a moment like that in his life, being that carefree with a woman. He had always been so cautious.

Tania slides her brown eyes to the sleepy Brandon, although the question is directed at Dan. "Since it's Saturday, do you want to just have hot dogs for dinner?"

So now he knows what day of the week it is, which explains why neither of them went to work that day, or his son to school. Tomorrow, Sunday, he'll have to figure out where he works, and what he does. Realizes he's looking forward to figuring it out. The three of them rise from the table, Tania heading toward the fridge to get the hot dogs going. Brandon walks sleepily over to his dad, resting the side of his head against Dan's thigh.

Tania slaps a skillet down on a burner, turns on the gas. "We'll put the game away tomorrow. Let's eat."

Dan pets his son's thick blonde hair, feeling the small skull beneath. The sheet of instructions for the game has somehow slipped to the kitchen floor, but he doesn't stoop over to pick it up. They'll get it tomorrow.

Wheezer pads out from the living room, nostrils lifted, flexing, at the smell in the air of hot dogs frying. Hard for humans or dogs to resist that smell.

TV on the wall talking about a traffic accident on Tamarin Boulevard in Duncanville, two fatalities, he lifted his bare legs, lowered them one by one, balancing on the other, into the soft circles of his pajama bottoms held by both his hands down by his knees, raising the waistband up and over his half-hard cock.

Tania came out of the master bathroom, sound of the flushed toilet behind her, that rush in the pipes behind the walls husbands and wives become so familiar with, in a short pink teddy, which he gut-reaction felt she didn't normally wear to bed, perfume behind her ears, averted eyes, blush on the tops of her cheeks, and he turned into a teenage boy.

Blurted it out before shyness stopped him. "Wanna?"

Her gush. "Gosh."

This time they took an unhurried slowness making love, pulling their eyes like Turkish taffy away from each other long enough, over the deepening late evening, to gulp from the glasses of ice water on each side of the bed, to refresh their throats, returning the glasses' bottoms to the wood surface awkwardly, distractedly, at angles, going back at it, slow and moaning, eyes closing, until finally, so much muscle tension in their limbs, trembling, first she came, then him.

Sprawled on his back, happy, she brought her head under his jaw, profile resting against his wet chest, him stroking her thick brown hair.

Eyes closed between his pale nipples, she grins to herself. "Twice in one day. Oh my!"

Dan's face looking up at the white ceiling. Blue eyes, wide mouth. "I've never been so happy. I've never been so happy."

He woke up in the middle of the night.
Banging, hammering.

Took a few sleepy moments before it registered.

Elbows switching by his sides.

Danger.

Gets out of his side of the bed. Tania still asleep.

Pads bare-footed, naked, to the kitchen.

Tousled hair, looks out through the glass of the kitchen's back door.

Silver curves gleaming in yellow moonlight, dozens of wheelchairs in his backyard, rolling up to the house, fists banging angrily against its windows, red brick outer walls.

They must have been rolling down the shadowed sidewalks for hours, to get here.

Standing on the dark grass of the backyard behind all those wheelchairs bumping forward against the house, the old white-haired man in the over-sized white jacket, spotting Dan's peek through the glass, clenching his dentures together, raising his fist at the house. "This is what you get when you aren't polite! This is what you bring upon yourself when you don't have any manners!"

Dan steps back as an old woman in a blue-flowered nightie rolls up in her wheelchair onto the concrete patio outside the back door, hands on top of the wheels of her chair propelling the front of her chair against the glass of the door, and again, again, until the glass cracks like lightening. Shards spilling inside, by Dan's bare feet.

Tania's frightened call from their bedroom. "Raymond? What's going on?"

Side window in the kitchen bursting inward. Arthritic hands reaching through, upward, raised blue veins across old knuckles bleeding from glass cuts blindly fumbling along the sill, finding the window latches, revolving them into an unlocked position, so the lower window can be raised.

Wheezer barking.

Elderly man with only thin strands of white hair combed over his pink skull smashing his tall forehead repeatedly against another window, milky blue eyes squinting with each painful impact, staring up at Dan with absolute rage.

Brandon shuffling past the furniture in the unlit living room. "Daddy, am I awake?"

"Run into mommy's room, Brandon! Right now! Run, run!"

Dan shoves the kitchen table against the two windows, trying to keep the elderly people out.

The old white-haired man in the backyard, grinning like a ferret. Lifting his arms from his sides. "Arise! Arise!"

The old rising shakily from their wheelchairs, toddling forward on their hairless legs, arms swaying for balance, white bands around their wrists spelling out their names in black type, collapsing against the windows, shattering them, dentures falling out of their mouths, lifting their bloodied knees over the window sills, pissing down their pajama legs from their pain, flopping over onto Dan and Tania's kitchen floor.

Dan running naked in front of the kitchen table, to push them back, slipping on the sheet of instructions for Monopoly he had lazily left on the floor, rising horizontally in the noisy air, landing on his spine, back of his head smacking hard on the floor.

Police sirens off in the distance, wailing.

Elderly hands grabbing his calves, five or six hands, with the long fingernails the old get, dragging him closer to the shattered back door.

And just when it looks like his situation is helpless, spine yanked, yanked again across the floor toward the door—

—he fights back.

Fists flying up at the chests, the faces, right, left, smacking knuckles across noses, clavicles, yelling loudly, kicking his feet free, stumbling backwards to his feet, banging into a side wall, snatching up the chair where Tania sat during their Monopoly game, smashing it down on the tops of white-haired heads, over and over and over.

I'm fighting back for Tania!
I'm fighting back for Brandon!
I'm fighting back for Wheezer!
I'm fighting back for me!
Maybe for the first time in my life?

Red and blue lights revolving across their kitchen walls.

Police forcing their big bodies through the broken back door, guns drawn.

Cop swinging his two-handed aim at Dan. "Hands up! Hands up!"

Dan shoots both hands up in the air. Bows his head. "I'm the homeowner! My wife called 911!"

Wakes up.

Has to pee.

Remembers all that happened last night.

But things seem peaceful now.

Reaches across the darkness of the bed. Can feel the curve of a woman's hip lying next to him, under a blanket.

The hip feels warm, not cold.

Reassuring.

Has to pee.

Gets out of his side of the bed, gropes in darkness down the bathroom, touching walls, left hand, right hand, until he reaches the hollow of the toilet alcove.

Pulls his limp cock out through the soft slit in his pajama pants, leans forward, right hand braced high up against the unseen back wall of the alcove, pisses down. The sound in darkness of bubbling.

Once he's done, and has shaken his cock a few times, and pissed a little more, he pulls his cock back behind the slit in his pajama pants, reaches his left hand down, slants the toilet flush lever down, releases it, turns to leave.

But the toilet keeps running.

Like it used to, in his old life.

We can't see his eyes, because it's so dark.

Shuffles back around in the alcove, tilts down the lever, but this time holds it down a long time.

Hands held out sideways, fingers feeling along unseen walls. Making his way back to the bedroom, the bed.

Lowers his knees, lifts himself up onto the mattress.

Pulls the top sheet over his shoulder, the blanket, the coverlet. Layers are so important to staying warm.

In the darkness, in his dread, reaches his right hand out to the woman lying next to him in blackness.

Heart beating in his Adam's apple.

Carefully swings his right hand out toward the sounds of the woman's exhalations in that black bedroom, questing for the woman's head.

Trails his fingers down the length of her sleeping head, trails them down her hair, fingers trembling, lips praying, eyes tearing, and at one point in that quiet trailing, when his fingers run out of hair to feel, he realizes this is still Tania, his young brunette wife. And not his original, long-haired blonde wife.

Police counted thirty-eight elderly people in his backyard and kitchen that night. Surprisingly, only two of them were dead. One from injuries sustained while Dan was defending himself, and one from an apparent heart attack.

They never found the white-haired man orchestrating the attack.

Wheezer died a few years later. He was a dog. It was going to happen sooner or later. The family accepted his death, buried him in the backyard. Put a pile of stones over the dirt where his body lay. Said 'Hi' to him whenever they went out into the yard to have a barbeque, or just sit under the sky, the stars, with some beers.

You can wish people happiness in a number of different ways. Good health, money, success in a career, but the best happiness you can wish someone is a great sex life. Dan and Tania had that. Once Brandon went to sleep, they'd shut their bedroom door, get into bed naked, and fuck each other for hours. They both lost weight because of all the sex they had, and that weight loss made them look even sexier to each other. Which meant they had even more sex.

A year after Dan became Raymond, Tania got pregnant. They went through the whole process, Dan getting her pickles late at night, the two of them picking out flattering blouses for her to wear as her lower abdomen expanded, helping her sit down by holding her elbow and wrist, but three weeks after their beautiful blue-eyed baby was born, no point mentioning the baby's name, he died in his crib during an otherwise normal weeknight. No crawling around in his crib with a stupid look on his big-eyed face, no holding his bottle of warmed milk up to his mouth while lying on his fat spine with his tiny fingers and toes, no looking up from the depths of the crib at his two hand-waving parents. Sudden Infant Death Syndrome. Four vague words that mean nothing.

But a year after that Tania got pregnant again, and that happy baby? She survived, and thrived. Brandon had a little sister, and as big brothers do, he was protective of her throughout her life.

Brandon, under Raymond's guidance, blossomed into a fine young man. At the time of this story's conclusion, he's in pre-med, planning to specialize in oncology.

Over the years, Raymond never asked his wife if she knew he wasn't really her husband, but instead a man named Dan who had suddenly showed up in her bathroom one night. He strongly suspected she didn't know. Nor did Brandon. Nor did Wheezer. But that was okay.

It had all worked out, to everyone's advantage.

For the first time in his life. He was truly happy.

One day, twelve years after he woke up in another family's home, in another wife's bed, he was walking back to a parking garage after a dentist appointment in Dallas, left lower side of his face numb, and saw his first wife, Monica, headed toward him on the sidewalk.

So what does he do?

He kept his face down, walking toward her, hoping she won't recognize him.

Feeling like he was about to have a heart attack.

Because he didn't want any connection with that former life of his, where he wasn't happy.

As she got closer, he bent his head even more, trying to remain anonymous.

Bent it so much, he accidently bumped into her.

Shit!

She looked right into his wet eyes.

Stepped around him with the fear all women have, moving through hundreds of strangers on city sidewalks, as the evening starts to darken.

Ralph Robert Moore's fiction has appeared in Cemetery Dance, Black Static, Shadows and Tall Trees, and a number of other magazines and anthologies. His website SENTENCE at www.ralphrobertmoore.com features a wide range of his writings. Moore lives with his wife Mary in north Texas.

The Smoke's Gotta Go Somewhere

Carmen Gray

It was another rainy day in April. Balmy with a bit of a chill hanging in the air as she rounded the corner of Chicon and MLK. She stepped into the coffee shop to grab a dirty chai latte. This was her respite after working all night cleaning the offices of nearby fancy workspaces that had sprung up recently in Austin.

She sipped the spicy, earthy drink concocted by an androgynous barista and divided her attention between this unclassifiable human and the gray street outside. He looked more masculine than feminine, what with the dark shadow of a beard coming in, but he had the smoothest, clearest skin and long, dark lashes framing almost black eyes. She noticed the large, black obsidian rings in his ears and multiple rings adorning his fingers. A scorpion ring on his right index finger caught and held her interest. Did it have significance? A meaning beyond simple adornment? Or was she just an unhappy woman, dissatisfied with her life and seeking distraction? She noticed a deck of tarot cards peeking out of the front pocket of the barista's tee-shirt. The Tower card looked imposingly at her.

"Do you read?" she asked before even realizing her intention to speak, her finger pointing at the beckoning Tower.

"Yes." He gracefully repositioned them in the pocket, the silver scorpion glinting under the halogen drop light.

"Cool," she replied, quickly glimpsing into his dark eyes before she looked down and walked away. She really wanted to ask for a reading, but thought maybe he'd think her too forward if she did.

She'd never had her cards read, but Irma, who worked with her, had. Irma knew all the ins and outs of the supernatural world. She'd sweep Rebecca's arms with bunches of rosemary after they cleaned the workspaces, telling her that she needed to rid her of any remaining *susto* that they may have acquired, so as to not bring it home with them.

"What the hell is *susto* anyhow, Irma?" Rebecca had asked her.

"*Susto* is all the bad, stressful energy that a person leaves behind, like dirt from outside on a *zapato, mija*. It comes from being scared or upset." Irma made her smile. She was a warm and nurturing Mexican mother figure to Rebecca. Always doing kind things for Rebecca when they worked together, even if they were foreign gestures to her. She would bring warm, homemade tacos with cut up hot dogs and eggs inside them rolled up in foil for snacks during their breaks. She complained that Rebecca was much too *flaca* and that she needed to gain some weight if she wanted to feel better.

Rebecca would laugh that off and tell Irma, "I don't think that's my problem, Irma!"

Irma was short, chubby and very cheerful. She made Rebecca's mundane cleaning job pleasant and was just the sort of quietly compassionate person to give her space when she came to work in tears, which happened all too often.

Rebecca sighed when she thought about going home to Anna, her alcoholic mother. There would be empty bottles of cheap vodka to pick up and cigarette butts to throw away. Anna would be passed out on the couch, the TV blaring Fox and Friends. She mused, how many hours of sweeping with sprigs of rosemary would it take Irma to cast off the *susto* that had accumulated in the apartment she called home?

She grabbed a Lyft, instead of walking home in the rain, granting herself this luxury today.

In her absence, nothing had changed. The scene at home was exactly as it had been the day before and the day before that. A bad dream, recurring again and again. Rebecca turned off the TV, retrieved the plastic pint bottles and tossed them into the overflowing recycling bin in the kitchen. The stench of sour milk lingered in the kitchen. A fly landed on top of the dirty dishes in the sink.

"What the fuck?" she yelled, to no one in particular.

How many times had she asked her mom to clean and put away the dirty dishes? She returned to the living room to clear away the cigarette butts and the half-eaten bowl of mac-n-cheese on the coffee table.

Why couldn't her grown mother pick up after herself?

Why did Rebecca have to take care of her?

Why did Anna drink herself into oblivion every damn night? She knew why, but it didn't change the fact that the burden ended up on her shoulders. For God's sakes, she cleaned other people's crap for a living. Couldn't she just come home and not have to clean up her mother's mess for once? She was so tired of all of this.

Working, going to school, taking care of her mother.

"Fuck it!" she yelled again as she swatted at the annoying fly, now hovering around the trash. She heard a *snip-snap-whoosh* and then a crackling sound coming from the recycling bin. She turned and looked for the source of the sound. *Ugh. Not roaches again!* she thought. Last spring they'd had an infestation. Her mother's inability to keep things clean prolonged the months it took Rebecca to get rid of the filthy insects. So tired, she wanted nothing more than to go to sleep. Instead, she picked up the recycling bin to empty it outside, keeping her eyes peeled for any unwanted critters.

She sighed, noticing a clenched sensation in her chest. As she tossed the items into the big green bin out by the dumpster, she heard that sound again, that crackle, and this time she smelled something burning; a chemical, acrid smell. She peeked into the green bin. A thin curl of smoke rose from the refuse. The crackling sound happened again, louder.

What? she thought. *Had her mother left a lit cigarette in the recycling bin?* God, that's all she needed -- her mother to burn down the damn apartment. They didn't have much anyhow. Maybe that wouldn't be so bad.

She went back inside to find her mother awake, hair sticking out in all directions, eyes bloodshot and her hand reaching for her pack of Virginia Slims.

"Ma, you need to be careful. I think you might have left a lit one of those in the recycling bin," Rebecca chided her.

"Recycling bin?? What's that? You know damn well I use this Dr. Pepper can for all my cigarettes." She lifted up a half empty can of Dr. Pepper. Despite not being coherent most of the time, her mother was right. She did have a habit of using the portion of the Dr. Pepper she didn't drink with her vodka as an ashtray. Whatever. Rebecca just wanted to get to her room as quickly as possible before her mother got too sober.

"You're right. I'm going to bed. I'm exhausted," replied Rebecca.

"Hey, honey, when you gonna get a regular job with some folks that look like you?" her mother muttered sneeringly to her. Might be too late. Her mother was starting to sober up -- snarky comments were a definite sign.

"Ma, quit saying things like that. I have a perfectly good job that pays well. It's just the graveyard shift, ain't no thing. As soon as I pass this massage therapy exam, I can start looking for a spa to hire me."

"Yeah, maybe you can get some of those fancy business people you clean for to hire you privately ... you know those guys would pay you a lot for a personal rub down ..." she cackled bawdily.

"Ummm … well, Ma, I don't think that's my plan," Rebecca responded, wondering why she even bothered, as she headed to her room, glad to be out of the suffocating living room.

She flopped into bed, picked up the Massage Manual for Therapists and thumbed through the chapter on lymphatic drainage techniques. But she couldn't concentrate on muscles and bones and the lymphatic system. Instead, she began thinking of her plan. Her plan to make a move into a better life.

That plan included leaving her mother, but that bothered her greatly, even though she could no longer stand the woman. She felt sorry for Anna and wished her older brother hadn't died 15 years ago, so drastically altering the course of their lives. She hardly remembered the woman from her childhood. The one she tried to think of as her *real* mother. Somehow, it seemed, she had been a lot nicer. There had been smiles and laughter.

Alex had been five years older than Rebecca. He was funny and adventurous. She remembered chasing after him on his bike to the park and swinging with him on the big swings, seeing who could go the highest and, even though she was so much younger and smaller, she had strong legs and would push herself high into the sky and he would shout, "You win, Becca!" And they would race to the 7 Eleven on the corner and he'd buy her a pack of lifesavers on the way home, giving her a pump on the back of his bike. They weren't rich in their modest little apartment, but life was nice and it was okay that they didn't have a dad, because they had each other.

She stared at the ceiling and reached under her mattress, feeling for the wad of cash she'd been withholding from her paychecks to save for a deposit on her own place. Sasha, who she met at Austin Community College in the fall, had asked her about getting a place together, come summer. Rebecca couldn't wait to do that.

Rebecca drifted off to sleep, dreaming of the pictures of muscles in the neck from her Massage Manual. In her dream, the pictures began to move. A whole body danced off of the page and ran out of her bedroom door. She chased this wild specter and followed it to that neighborhood park of her childhood. The body pushed her on the swing and she went high into the sky. She felt free. "You win, Becca!" she heard.

She woke up with a start and looked at her Massage Manual for Therapists. "Frickin' book giving me weird dreams," she said aloud.

The familiar clanking sounds of her mother searching for more vodka in the pantry came from the kitchen. It must be seven o'clock, Rebecca mused. Time for a liquor run.

"Becca! I need some money for more groceries!" she shouted. Rebecca sighed. She pulled a twenty from her wad of cash and met her mother in the kitchen. Anna grabbed the twenty and a pair of sunglasses. "Thanks, honey," she said.

"Ma, it isn't sunny outside," Rebecca's voice was weak as she spoke.

"Yeah, yeah, I know," her mother answered, rushing out the door.

Rebecca decided she would head to work early. She didn't want to be there when Anna returned. Outside, it was still overcast. The rain had paused and the streets were shiny. A red-winged blackbird chirped on a barbed wire fence that had a red rosebush growing beside it with blooms just beginning to open. She reached down to move one of the blossoms away from one of the barbs.

Then she looked up at the sky and thought she saw that body from her dream. "What the hell?" She rubbed her eyes. There in the sky was that body. It was just what anyone would look like, stripped down to muscles and bones. Like the illustrations in her book. It pointed in the direction of the coffee shop where she'd been early that morning.

"This is frickin' insane," she thought. "I need more sleep; I must be hallucinating."

Rebecca walked east to the coffee shop to grab a coffee to wake up a little more. Surely, she was just not fully conscious, yet. Maybe she'd work up the nerve to ask for a tarot reading.

She entered the familiar shop and made eye contact with the barista. "Hey, can I get a coffee and a reading?" she asked, after taking a deep breath.

"Long or short?" he asked.

"Long or short what?"

"Long or short reading? I charge $20 for short readings, $45 for long ones. Which one do you want?" he asked.

Well, that was easy, Rebecca thought. She'd been so nervous, and it was obvious he'd been asked to do this plenty of times before. It was no big deal. Why had she tried to turn it into an obstacle? "Whichever. I just need a reading." she said.

"Yeah, I can tell," he said, setting down her coffee. "Okay, I can do it in 15 minutes. Meet me at that corner table," he nodded toward the back of the shop.

Rebecca seated herself at the table he'd indicated. She sipped her coffee and waited. She anticipated work. It would not be fun, but Irma always made even the shittiest days a little brighter. Maybe Dolores would be there. She hadn't showed up last night. When the three of them, Irma, Dolores and Rebecca, were together they seemed to buoy one another with a more positive energy.

When he joined her, Rebecca found out his name was Tor. Tor had piercing eyes, even more so up close. He smelled faintly of Poison perfume -- that hint of amber with a sweet, cloying scent from the 90's. It reminded Rebecca of her mother long ago, when she cared about her hygiene. Tor stared at her, it seemed without blinking, for a full minute. Rebecca finally looked down at her hands. How was this supposed to happen? She wondered. Was she, once more, overthinking the situation? There was no real reason for her to feel uncomfortable. She'd just never done this before. As if he'd heard her question out loud, he said, "Look, let's start with your theme of the day," He slowly shuffled the cards. "You need to split the deck three ways and then make it whole again."

Rebecca broke up the deck into thirds and put them all back together.

"Alright," Tor began flipping the cards. The Hanged Man card popped out, facing Rebecca.

"Well, that's good. He's facing you." Tor stated

"Good? It's a Hanged Man! How is that good?"

"Facing upright from you, it means you are meditating on a change. Breaking a pattern, most likely a familial pattern."

"Wow. That's true," Rebecca said, her mind slipping into a deeper engagement with the process.

"Okay, let's go from there. What questions do you have about your day?" Tor asked gently.

"I want to know who the heck is this person I dreamt about today."

He nodded. "Let's ask the cards."

"Yeah, because … I keep seeing it."

"What? The person?"

"Well, yeah ... except it's a body. Like from a biology book. Sinews and muscles and bones."

"Hmmm, interesting. Let's find out. Okay, cards, who is this person that Rebecca is seeing today?" Tor asked. He flipped through the cards and two leapt out.

He gestured toward the first one. "Three of swords, pointed toward you. This means there is a deep emotional wound that was a necessary part of your life. You are being called to grieve it. This is necessary in order to facilitate moving forward. Next, we have the Six of Cups, facing you, also. This represents your childhood, getting in touch with the freedom and happy memories of your youth."

"That still doesn't answer who this body is!" exclaimed Rebecca.

"I think," Tor responded, "the message is this person is someone from your past, during a difficult time. They are asking you to surrender to the grief and retain the happy memories. Then, to move forward with your life."

There was a flicker, a movement behind Tor's shoulders.

"What was that?" She pointed.

Tor turned to look at the empty wall behind him. "There's nothing there. At least not on this plane of being. Perhaps it is that person you've been seeing. Who is a person from your past that you need to grieve, but also remember the innocent times with?"

There was no doubt in Rebecca's mind. Still, she couldn't bring herself to speak his name. "I think I know. What time is it? I need to be at work by 10." Rebecca wanted to change the subject. Enough of this mumbo jumbo. It made her feel uncomfortable. The delicate hairs on her arms tingled.

"It's 9:15," Tor responded. "I didn't get to do much reading here. We're just at the beginning,"

"That's okay, I think I got what I needed." Already, she had risen from her chair. Tor looked at her, his eyes puzzled. "I've got to go or I'll be late. Here's $20. Can I come get another reading again soon?" Rebecca asked, starting to leave.

"Yes, of course. Let's ask one more question." His tone was firm, almost insistent. "How about one about your future, before you go?"

"Okay, what's in store for me tonight, cards?" Rebecca paused, sitting down again. She forced a smile. Suddenly, she felt as if she may have seemed rude and that was not what she wanted.

Tor revealed the Fool card, facing Rebecca. "Well, it looks as if you are being invited to begin your journey."

"What journey?" Rebecca asked.

"A new expedition. Something completely different. Time for you to dance and be free again." Tor said, moving his fingers in the air like a ballet dancer. He smiled, gently, ready to let her leave. "Come back tomorrow and we can finish up your reading." Again, he stared at her with such intensity.

Rebecca met his gaze. She had a sense that she'd stepped outside the flow of time. Instead of the barista's, she felt as if she were staring into her mother's eyes. Not the mother she knew now, but the mother she had known from those early childhood days. She blinked and murmured an almost inaudible goodbye. Moving away, without looking back, she wasn't so sure she'd be coming back tomorrow to finish up that reading.

A cool breeze brought her back to the here and now. Night had fallen and the air was crisp after the rainfall from that morning. The sky was clear and the moon was full, as she walked to work. Rebecca thought about her sad mother and her own continuous enabling, day in and day out. She did not want to go home anymore. She wanted to be free of that burden. She thought about her brother, Alex. Wondering why she'd resisted saying his name. She remembered the silly songs they made up together as they played, all those years ago. And how, on the last night that she saw him, there had been a full moon. It was a clear, crisp fall evening. He had pointed to the North Star and told her, "That's the Peter Pan star, Becca. Make a wish on it."

What had she wished for that night? She was still trying to remember, when she met Irma inside the building they were to clean together.

"*Mija, que tienes*?" Irma asked, her brows furrowed in a worried look.

"What do I have? Nothing. I'm just thinking."

"Yes, me, too. I'm worried about Dolores." Irma said.

Dolores was usually with them during the night shift. Dolores was a very hard worker and did her job thoroughly. She would talk a lot about her daughter, Catalina, who was just a year older than Rebecca. Dolores had been the one to encourage Rebecca to go to school. "Listen, Rebecca, you don't want to clean offices the rest of your life. You can go to school. Make your life better," she told her, looking into her eyes, "You are a smart girl. Like Catalina."

Rebecca had decided to apply at Austin Community College. Massage Therapy would enable her to get started on a career quickly and she was good with her hands. Dolores helped her study when they worked together. She would mop the floors while Rebecca dusted, quizzing Rebecca on the latest muscle group that she was memorizing. Dolores was a good mother, that was certain.

"Where *is* Dolores?" asked Rebecca.

"Let's clean up the *basura* on this floor first." Irma gestured toward the trash bins in the break room.

It was clear Irma wanted to change the subject. Rebecca decided not to pry. Irma was always respectful of Rebecca's solitude when she needed it. She began picking up the trash cans in the first row of cubicles, while Irma handled the break room. *What a cold, boring place to work*, Rebecca thought. She could never have a desk job, even if it paid well. She suddenly felt a pang in her chest, she couldn't pinpoint what exactly this was. She tried to not think about her discomfort as she mechanically did her job.

Rebecca met Irma in the hallway where they combined all the trash from the first floor in one large bag. Something spilled out and rolled out onto the floor. Rebecca reached down to pick it up. It was a pack of lifesavers. A new, unopened pack. What was this doing in the trash? The uncomfortable feeling in her chest got worse. She grimaced.

"*Que tienes, mija?*" Irma asked her again.

"I don't know, Irma. I don't know." Rebecca began to sob, a flood of memories of her brother and her childhood hitting her all at once. Rebecca always tried to quell her emotions when this happened at work, but Irma's concerned look made it difficult. She was mortified, but try as she might, the tears kept coming. She sobbed, uncontrollably, it seemed.

"*¡Oh, Dios mío!* You need a *limpiezza,*" Irma told her as she patted her back, looking at Rebecca with a very troubled expression.

"What is that?" Rebecca asked between sobs.

"A cleaning. Like this building, *mija.* But for your spirit. For something you've lost, *mija.* You have grief. It's time to let it go. Come with me," Irma said. She led Rebecca gently to sit down in the break room. "Now just sit still. I'm going to get my *hierbas* and *vela.*" Irma dug around in her purse for the familiar bundle of rosemary. The herbal broom she'd always brush them with when they finished their job. She also took out a white candle with the Virgin of Guadalupe on it. She set it on the table beside Rebecca and lit it, whispering something under her breath.

"*Oye, mija*, I had to do this the other day to Dolores. She is fearful of being arrested by ICE." Irma said quietly.

"ICE? I hear about that on the news. But I thought Dolores was American. Her daughter speaks perfect English and is graduating from UT in May?"

Rebecca remembered all that Dolores had done to help her with school. She'd always talked about her daughter with great pride. Dolores had never missed a day of work since she'd known her for two years. Until now. What would ICE want with a middle-aged cleaning lady who had a daughter ready to graduate college?

"Oh, *mija*, no. She escaped a very bad situation 22 years ago from Mexico. Her daughter is a Dreamer. You know, so her daughter is protected. She's *segura*. ICE cannot touch her. But, Dolores, no. She is not free. Her soul is not free here. It is not free in her home country, either. She is *perdida*. She needed a *limpia* to recover herself and to ward off the *mal de ojo*"

"*Perdida*? What does that mean?" Asked Rebecca.

"*Perdida* … lost. Wandering, like a ghost in the living world. ICE is making rounds again, that is what we've heard. So, she is in hiding. And she must avoid the envy and anger of others." Irma responded.

Hiding. Lost. A ghost in the living world. Rebecca's chest tightened and she felt the anxiety rise up again. Where did she belong? Where did her mother belong? Her mother's spirit had died years ago. Anna truly was a ghost in the living world, not Dolores.

Irma lightly brushed Rebecca's arms as she chanted in Spanish, *"Dios te salve, María, llena eres de gracia, el Señor es contigo…."* She walked around Rebecca and continued to chant the Hail Mary as she blew a tobacco-smelling incense into the air. The uncomfortable feeling in Rebecca's chest eased. The tears continued to stream down her face, but quietly now.

Suddenly, Irma crossed herself and shouted, "*Mira*, Rebecca!" pointing at something above her.

Rebecca looked up and saw the body. She looked closer at the muscular form of it. The quadricep was too small to belong to an adult. She gazed at each muscle group. It was the body of a child. And it was dancing across the room and out into the night, up to the full moon. Free.

"You win!" She heard, somewhere in the distance, as Irma finished up the *limpia*.

"*Ya, mija*. You are cleansed." Irma declared as she blew out the candle and put things away. "Let's get back to work. We need to finish cleaning this building." It was as if this strange occurrence was part of everyday life for Irma.

Rebecca was still in quite a state of astonishment.

"Come on, now. We have to finish our job." Irma nudged her into motion.

Rebecca felt lighter. Something had changed, a weight lifted. She was determined to do what she needed to do this summer. Leave. She whistled while she gathered the trash, suddenly feeling ... what was this feeling? Hopeful? The shift passed and they managed to catch up for the missed time during the *limpia*.

Dawn was approaching, the pink sky opening up to a new day. As they were locking up, Rebecca noticed the familiar shape of someone she knew walking toward them. She couldn't exactly make out who it was. The woman had a scarf wrapped around her head. When she got closer, Dolores' kind, brown eyes met with hers.

"Oh, it's you Dolores! It's good to see you!" She smiled at Dolores, but Dolores was scared.

Irma turned around after locking the door and whispered fervently to Dolores, "*Cuidado*!" Irma looked nervously around.

"Nobody's around, Irma. She's safe, right?" asked Rebecca.

"I just need my last paycheck, Irma. I'm going to move with Catalina to California after she graduates. She already has a job working for Facebook," Dolores said softly.

Before Rebecca could congratulate Dolores, a car pulled up beside them.

A man stepped out of the car. He was holding a piece of paper and wearing a black jacket with "ICE" inscribed in white letters on the left side of his chest. "Dolores Hidalgo Rodriguez?" he inquired, staring into Dolores' kind, brown eyes.

All three women stood quietly frozen.

"Please answer me, or I will be forced to arrest all three of you," he demanded.

"For what?" asked Rebecca. She could not believe this was happening. "Are you Rebecca Hughes?"

Rebecca was stunned. How did he know her name?

"Yes," she answered.

"We were informed that Ms. Hidalgo-Rodriguez is working here illegally. We're federal agents. She must come with us. As a citizen of the United States, you must point to who Dolores is or you risk being arrested as well. Which one is she?" he asked.

This stranger was speaking about the two women who had mentored and helped her more in the last two years than her mother ever had. She could not forgive his harsh tone, speaking about these women as if they were inanimate objects she needed to identify.

Rebecca closed her eyes.

When she opened them up, another man stepped out of the vehicle. Same black jacket.

She noticed something in the sky behind him. A body. That diminutive body. Muscles and bones and sinews. And she heard, "You win!" again. The body was dancing.

"Ma'am? Excuse me? I have asked you a serious question. You need to answer it. I'm going to give you 1 minute. Then, I'm going to arrest all three of you," the first agent said firmly. The second one stood beside him.

Rebecca looked at Irma, who stood unflinching, as if giving strength to Dolores.

"You win!" Rebecca heard again. That body. Who was it? She wondered. And why was she still seeing it?

"Thirty seconds," the first agent said.

"What the hell are you doing? You're an American. What are you staring at?" The second agent barked at her harshly.

Snip-Snap-Whoosh. That sound. The same sound she'd heard in the recycling bin. There it was again!

All the fury and anger that Rebecca felt for the unfairness of her life and this new unfairness, it bubbled up, like a hot fire in her chest. She watched as the small body in the sky burst into flames. The flames grew larger and swallowed up the agents.

They melted into the sidewalk, muscles, sinews, bones. There was a crackling sound. A thin curl of smoke, not unlike the one from the recycling bin, rose from what remained of their bodies.

Irma was whispering in Spanish and crossing herself. Dolores' mouth was agape. Rebecca just felt exhausted. Still, she felt lighter somehow. Irma and Dolores gently patted her back. The three women turned and walked down the street together, arms around one another.

"You win!" The voice called out one last time. And this time they all heard, feeling free.

Carmen Gray is many things: mother, writer, teacher, reiki practitioner, yogi, and meditator.

Her Mexican-American heritage and work with English Language Learners is reflected in her characters and she often employs the Spanish language and Tejano culture in her writing.

Her first short story, *Daniel's Dilemma*, was published in 2016 in Road Kill, Volume I. In addition, she has many literary projects online, including *Mother's Day*, found in The Naga (Venom Vault, Prose, September 2017 edition) and on her blog: walkersonthejourney.com

The Chauffeur
Andrew Kozma

Joe opened the door to the Lincoln Town Car and slipped inside, instinctively stretching his legs out, relishing all the space taxis never offered. The car pulled away from the curb before he fully shut the door, the sudden jolt throwing him off-balance. But the rough beginning quickly leveled out into a ride so smooth he couldn't even tell he was moving without looking out the windows.

"Hey," Joe said, using his talk-to-secretaries voice. "Be more careful, okay, man?"

There was no response. There was no response because there was no driver.

Joe huffed in disgust. He'd heard about the driverless cars being developed by Uber and Lyft, but didn't think they were legal yet, at least not in Houston. But it shouldn't matter, and really, Joe didn't want to talk to anyone anyway. Drivers always felt the need to talk, as though friendliness was what he was paying them for, but that forced friendliness meant he had to pretend to be friendly in return. And he had enough of that at home and the office.

He leaned back and closed his eyes. Thought maybe he could sleep, just not-be for a few minutes. He thought about Jack and Vikram waiting for him at the office with their array of lawyers, their bristly, carefully-cultured stubble poking out into the air like porcupine quills. They had the contracts for him to sign. The papers for handing over his stake in the company. The news wasn't out yet, but they knew the intern Joe pissed off would be trying to get her story out to the local papers and TV stations. And once the reporters realized what she was peddling, that'd be it for Joe. The business in flames. His personal life a blasted ruin.

That's what they texted him and e-mailed him, what was endlessly repeated on the messages they wouldn't stop leaving on his phone. But Jack and Vikram believed the public runs the economy. Joe knew the public doesn't matter.

Joe opened his eyes and looked out at the people they passed on the sidewalks of downtown. These people were walking, and walking in Houston is the definition of *You Don't Matter.* That black guy doesn't matter. Those two Hispanic women in dress suits don't matter. That homeless white man huddled under a blanket in the doorway of an abandoned storefront doesn't matter. No one cares what they think because they don't have any power. Like ants underfoot.

He leaned back and closed his eyes again. The A/C blew cold air over Joe, chilling the sweat he'd sprouted walking from the restaurant to the car. He tried, but he couldn't remember what he'd just eaten. His tongue was numb and clean with vodka martinis. The alcohol seeped through him, flattening out his mood and his anxiety.

But he wasn't anxious. He flashed his eyes open and looked around the interior of the car as though for the first time. It was a wide back seat, the legroom large enough for him to lie down and take a nap, if he wanted. There wasn't a seat belt, though.

He wasn't anxious. The streets were full of cars, but the sidewalks were less crowded, almost bare, in fact. They passed by warehouses and four-story office buildings, not the skyscrapers and mountainous parking garages he expected. They weren't downtown at all. The car was heading into East Houston, a collection of hip new businesses and older, established Mexican and Central American neighborhoods.

"Hey, this isn't the right way," Joe said to the empty air in the front seat, knowing there was no one to talk to but hoping, maybe, the technologically-advanced car had microphones, like those phones his friends talked to, semi-intelligent apps ordering food, books, everything the modern person might need but doesn't want to go get themselves.

The car didn't respond. Or, if it did, the response was to turn off the main road onto a side street. This street was still well kept, and somewhat old-fashioned, a grassy median dotted with old and ragged pecan trees splitting it in two. The car was turning around, that was it, Joe was sure. The onboard GPS just knows a quicker way than a simple U-turn. That's all.

Joe relaxed, his muscles untensing, feeling as though he'd just sprinted down a dozen flights of stairs. That floating sense that you might never stop falling. He sloped his body across the seat to anchor himself, the cushion in the middle of the back seat rattling loosely as he brushed it with his left hand. Pulling on it, suddenly hopeful, he revealed a mini-mini fridge, crammed with half-size soda cans, tiny bottles of water, and even tinier bottles of liquor. To one side was piled a column of square ice cubes in a plastic sheath and a stack of rocks glasses.

Making himself a drink was a calming ritual, though he didn't need the calm. He was already calm. Outside the car, the air was starched with sunlight. With no breeze to riffle them, the trees might as well have been sculptures. Bourbon and Coke was sickening at first, after all the vodka martinis, but soon filled his stomach with sugary warmth. He felt heavy. Immovable.

Calmly, drink in hand, Joe eyed a woman on the sidewalk walking her dog. It was a medium-size mutt with a fur-puffball head. She held a leash in her hand, unattached to the dog, but the dog walked a few feet in front of her anyway, discrete and measured, just as though the leash was there.

As they pulled alongside the woman and her dog, the car jumped the curb—the bourbon and Coke sloshing out onto Joe's shirt and suit jacket—and slammed into the dog with a sickening crunch Joe could hear as well as feel. The woman moved out of the way at the last moment, the leash falling from her hand. She passed within inches of the car; her face so close to Joe's as they passed, he nearly tasted and felt her hot, shocked exhalation. The windows were tinted. She couldn't see him, but his eyes locked with hers anyway and he could feel her stare into the hollow of his body, and when she screamed, her tortured voice filled him up to bursting.

Then the car was back on the road, running smoothly over the newly-paved asphalt. Joe whipped around in his seat. The woman and the dog were one huddled mass close to the earth, the details already unrecognizable. Her face, so clear a moment before he could've traced it out on paper without mistake or hesitation, was now just a blur of dark skin. The car turned a corner without hurry, and they were gone. Joe turned back around and swallowed what was left of his drink. A spot of blood marked his window. He slid over to the other side.

"Stop," he said. "I want to get out."

Of course, the car didn't respond.

Joe checked the app he'd used to call the car, but according to it he never got into the car he'd summoned. He made another drink, one-handed, with two bourbons this time, not caring about the spills and tossing the empties onto the floor at his feet. There were no papers inside the car marking it like a cab, not a sticker on the window like Uber and Lyft drivers have. The customer service number led only to an automated menu which never connected to a live person.

Out the window, he tracked downtown Houston off to his left, the car circling back around to his office. His phone buzzed with a message from Vikram asking where he was. The same message had been repeated three times before, all within five minutes of each other. Joe thought about calling the police, but there was no driver. He was the only person in the car. Maybe they'd blame him for the dog's death, and he didn't need that right now. It was only a dog.

When the car paused at a red light, Joe steeled up his courage and yanked on the door handle, ready to tumble out, if he had to. But the door refused to budge. He tried to roll down the window, but it was stuck, too. He was a fish in an aquarium. He poured another bourbon into his half-finished bourbon and coke.

He was kidnapped. He admitted that now, and admitted, as well, that his hope the car was taking him to his meeting at the office was no more tangible than smoke. Joe thought he might be in shock, if only because it wasn't until now—only minutes after the car ran down the dog, though it felt like hours, like days—he remembered his own dog from when he was eight and how it was run down by a grey-faced man in a car who didn't stop, didn't even pause, in his hurry down the street.

What was the dog's name? Harry, he was suddenly sure, because at that age he was still utterly literal and the dog was hairy, the hairiest animal he'd ever seen, and so the name. And though his dad had made him promise to keep Harry on a leash, Joe had removed the leash as soon as they were out of sight of home because he liked it when his parents let him outside without watching his every move and he figured Harry would appreciate that kind of freedom, too. Minutes later, the dog was dead. Afraid of what his parents would say, he reattached the leash to the dead dog before running back home.

Ice clinked against ice at the bottom of his glass. Out the window, the top of a Ferris wheel rolled above some buildings, a restaurant's sad attempt at getting attention. Just after lunch, the cars were all empty. The neighborhood the car passed through was familiar, and getting more so by the minute. And when the car turned right, directly away from downtown, Joe knew the street because he'd been parking on it for years. This was where his mistress lived.

He fumbled her number on his phone, his tapping interrupted by another where-are-you message from Vikram. The phone rang and rang and he hoped she might be asleep. The street was empty of people, just tidy homes and townhouses clustered together like colonies of elaborate and exotic molds.

She answered, her tone both pleased and cautious. "Joe?"

"Evelyn, where are you?" He couldn't keep the anxiety from his voice.

She laughed nervously. "Have you been drinking?"

"No, I…no. I just need to know where you are."

"Joe, I'm not telling you," she said. "We've talked about this."

"Look, I'm not jealous. This isn't about jealousy."

"It doesn't matter what it's about. My life when I'm not with you is my own."

In the background, birds tweeted. A crunch, like metal being driven into raw earth.

"Are you gardening?"

"I told you, it's none of your business. And if you still want to meet up tomorrow night, you better leave it at that."

Out the window, he saw Evelyn kneeling in her front garden, back straight, face bitter with annoyance. For a second, he wondered if this is what she always looked like when on the phone with him.

"Listen, you need to—"

The call went dead. The car swerved over the sidewalk. Its tires ripped into the grass, spinning out as it revved up. Evelyn looked up from the phone but didn't move otherwise, didn't have time to, really, before the car smacked into her. Her head bounced on the hood before she disappeared under the car. There was none of the broken-body sound the dog had made, but the car stuck itself in her newly turned garden, tires roiling the ground and her body.

No one peeked from the windows of nearby houses. No front doors opened. Joe expected at any moment a jogger would come down the sidewalk and see the car digging ruts in Evelyn's lawn, the bloodied dirt scattering up behind it. It wasn't his fault. None of this was his fault, but he was in the car. He would be assumed guilty.

The tires caught on something and the car jerked out of the ground, flinging itself back to the street. Through the back window, Joe saw limbs rising up through the churned soil. Arms or legs, he couldn't tell. He was struck by the whiteness of her skin peeking from behind the mask of dirt. Or was it bone?

Without consciously making it, another drink was in Joe's left hand. In his right, his phone with Evelyn's number still on the screen. He drank and thought about calling 911. This wasn't the death of a dog. This was murder. And there was no way he wouldn't be held responsible for it. Who else could be?

But Evelyn was dead.

And yet, Evelyn was dead. What good would reporting her death do for her?

Even with the A/C blowing directly on him, sweat collected under Joe's armpits and around his waist. He drank until the glass was empty, then sucked on the ice until his teeth hurt.

The car stopped. The doors unlocked. He was outside of his company's building, and on the nineteenth floor Vikram and Jack waited for him. He wasn't going to sign their papers. There was nothing they could threaten him with, and without the company, what did he have left in his life?

He opened the door and the humid air of Houston struck him like a fist. He could smell everyone on the block, their nervous sweat, their bad breath. He wondered, before he stepped out onto the sidewalk, whether the car would be waiting for him when he came back downstairs. And, if so, whether he'd get in.

Blood and dirt crusted the Lincoln Town Car.

No one was driving.

He'd get in.

Andrew Kozma's fiction has been published in *Escape Pod*, *Reckoning*, *Daily Science Fiction*, and *Interzone*. His first book of poems, *City of Regret* (Zone 3 Press, 2007), won the Zone 3 First Book Award and his second book, *Orphanotrophia*, will be published by Cobalt Press in 2019.

Other HellBound Books Titles
Available at:
www.hellboundbookspublishing.com

The Toilet Zone

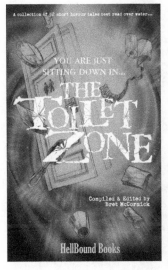

Compiled and edited by the grand master of 80's schlock horror, Bret McCormick, each one of this collection of 32 terrifying tales is just the perfect length for a visit to the smallest room....
At the very boundaries of human imagination dwells one single, solitary place of solitude, of peace and quiet, a place in which your regular human being spends, on average, 10 to 15 minutes - at least once every single day of their lives.

Now, consider a typical, everyday reading speed of 200 to 250 words per minute - that means your average visitor has the time to read between 2,500 to 4,000 words, which makes each and every one of these 32 tales of terror - from some of the best contemporary independent authors - within this anthology of horror the perfect, meticulously calculated length. Dare you take a walk to the small room from where inky shadows creep out to smother the light and solitude's siren call beckons you?
Dare you take a quiet, lonely walk into… The Toilet Zone

ROAD KILL: TEXAS HORROR BY TEXAS WRITERS - VOL 3

Everything is bigger in Texas - including the horror!

A Piney woods meth dealer clones Adolph Hitler. A nightmare exorcist meets an inexorable fined. An eyeball collector gets collected. The apparition of a lynching victim tracks down his executioners. A Texas lawman is undone by shades of his past. A Baphomet recruits converts as a local summer camp. The tales of the baker's dozen who appear in this anthology demonstrate why everything is scarier in Texas…

Including tales of terror from
Jeremy Hepler
Madison Estes
Bret McCormick
James H Longmore
ER Bills
Shawna Borman

And many more...

Schlock! Horror!

An anthology of short stories based upon/inspired by and in loving homage to all of those great gorefest movies and books of the 1980's (not necessarily base in that era, although some do ride that wave of nostalgia!), the golden age when horror well and truly came kicking, screaming and spraying blood, gore & body parts out from the shadows...

This exemplary 80's themed/inspired tales of terror has been adjudicated and compiled by one Mr Bret McCormick, himself a writer, producer and director of many a schlock classic, including *Bio-Tech Warrior*, *Time Tracers*, *The Abomination*, *Ozone: The Attack of the Redneck Mutants* and the inimitable *Repligator*.

Featuring stories from: Todd Sullivan, Timothy C Hobbs, Mark Thomas, Andrew Post, James B. Pepe, Thomas Vaughn, Edward Karpp, Jaap Boekestein, Lisa Alfano, L. C. Holt, John Adam Gosham, Brandon Cracraft, M. Earl Smith, Sarah Cannavo, James Gardner, Bret McCormick, and James H. Longmore.

Graveyard Girls

Female authors + Horror = something spectacularly terrifying!

A delicious collection of horrific tales and darkest poetry from the cream of the crop, all lovingly compiled by the incomparable Gerri R Gray! Nestling between the covers of this formidable tome are twenty-five of the very best lady authors writing on the horror scene today!

These tales of terror are guaranteed to chill your very soul and awaken you in the dead of the night with fear-sweat clinging to your every pore and your heart pounding hard and heavy in your labored breast…

Featuring superlative horror from: Xtina Marie, M. W. Brown, Rebecca Kolodziej, Anya Lee, Barbara Jacobson, Gerri R. Gray, Christina Bergling, Julia Benally, Olga Werby, Kelly Glover, Lee Franklin, Linda M. Crate, Vanessa Hawkins, P. Alanna Roethle, J Snow, Evelyn Eve, Serena Daniels, S. E. Davis, Sam Hill, J. C. Raye, Donna J. W. Munro, R. J. Murray, C. Bailey-Bacchus, Varonica Chaney, Marian Finch (Lady Marian).

The Devil's Hour

A new and altogether awesome anthology of all things horror!

Seventeen spine-chilling tales of the darkest terror, most unpleasant people, and slithering monsters that lurk beneath the bed and in the blackest of shadows…

An Unholy Trinity

3 TERRIFYING NOVELLAS, 3 SUPERLATIVE AUTHORS, 1 BIG, FAT, JUICY BOOK!

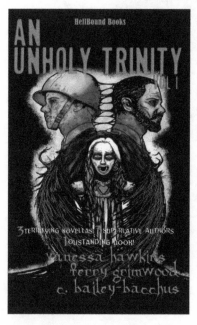

ENÛMA ELIŠ (When on High) – Terry Grimwood. The Babylonian Creation story is a tale of monsters and cataclysmic wars. An epic saga dominated by the gods Tiamat and Mardak, bitter rivals who battle for supremacy over the unformed universe. It is a story replete with Minotaurs and scorpion men, dragons and monstrous blood-sucking demons.

A myth, a fantasy...

But when a traumatized ex-soldier rescues a young woman, washed up and barely alive on the shore of a sleepy English seaside town, the fragile borders between myth and reality begin to crumble and gods and their legions wake from their long-slumber.

THE REMNANT - C. Bailey-Bacchus
When fifteen-year-old Bianca Baker is blinded by

rage and hatred, her inner demons take control and turn an ordinary school trip into a horrific tragedy. Witnesses to her violent act, succumb to Bianca's aggression and agree to say events were a terrible accident. Sixteen years later, those involved find the past clawing its way from the shadows to haunt them, and this time there is no way it will stay buried.

ALICE IN HORRORLAND - Vanessa Hawkins
Alice is an 11 year old orphan living within the veins of industrial England. When she meets a mysterious gentleman with the power to turn into a white rabbit, she finds herself tumbling down a manhole into Horrorland.
Here the creatures are strange and uncanny, lost in a revolution of madness. Drug addicted Caterpillars, grinning cats and homicidal Mad Hatters gambol around Alice like blood-drunk
mosquitoes. However, at the center of it all is the Queen of Hearts: said to have given up her own a long time ago…
Horrorland used to be so wonderful… Can Alice make it so again?

<u>AVAILABLE on AMAZON.COM</u>

Road Kill: Texas Horror by Texas Writers: Vol 1

An ancient demon plays cowboy and *takes on* the Texas Rangers. Three teenage girls sneak into a "body farm." An aging African American couple defies the Grim Reaper. An FBI agent discovers an entire city that's gone to the "dogs." A handyman learns that the fixer-upper he's working on has a doorway to the past that's way out of square. And a pack of possums burrow into the body politic. Join seventeen Texas authors for a harrowing spin on the twisting freeways and dark back roads that wind through the Lone Star State. Includes works from Joe R. Lansdale, David Bowles, Anna L. Davis, Stephen Patrick, Carmen Gray, Russell C. Connor, Michael H. Price, Tom Bont, Ernie Lee, David Robledo, Alan Beauvais, Michael Baldwin, Glen Coburn, Joe McKinney, Tom Alexander, Bret McCormick and E. R. Bills.

Road Kill: Texas Horror by Texas Writers: Vol 2

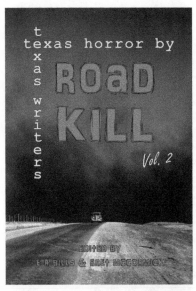

A hanging tree takes the law into its own limbs in "The Tree Servant." A mother's love is tested by the walking, crawling and thumb-sucking dead in "Mama's Babies." A famous author lays his process bare in "A Writer's Lot." Not for the faint of heart, this terrifying batch of Texas horror fiction delivers a host of literary demons who will be hard to shake once they get comfortable.

The second volume of the critically acclaimed *Road Kill Series* from Eakin Press, featuring seventeen Texas writers. Some of the writers are established and have been published in a variety of mediums, while others are upcoming writers who bring a wealth of talent and imagination. Edited by E. R. Bills and Bret McCormick, this collection of horror stories is sure to bring chills and make the imagination run wild. Writers include Jacklyn Baker, Andrew Kozma, Ralph Robert Moore, Jeremy Hepler, R. J. Joseph, James H. Longmore, Mario E. Martinez, E. R. Bills, Summer Baker, Dennis Pitts, Keith West, S. Kay Nash, Bryce Wilson, Bonnie Jo Stufflebeam, Stephen Patrick, Crystal Brinkerhoff and Hayden Gilbert.

**A HellBound Books LLC
Publication**

http://www.hellboundbookspublishing.com

Printed in the United States of America